Fr

I stumbled through the door. My poor mind felt savaged by a maelstrom of tangled memory and odd snippets of recollection. I wobbled a bit, meandering toward an alleyway next to the bar and rested my hand against the wall.

Steady, Bishop. I reached into my jacket pocket, my fingers trembling. More than anything, I wanted a cigarette—

But no. Of course I didn't have one.

In my other life, I didn't smoke.

I leaned into the cool wall, data singing electronic warbles into my mind as the intel packets blipped and booted, establishing a connection to Facility networks. Forgotten vistas opened before me, like a blind man who could suddenly see.

Focus. I took a deep breath and tried to ignore the dizziness. With a subtle *click*, my boot packet connected to the Lattice and ran its initial processes. The preliminary systems whirred in my skull.

When the greeting came, it resonated within my own thoughts, a whisper softly singing.

Welcome, Asset. The system prompt felt like sunlight after long darkness. ***Bishop, Michael, Asset 108.***

Rationality Zero

Rationality Zero

Novel One in The Dossiers of Asset 108
JM Guillen
Irrational Worlds

This is a work of wonderful fiction. All the characters and events portrayed in this book are fictional, and any resemblance to real people or incidents is purely coincidental. Except when not.

An Irrational Worlds book
Printed in the United States of America, where they make freedom.

A Myriad of Worlds...

This story is the first one in the series, *The Dossiers of Asset 108*, regarding the adventures and trials of Michael Bishop, a man who does not know his nature. It is a story of a shadowed world, a world where creatures of outer darkness are hunted by a faceless organization, the Facility.

This series is itself a strand in *The Paean of Sundered Dreams*, a multi-genre, universe-spanning array of tales.

Some of the strands of this work are technothrillers, some dark fantasy, and some Lovecraftian steampunk, but they share the same horrific universe. They weft and weave together, each leaving a breadcrumb trail of clues for the next story.

Each tale echoes a beating heart of darkness, cackling quietly in the shadows of existence.

These stories traverse space and time itself. They may be enjoyed as individual series or as part of *The Paean of Sundered Dreams* in its proper order.

If you are the kind of reader who cannot rest until every secret is found, for whom genre is unimportant, and who will travel a wide and vast multiverse to learn things man was not meant to know...

Welcome, wayward wanderer.

This was written for you.

Books in the Paean of Sundered Dreams

<u>The Dossiers of Asset 108 series</u>:
Rationality Zero
The Primary Protocol
Aberrant Vectors
Cascading Error: Critical

<u>Echoes of the Untold Age</u>:
The Herald of Autumn
The Harrowing of Twilight
A Culling of Shadow

<u>Judicar's Oath series</u>:
On the Matter of the Red Hand
Regarding Oaths and the Whispering Flame

<u>Other works</u>:
Handmaiden's Fury
Slave of the Sky Captain
The Wormwood Event
An Oath of Wintersteel
Wind Slinger

Free stuff? For reals?

You own a free e-book copy of this amazing book! As everyone knows, the internet makes everything better in every way, and my books are no exception!

Your e-book contains:

- *34% more evil sorcery designed to drive you irrevocably insane!*
- *The names of dark and terrible beings who will do your will.*
- *Free photos of the author sunbathing in a speedo.*
- *Money, money, money.*
- *A fidget spinner.*

To receive it, email me at JM.Guillen@irrationalworlds.com

Dossier # I63-1998

21 June, 1998
San Francisco, California
Earth

"Michael? Did you hear me?"

I blinked, realizing my mind had wandered. The urgent sensation that I had forgotten something—something fundamentally vital—gnawed at me.

"What?" I smiled and hooked my arm with hers. "Of course, sweetheart." I gave her a rakish smile. "I absolutely heard you."

I hadn't heard her.

"Then what did I say?"

"You were telling me how lucky you are to be with me. You were saying that your friends are all very jealous."

"No!" She playfully swatted at my shoulder, her smile widening. "I was not!"

I continued walking down the street, my brow furrowed.

"I'm certain you were," I mused. "You said something about the cute one."

"Michael Bishop!" She grabbed my arm. "I won't take *that* bait." She flipped her hair.

"You were telling me something about your feet?" I looked down at her dainty little toes poking through her sexy, strappy shoes. "I don't think they're *too* big, if that was it." I enjoyed our banter but couldn't help feel a bit distracted. I'd forgotten something—something that really mattered. It nagged and worried at the edge of my mind.

"I think you have a foot fetish, as often as you bring that up." She glanced at me wryly. "Just admit it. You were fantasizing

1

about my feet while I told you about your big surprise."

"Maybe." I kissed her forehead. "Sorry, Caprice. I'm a bit sleepy. I'll get with it."

Something. A meeting? It felt kind of like I was running late. Like I had forgotten an appointment with a very important person.

"Sleepy?" She wrinkled her nose at me, teasing. "Am I boring you?"

"Oh, no." I made a show of yawning and stretching.

"Jerk," she playfully jeered. "You're really going to regret this later."

"Nah." I put my arm around her. "Regret is for people with big feet."

The night lived and breathed around us, a sultry and inviting thing. People milled about the streets; cars drove by, brilliant with color and sound. Amidst it all, we stood alone. Just me and a woman so lovely that heads turned as we walked.

Caprice.

Tall and leggy, with a smile as if she knew every secret in the world, Caprice had long, dark hair the wind loved to dance in. Her eyes were like midnight, but when she gazed at me, they seemed to glow. She chatted happily along, our conversation wending and winding as if we were the only people on earth.

"Just so you know." She batted her wide eyes, feigning innocence. "I need you to be, um, 'not sleepy' real soon." She bit her lip, overtly flirtatious.

"Yeah?" I teased as I ran my fingers down her back. "Why?"

"It's a secret." Her gentle Italian accent curled the edge of her words. I couldn't stop watching her mouth and the way she nibbled her bottom lip.

"Oh man," I proclaimed with a shake of my head. "I don't like secrets."

"Hmm." She leaned in closer. Her breath tickled my ear. "I happen to know you *love* my secrets, Michael. Don't be coy."

"True. You caught me." I raised my hands in mock surrender.

2

Her unexpected adventures were always stimulating, often outrageous, and I greatly enjoyed them.

"You sit around in that huge apartment and wait for sweet Caprice to call," she teased. "You like playing all macho, but the other ladies are just floof and perfume compared to me."

"Other ladies?" I feigned confusion, though neither of us hid the fact that we saw other people.

"Ha!" She poked me in the chest. "We set the world on fire, Michael Bishop. Every time you see Caprice, it's some new chic restaurant or wandering barefoot on the beach with a 1923 Chateaux Margaux or dancing in some underground club—"

"I might remember some of those," I mused.

"You love watching me dance." She pressed herself against me, all curve and sweetness against my straight, hard lines. "I've seen it. I've seen it in your eyes. I've seen it in your body." She gave her hips the tiniest wiggle, making certain I knew exactly what she meant.

"Why are you always trying to seduce me?" I shook my head. "I'm more than just a gorgeous body, you know."

"Oh my God." She stepped back, trying not to laugh. "You're impossible. Tonight is special," she insisted.

"Special." I shook my head and chuckled. "Special like the time you set us up that room in Vegas? With all the—?"

"The entertainments," she finished for me and gave me a cat's grin.

"I *was* entertained," I agreed.

"You sound as if you didn't love every moment."

"I *did* though." I leaned into her and smelled the ocean in her hair. "Okay. *Maybe* I love every bit of craziness with you, Caprice."

"I'm glad." She glanced down.

Tonight's adventure led through the pulsing, throbbing city. Eventually, after dancing and a few drinks, we wound our way to a small unremarkable bar on Nob Hill. The lurid red sign, flashing in

3

the twilight, read Spoilz.

"Um." I gave her a skeptical glance. "Looks like a bar. This is the surprise?"

"Impatient." She leaned close to breathe in my ear, "Let me show you." She wrinkled her nose playfully and turned to talk to an immense, dark-skinned man at the door.

I nodded at the wall of muscle. He could probably break me in two.

"Evening." His voice positively rumbled as he gave us the once over. "Can I help you?"

"We are expected." She handed him something small I couldn't see.

"You are indeed." The man smiled, a white flash in the shadows. He nodded at me.

"Come on in, Michael." She glanced at me over a perfect shoulder. "Come and see."

I did, trying to forget the nagging in my mind. It might be an appointment. That seemed more certain as I pondered. The idea poked and worried at me, yet just one glance at Caprice...

She made it easy to forget any lingering responsibilities.

The moment we stepped inside, I saw the reality of my little minx's plan.

"Good evening," a red-haired young woman dressed in the barest hint of a silky, black dress greeted us breathily.

"Hello." Caprice glanced at me and then leaned over to the hostess. They exchanged whispers, and the young woman glanced at me, her eyes twinkling.

"Down the hallway." The redhead gestured, eyes on Caprice. "I'll make certain you aren't disturbed."

"Thank you."

Caprice pivoted and offered me her hand. I took it, and she led me into the shadows.

As we slipped through the twilight of the room, a different world opened all around us. Scantily-clad women danced with

4

well-dressed men in the low lights. Private alcoves where couples could be alone lurked just at the edge of sight. Several of them had four or five occupants in various states of undress. A few more featured people wearing leather harnesses, ball gags, or animal masks.

Most didn't seem to mind voyeurs.

"Oh my God." I couldn't keep the laughter out of my voice. "What is this?"

"It's an adventure," she responded. "A night you'll never forget."

"It's a fetish club." I shook my head.

"You don't like it?" She pouted, adorable and tempting.

"Caprice, I've got to be honest." I met her eyes. "This is absolutely awesome."

She led me through tendrils of incense and flickering candlelight to a private booth in the back. Soft, red curtains hung around us, and the entire place smelled like jasmine and musk. Someone played a violin, but I couldn't locate the musician.

"You will sit," Caprice stated as a matter of fact. She put a hand on my chest and pushed me backward onto the velvet seat.

"So bossy." I grinned at her, trying to ignore the certainty that something important had been forgotten.

A person? I shook my head. It seemed very important.

"Tonight, we are going to have a special kind of evening."

"No doubt." I arched one eyebrow. "I mean, look at this place!"

"You need to learn when to shut up, Michael." Her mouth pressed against mine, all pink sweetness. She slid onto my lap and pressed against me.

My hands found the curve of her hips, and I felt her softness beneath the short dress.

I forgot my worries.

Caprice tasted like fire and secrets. Her hair floated around me like wisps of midnight, and I became lost in her scent.

For long, blissful moments, I explored the secret curves of her.

She kissed like a thunderstorm, writhed against me like every man's dream. Her softness fit against me perfectly, as if her body had been crafted for mine.

"Hmm." A sweet voice sifted out from the shadows behind Caprice. "Did you decide to start without me?"

I glanced up to see a blonde woman eyeing us. She held a bottle of something expensive and wore a smirk like a knife's edge.

"Maybe." Caprice turned toward the woman, not moving from my lap. "I couldn't resist. He's delicious."

"Is she our adventure?" As my eyes drank in the woman, those urgent thoughts returned to tease and nag in the back of my mind.

I did have an appointment. A blonde woman. She didn't look like this woman, however. Had I been supposed to meet her? Something about her twitching fingers…

Yet, as I considered, lost in thought, Caprice's surprise glided sensually forward.

"You have no idea, Michael." Caprice didn't take her eyes off the woman.

"You say he's delicious?" The blonde's mouth quirked upward. "You'll have to let me try." She sat down next to me, and her lilac perfume immediately clouded over us. She traced a lacquered nail through my dark hair. "Surely there's enough to share."

"You don't think I will share *you* with him, do you?" Caprice grinned wickedly and then reached over to her friend's face and ran a finger along her jawline. "You're delicious too."

"So selfish." The blonde woman playfully turned from Caprice to me.

That moment froze, never to be completed.

Cold quicksilver boiled within my mind, and like a scarlet fountain, memory poured in to replace my vision. For less than a second, the alcove burst into brilliant light. The candles stopped flickering and gleamed.

Memory capered in my mind, rushed through me.

"Michael?" Caprice sounded concerned, but a thousand kilometers away.

"Um, yes?" I didn't even know what I responded to. I blinked slowly, drunk on concepts and ideas, things that felt alien in my mind.

Alien but certain. True.

I hadn't even noticed I lacked some of my memories but now the gaps became obvious.

The entire world shifted and changed. For a brief span, color faded into tones of gray, then burned, over-saturated, back into my mind.

The ladies continued their flirtatious banter, as if the entire world hadn't just slipped beneath our feet.

I sighed, delighting in the curve of Caprice's hips against mine. I had no time.

"We should discuss the terms of our evening." Caprice spoke to the other young woman but stared me in the eye. "Things are likely to get... rigorous."

"I hope so," the blonde purred.

"Ladies." I cleared my throat. "It seems as if we need to have a quick discussion."

"We do?" Caprice slipped her arm over my shoulders.

Despite her sweet distraction, the time had come. Already, initial protocols began to tick within my mind.

"As much as I want to never move from this spot, I need to step away. For just a moment. A bit of business."

"What?" Caprice stared at me, her lips pursed in an attractive pout. "Why didn't you handle it at the restaurant, Michael?"

"Will you ladies promise to be good until I return?" I kissed her cheek.

"No." The blonde woman's voice turned husky, tinged with shadows. Her hungry eyes shone. "I won't, at least."

"I won't be gone long." I tilted my head at Caprice and smiled.

"Hurry back, Michael." She frowned. "I won't wait forever."

"I know." I kissed her cheek. "Don't worry, love. I couldn't possibly stay away long." I slid out of the seat and walked away.

I felt her eyes on me as I went. Behind my left ear, that burning quicksilver urged me forward, toward my assignment.

It didn't matter how wonderful Caprice might be or what surprises she had planned for tonight.

I would probably never see her again.

Introduction Protocols

I stumbled through the door. My poor mind felt savaged by a maelstrom of tangled memory and odd snippets of recollection. I wobbled a bit, meandering toward an alleyway next to the bar and rested my hand against the wall.

Steady, Bishop. I reached into my jacket pocket, my fingers trembling. More than anything, I wanted a cigarette—

But no. Of course I didn't have one.

In my other life, I didn't smoke.

I leaned into the cool wall, data singing electronic warbles into my mind as the intel packets blipped and booted, establishing a connection to Facility networks. Forgotten vistas opened before me, like a blind man who could suddenly see.

Focus. I took a deep breath and tried to ignore the dizziness. With a subtle *click*, my boot packet connected to the Lattice and ran its initial processes. The preliminary systems whirred in my skull.

When the greeting came, it resonated within my own thoughts, a whisper softly singing.

Welcome, Asset. The system prompt felt like sunlight after long darkness. **Bishop, Michael, Asset 108. It has been three months and six days since you were last activated. Do you require full initialization protocols?**

"No." I spoke out loud before realizing I looked like a crazy person talking to myself in an alley. *No,* I linked. *Please play only my selected data stream.*

I'd heard the thing so often I had it memorized, but the system preferred a booting Asset perform at least a modicum of initialization.

Will comply. The system clicked in my mind. **Now preparing preselected introduction protocols.** The cool voice felt like a fresh

9

breeze. ***Initiating playback in three... two...***

Moments later, the smoky words of Gideon DuMarque, the Asset who had trained me for my early missions, grumbled into my mind. It felt as if he stood right next to me.

"It's always the same," Gideon growled. "You won't remember when you're in torpor. You'll just prance along like an idiot, living whatever life they give you."

"Why can't I just be active all the time? Or remember? Cops remember. Security agents and espionage agents remember their regular lives, and they go to work."

"Their work is nothing like ours," Gideon replied. "Their work won't shatter a mind, won't leave a person depraved and raving. It's better that we forget."

Gideon's career left him gruff as an old war veteran, yet his mind still sliced like a keen blade. This word-by-word recall, with my responses included, had been one of his earliest lessons.

I'd heard his explanations a thousand times. Honestly, it felt closer to a million. Still, should my memory fail to boot so that I needed the intel, I would be glad for it.

I let the words wash through me and waited for my favorite bit. I always enjoyed his description of the nanosecond of syncing:

"In high school, everyone learned about graphs: X represented left and right, Y showed up and down, and Z reflected near and far. With me?"

"Yeah. With you."

"Well, someday you'll be prancing along, happily listening to whatever ridiculous sound-track you play in that pretty head of yours, and they'll patch you in. It'll be sudden, with no warning. In the instant you connect to the Lattice, you'll stop being concerned with whatever idiocy you've gotten into, because it will be as if the world took a step in the direction of W. In that moment, you will see everything from a totally different angle."

10

"I just won't care about whatever is happening?"

"Fact. You could be in the middle of the world's best steak dinner, eating with the Hollywood starlet of your choice and it just won't matter. You'll stand up and you'll leave."

"I don't get it."

"Well, that's because you're stupid. You can't get it; that's the point. W exists outside your regular frame. But when it happens, all kinds of tiny mysteries will click; everything will make sense."

"Like what?"

"Things like, 'Why do I keep getting these cuts and bruises?' or 'What happened last Tuesday night 'round eight?'"

"Won't I wonder that before, like when I'm inactive?"

"Negative. You'll make up stupid excuses. Or they'll be made up for you; I can't tell the difference. Either way, you will instantly come to remember who and, more importantly, what you are."

The system carried on, informing me of current axiomatic readings in my area and reminding me of the nature of the Primary Protocol. Eventually, it came to a prompt.

Please acknowledge receipt of all data, Asset.

"Acknowledged." I paused. "Bishop, Michael," I muttered into the cool brick of the wall. "Asset 108. Authorization code 020798361. System green."

Welcome, Asset. The system greeting felt as brisk as cool spring water in my mind. ***Packet architecture initiating.***

"Acknowledged." I ran my fingers along the side of my head and imagined I felt the thin band of technology implanted in my skull.

I couldn't. The Crown fit perfectly.

A fine tremble ran through me, a result of an influx of hormonal stimulants and metabolic adjustments.

"I need a smoke," I breathed into the misty night.

From experience, I might have a bit of a wait before I got my first update. Perhaps I shouldn't hang out here, my forehead

11

pressed against an alleyway wall.

I needed to move.

Like a man coming off a four-day bender, I wandered into the shadows and slowly remembered everything I'd forgotten. Memories, stark and strange, began to fit together in a maddened jigsaw puzzle.

As disconcerting as it felt to realize I'd forgotten half my life, this remained an important protocol to an Asset's mental health. Once memories of my other life began to coalesce, it became suddenly clear why, most of the time, ignorance remained my best friend.

Without it, an Asset simply couldn't survive.

2

Wyatt Guthrie, my friend and fellow Asset, had a theory about our lives outside the Facility. Like most of the crazy things he posited, it made just enough sense to make me wonder.

"It's gotta have something to do with our biochemistry," he stated one day as we sat on a rooftop, staking out our targets.

"What does?" I whispered, trying to keep my focus on the two men in the alleyway below.

"Our lives. When we're all in torpor," he explained, as if I should know what he was talking about. "I think it's real important the Facility keeps some kinda hormonal balance within our brains." He scratched at his thick, neglected beard.

"You're not making any sense." I pointed at the men below us, as one of them handed the other a small package. "We need to focus."

"You can focus for me, Hoss." The man winked. "I'm over here bein' philosophical. When the shit goes down, I'm sure you'll tell me."

I shook my head. Arguing with Wyatt sometimes felt like playing catch with a well.

"Look at my life," he continued. "I customize stock cars from a shop in south California. I don't even have a house there; I've lived in the same trailer for the past decade."

"I thought you owned a house in Alabama?" I peered below as I whispered.

"I do," he agreed. "But I don't stay there. Instead, I live in a double-wide and spend every single day tinkering with the street stocks. Some nights, I go into town for a few beers, maybe watch some pretty thing dance." He shrugged. "It's what makes me happy."

"Okay? So what?"

"Gideon travels the world investing in businesses. You live in one of the most expensive cities on earth, acting like a damn fool with whatever cuteness bats her eyelashes at you."

"I'm still not following you."

"I think our tech requires certain hormones—happy ones. Dopamine, oxytocin." He paused. "Maybe the Facility has to keep our brains content and calm most of the time, just to counteract all the other bullshit they put our nervous systems through."

"Huh." I had to admit, I'd heard worse theories.

Most of the time, things were simple. I lived the perfect life, my days drawn from most men's fantasies. I didn't work; I didn't have to. I got a wire into my account every two weeks. It varied, but the amount surpassed what some people made in six months. Yet I didn't know where it came from. The sources had vague names like VRS Solutions or Apex Enterprises, throwaway companies that disappeared the next week.

Some might call me spoiled. Yet it got better.

I drove a new sports car. A candy-red thing that got me all kinds of attention. My wardrobe was perfectly tailored to me and quite expansive. My apartment in San Francisco should have run over ten grand a month, yet I never paid a dime of rent. It had a movie room, three separate bedrooms, and a small library, not to mention my personal white room for my Facility gear.

Oh. And... company.

I almost never spent an evening alone. I could have a different enchanting companion every night if I wanted. Or two. Not a matter of being some sleazy pickup artist, it was simply the way my evenings unfolded. I went to the right clubs, wore the right clothes. Before I knew it, I was dancing with someone like Caprice or her nameless friend. And the night's enticements had just begun.

As I said, I lived most men's fantasies.

There were other things though, odd things.

I never got ill. Never.

I never remembered my dreams.

I never worked out, ate whatever I pleased, and remained

14

incredibly fit.

I've never done taxes—in any country. A notation on all deposits read: tax paid.

I had no account with any public utility or phone company, yet I owned a phone and had electricity.

I never bought my clothes or books or diversions. A metallic white board hung on my fridge. Just now, it had "Men in Black" scrawled across it, indicating I wanted the VHS. As soon as I left, I felt certain it'd appear, yet I'd never seen anyone come into my place.

When in torpor I had no curiosity about any of this. *They* took care of everything. It was simple. I lived the perfect life.

Until activated.

Once active, I was a tool in the hand of the most powerful organization on Earth. I had access to devices and technology that literally shaped reality as we know it by the alteration of laws we termed axioms. In actuality, axioms were an analogy for the various laws of physics, some yet to be discovered by mankind.

To Assets such as myself, the axioms of physics were weaponry. They might be bent or altogether broken while on assignment. This awesome technology was an absolute requirement for what we did, the bare minimum of what we needed in order to come back alive.

Because dark, inhuman things lurked in the shadows of our world—things most people couldn't even imagine. Our very reality was under siege by beings older than humanity itself.

3

Events like my spoiled evening with Caprice practically dominated my life. Yet, regardless of my dalliances, when the Facility called, I came.

Earlier this year, while traveling in Oregon, the world had performed the same shift beneath my feet, sharp and jarring. At the time, I happened to be with Mira, an enticing young tourist, hiking to the top of Multnomah Falls. The start of a promising entanglement.

But no.

Just as had happened in the club with Caprice, my Crown protocols and system initializations rose like smoke in my mind. As we rounded the third hairpin curve of the trail, like thunder, I remembered the truth of my life.

The truth behind the world.

"I have to go," I told my companion.

"What?" The young lady pushed her dark hair from her eyes. "I don't understand."

"It's not going to work, Mira." I nodded once at her. "But enjoy the hike."

I turned and walked away, my new mission already bubbling in my mind.

The Facility had sent me to Idaho Falls to requisition Bill Iverson.

An innocent kid.

While a requisition might sound fancy, the simple truth of the matter loomed far darker in my mind. I said innocent, but Billy Iverson had earned classification as an Irrat—Facility shorthand for Irrational. He might have been innocent when the Facility identified him, but that wouldn't last. No, unfortunately for him and his family, the boy resembled a devastating time bomb far more than he did a child.

Irrats like Billy posed a primary concern.

Current axiomatic statistics have stabilized, Michael. The gentle Russian accent of Anya Petrova, Facility *Preceptor* seeped into my mind. She had sent me the link directly so that I heard it in my Crown as if it were my own thought. *The Irrational target currently reads as a 0.3 anomaly below baseline.*

Point three from Rationality zero. It's still too much. I frowned as I linked back, watching the kid play in the park. *What did you say the variance averaged out as?*

Over the course of the last thirty-six hours, Bill Iverson has shifted Rational physics seventeen times. These shifts were never larger than three points and were predominately sub-Rational. They averaged 2.7 points in variance.

Too much. I frowned, grinding my teeth together.

Affirmative, Michael. Anya's prim tone felt clipped in my mind. *Acquisition protocols remain in play.*

Understood. I sighed.

I saw no way out of this.

Bill had been slated for reeducation, a term that chilled me. Young Irrats such as Billy could often have their abnormality gentled before they became a serious danger. That was the best-case scenario. As young as he was, every possibility remained that I'd be able to return him to his family.

A long shot but possible.

Few older Irrats survived gentling and remained sane.

The fact that I'd been assigned to acquire him made this even more difficult. Yes, young Mr. Iverson might have been an innocent kid. But he was also an Irrat kid.

A dangerous kid.

Do we know if the target is conscious of what he's doing? I linked, hoping this would be one of my easier assignments. *Is he aware he's fracturing reality?*

Unknown. Over the link I felt Anya's brow crease just the tiniest bit. *According to dossier records, his mother did have a phone conversation with her sister two days ago that might pertain.*

His mother. I paused. *Ella Iverson?*

Affirmative. In that phone record, she spoke with her sister about hearing voices within their home. She teased that she thought their family might be haunted.

Damnit. I shook my head. *That's not good.*

His Irrationality had already progressed to physical manifestations. Perhaps Bill Iverson hadn't caused any significant problems yet, but soon he would realize he had twisted reality in some small, strange way. Maybe lights in the sky, maybe telekinesis easily written off as poltergeists.

Then his situation would become difficult.

Soon other entities—monstrosities hidden behind the world—would notice him. Bill Iverson's Irrationality already beckoned to them. Every time he used his power to shape the Rational world, he lit another candle in the infinite darkness. Their ancient eyes constantly sought people like him. Perhaps they would grant him artifacts from distant topias—other realities—or the talent to break the minds of men. Perhaps they would merely whisper madness in his dreams and show him shadows of the infinite future.

Or they could use him to rend the veil and pour into our world like burning maggots and shadowed carrion crows. Everyone who glanced into his eyes could become blighted and insane.

I'd seen how badly this could go. More than once the Facility had assigned me to a priority team to take out some threat to humanity's continued existence. Adults who'd started life just like young Bill became cultists and madmen, devotees to the unspeakable things beyond the veil of reality.

Target is on the move, Michael.

I see him.

Billy, laughing, had sprinted away from some of the other kids. He jaunted from the sandpit, running wildly toward the woods with his arms stretched out wide.

Happy. Not a care in the world.

Long-range telemetry shows him twenty-seven meters from your current location.

That seems correct. I tilted my head, making certain. Long-range telemetry could be quirky, but its accuracy still astounded me. Anya, after all, sat in Facility 17, several states away, yet she saw Billy on her visual array. Her readings were perfect, right down to the distance.

Recommend taking action, Michael.

Yeah. I get it.

I sighed and stood from where I crouched in the woods. From my pocket, I pulled the small injection module and fit it into the Maverick-class firearm I carried.

This wouldn't hurt the boy, and I could make it quick.

I engaged some of the technology docked in my Crown and altered the axioms of light around me. As if by magic, I completely faded from sight.

Slowly, I crept through the woods.

"You'll never catch me!" Bill Iverson called over his shoulder at the kids who weren't chasing him. "Too slow!"

"Bill!" Ella Iverson called from where she sat on a park bench with a tanned gentleman who wasn't her husband. "Don't go too far!"

Like a kid in an afterschool special who ends up kidnapped by bad guys, Billy pushed on, heedless.

Less than a minute later, he ran past where I leaned against a tree, unseen. The moment the dark-headed boy had his back to me, I raised the Maverick and fired an injectable into the center of his back.

Target acquired, I linked Anya the moment the boy's step faltered.

"What?" The kid spoke to no one in particular, and his hand scrabbled up the center of his back. "Mom?"

He should be out. This could be bad. I trusted the injectable

20

would render him fast asleep in a few moments, but that still left plenty of time to scream.

I toggled off the packet in my Crown, the one I'd used to pull my vanishing act. My favorite little trick, known as the *Wraith,* powered down. Light resumed its typical behavior, and I blinked into existence, Brooks Brothers suit and all.

"Hey, sport." I holstered the Maverick beneath my jacket. "You seem a little pale."

"I think I need to find my mom." He took a step back along the path, his pupils huge.

"I can help," I assured him. "Is she back over—?"

I hadn't even pointed before Bill Iverson collapsed, sagging to the ground like a rag doll.

I am patching you updated parameters, Michael. Immediately on the tail of Anya's link came the subtle whirring sensation of my Crown receiving a packet.

Copy that.

I stepped up to the boy. He looked so small, lying there. Like a puppet with its strings cut.

I bent over to scoop up the child. He felt light in my arms and smelled slightly of sweat and sunlight.

As I held Bill Iverson, I glanced back over my shoulder. In the park behind me, his mother laughed at something her gentleman companion said.

He placed one hand on her bare leg.

Ella Iverson would never forget today, I knew that. In all likelihood, she would never see her son again. Most families didn't survive this kind of thing; the trauma destroyed them. I heard her laugh again and couldn't help but think how many sleepless nights were on the horizon for her.

Michael? Anya linked me, reminding me that I still had a job to do.

I'm on it, Anya. I paused, gazing down at Billy. *Situation green.*

21

No, Michael. Rationality is spiking—!

The boy's eyes opened. Behind them, malevolent shards of despair burned. From Billy's eyes, nose, and mouth, shadowed mist drifted like greasy smoke.

"Um." I blinked.

No human eyes ever shone with that baleful green-and-violet light. Within them, blackened veins of ichor pulsed. No human tongue ever spoke the awful, twisted words that came from his mouth.

"Re'nach Par arre k'yarnak!" The boy lunged for my throat, drooling, inky veins writhing through his pale skin. **"Ooshu zhro nahlirghq!"**

Reality trembled around me. Distant whispers melted in my mind, burning like hot tar.

"Shit!" I offered eloquently, as I dropped the boy and scrambled back.

Billy Iverson landed on all fours, an umbra of tendril-filled twilight around him. He peered up at me like a feral child, then pounced.

—wo points. Three! Anya's concern pulsed in my mind. *Michael, I believe the Irrat to be unfurling!*

Think so, Anya? The sudden weight Bill hurled against me brought us both to the ground. *Do you?*

Most Irrats first awakened under stress; that fact had been well-documented. Their unfurling made extractions exponentially more difficult. I'd heard dozens of accounts of botched missions where the Assets believed themselves to be in the clear, only to find things had spiraled far, far out of their control in a single blink.

Like this one.

"Querizin," the no-longer-a-simple-boy hissed. Wisps of shadow boiled around him. **"Y-vulgtm ehye, ph'kn."**

"I understand." I fumbled for the Maverick, still heavy in my pocket. "I do."

I did not.

"**You,**" he spat, fingers scrambling for my neck. "**Heathens. Unbelievers.**"

I had the weapon in hand and pulled the trigger twice before I realized the boy had switched to English.

"**The Scarlet Star comes,**" he announced. Tendrils of misty twilight drifted from his mouth and nose.

"I see." I fired two more of the injectables, just to be certain.

Billy Iverson's eyes rolled back in his head. He slumped. The boy fell to the ground, the shadows retreating into him.

Rationality stabilizing, Michael, Anya reported as calmly as one might discuss the weather.

Understood. I pushed myself up. *Target achieved.*

You reported that previously. I felt her confusion.

I did. I sighed, gazing down at the boy. *I'm hoping it sticks this time.*

Bill Iverson didn't move.

4

A black van? I linked Anya. *I'm seriously taking this child to a black van?*

I do not understand, Michael. Like most *Preceptors*, humor and social cues often didn't land with Anya. *Does the color of the acquisition vehicle matter?*

I sighed.

With no time to explain, I approached the van. The moment I got within ten steps, I felt my Crown whir as it exchanged limited handshake protocols with the two Assets inside. Their names came to me in whispers behind my mind.

Olman, Edward, Asset 229.

Barmin, Miguel, Asset 872.

"He's your problem now." I nodded to Edward, who stepped out of the driver's seat.

"Looks like you have things under control," the young man responded. He smacked the side of the van, and the back opened. Miguel, burly and grim, reached from within.

"It was a close one," I replied as Miguel took Bill. "He's been hit with five class VII injectables."

"This little squirt?" Miguel raised one eyebrow. "Overcompensate much?"

"The situation required it." I arched my brow in return. "Watch yourselves."

"Will comply, Asset." Edward gave me a two-fingered salute. "We have it from here."

I nodded and then turned back down the street. The sooner I made my extraction locale, the sooner I could go home. The sooner I could go back into torpor—back into my normal, non-Asset life.

The sooner I could forget.

I hadn't made it a block before Edward's communique slammed across all channels, a flagrant breach of Facility protocols. An otherworldly shriek rent through my Crown, garbled with static and electronic noise.

Edward? I turned to peer down the block. *Miguel? Please respond.*

Immediately, a second communique came in, cool as quicksilver in my mind.

Asset 108. That hadn't been Anya or a system message; it'd been one of the Designates. *We require your attention. Please return to previous coordinates.*

Copy that. I'd already begun to sprint, adrenaline souring my stomach as I raced back down the street.

Toward the van.

I hadn't gone two meters before the Designate patched the data to my Crown. Due to the neural interface, the coordinates appeared in my field of vision, a burning blue indicator. Naturally, it only existed in my mind, but the directional indicators could be damned useful.

Telemetry reads local Rationality at negative five and sinking. The Designate's voice sounded calm, almost preternaturally so. *Negative six.*

Can you give me a direct read to my Crown? I asked as I got close. If the Irrat boy caused any large shifts, I wanted to know it ASAP.

Affirmative. Be advised non-local readings may vary by a factor of .006%.

I am aware. Thank you.

The Designate did not reply, but in the upper left corner of my vision, a blazing orange number flickered into existence.

Screams rent the air.

Those sounds belonged nowhere in the human world, wet cries of agony and terror, unlike anything I'd heard before. As I rounded the corner, the van tipped up. It rose over half a meter off the ground as something dented it from the inside.

"Oooooo-kay." I drew the only weapon I had, the Maverick-

class pistol. The gun had no real upgrades, just .38 ammo and the injectable module. This type of mission didn't often call for weaponry, and so I hadn't spec'd for it.

Foolish me.

Trembling a bit, I pulled the module free from the pistol. Bill Iverson—or whatever remained of him—would require more than a nap. The scream came again, along with a bellowing roar that made my bones shake. This time, the scream cut off with a sudden, wet finality.

Does telemetry have a status on the operatives in the vehicle?

Negative. The Designate sounded placid, as if nothing were amiss. *All Crown functions have ceased. Assets are assumed lost.*

"Well, gloves off then," I muttered as I took aim at the van. I'd equipped packets that might help me, neuralware that augmented speed and reflexes.

I hoped it'd be enough.

The van tipped up a second time as something far stronger than an eight-year-old boy slammed into the side, snarling.

"Oh man," I breathed. I raised my Maverick with one smooth motion and riddled the vehicle with bullets, firing again and again.

The front window glass of the van exploded outward in a shower of blood-covered shards and slivers. A terrifying darkness boiled within that explosion, amid the sharpness and sound.

Had that been... Bill Iverson?

The tiny orange numeral in the upper field of my vision slipped to negative seven, as mist and darkness roiled from inside the van. A dark whisper accompanied them, like what the mad might utter in the dark hush of night.

Within that shroud of living shadow, I saw furious eyes that burned with a feral, verdant hatred. The wisps of darkness coursed along on the wind, undulating like living things.

For a moment, those eyes stared squarely at me. The whispers pulled at me, words of blasphemy and sharpness. They cascaded into my mind, bringing visions of horror.

I reeled backward from the force of it, dropping the Maverick.

There is a darkness, a shadow across the face of the moon.
Within the sky, a brilliant star burns, crimson as blood.
The entire world has f—

"What?" I pulled myself away from those whispers, even as they sliced into me.

The misty tendrils of shadow reached for me, hungry.

"The Equation is not complete." Bill's venomous words made my ears bleed. I stumbled as the weight of them crushed me. **"It is because of your kind. You will repent, manling. You will know lamentation."**

"Fuck," I breathed. My fingers dug at the concrete, scrabbling wildly until they found the Maverick. I whipped it forward.

I fired and fired and fired.

As the bullets tore into Bill's silhouette, the boy screamed, a cry far too great for a child's lungs. That wail burned its way into me, gibbered with madness and the despair of forgotten things.

The shadowy abomination that had possessed Bill Iverson swarmed around me, and the entire world consisted of hollow darkness and fanged mist. Every time it touched my skin, I felt the cold, empty twilight, and the wailings of ten thousand madmen sliced at my mind.

An eternal moment later, it had swirled away, cast upon the wind.

Rationality zero reestablished. Baselines holding. The Designate's voice cascaded through me, sweet and calm.

I realized I had no idea how long I'd been lying on the ground.

The target is lost. I stared at the van and swore to myself. *Do you want me to pursue?*

Negative, Asset. The Designate's tone neither encouraged nor damned me. *Your dossier is complete. Proceed to extraction coordinates for debriefing.*

As I left, I gave the van one last glance and shuddered.

Events like these made me content with forgetting the darker truths of my life. I couldn't live with full knowledge twenty-four hours a day. I'd crack in no time. Billy Iverson had been just one example, and there were worse.

There were definitely worse.

The Rational World

I stepped out of the alleyway and tried not to pay attention to the burly doorman who eyed me as I left.

"Evening." I smiled to him as I walked past.

The man didn't smile back. He didn't quite scowl either, but I had the definite sense that he held one at the ready.

Yet no matter how fierce he might be, I'd been wrong about the large man. He couldn't break me in two. He couldn't come close.

An entire world loomed behind the one he lived in, a world he knew nothing about. He did his best to seem tough and formidable, but the man's hardest day ranked close to child's play when compared to even my simplest assignment.

I, on the other hand, slaughtered muscle like him when the dossier called for it. Fairly regularly, the Facility set me against bruisers—sometimes bruisers who had the power to shape reality in accordance with their will.

Those men ended up dead.

Or worse.

Those I brought into Facility Prime vanished, the rest of their lives spent in a Facility holding cell. Taken to some black site, they were endlessly questioned or simply eliminated.

For the good of humanity.

The nightly fog rolled in, and the city glowed with muted light. As I wandered through the San Francisco mist, I began to feel my way through the shadows in my mind, searching for the initial portions of the dossier.

Yet I didn't have it.

This struck me as unusual, a matter for some concern. The Facility had the capability to port me an entire packet, instantly, wherever I stood on the planet. The fact that they hadn't meant...

"Something's screwy." I sighed.

Five minutes later, as I passed a colorful synagogue, a bit of my past resurfaced in a blazing flash of memory and recognition.

I chuckled, remembering my earlier hazy recollections of a blonde while with Caprice. Now the truth showed itself, obvious. I'd been remembering one of the people assigned to this dossier with me. Anya.

Anya Petrova, the exact same *Preceptor* who had been assigned the Iverson case with me.

Preceptors utilized different gear than traditional Assets: a holographic readout they manipulated with their fingertips. Dozens of times, I'd watched Anya's dexterous digits do their work.

Looking back, it seemed obvious. My system had been queuing that I'd been assigned to a three-person cadre with Anya and the king of all smart-assess, Wyatt Guthrie.

"Wyatt Guthrie. That's wonderful," I mumbled to myself. "We'll be lucky to get out alive."

Other Assets, including Wyatt Guthrie and the late Miguel Barmin, made up my real friends in my regular life. We remained quite close, even if none of us could ever exactly recall why. Our bond had wound into our neural architecture, and we each acknowledged it, in our own ways, during torpor.

Our lives were vastly different than most.

That was why I doubted I'd ever see Caprice again. She wasn't one of us. Like a movie extra, her entire existence contributed little more than background texture to mine. Her role in my life didn't actually matter.

Even if I did see her again, a woman like Caprice couldn't ever be anything more than a diversion. Non-Assets caused problems. If she became too involved in my life, she became a liability.

A danger.

My training architecture dictated all this, primary behavior modules stored in my Crown. We were warned against non-causal relationships with baseline humans. Our habitual subroutines had even been programmed to push us away from emotional commitments. After all, relationships created no end of problems.

If Caprice and I got serious, she would eventually want to see my place. I had protocols against this, but I had no way of knowing how far those protocols would go to assert their directives.

Things could get far worse than that, however.

Sooner or later, Caprice and I might be at my place when I had a dossier imported to my Crown.

The world would change then.

With no rhyme or reason, it would be time for her to go. No explanations. *Get out, Caprice.* I wouldn't care what we might have been doing at the time.

Even worse if she arrived unannounced as I stepped from my white room. There I would stand, armed to the gills. I might be decked out in next-gen body armor, guns synced with my nervous system, holding bags of tri-polymer explosives. Depending upon what Facility architecture I had that day, I might be only partially visible, preternaturally graceful, or any other combination of reality altering effects.

And Caprice? She wouldn't mean shit to me. All I would see was a problem. The woman would know too much.

Caprice would have to be liquidated. My protocols would demand nothing less.

God damn, but I needed a cigarette.

I stopped at Ernst's Corner Convenience, one of the quirky shops that made Nob Hill famous. After waiting for what felt like far too long, the young Pakistani woman happily sold me a pack. I didn't have any cash on me, but my card never ran low.

I walked back into the mist and lit up.

"Oh, my God." In bliss, I leaned back against the wall of the shop and simply enjoyed it. This could be the last moment of quiet I would have for a few days.

Funny thing, I only smoked when activated.

2

Several minutes later, I crushed out the butt.

Already, my mind drifted, caught within the singing data processes of my neural architecture. As I walked through the mist, I didn't pay attention to where my feet took me. I apparently had a destination, and I'd learned long ago to trust my subconscious in these situations.

As an Asset, I knew more than I realized. My unconscious mind had already shifted into active mode, meshing with the worldwide Lattice. For a bit, I would use nudges and small intuitions to guide me down the proper path.

All Assets trained for this segment of our boot cycle. The important bit required one to allow their mind to relax and float along like an autumn leaf on the breeze.

In this state, choices came simply. They seemed obvious.

This time, it seemed reasonable to wait at a MUNI station— specifically the one by the bookstore at Nob Hill. I walked a couple of blocks, trying to decide if I should smoke another cigarette, before sitting next to an older woman to wait.

"Sprinkling again." She squinted at the sky.

"In this city?" I offered an incredulous gasp. "Never happens."

"Heh." She gave me a smile, taking in my suit with a long appraisal. "If it rains enough, maybe I should call into work."

She continued to chat me up, all the while obviously wondering why the man in the expensive suit was waiting for a Nob Hill bus rather than calling for a limo.

Yet here I sat. No rhyme, no reason. The urge felt like a reflex, like kicking a stone when I walked or fiddling with a worn button on my shirt. I knew I had free will; I could stand up and walk away from the station. But I belonged here.

Perfectly placed.

"Do you often take this route?" She peered back up at the sky.

"It's my daily trudge, but I don't remember seeing you."

"I don't typically take the bus."

With that thought, I checked my wallet. Did the MUNI even take cash? I had no idea.

Within my wallet I saw a brand new weekly bus pass.

"But you bought a pass?" She raised one eyebrow.

Yes, of course I had a weekly bus pass; I'd bought it… When did I buy it? What story had I told myself? I couldn't even remember the purchase. Pretty typical. I might have walked around with this pass for weeks now without realizing it.

"I did." I gave her an enigmatic smile. "Just for this trip."

The bus didn't take long to pull up. It featured an ad for the newest late-night action hero drama splashed all along the side.

"Blake Runner." I grinned at the image, my favorite action hero. A grim-but-handsome actor held his pistol while a beautiful blonde woman wrapped herself around his leg. Behind the two of them, a blossom of orange fire burned, an explosion that filled the ad.

I sighed. Blake Runner always had the exact kind of high-octane insanity I loved. I often argued with Wyatt that Blake's detonation-driven escapades reminded me of my own adventures, but the hillbilly laughed in my face.

I had to admit Blake looked nothing like me.

When I stepped onto the bus, I showed the older driver my pass.

He smiled at me, genuinely friendly, a rarity in a city this size.

I wasn't alone, naturally. The older woman from my stop sat two rows back, across from the driver. A young couple had claimed the back of the bus, and two skaters sat next to each other but bopped along, lost in the grunge blasting from their headphones.

I selected a seat equidistant from all of them, only because it felt like my place. Then I watched out the window, idly curious about my destination.

36

The city swam by, rain now falling in earnest.

I will join you soon, Asset. The Designate's words trickled through my Crown like a December stream. We'd only driven past three stops when I received the transmission. As always, she sounded as if she sat right next to me even though her words could have come from the other side of the planet.

You will? Here? I smiled at a young boy who had just gotten on with his mother, until I realized he looked a lot like Bill Iverson.

No. Not worth thinking about that.

Affirmative. The cool quicksilver of the transmission poured through my mind. *We require a system sync. Time is of the essence, 108.*

A system sync? Technically, that made me the voice of the Designates on this particular mission and, therefore, Asset-in-command. It wasn't quite the same as being mission Alpha, but—

It made me wonder what was up.

Understood, Designate.

By touching my system with hers, the Designate left a lingering trace of herself in my neuralware—a fingerprint, after a fashion. As I waited, I pulled up her trace in my Crown and mentally perused the data more efficiently than one might read a book.

Hmm. Designate Ling.

We never had first names for any Designate—Wyatt joked they didn't have real names, that they weren't even human.

"You ever see one when yer in the pisser, Hoss? Ever see a Designate smoke or cuss or even get a little mad?"

"Can we discuss this later?" He had begun the conversation as we slipped through one of the largest *haciendas* in Juarez. "I feel as if we should keep our eyes open for the inhuman cannibal who's been kidnapping local children," I whispered harshly.

"We'll be in torpor later." The large man peered around a corner and gestured. "If we don't talk about it now, when?"

At least link, then. I shot him a glare as I crept down the hallway, Maverick in hand. *Let's go ahead and use system resources so you can bullshit about the Designates.*

So you admit you've never seen a Designate take a piss. He adjusted his gear, a cumbersome pack he carried on his back.

Well, that's not the kind of thing I go looking for.

It's just a notation. The large man shrugged like a mountain shifting. *It proves th—*

"I heard something." A man's voice drifted down the passage.

We have company. He nodded at the wide hallway, and our conversation ceased.

The idea that the Designates weren't human came up often. Wyatt gnawed at the old argument like a dog with a worn bone.

I knew he didn't believe it, neither did I, but Wyatt loved hokey conspiracy theories. He'd even claimed the Designates were all gray aliens or reptilians secretly here to rule the Earth.

We laughed at his flights of fancy, which made our jobs easier.

In truth, the Designates were odd, yes, but every bit as human as we were. They simply used more tech, far more than a typical Asset. Perhaps because of this, they became distant. Crisp, perfect.

Too perfect.

Naturally, that prissiness threw Wyatt off. A rough and tumble barbarian, Wyatt took pride in having little class. Poking fun at the Designates came second nature to the man.

Add in how little we knew of the higher-tier Designates and their agendas…

"We're here to save the world. Obviously," I muttered to myself, and the young boy stared at me. For a moment, I thought he might ask what I had meant.

I smiled at him and shook my head.

3

I'd worked with Designate Ling on a few other occasions, according to her trace within my Crown. She'd always given me high marks during debriefings and I'd found her simple to work with, as far as such things went.

But the last time I'd worked with her, three years before, had been a small catastrophe.

Dossier 16-1995.

That shitstorm of a dossier had been nothing like my usual tasks of chasing down small anomalies and acquisition work. It began simply enough with myself, Gideon DuMarque, and another Asset named Maxwell Barnes hunting down intel in New Mexico on a small but growing cult, *El Camino Oscuro*.

The Hidden Road.

Within a few days, however, things spiraled south.

Following the trail of corpses and madmen, Designate Ling sent a full cadre into the Yucatán with four specially spec'd Assets and an Alpha. Gritty and grueling work, a maddened cabalist named Amir Cadavas summoned inhuman terrors that taunted us from the darkness. We delved into hidden caverns beneath the world and beheld visages of creatures no human had seen for thousands of years.

Truly horrific stuff.

The cult centered around a young Irrat who possessed the thankfully unique power of granting Irrational gifts to others—at a terrible price. We'd pulled survivors out of New Mexico, madmen who claimed the Irrat could channel chaos and enlightening horror directly into people's minds, irrefutably shattering their sanity.

Things had grown so serious that a second Designate had been assigned as onsite support.

The child is a Variance in Rationality. Designate Davis briefed us through our Crowns before arriving onsite. *I'm patching you the related reports. Please peruse them immediately.*

Copy that, Designate. Our Alpha had scarcely sent the response before the packet hit our Crowns.

Depraved madness bled from those packets, horror unlike any I'd ever seen.

The child emanated fell power that burrowed into cracks in human consciousness. Once driven mad, a subject fell into true depravity. Eldritch abominations from the shadows of the world whispered lost secrets into the minds of the broken ones. They would learn forgotten names no one should ever speak and master complex rituals and bindings involving creatures that dwelt in the aetheric tides. These poor souls were literally killed and born again as marionettes for terrifying monstrosities.

The cult followed a truly twisted cosmology, centered around numeric patterns, forsaken names, and comet trajectories. As we delved deeper, we found their entire philosophy hinged on one horrifying fact:

The world as we knew it would soon end in blood and terror and madness. Lamentations unimaginable would soon harvest our feeble world, and little of humanity would survive to face that incomprehensible future.

As typical, the cult sought to hasten the catastrophe through ritual slayings and beckoning otherworldly abominations into the Rational world.

They had to be stopped.

It had been messy, the worst kind of job.

Thankfully the Designate took control the instant he arrived. We waded into that jungle with five Assets. We only brought three out. And one of us, a brilliant young woman named Elle, had been driven irrevocably mad.

Only Gideon and I truly survived.

In the end, the cult had been liquidated. Unfortunately, the young Irrat escaped. As far as anyone knew, he still remained at large.

It wasn't a good memory, exactly the kind of remembrance that made me pleased to spend most of my life in blissful ignorance.

This assignment won't be like that, I assured myself.

But, of course, I had no way to be certain.

Nigh-Terminal

In Chinatown, the bus came to a stop. The boy and his mother stepped into the rainy night just before Designate Ling strode onto the bus, small leather case in hand.

I sat up straight and watched as she swiped her pass. The Mandarin woman didn't meet my eye, didn't smile. She strolled down the aisle with inhuman grace and pointedly ignored everyone on the bus.

Beautiful. Cold. Efficient.

She sat directly across from me and nodded crisply.

As always, the Designates met with me in the strangest places: a biker bar, an abandoned warehouse, an isolated greasy spoon. Once, I'd met one in a strip club in the Tenderloin. She'd waited across the room at the bar, while I sat and drank. The entire time, she briefed me through my Crown.

Good evening, Asset 108. The cool words blew through my mind like an early spring breeze.

Good evening, Designate.

Around us, the rest of the passengers gazed out into the city or engaged in small talk. One man, who had gotten on the stop before, read a ratty-edged paperback. Yet we might as well have been alone. Sitting straight across the aisle from each other, Designate Ling and I had all the privacy we needed, even in such a public place.

Let us get synced. She opened a small leather case and pulled out an Ordinal slate—a stark black device that appeared somewhat like a book.

Unless one took a closer look.

Understood.

I glanced at her. The sterile light made her sable hair gleam above her perfect suit. She crossed her long legs and tapped the dark surface, manipulating the small piece of Facility tech.

In the visual array provided by my Crown, scarlet system symbols initialized on the surface of the slate. From the passengers' perspectives, however, nothing unusual shone within the visual spectrum.

We trust you have been ported the initial packet? She arched an eyebrow but didn't so much as turn her head.

I have, Designate. My mission details were already stored in my Crown, but I hadn't been able to access the information in full.

This dossier requires on-site Designate support. You will be briefed, rather than ported the intel, since the sync monopolizes sixty-seven percent of your system resources.

I see. I kept my gaze straight ahead.

Not every dossier required a sync. Far more often, I simply received my packet, geared up, and went on my way. Apparently the Designates desired something more. I couldn't imagine why they'd chosen me for extra responsibility though.

Initiating phaneric relay. She gazed at me then. *Are you prepared for the sync?*

I am. I focused on the city outside the window. *Situation green.*

The technology in my Solomon's Crown interfaced seamlessly with my nervous centers, optic nerves, and perceptual nodes. As a result, the Designates retained the ability to use my own senses and synapses to brief me and transfer information. It felt like having a private readout, a screen only I saw.

This incredibly useful trick meant that, for the most part, a Designate had the ability to patch us our entire dossier from afar. We could then process it as we would our own memories. However, a Designate sync could only be performed close at hand.

Mark, she linked.

In that same moment, the world transformed around me.

Designate Ling still sat in place, yet now a nimbus of pulsing meridians surrounded her, glowing channels of the Lattice that constantly updated and soft booted new packets as required.

44

Dataglyphs briefly glimmered in her vicinity, crimson symbols that burned into place as she sent system commands and received packets from Facility Prime.

All invisible to my fellow passengers.

Initiating data sync and packet update, she linked. One of the dataglyphs, a glowing symbol which appeared a bit like Japanese kanji, drifted from her slate toward me. I felt my Crown respond, a series of clicks only I could hear.

Copy that. Those brilliant channels of scarlet radiance bent toward me, filaments seeking their connection. They meshed with my Crown, and something whirred behind my right ear.

Radiance flashed in my mind.

It sang. It burned.

Sync completed, 108. Initiating briefing.

I nodded. Outside, the mundane world drifted by.

This is an atypical mission, Asset. Facility 17 has run deep telemetry tests beginning twenty-two days ago. Preceptors *are experimenting with bandwidths that might allow more effective, long-range monitoring of Rational integrity.*

I've heard. Anya had almost expressed excitement over the experiments, which floored me. Intense emotion remained an unheard-of anomaly for a *Preceptor*. Upgrading long-range telemetry might mean the *Preceptors* could remain within Facility 17 while still providing us with worldwide Rationality readings.

Success removed them from the danger of a dossier entirely. I approved; Anya had always proven capable but would never be a primary combatant as she could never equip enhancement packets.

During one of these tests, the operatives detected nigh-terminal levels of Irrationality, intense spikes of activity. Initially considered a systems error, a small cadre investigated. When these outliers returned during that excursion, Facility 17 alerted their superiors.

Nigh-terminal? I furrowed my brow. Hardly subtle. Someone had bent reality nearly to the breaking point. Such extreme manipulations couldn't help but be noticed. With Rationality spread so thin, some abomination could sunder the axiomatic realmwall and break through into our world.

Ambient Rationality levels spiked for little more than nanoseconds, varying between R -90 and R 36. Then, typical Rationality resumed, albeit with some lingering effects.

Such as? I glanced at the Designate.

She gave a nearly imperceptible shrug. *Small gravitational anomalies and variations in local space-time. There are no locals, and the anomalies seemed to resolve themselves. They were little more than eddies in physics and have been classified as non-threatening.*

So, no ripples in Rationality itself? No echoes of otherworldly horrors?

No. Just slight and temporary alterations in physics.

Hmm. I glanced out into the rainy night, processing what she had said.

Designate Ling's casual attitude spoke volumes.

Typically, small variations would be seen as a problem, even if they'd been short lived. Assets would be dispatched. Hell, I'd had entire dossiers regarding events that scarcely registered two points above Rationality zero.

Yet these were to be overlooked.

Where did this happen?

Sixty-seven minutes southwest of Las Vegas. An unpopulated area in the middle of the Mojave Desert. She tapped the Ordinal slate, and two crimson pulses burned in my vision.

A scarlet dataglyph briefly flashed between us and then vanished.

I sat back and crossed my arms.

You seem disturbed, Asset. The Designate finally met my gaze.

It's just a bit beyond my typical assignment. I shrugged slightly to adjust my jacket. *Usually I'm little more than a courier; maybe muscle if an undesirable is suspected of Irrationality.*

You've been on several dossiers that involved intense action. She tapped at her slate again, a furrow between her eyes.

True. Situations like the Yucatán came along pretty rarely—but they did happen. *It's not exactly the idea of danger that concerns me, Designate. I'm simply accustomed to better understanding my assignments.*

That is reasonable. She nodded again, just a bit, and her furrow vanished. *And the primary cause for our data sync. As Designate support, I will provide intel to Facility 17. Once appraisal is complete, your cadre will have nearly instantaneous updates.*

I suppose that will have to be enough. I popped the knuckles on one hand.

The atypical nature of this mission made me grind my teeth. Most of my dossiers dealt with minor things: a girl with some extra-cognitive capabilities or an insurance salesman who always drew aces. They bent reality without really realizing they toyed with the fabric of space-time. These Class IV events could be dealt with in an afternoon.

But nigh-terminal Irrationality? Hidden in the desert?

I popped the knuckles on my other hand.

Where will the conduit insertion point be, that far in the desert? I hadn't considered it until now. Typically, Facility teams worked with a *Gatekeeper* Asset to reshape physics for our transport. These conduits took many different shapes and classifications, yet the result of all the work ended up with our own personal wormhole depositing us in the Irrational hot zone.

You will take a commercial aircraft. We've been caught unprepared for this eventuality, and there aren't any conduits available in the area.

A... commercial flight? I shook my head in disbelief. I didn't remember a single mission where a transport conduit hadn't been arranged.

Screwy indeed.

Okay. When will I join the rest of my cadre?

Preceptor *Petrova has already departed Facility 17 and is well apprised of the situation. She will meet you at the airport. Asset Guthrie is already on the ground. You must leave immediately.*

How will I be outfitted? I frowned. All my gear still sat in my white room. My personalized stuff, the gear that had seen me through, stayed at my apartment. I had personalized katana, weighted and balanced just for me, along with my Maverick, and kinetic disruptors. Hell, the suit I wore wasn't even one of my specialized quasi-steel jobs—I'd stepped out with Caprice in a well-cut Brooks Brothers.

However, immediate departure precluded the time to run home to change.

Your cadre will equip on-site in Las Vegas. Time is of the essence.

I ground my teeth again.

Understood, Designate. The packet still wasn't fully sorted in my head. *Will this be simple reconnaissance? Or are we expected to pull an incursion?*

Your primary objective is to accompany Preceptor *Petrova. As long-range telemetry is unreliable in the region, she will gather further readings on localized Rationality and seek the cause of this event.* The Designate paused. *Expect objectives to adjust to mission requirements.*

The bus slowed to turn into the airport. With a dawning comprehension, I realized we'd arrived at my stop.

All pertinent details are in your Crown. Review the dossier during your flight.

I will, Designate. I stood and grabbed at the handhold. *I will be prepared by the time I touch down.*

She smiled at me. *We're certain you will be, 108.* As I walked away, I heard her one last time.

As always, Asset, we wish you well in the days ahead.

Barbaric

"Thank you, Mr. Bishop." Tricia, the bouncy young lady who waited for me at the terminal, helped me to my seat as if I couldn't find my own way. "If there isn't anything else?" She smiled and leaned in close to adjust my seatbelt. Enveloped in the violet of her perfume, I wondered for the tenth time who she imagined I might be.

"Nothing, Tricia." I offered my most reassuring smile and settled in. "I should be fine." *Fine for having to fly. Like a damn barbarian.*

"Wonderful." She graced me with her dazzling smile once more, then turned down the aisle and walked away.

I sighed and leaned back into my chair.

Tricia had met me outside the airport with two large men to handle my bags, a courtesy the airline provided though I carried no bags. No wait at the ticket counter, they escorted me straight past security.

Obviously, Mr. Michael Bishop had been classified as a very important person. Or, at least, someone on important business.

"Not important enough for a conduit though," I grumbled to myself.

Typically, the Designates set conduits up long before they ever tapped an Asset, one of the first points listed on the dossier. Often, these proved to be odd little locations like 'the second story exit of the abandoned mattress warehouse on Fifth and Powell, from 11:38 PM to 11:40 PM.'

It couldn't ever be simple.

An individual Asset's Crown data always keyed to whatever specific conduit was designated for their use. This safeguard protected the public, preventing random citizens from opening wormholes in reality.

A wise precaution, I thought.

Conduit creation bent the axioms of Rationality far beyond their typical parameters, hence the short window for their usage. Assets equipped with *Gatekeeper* packets synced with various pylons situated in Facilities around the globe, which allowed instantaneous transport. Conduits rarely made for a long trek, but the far end might be thousands of kilometers away or across the ocean or in a white room at one of the Facilities.

As long as an Asset kept to the schedule, all went well. I'd typically step into a twisted sphere of light and find myself along a short path or hallway or moonlit road. It might take ten steps to travel from Austria to Australia. At other times, the conduit provided an instant experience, literally one step away from wherever I needed—

"Would you like something to drink?"

"Oh." I glanced up, startled. "Um—" I mustered a grin as I turned.

The stewardess smiled and tilted her head. Red hair spilled around her face, and she gestured at the cart. "Need anything before we take off?" Her blue eyes fascinated me.

"Not just now." I cleared my throat. "Could I get something later?" I peeked at the cart, then at her. "If there's something I want?"

"Maybe." She wrinkled her nose, her smile broadening with nuanced meaning. "I'll be around, Mr. Bishop."

I watched her walk away, wondering again who the airline believed me to be.

Making the mental tick that opened the options within my Crown, I settled back into my chair. The device responded instantly, subtly clicking as it engaged the Lattice. I opened the Adjunct dialogue and, instantly, a chipper voice whirred in my mind.

Good evening, 108. How can I assist you?

I considered for a moment. My most impressive piece of technology, the Solomon's Crown lined the inside of my skull and remained constantly connected with the Lattice, the worldwide information network used by the Facility.

Through the Lattice, my Adjunct helped process the vast amount of data I might require.

Its base personality never failed to be ridiculously cheerful. I had other aspects for the device, secondary personalities I could equip. For now, however, I decided to stick with the initial settings.

I needed to focus on work.

I used the seamless technology as effortlessly as my hand, with no pointer or keyboard input. It normally presented whatever I wanted, how I wanted it, faster than I could give voice to the desire.

My system just underwent a soft sync with Designate Ling. As a result, my Crown has yet to process my dossier packet.

Affirmative, 108. The Adjunct happily whirred. **However, due to the additional processing time required by Designate 094's integral connection, your dossier is due to be fully ported by 0425.**

That won't do. I frowned. *I need to have this down by the time I reach Las Vegas.*

Understood, Asset. That whirring sensation came again. **How can I help? Would you prefer manual perusal of the packet?**

Not really. More knuckles popped as I sighed. *But it's my only choice, I suppose.*

Will comply. I felt the thing practically beaming with joyful purpose in my mind.

The Adjunct engaged my phaneric node—the same node the Designates used to place indicators over my visual array. I felt the slightest *snick* behind my left ear.

You prefer visual overlay. This hadn't exactly been phrased as a question.

Copy that. I could port data into my memory, at least when my

51

resources hadn't been tasked by a Designate. Now, though, that didn't seem to be an option. With adequate time, however, I could absorb the packet the old-fashioned way, one tidbit at the time as if I were reading.

Reading. Commercial flights. What could be next? Why not hand me a club, point me toward the incursion, and send me tottering off on foot?

With a smooth vibration in my head, my Crown meshed with several areas of my cerebral cortex. I relaxed my gaze and stared at the back of the seat in front of me.

Visual interface initiating now, the Adjunct merrily reported.

I watched as the packet's visual dialogue opened before me, a series of vibrant, colored spheres only I could see. Burning dataglyphs identified each ball. They moved with little more than a thought.

Initiating "Overview" on your mark.

Mark, I agreed.

The middle sphere moved closer to me, appearing to hang in the air between my face and the seat in front of me. It rotated. On its surface, a crimson dataglyph glimmered. A synthesis of numerical symbols, it resembled the astrological sign for Mercury, ☿.

The Adjunct began to speak, relaying the packet data in a more neutral tone. *Twenty-three hours, nine minutes ago, Assets in the Death Valley region noticed several sharp spikes of near-terminal Irrationality. These spikes showed at the edge of their data range but remained significant. This report led Facility 17 to scan the area with axiomatic telemetry as part of new protocols.*

The interface resolved to a map of the American southwest, superimposed over my vision, yet a simple shift in focus would allow me to see the plane's cabin faster than I could blink, if required.

As the map clarified, I saw the team's location, the readouts on their gear, and the Irrational spikes. Swiftly, the view resolved, focused on two unfamiliar Assets in the desert.

Something's wrong, the dark-haired Asset linked while he scanned the area. His *Artisan*-class neuralware glitched in time with the spikes.

"My gear seems to be misqueueing," said another Asset, a *Preceptor*, Russian and blonde like all the others. She didn't bother to link as she stood in place, twitching. "Is this right?"

I watched both the gear readouts and the spiking levels of Irrationality. The two appeared intimately connected. The spikes were incredibly focused, intensely powerful, and only occurred in extremely short bursts.

With a scarlet flash, the entire readout burst with static.

Wait. I shook my head. *What was—?*

Before I could complete the thought, the Adjunct replied: ***A spike in Irrationality of R -90. The bursts lasted nanoseconds, in some cases picoseconds, but spread over the course of the next hour and twenty minutes, with no discernible patter—***

Pause. I wound the data stream back a few seconds. In 1/10,000 time, I watched the bursts in the middle of the desert.

It fascinated me.

The readout showed Irrationality spiking dangerously high yet not rippling throughout the area. It did cause small anomalies, but it surprisingly didn't echo and create other, smaller spikes.

"Strong," I muttered. "Localized."

"Excuse me?" I hadn't noticed the attendant walking by. "Did you want that drink now, Mr. Bishop?"

"You know…" I gazed up at her, and the edges of my mouth quirked up in pleasure at the sight of those lovely blue eyes. Between us, I still saw the faint outline of those spikes in reality. "I might need one after all. Whiskey, if you have it. On the rocks."

As she stepped away, I turned my attention back to the dossier.

Those bursts seemed surgical in their precision. Hell, they almost ripped through the axiomatic realmwall—the fragile veil of reality.

Did these bursts threaten realmwall integrity? I turned sideways a bit to take the drink from the stewardess, nodding genially at her.

Happily, no fracture occurred, the Adjunct responded promptly. **Current speculation categorizes this event as a near incursion.**

Yeah. I rubbed my sweaty palm on my slacks. *I bet.*

If this event had been enough to fracture Rationality, it would have exposed us to… whatever waited on the other side. We'd been a hair's breadth from a breach.

No single Irrat could cause bursts that large.

Adjunct. I peered at the data. *I see absolutely no echo effect on these bursts. With something this large, I would expect ripples of Irrationality across the region.*

I frowned at the thought and peered harder at the data. Spikes less than a tenth that size cascaded and rippled. Something of this strength should have created other bursts to spread across the Mojave Desert and leave inhuman aberrations and small rifts in its wake.

This had not. It'd been controlled.

By someone.

Cascading effects, a reasonable expectation, have not been recorded. Facility 17 and Facility 6 have both monitored ambient Rationality in the area since this second set of spikes, but there have been no further variations.

Really. I scrolled through the dossier until I found satellite pictures of the location. It only took a few moments to enhance the photos to the point where I saw an old structure, hidden in the shadow of a cliff.

A missile silo?

I took a sip of my whiskey, thinking. Who could possibly do this?

Perhaps I needed a different kind of intel.

Adjunct, I require data on local persons of interest.

Will comply, 108. The Adjunct again whirred merrily.

The visual data collapsed into wispy shadows, swallowed up by the emerald sphere. It spun away from me, and an azure orb moved closer, its dataglyph shining brilliantly on the surface.

Known Irrationals and their locations, the Adjunct cheerily reported. *No Irrationals are known in the selected area.*

None? The moment I sent the link I realized what I'd done. Still centered on the missile silo, the program had searched only that region. Unsurprisingly, no known Irrats had been sighted in a single abandoned structure in the middle of the desert.

Expand parameters to include Las Vegas, please.

No problem! I'll place the list over here. On the right side of my visual array, a rectangle appeared. White letters began to scroll within it:

The known and wanted Irrational variations in the Las Vegas Metro area during the last month include:

Clyde D. Gordon- Irrational 1854
CLASSIFICATION: Human with Bound Affinity
***

Harij Nasan- Irrational 1458
CLASSIFICATION: Human with Bound Affinity
***

Thomas LeManns- Irrational 7704
CLASSIFICATION: Human with Bound Affinity
***

Rudolfo Firenzei- Irrational 2187
CLASSIFICATION: Human with Bound Affinity
***

Leticia Del Toro- Irrational 6723
CLASSIFICATION: Human with Bound Affinity
***

Earl "The Masque" Princely- Irrational 3420

CLASSIFICATION: Practitioner of the Heretical Art
***

Nicholas Eidon "The Padre"- Irrational 0081
CLASSIFICATION: Archonic Legacy
***

Unnamed Crimson Dedicant- 1107
CLASSIFICATION: Sorcerous Malfeasant
***

Rebecca Thorne- Irrational 9108
CLASSIFICATION: Baseline Outlier
***

"The Carrion" Irrational REDACTED
WARNING: COGNITOHAZARD
REDACTED
***

Fredric Bowman/Kali-Kajin- Irrational 2736
CLASSIFICATION: Aetheric Deviation
***

"The Gaunt Man"- Irrational 13563
CLASSIFICATION: Primal Construct
***

"Errg'hul," Screi- Irrational 098145
CLASSIFICATION: Interstellar Anomaly...

I stared at the scrolling display, my eyes wide. I hadn't expected nearly so many results to return.

Is this the typical number of known Irrational beings within the selected area?

Sorry, that query is undefined. The Adjunct clicked. ***Average rate of Irrational humans remains steady at .4 per million. Incidence of Aberrations or other Deviations is unknowable.***

Right. I expanded a selection at random.

Its miniature image, about half a meter high, resolved on my visual array.

Aberration 13563, the Gaunt Man, has been frequently reported since 1974, although it may have existed longer. Basically humanoid in appearance, it is unnaturally slender. It wears a gray suit several years out of date and can easily pass for an older man by any who do not pay it special heed.

Pause. I peered at the thing. Its eyes shifted in color and its pale skin sagged, sallow and flabby.

Looks like a tough customer.

This creature is truly monstrous.

Continue. I sat back and took a drink.

Aberration 13563 is a collector, both of rare items and creatures. It often appears as a peddler or a shop owner, a person of legitimate business. First encountered by Asset 71, Leo Telesco, in Romania in March of 1974, during Dossier P76-1974. The aberration pursued a trader who had found an item of particular rarity: a small statuette of unknown origins with an affinity for bestial astral aberrations. As a result of this...

In an attempt to process the vast information available, I let my vision drift. I learned about the Gaunt Man's tendencies toward flight and trickery rather than confrontation. It tended to create alliances with other creatures and then manipulate them into doing its work.

...most recently in a small shop within Las Vegas on Sahara Avenue called Fallen Leaves. This location is believed to be an entrance to an extra-spatial realm Telesco named "The Menagerie." Here, the Gaunt Man keeps living prisoners—

Pause. Perhaps something here could be of use after all. *Did an Asset recover this latest intel?*

The answer might matter. We often had Assets in the field, simply on reconnaissance. If we had feet on the ground in Vegas, I might have a useful resource available.

Negative, Asset, sorry to say. A Hornet-class drone, XS-761 recovered this data.

Fine. I finished my drink, irritated.

Previously, Fallen Leaves operated within New York City. Asset 341, Garret Valis created a record of the encounter, accompanied by an Asset you may be famili—

No. Let's move on. I wished, again, that I could simply port the packet to my Crown's memory, so I'd be able to draw on it as simply as any other recollection.

But my system still processed the Designate's sync. It didn't matter how much I wanted to take the easy way out, it just wasn't happening.

I needed to keep things simple.

Instead I closed the Irrat data and went back to study those spikes overlaid on the map. I couldn't help but marvel at how tight they were. That much Irrationality should have created some lingering effect: hauntings, lights in the sky, lost time...

Something.

I dug deeper into my Crown's database and perused the telemetry data. There had to be something, some echo, some lingering malaise due to such a sharp anomaly.

Moments later, I reached a dead end.

There have been no further reported Irrational readings as a result of the events of 21 June.

"So strange," I muttered. Nothing about this made sense.

I'd been on dozens of assignments where aberrant creatures knocked Rationality out of whack. Once, in Saskatchewan, I'd been on the trail of an aberration, a native of the aetheric tides that had somehow slipped into our world. In the distant wilds of Canada, I'd spoken to a native man, a First Nation resident, named Oki. Over a beer, Oki told me something had passed through his small town, something definitely inhuman.

"A wendigo." I took a sip of my beer, trying to seem credulous.

"That's what my grandfathers would have called it." Oki shrugged. "A ravenous, cannibalistic spirit. She probably began her life as a human."

"You saw her?" I raised one eyebrow.

"I did." He met my gaze. "Out near the Reaches." He poked me in the chest. "She's the one who killed that little boy. I guarantee it."

Oki's story ran deep with horseshit. Entire mythologies had been built by people who told stories to make sense of what they had seen.

Wendigo didn't exist. Not really.

Three days later, I found the aberration east of the Athabasca Sand Dunes. By then, I'd lost my *Preceptor* and I had to creep into the village alone. The forlorn little town sat desolate in the frigid night.

The wind howled. It sang with the voice of minds lost to depravity and despair.

The aberration had devoured the sanity and vitality from the people, leaving them as shambling, rambling husks. They lived, but theirs was a shattered life, little more than half-mad cadavers that muttered and whispered as they served the gray, emaciated figure. A local church served as a filthy nest for the creature and her thralls who only went afield to fetch unwilling victims to service the aberration's hungers.

The Facility had little choice. We purged the entire town from the map. Every sentient being had been liquidated. We wiped the townsfolk from the minds of their relatives. We razed the town. The Earth was salted.

Nothing survived.

Unfortunately, the assignment hadn't been completed before the inevitable ramifications began to appear. In the village of Stony Rapids, 107 kilometers to the east, the local mechanic completely snapped. The gray-haired man began to lure his neighbors into his shop, where he would bludgeon them to death with his tools while shrieking in an inhuman tongue.

He ran for two days into the wild before another Asset and I found him, babbling and building bloody shrines in a hidden cave.

I put him down.

Meanwhile, an entire herd of caribou went on a bloody, stampeding rampage only sixty-five kilometers west of the small village. It lasted for three days, and survivors said the animals ate the flesh of those they killed, devouring the carnage with what seemed like glee. They tore through the homes of rural natives, frothing and screeching, attacking the residents as if driven by an intelligence not their own.

The event had been publicized as rabies.

In a small village ninety kilometers to the northwest, an entire school committed mass suicide. Investigators found the student body had scrawled messages upon the walls of their classrooms, warnings written in Hindi, of all things. These warned of the Kali Yuga, the age of destruction, and spoke of the coming of a crimson star, which would herald the end.

Irrationality worked like a cancer in the world. It spread.

Yet echoes like these weren't the only dangers.

The "wendigo" had also drawn other Irrational creatures to the area, some from native myth and legend, some from beyond our world.

The entire situation took months to quell.

The Facility classified that event as a typical incursion, and its parameters scaled with Facility expectations. With such Irrational incursions, ramifications always followed.

Always.

"But not this time." I frowned as I again flipped through the data. Every piece of telemetry read as flawed or incomplete. These surges pulsed at least ten times larger than the one that began my Saskatchewan adventure.

Yet no echoes. Not one.

Impossible.

I flagged the red-haired stewardess only a few rows up from me.

She gave me a quick nod and headed in my direction. "Yes, Mr. Bishop?"

"Could I get another drink?" I gave her my most charming smile. "I think I could use it."

"My pleasure." The stewardess sashayed away and returned with another tumbler.

"Obliged." I accepted the glass, took a sip, and settled in again. *Adjunct?* I linked.

Yes, 108? The cheer made me want another drink.

Please display all known telemetric disturbances, worldwide, during the time of these spikes. I sighed, knowing exactly how much data I requested.

Understood, Asset. Will comply.

As the field began to populate, I shifted forward in my seat and took a longer sip, not quite gulping.

Then I resumed the long trawl through my dossier.

A Horror Out of Time

"Mr. Bishop." The red-haired stewardess stepped up from behind me and spoke just above a whisper. "We'll be landing soon."

"Oh." I managed a half-smile. "Thank you." I handed her my empty glass, trying not to grind my teeth.

This entire exercise had been pointless.

"Nothing," I muttered as she walked away.

If anyone had been watching me over the last hour or so, I certainly would have appeared cracked. For the entire time, I stared intently at the back of the seat in front of me and muttered my dismay under my breath.

Yes, completely normal.

I popped the knuckles of my right hand, trying not to glare at my interface. My Crown held wonders of little-known technology, but I felt awfully limited by the quality of available intel. The data, though plentiful, had been useless.

Do you wish to shift your viewpoint, 108?

I'd again pulled up topographic maps of the area adjusting my perspective all around the small structure. I confirmed the building as an abandoned missile silo but learned nothing more.

No. I massaged the back of my neck. *Do we have telemetry on ambient Rationality in the area?*

Long-range telemetric readings can often vary by—

I know, I snapped through the link. *What do they show?*

.0067 below Rationality zero. Completely within normal range, the Adjunct assured me cheerily.

I sighed.

Within the past hour, I'd combed the profiles of every Irrat sighted locally. Each seemed a poor fit for this magnitude of Irrationality. Even if they all worked together, they'd be unable to create these spikes. The precision and the speed at which the events had occurred remained impossible to comprehend.

This didn't feel like the work of an Irrat at all. My mind drifted to the aberration I'd destroyed, the wendigo. We hadn't come close to classifying all the abominations of the aetheric tides. Could it be something behind the axiomatic realmwall? Some aberration trying to slither through?

Would you like to continue this query? System resources are tasked to 98%.

No. I closed the dossier. Conjecture from the current info had proven pointless. Hopefully, Anya or Wyatt would know something I didn't.

Ten minutes later, we touched down. I stood and began to move toward the front of the plane.

"Do you plan to fly with us again?" the stewardess asked, as I made my way along.

Her nametag read: Claire.

"I just don't know." I shrugged, again captivated by those stunning eyes. "My business takes me all over."

"Maybe I'll see you later, Mr. Bishop." She gave me a little wave.

"Maybe." I sighed as she walked away.

Such laters never happened, not for an active Asset. Later, my Crown would be in torpor mode, and I wouldn't remember myself, much less the stewardess. She would be a stranger to me.

Too bad.

While in torpor, my adventures with Caprice, and seduction in general, were just another part of my Crown architecture. It required no skill, no wit or banter.

I had nothing to lose.

When awake and online, I enjoyed relationships much more, fully myself and in control of my debonair charm. Unfortunately, this remained a practical impossibility. Neither of my two states proved ideal for romance.

"No place for love in a Rational world," I sighed.

I made my way into the airport. Everything checked out, as it always did for Assets, and I moved along without issue. I had no bags, so I didn't need to—

My Crown whirred. In less time than it took to think, I realized I had an incoming link.

Michael, we have a small concern, Anya sent. I felt the tiny furrow between her blue eyes.

Worried, Preceptor? *I just made it off the plane.* Happy to hear from her, I beamed with full knowledge my emotion would transmit through the Crown. *What's the problem? Is Wyatt in the airport bar?*

Nothing so simple, Michael. Even though she knew me well, Anya's tone contained no warmth, standard among *Preceptors*. Sometimes, Anya seemed even more robotic. Wyatt called her the ice princess behind her back.

Fine. I sighed. She would be all about work. *Apprise me, Anya.*

Michael, her tone softened a touch before she continued, *there is an aberration of an unknown type within two hundred meters of your current position. It has been motionless for the past half hour at least.*

What? I stopped in place. *Unknown type?*

I have run it through every aberrant directory in the Lattice. I also cross-referenced my readings with telemetric databases. She paused for a moment, hesitant.

A hesitation that concerned me.

Michael, I found no known classification.

Does Facility Prime think this involves our dossier?

I have no indication of that. Anya paused. *I believe the consensus is this is a separate issue.*

Fucking brilliant. I am completely zero-geared, Anya. I don't suppose Wyatt chose to come with you?

Asset Guthrie is not present, Michael. We are to meet him at a different location.

I know that was the itinerary. I ground my teeth. *I simply hoped that, along with this news, you might tell me Designate Ling had altered the plan.*

I'm afraid that isn't the case.

One can always hope. I sighed. *Can you put in a request for tech disbursement? Otherwise, we really aren't equipped.*

That request has been filed and approved, Michael. She seemed pleased with herself.

Really? I shook my head and grinned ruefully. *At least I have you here to take care of things.*

Of course. I felt the little crease between her eyes again. *What else would I do, Michael? The disbursement was easily handled.*

Well, that's something at least. I'd been concerned a disbursement would be impossible. After all, that involved conduits, and here I was flying commercial. *Where do I need to go?*

Ahead, you should see the airport bookstore. There is a small restaurant next to it.

I see it. I smiled at a young girl who stared at me as I passed. Realizing I'd been standing in place like a loon, I started to walk.

Between the two of them is a gray access door marked Janitorial. You will find it unlocked.

Perfect. What's my time frame?

This is an emergency conduit. It will be available for the next four minutes and thirteen seconds only. I would advise haste.

Got it. Thanks, Anya. I broke into a run.

A couple stepped out of my way, and an older man shot me a glare as I took off with no apparent cause.

I didn't have time to worry about them.

Four minutes, Michael.

I sprinted past the bookstore, turning on a dime as I came to the janitorial door. I reached for the handle. It wouldn't be locked, simply coded for me.

Bishop, Michael. The Adjunct sunnily spoke in my Crown. ***Do***

you wish to initiate conduit?

"I do," I muttered, peering around the airport. "Asset 108. Authorization code 020798361. System green."

For a moment, I wondered how many times this location had been used. Conduits typically only existed between previously established locations.

I opened the door and felt the subtle *snick* in my Crown. The door shimmered for a moment, but only on my personal visual display. No one walking by saw anything odder than a man in a suit stepping into a janitor's closet.

A scarlet dataglyph appeared within my vision. Light danced around the edge of the doorway and burst around me, a brilliant display only I could see.

My Crown clicked, acknowledging the conduit.

I stepped into the white room.

The exact dimensions of the white rooms remain difficult to ascertain. Wyatt claimed they weren't in any of the Facilities but that they actually existed in some kind of non-Euclidian space.

I tended to believe him, as every time I stepped within one, I felt as if the world tilted sideways.

It looked like every white room I'd ever seen, a lab with white tile on the floor, white walls, and stainless metal tables and counters. Several different workstations held various pieces of equipment that presaged humanity's scientific knowledge by decades.

It held no visible light source, yet the room glowed with brilliant, cool light. I'd never determined exactly what the white rooms smelled like. They smelled clean but not harsh like disinfectant. The scent comforted me, reminded me of safety in some way I couldn't explain.

"On purpose, I'm certain," I muttered as I stepped inside.

I trailed my fingers along one of the stainless-steel tables and peered at the weapons cabinets.

Empty?

Those two bare weapon cabinets normally housed menacing, black firearms, while another cabinet held bits of body armor and various tools. A couple of duffel bags hung on the wall with some luggage and briefcases on the shelf beneath.

Bishop, Michael. Asset 108. The Adjunct clicked twice. *Do you wish me to initialize packet sync?*

I do. The moment I sent the link, a brilliant crimson indicator appeared in the lower left corner of my visual array. It blinked, indicating Facility system emanations had been detected within the room.

Do you have preferences regarding packet allocations?

I do. I stepped further into the room. The walls and gear racks still appeared quite sparse. *Please set up all packet operations in accordance with my personalized disbursement allocations per Bishop 23-67t.*

Will comply. Across the room from me, a bank of Facility subsystems began to power on.

I don't see much in the way of options. I opened a small locker and peeked inside. Where several pistols should be, the locker sat bare.

The situation has been classified as high risk, just so you know. Due to the location of the aberrant creature, there is an 83.2 % probability you will encounter baseline humanity while on site.

Well, I am in an airport. I frowned. Now that I considered it, I probably shouldn't be packing heat while there.

Perhaps I'd been spoiled. The white room connected to my apartment never lacked for anything. A drawer held cash, credit cards, and various bits of ID: passports, driver's licenses, national ID cards. If I needed something special for a mission, the computer and ultrahigh-quality printer allowed me to download and print pretty much any piece of government paperwork possible. I didn't have to load paper, it printed that too. Fancy. They might be on the market in fifteen years or so.

But here…

My choices were short, to put it kindly. I saw no guns at all, neither general issue nor Facility specialized. No blades of any kind, either, not even the smallest knife. No body armor.

"I'm not certain what I'm supposed to do here," I muttered. Going up against an aberration of unknown classification was one thing. Doing it with nothing more than the suit on my back felt a little reckless.

I stepped deeper into the room and opened up several drawers and cabinets. It seemed the Facility suggested equipping pepper spray and flash bangs, as I had plenty of each. A small black case proved to hold temporal anchors, rings one could suspend in space-time itself. These I picked up, wondering how the stationary rings continued to move with the Earth.

"Erm… no." I put the case back down and shook my head. I probably wouldn't find those useful in the middle of a battle.

I found sonic incapacitators, gravimetric snares, and drone perceptual systems. I considered that last one. It might be helpful to have drones the size of a quarter that fed me sensory data.

"Oh." I changed my mind as I went over the specs. I'd need to load the *Falconer* packet to make that work, and I'd never used it. Pass.

I opened a third metallic case before I found something useful.

"Dampening grenades!" I picked one up, enjoying the heft of the spherical device. The case held four of them, and I felt confident they would come in handy.

Beyond that, however…

I tapped into the system to link with other Assets. Through Designate Ling's sync, I had access to her secured channel. It pulsed in my mind, a tremor of cerulean coolness.

Designate, I need guidance, I linked. *Anya has apprised me to our situation, yet I am uncertain of my intended response.*

Understood, 108. Her voice burst into my mind like a December wind. *The aberration is not our primary objective at this time. In 88% of all simulations, its ejection is the preferred outcome. This is a random event, and you are not to jeopardize your primary mission to resolve it.*

Do we know it's random? I pocketed two of the dampeners. The grenades would be the simplest means of ejecting the creature.

We cannot be certain, she clarified.

It strikes me as coincidental we're dealing with an unrelated aberration, just when other matters have arisen.

Asset, we cannot ignore the aberration, yet events do require your attention elsewhere. If we were to give direction, we would suggest using the dampeners to restore ambient Rationality. Take the aberration if you can, but if the dampeners eject it to the aetheric tides, you are to let it go.

I see. I bit my lip. I hated to leave the creature loose.

Understood, Designate.

Just like that, she vanished, a whisper on the wind.

Glancing around, I weighed my limited options. I grabbed two more of the dampener grenades. For their size, they contained quite a punch. They weren't explosives; instead they reasserted the axioms of Rational physics, creating a burst of stability within a certain sphere.

Quite handy indeed.

I passed over a Neural Lacuna, designed to stun a human target and induce amnesia and suggestibility in order to create new memories. I also dismissed a pair of axiomatic shackles. I considered a photic baton, figuring it would be simple to conceal. My hand hovered over it, but then I changed my mind.

"I think that's it." Truly, I didn't relish the thought of going after an inhuman horror with nothing but dampening grenades on my side. I found it easy to understand why the Designates wouldn't want me running around an airport packing heat, yet—

Something caught at the corner of my eye.

There, resting within a small case next to the wall, sat a smooth disk, no larger than my fist. Several dials gleamed along the surface, and I felt certain it had already been queued to me.

"A Tabula Rasa," I mused with quiet wonder I stepped closer, certain I had been mistaken.

But no. There, in the middle of a white room almost bereft of weapons, sat one of the most powerful devices an Asset had the clearance to wield.

I picked it up. With the cool smoothness in my hand, I only trembled a bit. I'd never actually used one myself.

The Tabula Rasa completely removed all matter within a certain radius, leaving a spherical void in its place. The device created an unstable axiomatic field, then vented the matter into the aetheric tides. It treated organic matter and inorganic matter exactly the same: complete banishment from our reality.

Once detonated, only a sphere of nothingness would remain. Thunder would crack as the atmosphere surrounding the device slammed back into place.

Lethal. Devastating.

"And maybe a bit of overkill?" I mused as I tossed the device from one palm to the other. Obviously, the thing could come in handy to banish the deviation—the most common purpose for the Rasa. Yet I found it difficult to conceive how I might covertly use a Tabula Rasa while standing in the middle of the Las Vegas airport.

"Not today." I set the device down and stepped over to the silver refrigeration unit against the far wall. I pulled the door open and peered inside to peruse the dozens of pressurized injectables within.

Three minutes, twelve seconds, Michael.

Thank you, Anya. I reached into the unit and pulled out three small cylinders—Facility injectables. The small, pressurized syringes held viral mecha—Facility specialized nanomachines. The vast majority had been designed to interface with the Solomon's Crown and give short-lived boosts to the human body. Oftentimes, we needed these boosts to do far more than what

simple chemistry could provide. Hence, viral mecha had been created to make small
changes within an Asset's body.

The things performed miracles. I'd seen the mecha knit someone's face back together; I'd seen them create bone from spit and nothing. They altered reality itself within the human form, creating spectacular effects. Here, in the white room, it felt a bit more subdued.

Mechanical.

The moment I touched them, my Crown Adjunct initiated.

Asset, do you require assistance with the injectable selection?

I'm not certain which types are included here. I peered at the small device. *Typically, a* Caduceus-*class Asset provides my injectables.*

You are currently holding two type IV injectables and one type II-B. Both are indicated for physical alterations.

They both have the same specifications?

Type IV repairs wounds. The viral mecha will assist with tissue repair, shock, and fatigue. Type II-B alters metabolism, reaction times, and grants superhuman levels of hand-eye coordination.

Similar to the Adept *packet?* I hadn't been provided the means to download packets into my Crown. Odd.

Affirmative, to a lesser degree. If you note the numeric coding on the bottom of the devices, you can see what variation you're holding.

I did note that and scooped up seven of them.

I checked the codes on the side and selected one of the II-B injectables. Dozens of variations on II-B existed, but this one augmented speed and grace. It allowed short bursts of each, all at the cost of a little muscle soreness.

Useful in a pinch.

I thrust it against my bare arm. It made a tiny hiss as thousands of dormant viral mecha flowed into my bloodstream.

Then my gaze settled on the Tabula Rasa again.

"Fine. Just in case I need to banish part of the airport into the aether." I grabbed it. "It's not as if I have much choice," I muttered.

Two minutes, Michael, Anya piped up.

Understood. I'm finished. I walked toward the door. *There's little to be had here.*

Acknowledged. I will be standing by if you require me.

Can I get a visual overlay of the aberration's location? Already I felt the effects of the mecha as the tiny devices stimulated my neurons and endocrine system. Everything felt faster, even my head felt clearer.

Patching you the intel, Anya replied.

I felt a subtle shift in my Crown.

Thank you.

I stepped through the door, back into the busy airport. My ears popped, and for an instant a scarlet dataglyph burned in my mind.

The Solomon's Crown created intricate axio-static connections to each hemisphere of my brain. Several different nodes had been installed in and around the nerve plexi there and within my peripheral nervous system.

Anya used them to display her telemetry data as sensory input.

My visual cortex created a burning red marker over my field of vision. One hundred and eighty-seven meters away sat a figure shaped like the letter *J*. It hung, unmoving, in the air.

Advancing toward target.

I held two dampeners and kept one more in each pocket. Hopefully, the aberration lurked in some out of the way place, so I could trigger the devices without drawing too much attention. If that worked, the thing would be ejected back to the aetheric tides.

We'd be off to find Wyatt in a matter of minutes.

I hurried toward the aberration. *I read the target as in the nearest men's room. Can you confirm?*

Affirmative, Michael.

73

At least it's not out in the terminal.

With the door in sight, I hefted a dampening grenade.

The hairs on the back of my neck prickled, and I froze in place. I turned, certain someone watched me.

There.

A man leaned against the far wall, casual and confident. He had the dusky skin of someone born in the Middle East, yet even from here I could make out the keenness of those eyes.

I knew him.

I couldn't say how I knew him or where I recognized him from. Yet the young man stared at me, his eyes fixed on me as if daring me to speak to him.

"Excuse me," a second young man said as he stepped past me. The scarcest smile lurked at the edge of his mouth as he pushed into the airport hall.

I gaped at him for a moment, realizing he had no clue he had just used a restroom occupied by an extra-planar creature.

When I gazed back across the airport, the first man had vanished.

"I don't need extra puzzles," I muttered.

I pushed open the restroom door and stepped inside.

No one else stood within. For the scantest moment, I thought I heard wind howl, but—

But no.

All clear. I checked under the stalls to be certain. Then I flipped through the optic settings on my Crown. Still nothing.

Wyatt will love to hear about the aberration that got caught in the john, I mused.

No matter how I snarked, however, my hands trembled just the tiniest bit. The hair on the back of my neck rose, and my heart pounded in my chest.

The glowing marker indicated the third stall down.

Focus, Michael. Facility Prime says your adrenaline levels are spiking, Anya cut in.

I'm sure they are, I sent. *Are you saying we have a* Caduceus *watching our vitals?*

Asset Gardener is on remote vigilance, Anya confirmed. *I have a live link with her data.*

Good to know. I took another step. *Honestly, I wonder if we're getting a glitch. Anya, do you read any residual Irrationality other than what the marker shows?*

Ambient Rationality readings are nominal to .0026%. She paused, but I heard a touch of uncertainty in her cool tone. *Yet the figure remains, Michael. The data seem accurate.*

Understood. I placed my hand on the outside of the stall door, my thumb still on the dampener, ready to set it off in an instant.

Carefully, I pushed the door open, my heart thundering.

Empty.

Nothing, Anya. I peered at the strangely bent marker that hung in midair. For a moment I simply stared at empty air. *This makes no sense.*

When my system showed an aberration, it usually gave me an outline of the creature. Now it just showed a curved marker somewhat taller on one side. Whatever caused the aberration wasn't physical in any way; I only saw the marker through my Crown. I peered closer with the knowledge that my Crown recorded everything.

Ambient Rationality fluctuating, Michael. Rationality negative point seven five.

Copy that, Anya. I edged closer, holding the dampener tightly.

The indicator twitched, almost a spasm. I leapt back a bit, startled at the sudden movement.

Michael. Anya's link conveyed a bit of wariness. *I do not like these readings.*

Me neither. I eyed the indicator, then glanced around the stall. I saw nothing unusual, not a single thing out of place.

The marker undulated, twisted and bent in the air.

I'm initiating the dampener, I linked. *This aberration unner—*

The thing struck like an angry serpent. Quicker than thought, it flicked toward me and buried in my chest.

I screamed, expecting pain and gore.

No. Nothing. I gaped at it, stunned.

Michael! Use the damp—

It pulled, as if hooked between my ribs. Agony, like nothing I'd ever felt, sliced through my chest.

Michael! You—! Anya's link cut short, torn from my mind so suddenly, it felt like I'd lost a part of myself.

Wind. Howling, screaming wind wailed around me, wind that had wailed since the beginning of time. It cried my name and whispered things best forgotten. It cut, sliced with a keenness I had never known. It smelled like alien vistas, like a world that had never known the light of a warm and living star.

Cold.

I fell.

2

Stunned, I grabbed at my chest, scrabbling madly. My hands desperately sought the place the hook had sunk in.

Nothing. No pain, no wound.

I gasped and panted. Around me, lonely wind blown from the corners of existence cut against my skin.

Anya? Tell me you're there, Preceptor.

A long moment passed yet no response came.

Designate? Do you have my position? Panic began to boil in my mind. *Initiate Crown Adjunct.*

Nothingness. I felt only silence from the other side of my link.

I desperately tried again, yet I knew the truth. The emptiness in my mind told me my link to the Lattice network had been severed. I had no connection to the Designate or my personal Adjunct. This likely meant I found myself adrift in another topia—a reality altogether different than my own.

"Well, great."

I blinked and gazed up into a strangely tilted night sky.

The stars overhead were mad, screaming eyes that sought to burn away the world. A sharp, angled sea of jagged onyx made up the ground underfoot.

I'd landed hard and broken several of the crystalline structures. My leg bled.

"Okay." I took in a breath and winced against the cold. "Okay, okay, okay. What now?"

The wind blew fierce and cold. I would freeze if I didn't find shelter.

At my feet lay a bent, barbed hook.

Still in shock, I reached for it. A black filament stretched out behind the hook into the unseen distance.

I dropped it in horror as thought returned.

"A trap." I shook my head as the logic fell into place. Only

Assets would have noticed the wicked hook-aberration—only a *Preceptor*, with her hard-wired neuralware. Something so small would never have been found with deep telemetry.

It had been left there. Someone had known we would be in the area. Now they'd caught me, and I'd been pulled—

Where?

I pushed myself up, still wobbly, and again checked my chest for a wound where the hook had been. I couldn't quite believe myself whole.

"Not a physical hook." It must not have been solid in the Rational world, must have been some kind of Irrational force.

A small blessing, at least.

Anya, I'd love a response, I sent again but with little hope.

Nothing.

I stared around in a stupor at my otherworldly surroundings.

On a vast plain, obsidian jutted from the ground in gleaming, razor shards. Several ziggurat-style pyramids loomed in the far-flung distance. Amid the shadows, violet stars and a bloated, angry moon provided pale outlines.

Odd clicks echoed from my left, as if many legs skittered along the stone. Those scuttling legs had to be just behind me.

I turned quickly.

Only emptiness and darkness stretched in that direction, the vastness of an empty plane.

"What?" I turned slowly about, searching for anything, anything at all that might help me. Other than the hook at my feet and the shattered obsidian, only the empty madness of that world met my gaze.

Softly at first, words I couldn't make out slithered about my ears. Those sounds taunted me, teased at the corners of my memory. When I listened closely, the howling wind whispered names and words so foul they made me shudder. Angry words, words of spite and barbed flame, they seemed to drag and slice through my mind.

"No." I shook my head to throw off the strangeness. Scrambling to make something whole and sane out of this place, I pivoted and desperately sought any touchstone that would let me hold onto Rationality.

"Okay. That's it. Okay." Trembling, I put my hands back into my pockets. Three of the dampener grenades still nestled there, along with the Tabula Rasa. A brief glance revealed the fourth grenade, which I'd apparently dropped as I came through.

"Came through." The thought gave me a tight, hard smile. A few moments consideration and the beginnings of a plan started to shift together. "Came through. Came through…" I muttered as I ran the spectrum of optics in my Crown to see if I could locate the cleft back to Rationality. Some kind of hole must exist after all, and if it remained open, I might have a chance.

All the readings came back twisted and wrong. Infrared showed shifting, ominous shapes around me, lost specters that drifted on the wind. The x-ray spectrum actually made my head ache. Pain lanced through me as I stared into nothingness.

"Damn it," I swore to myself. This wouldn't do.

I attempted to cycle through x-ray again and felt my Crown grind. The headache pulsed, angry in my skull.

I powered my optics down, trying to ignore the obvious. Something interfered with my perception. Something had clouded my mind so I couldn't see the way back.

I paced, trying to ignore the whispers and the uncanny skittering. If the passage between worlds remained, I couldn't find it. If I'd been snared and pulled here, I might not have much time to locate it before I became trapped.

Again, I wrapped my hand around one of the dampener grenades. I pulled it from my pocket, mind racing.

Unlike a traditional explosive grenade, it would anchor the local axioms of reality to match the baseline Rationality of Earth. Immensely useful when dealing with Irrats or aberrations, the devices made it exponentially more difficult to alter the Rational

79

world, at least within the dampener's range.

I furrowed my brow. If only I'd been able to trigger one while in the stall, the cleft between worlds would have closed. That gateway had been unnatural, and the axioms of normal physics wouldn't allow it.

"But what happens if you use a dampener while adrift in some other dimension?" I hefted the device, contemplating.

Both Wyatt and Anya would have long, mathematical answers to such a question, especially given the Lattice connection.

I didn't even have the Adjunct at this point.

As I attempted to juggle axiomatic coefficients, coldness poured into me, looming like a shadow in my mind. The sensation came suddenly, and I stumbled backward, raising my arm against...

Nothing. I stood alone in a field of obsidian and wind.

My heart thudded against my ribs.

"Damnit." I couldn't help but feel watched.

Toyed with.

I shook my head and warily glanced around as I again began to factor my Rationality variables. If I could just work this right, then perhaps the grenades could banish whatever mindfuckery kept my optics from full functionality.

Yet no matter how I tried to ignore it, that alien coldness remained. I felt it, scrabbling around in the back of my head, all bristled hair and gangled legs. Huge and bloated, it hid in the places where the waking mind never went, behind memory and dream, and cast forth threads of terror.

I turned again, half expecting to see some loathsome thing creeping up on me.

Nothing.

"Show yourself!" I screamed into the wind, though it stole my voice. I spun wildly, searching all around for the creature, a dampener in one hand and the Tabula Rasa in the other.

I needed to find some kind of cover. Whatever aberrant thing had lured me here, I felt its shadow on my mind, an eldritch intelligence alien to my own.

I turned again, breathing hard.

Nothing.

Yet I felt it, as if the shape of it could echo through my senses. Neither a spider nor a scorpion, yet somehow both. It had scrabbling legs, each longer than my arm, a hairy carapace, and a wicked, pincered tail. A visage on the edge of my imagination showed a female with a gaping maw on her face and eight shiny eyes.

"Nothing." I bit the word short as I glared into the darkling shadows. "There's nothing there."

Now my breath came in great, shuddering gasps. My heart still pounded in my chest. No matter what I said, I knew the truth.

She came.

Insectine and sharp, she had been called from the far corners of the aetheric tides, called here for me. The certainty that the creature had been meant for me specifically terrified me. Yet it felt true, irrationally true.

Gifted with feral intelligence, she wanted more than sustenance. I felt her desire envelop me in heat.

More than flesh, more than food. She doesn't want, she desires.

I almost retched at the raw lust of her flooding my mind, burning in my veins. The sensation scorched me like boiling honey drizzled across my flesh.

She wants to drag me away to mate. After days of coupling in the darkness, I will have fertilized her brood. Then, and only then, will she sink fangs into flesh. She will devour my eyes while I scream in the dark. She will make certain I cannot escape.

I must be alive when our eggs hatch inside me...

"No." I shook my head, wildly negating the abomination's lustful hungers. "No!"

The sensations washed over me again, shadowed memories of what would be. I felt the way her body convulsed around mine while she mated with me; I smelled the scent she coated me with, the scent that would tell our young to devour my flesh.

"Come on!" I pocketed the dampener for the moment and reached for one of the broken shards of obsidian. "You've got me here, bitch! Come take what you want!"

Nothing answered. I sensed only darkness and wind.

I turned again. I knew—

There!

She skittered through the shadows on more legs than I could count. When she opened her impossible mouth to screech, I saw teeth lined her throat all the way down.

The horror of it struck me like a maul in the face. I scrambled backward, falling as she rushed forward, her many legs ticking against the unyielding stone.

I screamed.

She lunged for me. Yellow, wicked teeth sought my flesh. Her rotten breath created a miasma of despair that left only hopelessness and loss.

Blindly, wildly, I swung the obsidian shard.

Yet I couldn't seem to touch her.

She wasn't truly solid, some astral predator created only of nightmares and mad visions. Yet she remained real.

Her deadly pincered tail arched up behind her.

She'll tear into me with that. I couldn't say how I knew, yet I envisioned the scythe-like tip cutting the chilled wind. *After mating, she'll rip into my stomach to lay her eggs. I won't die, though, not until they hatch—*

She emanated fear and broken imaginings. Without words, she explained my fate exactly.

I swung the shard toward her face. This time, I made some vague connection, but it felt useless, like I'd thrust a butter knife at porcelain.

She lunged again, those scratching, twisting legs propelling her forward.

I screamed in blind panic and terror. *She has me! She has me, oh—!*

I hurled myself backward, cutting my arms on more of the obsidian. The wind felt frigid against my skin and scoured my flesh.

I didn't notice any of that. Her mad eyes and the mesmerizing dance of the pincer at the end of her tail made up my entire world.

She gave a harsh rasp, an inhuman, chittering cry of victory. Stringy mucus drooled from her mouth, brown and thick like old grease. She reared on her back legs and lunged at me, all horror and insectine grace.

I couldn't harm her—not in this shape. She held no resemblance to anything real, anything that could be wounded.

No, I needed to shift the playing field.

I waited. I held out until the last possible second as the obsidian shard sliced into my trembling hand.

When she came so close that her stench boiled around me, I fumbled for my pocket. I found one of the dampening grenades and pushed the button.

WHUM. The device pulsed to life.

I felt the world tremble around me as Rationality cascaded into this bent, dark world. The local axioms warped as they underwent instantaneous change.

The screaming wind ceased around us. The ground became softer, the air more breathable. Gravity shifted, and the stars twinkled. The creature itself—

Light. God, there's light! I spotted a bright crevice behind the abomination.

The thin, antiseptic light of the men's washroom filtered into this world.

The aberration had hidden the rift from me through some fell power. She'd dangled her lure through that crevice. I just hadn't been able to see it, not with the mind-bending physics of this place. But with the dampener altering reality—

83

I didn't waste a breath. Even as the spider-scorpion-bitch reached for me, I rolled to the side and stood. With animal panic and deep, unreasoning fear, I sprinted toward that sliver of light. The viral mecha in my blood sang and allowed me to push a touch harder…

I hoped it would be enough.

It wasn't.

One of the creature's legs caught me across the back, striking with razor sharpness. I felt a brief sliver of fire and pain.

"Come *on!*" I roared as I stumbled forward. I bit my lip, focusing.

My pain became irrelevant. That light shone, the only thing that mattered.

I felt the aberration turn, sensed her as she chased me. Monstrously fast, I heard her hard carapace click against the stone as she launched after me.

I hurled myself into that light and slammed onto the tiled floor. My back screamed where the aberration had ripped at me.

—twenty-seven minutes and nine seconds, the Adjunct droned in my mind. *Asset 108, please respond. You are location-unknown and tech adrift. You have been offline for three hours, twenty-seven minutes and twenty-six seconds. Asset 108—*

Anya! I linked her in a panicked scream. *The rift is still open!* I turned and stared. The aberration had reached the crack. The air that sang through from that other place reeked of death and lost things.

Michael?

The spider-scorpion pushed three legs through the cleft. As I watched, she lowered her maw to the rift and pulled herself through.

The aberration emerged into Rational space. Between the dampener and the parts of her that straddled the rift, she no longer occupied her shadowed, shattered world. Now she burrowed into mine.

Rational physics applied.

I still held the obsidian shard. Hand trembling, I clenched as it bit into my flesh.

She lunged at me.

I plunged the shard into her gaping, tooth-filled maw with a scream, all savagery and victory and hatred.

"—fucking right, you bitch!" I hadn't even realized I shouted. "You take that!

This time, she wasn't some half-physical astral monstrosity. She writhed, all meat and chitin, blood and gristle.

She screamed and sprayed gore as the shard exploded out the top of her head. Brown, stinking viscera splattered all over me and sullied the white walls of the stall.

I pulled back and lunged forward again, driving the sharp stone into one of her eyes.

Her screams no longer manifested only in my mind. Now they echoed through the tiled room as rasping, howling wails. Her legs twitched madly. As her body convulsed, the horror dragged herself away from me.

"No. You don't get to run." I tried to pull the shard free to attack her again but found it slippery with her gore. I spun toward her, reaching forward with the Tabula Rasa in my other hand.

Quickly, she retracted into the rift, leaving only the hole between worlds.

Slowly, it faded from sight.

"Oh God." I slumped against the side of the stall, covered in her viscera and my own blood. "Oh, fuck me."

With another instant, I could have jammed the Tabula Rasa down her throat. I grinned at the thought, feral and half mad.

I smelled like grim death.

Michael, I need you to respond.

I laughed, more than a bit manic. For a long moment I couldn't even link, the calm reason in Anya's comment striking me as too catastrophically funny.

Finally, I found the will to answer.

My system is green, Preceptor. *I am wounded but whole.*

You are at Rationality zero, Michael. Caduceus *Gardener reports that your Crown reads blood loss, fatigue, shock, and several torn muscles. Recommend immediate inoculation of type IV viral mecha.*

Right. Okay. The wild grin wouldn't leave my face.

Are you well, Michael?

No. I chuckled as I linked. *Not at all.* I pulled the injector from my shirt pocket. The device hissed slightly as I injected the mecha into my leg.

The door to the restroom opened, and some poor fellow gagged.

"Oh God!" He sounded as if he might retch.

"Sorry man," I chuckled. "I must have had some bad sushi."

"Are you—?" The voice choked. "Are you alright in there?"

I couldn't decide whether to laugh or cry.

Anya Petrova: *Preceptor* Second Tier

Three hours and twenty-eight minutes in total, Michael. Anya's crisp tone contained no judgment; she simply reported facts.

Gone that long? I shook my head. *The Designates seem irritated about the delay?*

It is an imperfect situation, she responded. *We had no way of knowing the coefficient for temporal slippage. You were in an unknown topiatic realm.*

I understand.

I sat on the far side of the McCarran food court, watching as Facility Factors contained this portion of the airport. The entire area had been sectioned off, and security kept the public away.

Designate Ling certainly seemed insistent regarding our timeline.

If you had not been recovered within the next thirty-two minutes, Asset 087 would have been tapped for this dossier.

Michele? Out of LA? I wrinkled my nose. *Lady's hard to work with. She's a bit persnickety.*

I have never had difficulty with her.

You must have never worked with her and Wyatt together. I couldn't help but chuckle. *They fight like wet cats. Trust me, Anya, you're better off.*

In front of me, the last of the Facility Factors stepped out of the airport restroom and signaled that the area had been cleared. They branded the incident an environmental hazard, which served as well as any excuse.

"Bishop?" The deep voice from my left surprised me.

I turned. "Oh, hey." I smiled at Reid Lockwood, Facility Factor 56, a regional enforcement agent for the Environmental Protection Agency.

I gestured at the chair next to me. "Have a seat."

I'd worked with Reid before—several times in fact. The man held distinction among Factors: few others had attained his clearance. After working with the Facility for many years, the man knew almost as much as an actual Asset.

Almost.

"I just wanted to let you know that everything here looks tidy." Reid grinned as he sat, the swarthy man projecting an almost inhuman level of confidence. "We only tinkered with the memories of a few people, and there's no further sign of Irrationality."

"I'm a little curious why the Designate signed off on you guys detaining me?" I took a sip of awful airport coffee. "I'm starting a dossier, and apparently time is of the essence."

"We had to promise we wouldn't keep you long." Reid shrugged. "The thing is, some jerkwad summoned the aberration you encountered. Called it straight up, right there in the airport restroom."

"Are we sure about that?" I set the coffee cup down.

"Absolutely!" Reid chuckled as he spoke. "I don't know what you're in the middle of, but apparently Facility 17 has the whole area under scrutiny. Every kind of experimental telemetry the Facility has is being brought to bear."

"So the *Preceptors* have data on this thing?"

"They do." He shook his head slowly. "Seems someone expected us to find it. There are all kinds of traces left, sloppy work really."

"Have the Designates changed their minds?" I picked the coffee back up and took another sip. I had to pretend as if it didn't taste like mud. "Do they think this had something to do with my dossier?"

"Who knows, man?" Reid paused for a moment. "Awfully convenient, though."

"You think it might have been an ambush." I didn't exactly ask because the answer seemed certain.

"Maybe." He sighed. "Just don't be surprised if we have to

have a discussion about this later. I'll replicate the data and attach it to your dossier report. If you remember anything else, we need to know about it."

For a moment, I couldn't help but think of the vaguely Arabic man who had stared at me across the concourse. I had absolutely no reason to believe he might have anything to do with the she-bitch spider-scorpion...

"Will do." I smiled and offered Reid my hand. "You need anything else, you let me know."

"Understood." He took my hand and we shook.

2

Factor Lockwood thinks someone set a trap for us—left that creature as a party favor for us. I still stank of otherworldly filth and gore as I walked through the airport. Now that I had moved outside the Factors' quarantine area, I exposed the public to a wonderfully unique stench.

Does he? Anya didn't have to communicate her disbelief; I could feel it.

He may be right. Only a Facility Preceptor *would have found that snare.*

Unlikely. Anya's coolness bled across the link. *The probability does not play out. Facility Assets do not typically use citizen transportation. Leaving such a snare here is inefficient.*

Except, I frowned, my exasperation obvious through the link. *Except it did, in fact, catch me, didn't it? I'm not suggesting this is the only location, Anya. It might have been one of several.* I stopped and took a drink at a water fountain, trying to wash the taste of that bitter coffee from my mouth.

You believe the Irrationals responsible for our strange telemetry readings summoned not one but several aberrations for surveillance?

Yes. I paused. *No. Not exactly. The aberration wasn't immediately on the scene when the snare pulled me driftways into its topia. I think it might have a web of those snares, likely spread across the city. In fact, I suspect the Irrats know we triggered one.*

I see. She stayed silent for a long moment. When she linked again, I felt her cautious logic. *If what you say is true, the implication is that we are dealing with an operation of higher sophistication than we are accustomed.*

Correct. I nodded, even though anyone around would think I nodded to no one in particular. *It means our Irrats know of the existence of the Facility and understand our protocols enough to*

91

lay a trap.

That is a dangerous possibility. She paused again. *I will bring this consideration to the Designate and patch the details of our conversation to Wyatt's Crown.* She hesitated. *Do you have anything you would like to add to the packet?*

Only that I reek and need a wash.

That seems unrelated. It is an added difficulty if you require clean clothing.

I do require. Also about a gallon of cologne. I headed down the steps, ignoring the disgusted glares of the people I passed.

I am pulling around to the south gate. I will be there momentarily.

I'll be the handsome, smoking guy who smells like monster viscera. You can't miss me. I skipped the luggage terminal, as I had none with me. Once to the door, I reached into my pocket for a cigarette and lit up.

Asset Gardener reports the viral mecha in your bloodstream are tasked to 88% maximum, Michael. You might consider waiting before smoking.

I don't care, Anya. I took a long, satisfying drag. *You can tell the* Caduceus *I said so. Pick me up. Let's get Guthrie and get this done.*

Affirmative, Asset. Her normally cool tone went frigid.

Anya hated it when others ignored her advice.

3

Anya drove a black sedan, one of our *Legacy*-class vehicles. The car contained several axiomatic upgrades woven into the body, making it one of my favorite vehicles. The moment I stepped close to it, I felt the sedan ping my Crown.

My Adjunct immediately responded.

Bishop, Michael. Asset 108. You have been recognized as an operator for this vehicle.

Good to know. As Anya pulled up, I put out my cigarette and hopped in, shotgun. *However, I will allow the* Preceptor *to continue her role as operator at this time.*

Current mission-specific upgrades to this vehicle include a Wraith *system as well as a contingent of* Raiju-*class drones hidden within the chassis. Telemetric relays have been activated within the dashboard to strengthen readings. Each seat also generates type seven emanations designed to sync with all active viral mecha. The message paused. **Would you like the full list of specifications?**

I'll check the specs later. I shot Anya a boyish smile as I fastened my seatbelt. "Did you miss me?" I asked, nodding even before I finished the sentence. "Of course you did. You missed me."

She said nothing but crinkled her nose ever so slightly. Then she shook her head, as if to clear the scent from her sinuses and pulled away from the airport.

"You know, other coworkers exchange pleasantries when they start a day's work." I slumped down in the seat a little and gazed at myself in the car's mirror. With a little tousle, my hair regained some semblance of acceptability.

"You smell like a sewer," Anya opened conversationally. She didn't add any sting to the words, simply spoke them, matter of fact, as always.

"There it is." I chuckled, opening my arms as if to hug her.

Anya's voice always sounded so strange when she actually spoke. Many times while on dossier, I could only communicate with her through the sterile utility of our links. But when she spoke in person? Anya's soft voice had a musicality to it, a sweetness.

I thought it quite beautiful.

"We are running late." When she shook her head, her straight, blonde hair bounced partially over her face. She pushed it back behind the white tactical gear covering her shoulder and glanced at me with winter-blue eyes.

"That's not exactly my fault," I explained. "The Factors demanded I hang out for a little bit."

"Fault does not come into play here." Anya watched the road, her mouth a smooth line. "We have a task to complete, and we are running behind."

"This is why you're my favorite *Preceptor*." I pointed at her. "I missed you too."

"I did not indicate I missed you." The tiniest furrow appeared between her eyes, the scarcest shadow of confusion.

For my ice-princess, this spoke volumes.

As a *Preceptor*, Anya had permanent Asset enhancements. Much of her internal nervous system had been built, cell by cell, toward the purpose of altering her sensitivity to ripples in reality itself.

No small feat, that. The *Preceptors* were living diagnostic operatives. Specifically, these diagnostics included the capability to read telemetric relays and therefore coordinate a cadre while in Irrational situations.

Anya amazed me in action, a genius in a tight spot. More than once I'd been surrounded by otherworldly horrors, certain that events were headed south, but she had stood with me. She could remain cool in the center of Irrational hell itself, all the while calmly updating me as to how deep the shit had actually risen.

Unlike Wyatt and me, she never got to turn off her life with the

94

Facility. Anya's position could not be negotiated. She lived this life, twenty-four seven, three sixty-five.

I would say I felt sorry for her, but emotions weren't her strong suit. I genuinely didn't know how much she could suffer. In fact, when it came to *Preceptors,* I didn't know much at all.

"It's Facility 8," Wyatt had once observed while we waited to be debriefed. "I know it's gotta be somewhere in Moscow, but I just don't know where. That must be where they receive their fancy-schmancy modifications."

"Schmancy?" I let one eyebrow rise. "Are you saying Facility 8 can make me into a super-genius?" Every *Preceptor* I ever met scored off the intelligence charts. "If Facility 8 can pull that off, sign me up."

"Oh, Hoss." Wyatt shook his head. "Making you a genius? I'm bettin' some things are even beyond the Designates' capabilities."

"Why do you think they're always women?" I furrowed my brow, trying to sort it out.

"Why are they always gorgeous?" Wyatt winked at me. "Have you ever seen an ugly *Preceptor*?"

"I've never even seen an *average*-looking *Preceptor*," I mused.

"Here's how I figger it." He leaned close, conspiratorial. "I wager they have to be genetically perfect to accept the neural architecture. That's the only thing that explains it."

"Could be," I replied.

Preceptors were wonderfully fit in all the most enticing ways. Perhaps specific genetics had become a requirement in crafting their telemetric relays. Were that the case, then their physical characteristics might be a side effect.

"Now, if only the Facility could ingrain a sense of humor." Wyatt toyed with his beard as he chuckled.

"It would be nice if she understood more of my jokes," I agreed. "It truly is a shame for someone to miss out on my amazing wit."

"I'm gonna nod and pretend you said you were an 'amazing

twit.'" Wyatt sank back in his chair, grinning to himself.

We'd had that conversation almost three years ago. In all that time, Anya had never been anything other than courteous and highly professional. No matter how I might try to tease her or crack wise, she remained aloof.

It drove me crazy. I'd made it a personal goal to try to make the *Preceptor* laugh out loud.

Of course, I had other concerns also weighing on my mind just now.

"I require a sink of some kind," I announced as I held my ruined jacket on my lap and used one of the cleaner parts to wipe my face. "Stop at a gas station or something, and I'll wash."

"I would like to remind you we are running late. Perhaps we should wait until after we rendezvous with Asset Guthrie." She cracked her window.

"I don't think that will do." I took an experimental sniff of my shirt and recoiled.

"I am sorry you are uncomfortable." She didn't meet my eye, simply stated the words firmly and concisely. "Unfortunately, we need to make up for lost time."

"Well, that makes perfect sense." I unknotted the tie hanging around my neck, wincing at the sensation of freeing the gore-slicked fabric from my skin. I rolled down the window. Without saying another word, I threw my tie outside, where it came to rest alongside Highway 95.

"What are you doing?" Anya glanced at me now, her blue eyes wide.

"We don't have time for me to clean up." I nodded to her as if we'd reached agreement. "I totally understand." I met her gaze in the rearview mirror. Without breaking eye-contact, I started to unbutton my shirt.

"You cannot simply throw all of your clothing out onto the highway." Each syllable became more clipped.

"I'm sorry you feel uncomfortable taking a few minutes to

stop." I continued unbuttoning my shirt.

"You are acting like a child."

When she went to close the window, I already had my finger on my button. I held it in place so hers wouldn't do anything.

She stabbed her button with one finger, three times in a row.

When I spoke, I kept my voice measured and calm. "The Facility requires professionalism. It is intolerable being covered in the guts of an aberrant creature. We don't have to stop so I can wash up, but I'm not going to continue to wear these clothes." I undid another two buttons with my free hand.

"You cannot expect a person to sit unperturbed while you undress in the car." She stared at me as if she thought I'd lost my mind. "It violates several Facility guidelines."

"I'm open to whatever options you can create, *Preceptor*." I smiled as I undid the last button.

"Fine. There is a small convenience store .23 kilometers ahead. If it will keep you from dispersing your clothing along the interstate, we can stop for five minutes."

"Reasonable." I nodded. "If I can get a quick wash, I'll keep my pants on."

"I will also ask you to contact Asset Guthrie." She gave me a sideward glance. "As we will be further delayed."

"That's fair." I opened a channel as I spoke. *We're en route, Wyatt.*

Wyatt Guthrie is currently unavailable, the Adjunct informed me.

"It seems he's not taking calls." I couldn't help but frown at the thought. I'd known Wyatt long enough to suspect his nature. If he thought he had extra time to shoot a game of pool or head down to some stock-car race before our dossier, he'd happily take the opportunity.

"Asset Guthrie's behavioral quirks are well documented." She pushed a stray strand of blonde hair from her face, her head twitching slightly as she accessed the Lattice. "Even though he is

97

offline, his latent signal remains public."

"That's quite responsible actually." I gave her a glance. "For Wyatt, anyway."

"I can contact Designate Ling if you feel the situation might be an emergency. I am certain she would allow me to override his Crown settings."

"If it gets to that point, I have a direct sync with Ling."

"I know that you do." Anya shifted in her seat. "It is an odd choice."

"Yeah. A damned sight odd."

"Do you expect a problem with Asset 423?"

"No." I sighed. "It's just his nature. I'm certain Wyatt considers it the height of courtesy that he even let us know where he is."

"Asset Guthrie's latent signal indicates he is currently located approximately 25.2 kilometers northwest of here." She paused for a moment, her head ticking to the left just the slightest bit. "He is waiting in a restaurant named The Booby Trap."

"What?" I snorted. "I doubt that's a restaurant."

"It is possible this intel needs to be updated." Anya didn't even blink. "Regardless, without stops, it will take us close to half an hour to arrive at The Booby Trap."

I had nothing to say to that.

"There!" I pointed at the small convenience store at the side of the highway. A large yellow sign proclaimed them to be the friendliest gas for the next hundred miles.

Without saying a word, Anya pulled off and parked.

"I'll only be a moment." I hopped out into the morning sunlight, blinking in its brilliance. I didn't yet notice fatigue setting in, even though I'd been awake all night. *Caduceus* Gardener had something to do with that, I would guess.

I shut the door and trotted over to the small building. Less than a minute later, I realized the door to the restroom was locked.

"Oh, come on, man." I scowled and stomped over to where the

attendant waited behind thick glass. "I need the restroom key."

"Are you buying anything? The restroom is for customers only." He nodded at the *Legacy*. "I can let you in if you get some gas."

"I don't need any gas."

"Then you can piss by the side of the road." He gestured down the highway.

"Dude, you just don't get it." I gestured at my filthy shirt. "I don't need to piss; I smell like a charnel house."

"Not my problem," the young man replied.

"Friendliest gas in the next hundred miles?" I queried.

"You aren't buying gas, man."

"I'm getting sick of this bullshit." I patted my empty pockets, then threw my jacket on the ground. "How about I just leave my filthy clothes right here for you to clean up?"

You cannot solve all your problems by getting naked, Michael, Anya linked.

"You don't know that!" I turned around pointing at the car, not at all like a crazy person.

"How about a candy bar?" The attendant ground his teeth. "Pack of cigarettes?"

I glared at him.

"Fine." I snatched up my jacket and stalked over to the small window. "I'll buy a pack of cigarettes." I pointed. "Those."

Even through the window, the man wrinkled his nose as I got close. "Thank you very much, sir," he said tightly. "Here's the restroom key."

I snatched the key and stomped back to the restroom. Moments later, I splashed cold water on my face and arms, sighing in bliss.

Michael, I had hoped to show you some analysis I did on the dossier while you were on the plane. I compiled some data I believe you will find fascinating.

That sounds lovely. I scrubbed my face with a paper towel, desperately trying to remove the dried gore. *It sounds as if you got far more done than I did.*

Would you prefer to receive the intel in a patch?

That seems reasonable. I finished up and ran my fingers through my hair. When I stepped outside, I dropped my suit jacket in the trash. I handed the attendant the key.

Patch 11.7A is not as large as the dossier. I've configured it to load to your memory for simplicity, Anya linked

"Thanks for the warning," I said as I headed to the car. I'd scarcely finished the sentence when I felt the jolt on the left side of my Crown. Uncomfortable and jarring, I disliked the sensation.

Unlike the dossier, Anya's patch immediately became something I'd always known, as if it had happened during my childhood.

"Patch received, Anya." I blinked as the data instantly meshed with my knowledge of the dossier. "That *is* interesting."

Interesting didn't begin to cover it.

Anya had caught something I never would have in the series of Irrational spikes. As I picked through her notations regarding how far from Rationality zero those spikes had strayed, a pattern materialized.

Anya started the car.

"Are these Fibonacci numbers?"

I didn't actually need to ask. The obvious mathematical pattern lay before me; each number equaled the two before it. I'd noted the intense, exact bursts, but this held more than exactness. This showed the perfect precision of automation.

"Indeed. Understand, however, the Fibonacci sequence may have occurred without undue influence." She'd given this some thought. "It is a pattern that occurs often enough in nature."

"Yes, I know it occurs in nature." I shook my head, dismissing the idea that this might be an accident. "This just seems too coincidental."

"If you look at frame 13:05, you will notice the spike comes close to overwhelming the localized axioms and creating perforations through reality." She glanced at me in the rearview mirror. "At 13:23, the spike reaches the next Fibonacci level down. Because the previous spike weakened Rationality at this location, this spike is as strong as it can be without creating a rift in the local realmwall."

"The next is the same," I realized. "They first weakened ambient Rationality, just to the breaking point. The second struck again, almost to the new tearing point, but much smaller and much faster."

"They only lasted for picoseconds in some cases."

"Hmm. Our Irrats could have easily created a rift if they'd wanted."

"My conclusion as well."

"So why didn't they? Why go to all this trouble and then stop?"

"It is confusing." She shook her head, just a bit. "They create Irrational events so massive we cannot help but see, but at the same time, seem careful not to damage the realmwall."

"Maybe it's some kind of warning?" Even as I spoke I shook my head. That didn't feel right.

"With the speed these alterations manifested, it seems obvious they could be replicated at any time." Anya rolled her shoulders. "At this rate of axiomatic manipulation, similar events could take place anywhere within Rationality. It would be over before we could assemble a dossier."

"They know about the Facility, if my theory about the snare in the airport holds true."

"That is only a theory." She glanced at me. "You possess no evidence." I watched her fingers twitch in the way they sometimes did when she compiled data. "Once I get further readings, we may be able to draw a conclusion."

"I hope so." I slumped back into the seat. "I don't like mysteries."

In our line of work, few things posed more danger than mysteries.

101

Wyatt Guthrie: Asset 423

As Anya pulled the *Legacy* into the parking lot of The Booby Trap, I watched her out of the corner of my eye. First sight of the building confirmed my suspicions on the nature of the place. I keenly wanted to know if Anya would pick up on the clues.

"Asset Guthrie's latent signal still shows him inside." Anya took no particular note of the buxom woman in red neon that loomed over the door. Beneath her, the words ALL DAY EVERY DAY flashed in blue.

"Lots of pickup trucks and motorcycles," I remarked as I peered around the parking lot. "I'm kind of surprised it's open."

"Lattice records show this restaurant to be open twenty-four hours a day."

"Makes sense. We are still in Clark County."

A young woman walked outside in the strippiest stripper heels I had ever seen. She strode to her car as if born to traipse around in the fragile things.

While Anya parked, I cleared my throat. I'd already decided this might go more smoothly if she stayed outside.

"Anya, I wondered if you would review the data again while I corral Wyatt?" I gave a hopeful smile. "I'm impressed at the patterns you found. I found nothing of real import on my entire flight."

"If you think that's best, Michael." Though her tone remained neutral, her pleasure from my praise electrified her gaze. "I had considered running some area background checks as well. Other Assets may have documented data that could help us."

"That sounds great. I'll step inside. We should be right out. Otherwise I'll let you know."

"Please do. Time is of the essence."

"Copy that." I breathed a sigh of relief as I stepped from the

103

car. Anya inside a gentlemen's club might have been a bit more than I wanted to handle just now.

Before I stepped inside, I sent one last link, hoping the smartest man I'd ever met would answer this time. *You there, buddy? You're not gonna make me come inside there, are you?*

Wyatt Guthrie is currently unavailable, the Adjunct reported in a chipper tone.

Fine. I would have to go inside the strip club to find the jackass.

Just another burden I had to bear.

DING! DING! I opened the door, immediately awash in the clanging and chiming of over a dozen small slot machines and video game-style diversions. The entire foyer rang with the sounds of the games and the curses of the charming gentlemen who played them.

As I meandered through the haze of cigarette smoke, a short man with a shaved head and a sleeve of tattoos awaited me at the inner door.

"No cover, not this early." He arched one eyebrow at me. "You like to start your party in the morning?"

"I'm here to pick up a friend. His party is probably just ending."

"That makes you a good friend." The man wrinkled his nose just a touch. I saw him consider that, maybe, I shouldn't be allowed inside.

"Hey, I get it," I spoke quietly. "My suit reeks. Our other friend got sick in the car."

"Damn, man." He turned away with a grimace. "You're a better friend than I am."

"Let me grab my buddy, and I'll get out of your hair. I know the girls don't want to have to deal with—" I waved my hand down my body, indicating my clothes.

"Yeah, yeah, whatever." He wrinkled his nose again. "Go on in."

The Booby Trap met my expectations exactly. I knew Wyatt's tastes, so I wasn't surprised at the haze of cigarette smoke or the men sitting at the bar. Four mirrored stages were scattered around the dim room, yet only two of them held dancers just now.

I hadn't taken five steps inside before two half-clad girls met me. Both of them wore stilettos, but after that, their similarities vanished. The shorter one, a pretty brunette, did an amazing job at pulling off the naughty schoolgirl look—complete with plaid skirt and knee-high stockings. Her friend's hair had probably once been blonde but now burst with wild color, just an accessory to her leather 'rave-girl' getup.

I ignored the way the not-blonde wrinkled her nose at my unique aroma.

"You seem like you've had an interesting day." The pretty brunette smiled through my stench.

"You can see I'm playing with a handicap." I gestured at my slacks and stained shirt.

"What?" The rave-girl blinked in confusion.

"Any guy can walk into a place like this and dress nicely." I gestured at some suited guy at the bar, dismissing him. "That's easy. Child's play."

"Okay?" The Catholic schoolgirl smiled, seemingly genuine.

"Ladies." I held my arms wide. "You need to understand. When *this* is what you bring to the table, it's far too easy if I strut in here in a nice suit throwing money around."

"But we like it when you throw money around," Rave-chick stated, but she had started to smile too.

"That's kinda the point," Schoolgirl said. "Is that what you're here to do?"

"I can't be responsible for what might happen." I shook my head sadly. "If I came in here, bringing my full game?" I scoffed. "Wearing my best?"

"What would happen?" Dimples blossomed on the brunette's cheeks as she smiled wider. I appreciated how fresh and bright she seemed, not at all worn down by the challenges of her job.

"Well, none of you would get any work done, that's for damn sure." I glanced around, gesturing at all the other patrons. "And these guys? I mean, these are men who have to pay for their entertainment. Who's going to take care of them?"

"Oh my God!" Rave-chick barked a laugh. "You're hilarious."

"So what are you doing, then?" The schoolgirl tilted her head as she spoke. "Coming in here, in the morning, not bringing your full game?"

"I'm here to retrieve an Asset." I dropped the tone of my voice, completely serious. "I and my friend are highly trained agents of a world-spanning secret organization."

"You are?" Rave-chick glanced at Schoolgirl. "I admit, I haven't heard that one before."

"Maybe your friend can wait." Schoolgirl gave me a wicked smile. "We can be friends."

"I'd like to be friends," Rave-chick stage-whispered. "The private stages are around the far side of the bar. Maybe the three of us could step back there and get friendly?"

"It's a good thing you wore that disgusting shirt." Schoolgirl trailed her gaze along its front. "I can't imagine what I might want to do if you had brought your A game."

"If only I had the time," I said mournfully. "But quite literally the safety of the free world is at risk here."

"My goodness." Schoolgirl turned to Rave-chick. "I'd hate to endanger the free world."

"My name's Tatiana." Rave-chick arched one eyebrow at me.

"Archibald." I extended a hand and, naturally, she shook it. "Archibald Moneycock." I paused. "No, Dr. Archibald Moneycock."

"You are not!" Tatiana guffawed, one hand over her mouth.

"Like your mother actually named you 'Tatiana.'" I gave her my best grin. "I should get a stripper-name too, just for when I'm here."

"You're crazy." Schoolgirl couldn't stop smiling.

"Listen, my friend is hairy and has a loud mouth." I turned from one to the other. "Also, he likes strippers, just between you and me."

"You just described every guy in here," Schoolgirl interjected.

"Maybe you should forget him," Tatiana suggested again.

"I still have to save the free world." I put my hand on her waist. "Tell you what. Let me get settled in and do a bunch of sexy secret agent stuff. Afterward, I'll give you some attention."

"That seems fair." Tatiana smiled. "But remember, we're supposed to give *you* the attention." She bit her lip playfully.

"That sounds nice. For now, can you bring me some bourbon?"

"I can." She nodded, her lips quirking into a smile. "But don't think you're getting off the hook so easily, Dr. Moneycock."

"Understood." I gave her one last smile.

On the center stage, a young woman undulated beneath lights that flashed blue and purple in strobing array. The shorts she wore had once been blue jeans but had been cut so high she might as well not wear them at all. A tied off flannel shirt scarcely covered her chest, completing the look of young country girl gone wrong.

Over the speakers, "Friends in Low Places" blared, which she mouthed along to in perfect timing as she swung her hips. The chorus began, and the men at the stage sang with her, shouting the last word.

"I'm not big on social graces—
Think I'll slip on down to the O-O-A-SIS*!"*

In front of the stage, a college kid stood, agape. He held a cluster of bills loosely in his left hand.

Even over the music, I heard the dancer say, "Want me to show you where you can put those?"

A group of young guys, drunk beyond all sense, hooted from a table behind him.

The poor guy didn't even know what to say. He just nodded dumbly as the performer took his hand to show him where his money belonged.

Guthrie, seriously. I glanced around the room but didn't see him. I made certain to include a bit of irritation in my link. *We've got to get to work.*

Wyatt Guthrie is currently unavailable, the Adjunct replied.

"Thirteen-fifty." Rave-chick had slipped up beside me. She held not one but two tumblers of bourbon. She handed one to me, which I took.

"What?" I stared at her, taken aback by the price. "Are you kidding me?"

"Nope." She gave me a winsome smile. "That's how much two drinks cost." Without another word she took a sip of the second one.

"I wasn't aware I was buying one for each of us."

"If you brought your A game, I wouldn't need a drink." She gestured at my shirt. "Think of it as a companion tax."

"Isn't this whole place a companion tax?" I gestured around us but couldn't help smiling just a bit. The girl had cheek.

I liked that.

"Where are we sitting?" She gestured around at the tables in front of us. "If we sit close, I'll be able to tip the dancers for you."

"I'm not here to tip the dancers; I told you I'm looking for my friend."

"I'm not asking you to tip the dancers," she retorted. "I'm pointing out you might like watching *me* do it." She gave me a wicked little smile.

"I won't be here long; I'm not opening a tab." I handed her my card. "Why don't you take this to the bar, so you can pay for these two drinks?"

"Take this to the bar," she repeated as she took the card, her eyes holding mine. "Don't open a tab. Go ahead and pay for four drinks."

"Damn." I couldn't help but shake my head. "I bet you make a killing here."

"I'll be back." She gave me a small little wave as she stepped away. "Why don't you take a seat, right there?"

I did take a seat, craning my head and peering all around the club. Even though the time of day hadn't crept much beyond breakfast, the little place hopped. I counted eight young ladies working the stages and the bar, yet even this didn't seem to be enough for the two dozen or so men strewn around the floor.

Only a few of us were stalwart enough to drink liquor at this time of day, which seemed like a shame to me. Then again, not everyone had nanotechnology to scrub their bloodstream free of toxins.

"Where the hell are you, Guthrie?" I took a sip from my tumbler, enjoying the best watered-down bourbon the county had to offer.

I didn't see the bear of a man anywhere.

Anya, are we certain about that latent signal?

Confirmed, Michael. She paused. *I take it you have yet to encounter Asset 423?*

I'm working diligently on the task. I turned toward the far wall, wondering if he might be in the men's room. *I'll let you know if I need help.*

Designate Ling has the capability to override his Crown settings, she reminded me. *If you require, I will link the request.*

Not yet. I popped the knuckles on my left hand. *I'll keep you apprised.*

Understood.

I felt Anya's presence slip from my Crown and considered her offer. Because I'd been sync'd with Designate Ling, I could also easily contact her. It wouldn't be anything at all to request an override for Wyatt's Crown.

Except… I didn't really want to. He had turned on his privacy settings. If I could honor that, I would.

Facility Assets lived with a level of connectivity baseline humans couldn't possibly comprehend. If the Designates wished, they could pull our sensory data from our Crowns without a moment's notice. They had the ability to download the dialogues of our very thoughts, thankfully a rare necessity.

All of this meant Assets didn't exactly possess a measure of true privacy. Protocols existed to ensure these initiatives didn't take place, but this offered little comfort, especially to a paranoid man like Wyatt Guthrie.

"Okay." Tatiana slipped up next to me and sat down. "Right after this set, Lilith will be dancing."

"Lilith?" I rolled my eyes. "Seriously?"

"Lilith." She stared at me as if I might be crazy. "My friend. The one you met when you first came in?"

"Oh." I smiled. "The schoolgirl."

"I know." She put a hand on my arm. "The other girls are absolutely forgettable compared to me."

"Oh my God." I chuckled. "No, it's just that she didn't tell me her name."

"Anyway, she has the next set." Tatiana leaned close so I could hear. "If you give me some bills, you can watch me tip her."

"You said that before. But I'm telling you, I'm not here to tip or watch the dancers. I'm looking for my friend."

"You don't understand," she explained. "It's one thing when one of our gentlemen guests tips a dancer. There are rules. There are places you can and cannot touch."

"Okay?" I didn't follow her.

"Those rules don't apply to *me*," she said with a sunny smile. "And Lilith is my friend. I can touch her however"—she poked her finger into my chest—"you. Want."

"That sounds…" I let my words drift off as I gazed into Tatiana's mischievous eyes. "…wonderful."

She smirked. "It *is* wonderful, Archibald. I can promise you that."

"I…" I shook my head. "I can't. I'm here on business."

"So you can't have any fun?" She shook her head as if disappointed. "You strike me as the kind of guy who likes to have fun."

"I told you, the fate of the free world hangs in the balance." I stopped peering about the room and turned to her. "I do like having fun. Just now, however, I need to find my friend."

"Well," she replied holding one hand out, gesturing at the room, "where is he?"

"I don't know." I shook my head. "I mean, I know he's here, in the building. But I don't see him."

"You think he's in the men's room?"

"I wondered that. Maybe I should step over there and wait for him to come out."

"Unless you think he's the kind of guy to spend time in the private room?" She tilted her head.

"The private room?" I repeated, certainty settling into my bones. I had to admit that sounded an awful lot like a feature Guthrie might enjoy.

"It's where we offer our platinum-tier services."

"You mentioned that before," I mused. "Back behind the far side of the bar?"

"The bouncer would have to let us in." She gave me a sunny smile and arched her back just a bit. "I mean, if you were going to pay for a private experience."

"What?" I shook my head. "Seriously, Tatiana, I appreciate what you're offering." I made a general gesture in her direction. "But I'm dead serious. I didn't come here to enjoy myself."

"I don't even know why you're talking to me then," she teased. "I'm very enjoyable."

I couldn't help but laugh. Taking another drink, I shook my head at her sheer gall.

"If my friend is in the private room, I need you to get him for me. It's a little bit of an emergency."

"So you said." She took a sip of her bourbon. "Fate of the free world."

"Right." I pointed at her. "You'd be doing me a favor if you went back there to get him. I'd tip you for it."

"Here's the thing," she said with a wry little quirk of her lips. "The ladies who work here are quite competitive. In your eyes, you leave me a tip and I do you a favor. However, whatever entertainer your friend is currently with will perceive me as someone distracting her current client."

"And that causes problems?" I took another sip.

"Have you ever met a woman?" She chuckled earthily. "People around here hold grudges for a very long time. Let's just say you'd have to give me one hell of a tip to step back into the private areas and interfere with someone else's income."

"How much are we talking?" I narrowed my eyes.

"That's tough," she admitted. "You might be asking me to have problems with a coworker for months, maybe years. People get catty about that kind of thing."

"That definitely doesn't sound as if you are angling for more money." I gave her a wink.

"Only a little bit," she admitted. "I do have a better idea."

"I'd love to hear it."

"Let's step over there and talk to Stu." She pointed at the bouncer standing at the doorway to the private rooms. "Tell him you want to take the prettiest girl here back into the privates."

"I thought you said Lilith was going to be on stage?"

"Hey!" She gave me a punch in the shoulder.

"Oof." I made a show of rubbing my arm.

"Take me into the back as if you have procured my services. Paying for that will be a lot cheaper than trying to bribe me into pissing off one of my coworkers."

"Okay."

"Once we're back there, if you see your friend, you can be the one to interrupt his personal party." She shrugged one smooth shoulder. "I won't have anything to do with it."

"That's actually a brilliant idea f—"

"For a stripper? Please tell me that's not where you were going."

"No!" I held up both hands in mock fear. "I've been beaten enough."

"Good." She took the final sip of her drink and gave me a sweet smile. "Now let me go get that second pair of drinks you paid for, and then we'll make our way into the back."

"Seems reasonable." I took the final sip of my own drink and shook my head ruefully.

On the stage in front of me, Lilith began her set. I sat attentively, thinking about all the things I had to say to one Mr. Wyatt Guthrie.

2

"That's an even $150.00." Stu stared at me with a firm, expectant expression.

"You kidding me?" I turned to gape at Tatiana. "For that much money you'd better be the best dancer in Nevada!"

"It's not just for the dancing," she informed me flirtatiously. "That's the door fee for our platinum-level services."

"Do you have, like, bronze-level services?" I raised one eyebrow. "Copper?"

"Other girls might." She crossed her arms. "Pay the man, Archibald. Or you can sit out here and wait for your pal."

"Fine." I handed Stu my card, wondering how often the Facility paid for strippers. "But I expect platinum service from here on out."

"You got it, big guy." She wrapped herself around my arm, and Stu let us inside.

The back area easily took up as much room as the rest of the club, including the small casino in the foyer. Darkness and velvet curtains draped around us, and the place seemed positively labyrinthine with small, secluded booths.

"There's one mainstage in the middle, but they won't open that until this evening," Tatiana informed me. "For now there's just a lot of comfortable little nooks where our guests are treated to platinum services."

"I'm not certain if I want to watch my friend receive platinum services."

"What we'll do is walk around." Tatiana ignored me. "A lot of the girls don't completely close the curtains, it makes them feel safer. That way they know when Stu walks through, he'll notice if they're in trouble."

"Smart." I nodded.

"Keep an eye out for your friend. If anybody stops us, we're just headed to your favorite little booth."

"Fair enough," I agreed. "Let's do this."

I needed a moment to get accustomed to the soft light in the private room, but once I did, I found it quite soothing. The deep bass of a bluesy groove resounded through the room in a low, earthy beat. In more than one of the alcoves, I heard muttering, giggling, and other, more intimate noises.

"I just love peeping in on these people," I muttered.

"You're the one who doesn't like fun," Tatiana responded.

I had nothing to say to that.

"Let's step back this way," she whispered. "The inner row of alcoves is popular. Stu checks those every ten minutes or so."

I nodded and followed her through the shadows.

We rounded a corner then took a few more steps. In one of the alcoves, I could just make out the large form of Wyatt Guthrie, sitting on one of the plush seats. On his lap, a young Asian woman giggled, writhing suggestively.

I felt fairly certain she wasn't wearing a top.

"Oh God." I froze for just a moment and then continued walking.

"You found your friend?"

"Yeah, but..." I shook my head. "I guess I didn't exactly think through what he might be doing when I found him."

"Our platinum-tier services are popular," she teased.

"Apparently."

"You're going to have to do something here, Archibald," she informed me. "I don't think Stu would like it if we just walked around peeping."

"Okay," I said, coming to a conclusion. "Okay, let's go in here." As I spoke, I drew back the curtain of the alcove across from Wyatt.

"Good." Tatiana tittered, giving me that sunny smile. "I hoped you might be up for some fun after all."

"Just hold on." My situation had become intolerable. It seemed as if no matter what I did, I'd have to invade Wyatt's privacy.

That being the case, I had a preferred method.

Adjunct, activate my sync with Designate Ling.

Will comply, 108.

Just above and behind my left eye, I felt a subtle click, and a scarlet dataglyph pulsed briefly over my visual array.

The Designate flowed into my mind like a mountain stream.

"If we're going to be in here we need to make it look good." Tatiana put her hand in the center of my chest, pushing me back into the seat. "I have a job to do."

"You do not have a job to do!" I hissed. "Just hold on."

108, do you require assistance? Designate Ling synced into my Crown, perceiving everything from my sensory nodes in real time.

Even as Tatiana began to remove her shirt.

"Stop it." I frowned at her. "I'll only take a moment."

"You say that like it's a bad thing." She winked.

Designate, I need to rendezvous with Asset 423, I linked, scrambling to send the entire thought before Tatiana began removing more clothing. *He is indulging himself just outside Las Vegas and currently has his Crown communications blocked.*

Understood. I felt the Designate's confusion. *Asset... what are you doing?*

This question came as Tatiana snuggled her way onto my lap, wiggling impishly.

I had to pay to get inside this place, Designate. I made certain to convey world-weariness in my link. *If you glance back through my mnemonic trace, you'll see I've been attempting the rendezvous but found it impossible while Asset Guthrie's lock is active.*

I see. I didn't know if it was my imagination that her link felt chillier than it had. *You require an override for his Crown.*

Please. I frowned at Tatiana and shook my head just a bit. *Then I can move on.*

"Look, Archibald." She gave a frown in return, mocking me. "You're either here to get your friend or not. If you're not going to pick up your buddy, I have a job to do." She jerked her chin at the corner of the room. "There are cameras. Management is real picky over what people get to do back here."

"Give me just a minute," I hissed.

"Fine. You take your minute, and I'll cover for you." Slowly, sinuously, Tatiana began to dance on my lap.

Override approved. The Designate felt distant, even though she spoke within my own mind. *Tracking code 657-986. The lock on Asset Guthrie's Crown has been removed.*

Thank you, Designate. I made certain she felt my relief. *I will requisition Asset Guthrie immediately and we will move forward.*

See that you do. She still felt distant. *Time is of the essence and the dossier did not account for... dalliances.*

Understood.

She vanished then, drifting out of my mind like an autumn wind. Briefly, I hoped she had, in fact, peeked at my mnemonic trace, so she knew I hadn't come in here just to mess around.

"Come on, Archibald." Tatiana snuggled closer to me, wrapping her arms around my neck. "You found your buddy. Surely the free world can wait a minute or two, right?"

That sounded like a really bad idea. If the Designates later chose to scrape my Crown for data, I certainly didn't want them to find I had chosen a... dalliance.

I didn't answer Tatiana. Instead, I sent a link to Wyatt.

Hey there, buddy.

"Oh my—!" He exclaimed from across the aisle. "Seriously? Are you serious right now?"

"What, baby?" His slender companion stopped her writhing and ran one finger down his face. "What's wrong?"

"I have to go," I whispered to Tatiana. "It seems my pal has realized I'm here."

"Are you sure?" She nuzzled against my cheek, her breath warm on my ear. "We haven't really gotten to know each other yet."

You're some piece of work, Wyatt linked, irritation plain in his tone. *How do you not know to give a man a little privacy?*

We've got a job to do, buddy. I put one hand on Tatiana's lower back, trying to hold her in place rather than allow her to continue to "encourage" me. *If you had answered my link, I wouldn't have had to come searching for you.*

This is just amazing. He shifted in his seat.

"It's not my fault," I said, loud enough so he could hear. "Our client requires some attention."

Wyatt sighed. "Honey, papa bear's gonna have to step away," he informed the dancer. "I have some business to deal with."

"No..." The young Asian woman pouted. "You don't have to leave yet."

"You know," Tatiana whispered, wriggling her hips as she glanced across at Wyatt's alcove. "I don't mind working with Jasmine. We could make it a party."

"Jasmine?" I arched one eyebrow at her. "That girl's name is not Jasmine. I don't believe it."

"You can't just leave, Archibald." Now she pouted too. "You know how much money I could have made if I'd focused on another guest?"

"We'll make it right," I assured her.

"I'm not leaving here sober." Wyatt stood, one hand on Jasmine's hip. A grizzly of a man, he stood nearly a head taller than me. He had the broadest shoulders I'd ever seen but always dressed as a good ol' country boy. Today he wore jeans, a beat-up Stetson over his close-cropped head, and wide sunglasses that might be a full decade out of fashion.

"Two fingers of Jack." He reached out and kissed Jasmine on the cheek. He held up a fifty and pointed at me. "For each of us."

"That's gotta be it, man." I stood as well. "One last drink at the bar, but then we're out."

"Then we're out," he agreed wearily.

3

Less than five minutes later Wyatt and I sat at the bar, enjoying one last drink. I'd run my card again, ensuring Tatiana got a hefty tip. We'd assured Jasmine and Tatiana that, no, we definitely weren't staying any longer and therefore weren't their best options as guests to entertain.

"Too bad, though." Tatiana toyed with my hair. "You're a lot of fun, Archibald."

"That's Dr. Moneycock to you," I responded airily.

"Right," she agreed. "Come back and see me? Maybe after you save the world?"

"Maybe after I save the world," I confirmed. "It's a dangerous life I lead, though; it might be a while."

"I'll wait." She giggled. "I don't really have anything else going on." Then she kissed me on the cheek before walking away.

"You couldn't wait another hour?" Wyatt scoffed. "I was having a hell of a time."

"I've had a hell of a time, all day." I took a sip of my Jack. I hadn't even swallowed before I felt the incoming link.

Michael, I see Asset Guthrie is active and green, Anya linked.

"Give me a minute, man." Wyatt waved one hand at me. "Let me shift modes."

Yep. We'll be outside in just a minute, I linked back with a nod at Wyatt.

I have been communicating with Asset Gardener ever since 423 came back online, she informed me.

The Caduceus?

Correct. She paused. *She would like a quick word with you, if you are available?*

Okay. I furrowed my brow. *What does she want?* I couldn't imagine why the medical Asset would be interested in speaking with me.

Anya didn't respond. Instead, I felt the clicks and whirs of my Crown's handshake protocols. In less than a second, Asset Gardener's Facility profile merged with my dossier and available Asset information. As if I'd known her for my entire life, I remembered her basic personality and Facility specs.

I felt her the moment her trace touched my Crown.

She felt pissed.

Hello, Caduceus! I did my best to exude cheer. *How can I help you today?*

Hello, 108. Asset Rachel Gardener sent irritation along with her link. *I'd like to discuss the current status of your cadre.*

Understood. I took another sip. *I have just rendezvoused with Asset 423, and we will shortly make our way toward our white room. From there, I expect our dossier will begin.*

108, you should be aware Guthrie's current blood alcohol level is .08. He is impaired and unfit.

Really? I took a long, sideward glance at Wyatt. *You'd never know it to look at the man.*

You'd also never know it if your own BAC registered somewhere around .11, she replied. *Neither of you are fit to engage new packets in a white room.*

I... didn't intend to drink, I explained lamely.

You accidentally got drunk in a strip club? I felt her eyes roll to the ceiling. *I completely believe that. You are completely believable right now.*

We'll take care of it, I assured her. *We won't hook our Crowns to the Cradle while drunk.*

Um, that is correct. You will not. She paused. *Anya Petrova has viral mecha prepared. Both you and Asset Guthrie will take two injections of type III viral mecha upon returning to the vehicle.*

Understood, Caduceus. I finished my drink. *You can count on me.*

You just took another drink! I felt her shake her head, gaping in disbelief. *You know I can watch your physical reactions in real time, right?*

I... did not know that, I admitted. *That was my last swallow. I'm retrieving Guthrie now and removing him from the premises.*

That would be best. Do not engage new system packets while in your current state.

Copy that.

I have also defered your body's sleep requirements. If this dossier can be completed within the next forty-eight hours, that would be preferred.

Understood, Rachel. I smiled over the link. *Thank you.* The moment I sent the link I felt her fade from my Crown.

I guess the ice princess is waiting outside? Wyatt glanced at me.

You know she is. We have to get moving. I've already had a rough day.

You and me both. He smiled, a flash of square white teeth. *Almost got into a bar fight.*

You've been offline, so I couldn't send you my day. I sucked on a piece of ice. *Let me catch you up.* I sent him the patch, porting it to his memory.

In that instant, Wyatt remembered my day, as certainly as if it had happened to him.

Wow. His eye momentarily widened. *That's a truly messed up day.* He took another sip. *You aren't the only one though. Here.*

I felt the slight whir of his patch. Instantly, as if I'd lived the memories myself, his recollections formed in my mind. During Wyatt's long evening in The Booby Trap, each moment loomed sharp and horrifyingly intimate. I remembered every sight, scent, and sound in full, three-dimensional technicolor. Every beverage he'd drunk, the five women he'd dallied with...

And yes, he'd gotten into a bar fight with a lean guy topped by a shock of red hair. Apparently Wyatt caught the guy staring at him, and then the guy had been rough with one of the ladies.

Wyatt and the bouncer threw him out.

Afterward, Wyatt had celebrated.

My friend certainly made use of his time and money, and I experienced every second as if it had been my party instead of his.

Wyatt's tastes were... eclectic to put it mildly.

He grinned widely at me.

Dude. Not cool.

You just try to forget that. He finished his drink, adjusted his hat, and stood. *Let's get out of here.*

I blinked and tried to push the images of Wyatt's long night to the back of my mind.

When I stood, he recoiled, his nose wrinkled.

Damn, Bishop. You reek.

I sighed and followed him out of the bar.

4

"This is not my place of employment." Anya's quiet voice grew firm. "Not at this time."

"All's I'm sayin' is maybe you should. It should be. That's what I mean." The man leaned against the *Legacy*. After too much time inside The Booby Trap, he slurred and stumbled, in no shape to drive.

"She'll take your idea under consideration, I'm certain." I walked around the man and opened the back door.

"Hey, I jus'—"

"We don't care, pal. We gots to go." Wyatt tipped his hat to the man as he got in the passenger side.

That man offered me a job in the restaurant. Anya blinked in confusion.

She doesn't get it? Wyatt stared incredulously.

I shrugged.

He said I looked like a perfect fit. Anya continued, *He told me he thought I could do just as well as any of the other women in there.*

"Ha!" Wyatt patted her knee. "You could, Petrova. I just bet you could." When Anya moved his hand, he laughed again.

Let's go, I linked them both. *Anya, do you have viral mecha for us?*

"I do." She threw the *Legacy* into reverse. "Asset Gardener has made it clear that each of you require two."

"Two?" Wyatt gasped. "Princess, I'm just fine, I promise you."

"This isn't a negotiation." I leaned forward between the two seats to glare at him. "We've had too much to install any packets."

"That might not be so bad." He raised an eyebrow at me. "Maybe we should step back inside? Take a couple hours to sober up?"

"Maybe another time." I shook my head.

"White room dispersal is on a very limited timeframe," Anya informed him. "Going back into the restaurant is not the best use of our time."

"I dunno..." Wyatt gave her a teasing smile. "I really think you'd fit in well there."

"The injectors are in the glovebox," Anya stated. "Taking them immediately would amplify their effectiveness."

"Yes, Mom," Wyatt mocked.

I opened the glovebox and handed him two injectors.

"Michael," she went on, "I have made certain you will be equipped with a shower and clothing exchange."

"Thank God for that." Wyatt rolled down his window. "Seriously. You smell like raw sewage."

"Well, some of us had to work today." I sat back with my injectors, hoping to protect my cadre from the worst of the reek.

We drove into the desert.

The world fell away behind us.

Cradle and Crown

Several kilometers outside of Las Vegas, Anya turned south on 160. Somewhere past Pahrump, she pulled into a small, abandoned gas station. Wyatt had been half asleep, but now he sat up and pulled his hat back.

How about a beer run? he linked to me alone.

I'm pretty certain I haven't seen you take your injections yet. I'd say now's the time.

We were a few hours outside Barstow, on the edge of the desert, when the viral mecha began to take hold. He pulled his pant leg up and took the shots.

"Gentlemen," Anya began, "for the next fifteen minutes, the washroom behind the station will function as our white room."

"Really?" I rolled my eyes. "All my best stories today seem to involve extra-dimensional restrooms."

"From here," Anya continued as if I hadn't spoken, "it is less than two hours to the hot site. Extraction teams have been readied, but they are also using mundane transportation. We have no conduit support for this location."

Still? Like myself, Wyatt held out hope that a Facility team might be able to set up an extraction conduit.

"The unstable Rationality levels of this region have made that an impossibility," she stated firmly. "No matter how we run the topiatic coordinates, the *Gatekeeper*s cannot guarantee the stability of a conduit due to aberrant vectors."

"That's brilliant," Wyatt grumbled, annoyed. "So when we're in the thick of it, and some 'Rat is summoning horrific lamentations, we just gotta… what, out run them?"

"No Irrational with that capability has been confirmed on-site, Asset Guthrie." Anya's head twitched the smallest amount. "Our primary objective remains getting close enough to Locale One for me to read ambient Rationality. If there are further directives, the Designate will update us as required."

"In and out." He shrugged. "Shouldn't be a big deal."

"Due to the unusual nature of this event, Michael is in possession of a sync with Designate Ling." Anya nodded in my direction. "We are to activate the sync when we are one kilometer from Locale One."

"You have a system sync?" Wyatt's eyes grew wide. "You're Asset-in-command?"

"Not really," I assured him. "Ling just wanted a ride along."

"We're all going to die," he lamented.

"This is all old news to me." I smiled at Wyatt. "I haven't spent the last several hours offline at The Booby Trap." I opened the car door. "I do, however, smell like monster viscera, and a shower is on the offer."

"You need one, Hoss," he replied. "My mama would say you smell like chitlins that done went bad."

"I shall remain here while you get equipped." Anya met my eyes for just a moment. "I thought I might continue my research into the Irrational spikes to see if I can identify any further patterns."

"Brilliant." I gave her a thumbs-up. "Make certain you patch Wyatt what you found with the Fibonacci numbers."

"I have not done that yet, thank you." Anya turned toward Wyatt, and I watched his miniscule tic as he received her patch.

"That's flipping weird." He scowled. "I like all of this less and less."

"Good." I clapped him on the back. "At least we agree."

Together, we walked toward the abandoned structure.

The grit and dust of Nevada had leeched all the color out of the gas station, and one of the dirty windows had a crack all the way across the top. Overhead, the morning sun fell like a hammer on the anvil of the desert.

"I assume you're going to pick up the Tangler?" I knew

Wyatt's answer. For all his rough charm, Wyatt remained one of the few men I knew with the intellect to absolutely master that piece of tech. I hoped he'd take it; the man was an artist with the device.

"If I can get it. I'd love to walk in there and see a couple of pistols though, just in case. Maybe a Maverick, if I have Crown space."

"Sure." I considered. "I'll probably take kinetic disruptors; I've gotten fond of them lately."

"Stilettos?" Wyatt gave me an askance eye. "I dunno, Hoss, I like my guns to have bullets."

"Me too," I agreed. "Right up 'til the bullets run out. Firing blasts of kinetic energy, I won't have to worry about that."

"Sure." He nodded. "I get it."

"It's a sneak mission though, so I'll poke around for an emitter."

"The diaphanic emitter." Wyatt shuddered. "Nope."

"Really?" I squinted at him, trying to shield my eyes from the sun. "What's not to like about nigh-invisibility?"

"Can't stand the things. I don't know what they do to my metabolism, but I'm always starving afterward."

"It's what keeps me trim."

"Heh." Wyatt kicked at a stone and then changed topics. "You understand, we're in some deep bullshit here."

"Are we?" I squinted at him. "I don't think the Designates know what kind of bullshit we're in, not yet."

"They know enough to send you in with a sync," he replied. "And that Fibonacci garbage Petrova found?" He shook his head. "Something huge is happening."

"Maybe," I replied airily. "I prefer to keep my predictions of doom and gloom to myself until we're up to our necks in Irrational horror."

"Mark my words, Hoss." Wyatt stopped in front of the door and turned to gaze at me. "This may not seem like much now. But we're potentially looking at the largest Irrational event within modern Facility records. There's bound to be repercussions."

"Yeah," I nodded. "You're not wrong."

Bishop, Michael, the Adjunct chirped in my Crown. **Do you wish to initiate conduit?**

In a moment.

For that moment, Wyatt and I stood in silence.

Then I rapped my knuckles on the door. "After you, my good man?"

"Yep." He grinned. "Anything to get away from that smell." Wyatt opened the door, muttering his clearance codes. Unlike when I used a conduit, I didn't see the sudden flash of a crimson dataglyph. Instead, Wyatt simply opened the door and strode into a dilapidated public restroom then shut the door behind him.

Wyatt's gearing up, Anya. I'm headed in.

Affirmative, Michael. Remember, we only have fourteen minutes remaining on that conduit.

Understood.

I touched the door and cleared my throat.

"Asset 108. Authorization code 020798361. System green."

I opened the door. This time, ruby bursts of light flashed around the edges of the door, and the dataglyph burned into my mind.

I walked into the white room. The door closed behind me, leaving me in another place altogether.

2

Inside, I blinked the harsh desert sunlight from my eyes. This room had been set up differently than the last. Anya had indeed requisitioned a shower, and a fresh set of clothes hung beside it. The suit wasn't in my preferred colors, but it seemed a perfect fit with lots of flexibility.

"Quasi-steel," I noted as I fingered the cloth.

To look at it, no one could tell the difference from a typical suit. Except the quasi-steel breathed more easily than linen and could take a bullet or six.

Offhandedly, I wondered how much thought Anya gave to the clothing she requisitioned.

Probably none.

I stripped off my slacks and button-up, then slipped into the steaming water.

"Oh, God yes." The water felt like heaven itself.

I didn't dally, however. I showered up, splashed on some expensive cologne—Anya's idea of a joke?—and slipped the gear from the ruins of my old suit into fresh pockets.

Wyatt always giggled at my tendency to wear a suit jacket and slacks regardless of the mission, but it felt appropriate.

"Hard to play super-spy without the proper attire," I reasoned to myself as I gazed in the mirror. I tousled my hair and gave my reflection a grin then turned toward the back of the white room.

"This," I said to myself as I glanced around at my options, "is more like it."

The weapon's cabinet had been loaded with various firearms, both mundane and Facility specialized. I saw more than one model of Maverick, as well as two different Talons—Facility sniper rifles, broken down for easy transport. A display off to the side held four different models of Vulcan, our own high capacity TASERs.

I passed those over, searching for a pair of Stilettos, my current favorite pistols.

"There we are." I picked up the sleek, black weapons.

Stilettos required no ammunition, one of the things I preferred about them. Instead, they fired compressed bursts of sheer kinetic force—force I modulated at will. I enjoyed being able to fire *ad infinitum*, as well as the capability to choose how hard I wanted my shots to hit.

The hilt of each encased a small, blue injector, exactly like the others we used for the viral mecha. I popped both out and pressed them to my forearm. They hissed as the specialized mecha flooded my bloodstream.

The moment they hit my Crown, I heard the Adjunct prompt. ***Bishop, Michael. Asset 108. Do you wish to initiate weapon synchronization?***

"I do," I spoke out loud. "Please synchronize both for item possession and neural link."

Without the mecha, the guns became paperweights. However, if I burned their operational reserves, those mecha could give the weapons a significant boost, create a shot exponentially stronger than typical.

Synchronization initiated.

My Crown tingled as the mecha altered the parameters of my nervous system. The sync would progress regardless of what I did, so I opened one of the weapons' cabinets.

Inside, I found various throwing knives, tonfa, and even a set of injectable brass knuckles.

I considered the tonfa for a moment, as I enjoyed using them. Still, if I had my choice…

My gaze fell upon a set of katana, resting delicately on a display rack.

"See, that's what I'm talking about!" I gazed longingly at the mated pair of katana on the wall.

Yet I couldn't be certain I would have the neural space. I didn't exactly have any sword training, but one of the packets I often took came preset with the required skills.

"Maybe," I told myself. "If I have the space."

I continued my perusal, noticing I hadn't been provided with any dampening grenades or *Wrath*-class explosives. I shut the door and peered in the next cabinet. No, it only held ammunition for traditional weaponry.

I preferred weapons that wouldn't run dry, thank you.

Synchronization complete, 108. How else can I help you?

I think it may be time for Cradle harmonization.

Understood, Michael Bishop. Will comply.

An otherworldly, high-pitched whir began on the other side of the room. I grit my teeth. The sound set me on edge, made me feel nervous in an illogical way I couldn't quite explain.

"Let's get this over with," I said, resigned.

The Cradle loomed at the far end of the room. At first glance, it appeared to be a stainless-steel table stood upright on one end. Closer inspection revealed handholds at the side and swivel capabilities. Along its left edge ran a dizzying array of LED lights, data readouts, and biogenic resonators. A white metal halo encircled the Cradle, its surface engraved with grooves. A swing arm attached to the halo via a hinged joint. At the end of it hung a blue-tipped silver rod, sleek, about the size of a ballpoint pen.

A polished chrome plate with an obsidian inset labeled the halo. I traced my fingers along the markings used by the Facility. I had no idea what they said, and I'd never met an Asset who could read them.

Not that it had never been tried.

"Designate stuff," Wyatt confided in me once. "Some kind of secret language."

"Yeah?" We slipped through the old Chicago underground, searching for a small cult holed up in an old speakeasy. "How do you figure?"

"I've seen the markings," he said with no small amount of glee, "on one of their Ordinal slates."

"You saw one of the slates?"

"Designate Johanson is a bit slow sometimes." He paused. "I wasn't trying to look; it just happened that way."

"Aren't they the same as the dataglyphs?"

"I think so. I use a few for the Tangler but not many." He took a few more steps through the darkness before continuing, "I don't know where they came from, but it's an entire language. I'd kill to know it."

Initiating now, 108. Several of the lights along the side of the Cradle pulsed in a triggering sequence. *Prepared for Crown entanglement.*

With this last link, the white halo slid to the bottom of the table. Verdant lights blinked amidst clicks and whirs. I walked over to it and stepped inside the halo.

Initiate entanglement.

Will comply.

When I first entered the halo, I felt the subtle *snick* as it entangled with my Solomon's Crown. I leaned against the table and held onto the side handles.

Noiselessly, the table began to shift beneath me, leaning backward.

The halo began to move of its own accord as it calibrated to my settings and system. It positioned the rod around my head, paused, and then darted to another location, lightning fast.

Bishop, Michael. Asset 108. With each word, the end of the rod pulsed a brilliant cobalt blue. **Would you like to peruse sanctioned neuralware? Your current classification will allow for three packets slots.**

Three? The extra slot made me grin. The Designates had decided to let me have some fun. *Peruse packets, please.*

I noted the system time; eight minutes remained.

The world around me resolved into a shimmering whirlwind of scarlet dataglyphs; a maelstrom of symbols. Many of them moved along strands of shimmering light, the closest representation of the Lattice my mind could conceive.

Opening neuralware channels now, 108.

As I received the link, several of the strands bent toward me as if attracted by magnetic force. My neuralware channels entangled with these, and with a solid KA-THUNK in the back of my skull, my entanglement sequence completed.

Initiating packet selection, it chirped.

A collection of dataglyph-marked spheres appeared in my mind's eye, each a different packet of Facility firmware. They could grant me battle skills, control over exotic technology, even limited mastery of localized axioms.

Not complete mastery, of course. The Facility would never license us to warp and rend reality ourselves. We weren't Irrats, after all. First-tier Assets such as Wyatt and I were typically kept on a pretty tight leash.

Heck, most of the time my assignments didn't stretch much beyond low level psychics and cultists.

Mentally, I thumbed through the packets. The sheer number of them left me confused. *Fury, Adept, Raptor...*

I even found a *Seraph* packet. I hardly ever saw that one. "Weird."

I thumbed past *Titan* and *Juggernaut*, my hackles rising. Most missions offered one or two possibilities. Often, the Designate selected packets for the Asset pre-incursion.

What did this freedom mean?

The system also offered a *Caduceus* packet, designed to direct and bolster the viral mecha in our bloodstreams. A sweet option, but it would take up all three of my Crown slots.

Besides, I had the feeling Rachel Gardener would be all the *Caduceus* I needed.

"What is all this?" I shook my head, a bit overwhelmed.

I thought back to what Wyatt had said about this being the largest Irrational event on record. He'd mentioned repercussions.

Were we being prepared for those repercussions or for the expected danger-level of the current dossier?

"Doesn't matter." I ground my teeth. "Choose something and move along, Asset."

The *Spectre* packet caught my eye. I hadn't ever used it, but I knew the specs. The idea of being physically insubstantial appealed to me, but I needed to be on hand if Anya required assistance. If Wyatt geared the *Artisan* to counteract Irrats, then my cadre needed me to be a bit more of a bruiser.

This wasn't the time to experiment.

In seconds, I drifted through the array of choices. *Cavalier, Rapier, Tempest...*

"The *Wraith*." One of my most frequent packets, I brought it forward. I manipulated the packet interface and glanced through its specs. The *Wraith* only took up one of my slots and had always served me well.

The diaphanic emitter, the Wraith's firmware, had saved me on more than one occasion. It employed a simple axiomatic change but a potent one. When engaged, the vast majority of my surface area would no longer interact with most bandwidths of light. Practically identical to invisibility. Handy in a pinch.

However that barely scratched the surface of the *Wraith's* utility for stealth and subterfuge. The emitter dampened noise as well as bent light. I didn't know all the specifics, but on more than one occasion, the packet had enacted preinstalled subroutines, assisting me in unexpected ways.

"Bullshit," Wyatt had said when I brought up the possibility. "You're just the luckiest asshole alive."

"The *Wraith* can alter sound; we know that," I insisted. "So when an unexpected noise distracts a guard—an unexplainable sound with no cause—what else could that be?"

"You're implying a packet can make choices, think for itself." He shook his head. "Even if it could, it's not worth the metabolic alterations."

He had a point; it definitely stoked the metabolism even when inactive. Protocols dictated the emitter not be active for longer than fifteen minutes at a time.

Do you wish to install the **Wraith?** The Adjunct sounded chipper.

I do.

Crown slot 12-b is currently configured for this class of packet.

Do it.

The swing arm darted to my left, coming to a stop level to my neck. The small rod swung closer, flashing with cobalt light.

Crown dock 12-b engaged. Packet transferring to iteration 108. A series of clicks whirred. **Packet installed, Asset.**

One choice down.

I gazed longingly at the *Gatekeeper* packet for creating Facility conduits. The standard process followed smooth lines of logic. An Asset geared with *Gatekeeper* would be deposited into a hot zone. From there, the Asset would establish a conduit available for extraction or reinforcements.

Then I remembered what Anya had said about aberrant vectors. In an unstable area, a conduit might not open in the intended location. It could open anywhere at all.

I remembered the deafening, screaming wind of the spider-scorpion's lair, and shuddered.

So no, not today.

Instead I accessed the *Adept.*

This packet requires two slots to function. Do you wish to—

Yes. Continue, I urged, impatient. *Begin packet installation.* I glanced at the system time, four minutes.

Crown slots 12-c and 12-e are currently configured for this class of packet.

Perfect. Use those.

The halo moved a few centimeters, and the arm darted wildly. Its tip pulsed, bright blue.

The *Adept* packet altered reaction times and concentration, making the user superhumanly fast. It also came with a plethora of preprogrammed combat routines, including various melee moves perfect for the katana. It even generated proteins to keep the user alert and intensely focused. Wyatt and I theorized it created natural caffeine or an adrenaline alternative.

Of course, Wyatt also theorized I might be addicted to the intense rush that came with the packet and suggested I needed professional help for it.

Personally, he wouldn't be caught dead with the *Adept*.

"I prefer fighting the 'Rats from as far away as possible." Though this had been one of our earliest discussions, I still saw his grin. "I prefer not to fight at all, actually. Set it up so you win before you start. Sun Tzu and all that shit."

I felt differently. I'd never learned any true martial art, but with the *Adept* packet, I never had to. When activated, everything I needed coursed through my body like sweet quicksilver. I had speed, muscle memory, and fighting styles.

With the *Adept* and the *Wraith* cybergeared into my Crown, I could be devastating. I became a character in a bad anime, without the need to power up.

Crown docks 12-c and 12-e engaged. Packet transferring to iteration 108. Another series of clicks whirred. **Packet installed, Asset.**

Perfect. Please disengage Cradle.

Disengaging, Asset.

One minute remains, Michael, Anya linked. *Wyatt is complete and has emerged.*

I'm finished. Grinning, I grabbed both katana on my way out as well as a few more injectables. When I stepped into the brilliant desert sun, Wyatt laughed.

"Playin' a ninja again, I see. What's the sound of one hand clapping?"

"What's the sound of one man handing you your ass?" I

offered.

Chuckling, we walked back to the car.

I glanced at him as we walked.

"Tangler again, huh?" The *Artisan* might as well be a permanent install for him.

Wyatt wore a sleek, black backpack with several readouts along the side. A semi-circular keyboard hung from his belt at his right hip. The keys were in no tongue I understood—mostly dataglyphs. It calibrated the rivet-gun-like attachment hung over his right shoulder.

"I stick with what I know," he replied.

Technically, it wasn't named the Tangler. The single most complex piece of equipment at the disposal of an Asset had an appropriately grand name: the T-90 Axiomatic Redistribution Algorithm. With it, Wyatt could temporarily alter Rationality within a given radius to almost any specification. Defensively, he could set up fall back locations by changing the laws of physics on the battlefield. He just had to choose a radius and input the alterations. An *Artisan* could shift gravity or alter the density of stone. He even had the capability to convert one element to another.

Wyatt's skill with the thing amazed me.

"You go ahead swing your swords at the 'Rats. I'll stay back, thanks."

"You're cheating," I countered. "At least I engage straightaway. Boiling your opponent's blood or turning his bones into acid seems unfair."

"It *is* unfair." He grinned at me. "There's a reason we aren't allowed to do that crap, typically."

"Typically." I snorted. "You like to skirt the regs with that thing and you know it."

"Heh," he replied. "Whatever gets me home."

Wyatt seemed like an unlikely choice to wield such a complex device. To look at him or even speak with him for a few moments, a person might walk away believing Wyatt to be a shallow redneck who loved beer, stock car races, and strip clubs.

One would be correct.

But the Tangler required a genius-level grasp of mathematics and a mastery of particle physics. I'd seen him alter the rate at which wounds healed, transform the oxygen in a man's bloodstream into red-hot plasma, and even shift the direction of gravity right underneath an Irrat's feet.

Typically, offensive uses of the device remained prohibited. But sometimes…

Suddenly, I realized Wyatt didn't have any guns.

"What happened to the pistol you wanted? A Maverick, wasn't it?"

"Nope." His expression appeared grim. "Not today."

"Why not?"

"This is an entirely new *Artisan* packet. Took all my Crown slots. Plus a shitload of injectables." He paused. "I even have to be cautious what mecha I use."

Unusual. Most of our weaponry required either a Crown sync or viral mecha. Both said something.

"So today you're not running anything but the *Artisan*?"

"You got it." He nodded. "Tangler only. It's an odd packet. I won't need near the Designate clearances I have in the past."

"And that means…?" I arched an eyebrow.

"Means I'll be able to mix it up quicker, have more authority on the fly."

Wyatt wasn't saying something.

"That's good for us, at least," I probed.

"Right." He gave a rueful grin. "Sure. Sure it is. Makes a man think, is all. Interesting time to let up on the reins a bit."

I thought back to all the available packets. It *did* feel like the Facility had allotted us more than standard resources. I took another few steps before probing again.

"Does feel like this is more than a typical insertion, doesn't it?"

"You never geared the *Artisan*, so you don't know." He spat into the dust. "While I'm in the white room, I typically have to clear ten to twelve algos with the Designates, while the Tangler equips." He met my eye. "Most of the crap you see me pull is precleared hours before I do it."

"That makes sense." I nodded thoughtfully. If the Designates gave preclearance on whatever weird physics fuckery Wyatt pulled, it might be easier for them to create equilibrium in Rationality once he'd finished.

"When I geared this packet, the Adjunct said no preclearance required." He scratched his beard. "I'm supposed to patch a record of every algo I use on this dossier. After the fact. I have general clearance to act as required."

"That's—" I shook my head. "That's a ludicrous amount of leeway. They've given you the capability to alter Rationality as you see fit?"

"I've never seen the Designates hand over so much control." He shrugged. "I kinda figgered you'd go all ninja on me, so I took the upgrade. If I snagged a gun, I'd be shootin' offa skill alone, no fancy tech."

"Probably not worth the weight."

"Didn't seem like it, not when Rosie here can just as easily take someone out—even without any special mojo." He patted the 'rivet-gun' end of the apparatus.

Ten centimeter titanium spikes could make anyone's day rough.

"That makes sense," I agreed.

We walked in silence back to the *Legacy*, both in our own thoughts.

Anya popped the trunk for Wyatt's gear. I set the katana in the back as well.

"I thought Michael might drive." Anya stared off into space, a touch distracted. "I have perused the initial readings, and I would like to continue as we approach."

"Fine by me." Wyatt gave a cat's grin. "As long as I can nap on the way, I don't care."

"If you're asleep, I won't have to listen to your rambling." I teased. "Seems perfect all around."

Phage

I drove into the desert, and time began to drift. As promised, Wyatt lay in the back and snored, hat drawn over his face. Anya stared off into space, reading holographic telemetry only she saw. As the sun rose higher into the sky and the day grew hotter, I periodically rolled down my window.

I didn't want to disturb them as I smoked.

We passed into the Mojave along Nipton Road sometime around ten a.m. We cut south on Ivanpah and drove straight for the New York mountain range.

'Desolate' didn't begin to describe this place. The wind skipped across the barren landscape, soughing through the emptiness. As far as the eye could see, only rock, sand, and empty sky lay around us, broken only by the occasional Joshua tree.

Anya sat in silence at my side. Occasionally, her head would twitch, accompanied by that marionette-like finger motion all *Preceptors* did while they viewed telemetry, as if she played a harp that wasn't there.

I drove, enjoyed my second cigarette, and looked amazingly cool beneath that brilliant sky.

I'd just put out my smoke when Anya sat straight up and stared wildly off to our left. I peered in that direction myself, not realizing that she gazed at something on her visual array.

"Michael," she whispered, her eyes wide. "Adjust by 42 degrees."

"The temperature?" I reached for the AC. "I don't think it can go that—"

She screamed.

Her left hand clawed into my pantleg, and she whipped her head to the side. Her right hand went positively mad, plucking and picking at her holographic controls.

143

"NO!" Anya screamed, panic reedy in her voice. "Michael, it's too—!"

Bishop! Wyatt's link held all the confusion of a man jerked from sleep. *Where are—?*

"Anya, what?" I stared at her, stunned.

She whirled back to me, her eyes gone wild. Her link slammed into me, the sensation like a patch too large to be accepted into memory.

It didn't even feel like her. The link felt more like something sent by the Adjunct.

—elemetric relay 345-t offline! Telemetric Relay 345-u offline! Situation critical! Rationality spiking at R45, R46. Facility 17 Terminal Prime OFFLINE. AXIOMATIC STRAND 542-8 uncalibrated. Resonation state critical—

"What the hell?" Wyatt bellowed as he shoved at his hat and pulled himself upright on my seatback. He pointed ahead. "Bishop, what in the name of—?"

I turned from Anya, back to the road.

A shimmering plasm of color burned and trembled, hovering about three meters in front of the *Legacy*. It exploded all around us in a whirlwind of unnatural tints.

"Oh, shit!" I gaped at the brilliant hues, rapt in the oddness of them, the wrongness.

"Michael!" Anya stared at me, horror stark in her eyes. A ringing cacophony punctuated her cry, and it felt as if my skull split open. For a moment, the desert wavered around us, trembling like a leaf caught in a thunderstorm.

I jerked and spun the car to the side. We careened off the road. The world whirled around us.

It felt as if I'd plunged underwater, as if embers burned at the center of my bones.

Everything slowed, and my mind felt full of mud.

"Sub-Rational." Anya sounded forlorn, infinitely far away.

"Bishop," Wyatt warned.

"I see it, man, I do." I peered out the windshield in disbelief.

We weren't exactly in Kansas anymore. We'd driven through to somewhere else entirely.

The world flickered around us, shifting us between the California desert and—somewhere empty. Somewhere wrought with shadows and stone. Somewhere dark with furious fires in the distance.

"Rationality negative thirteen!" As if in pain, Anya grunted the statistic rather than spoke it. "Negative twenty-one! Negative thirty-four!" She shook her head wildly, like a horse trying to tear loose from its traces.

"Understood, Anya." I put my right hand on her shoulder, leaving the other holding the wheel.

"Hurts," she whimpered. "Michael, it hurts."

That hit me, square in the chest.

Hearing Anya scream statistics didn't matter; I couldn't decipher their meaning. If I'd given it a moment's thought, I would have realized her panic did as much to throw me off center as anything else.

I'd never seen Anya truly afraid. Truly hurt. That pain in her voice…

"Bishop!" Wyatt pointed at a gully that loomed in front of the *Legacy*.

The air boiled and the way ahead writhed, swirling while the sky shifted through a sickening violet-red into a smothering darkness.

For an instant, we faced the Rational world again. The Mojave Desert flickered around us, immediately followed by that lost, unearthly place.

The flickering stopped, as suddenly as it began. We no longer drove through the Mojave. Emptiness lurked around us in a sky with no stars. Colossal, limbless trees reached for the forlorn heavens.

Abruptly, hungry, oppressive night shrouded us. I flicked on the car's headlights, but it took my eyes a moment to adjust.

No, not night. We drove through a cavern, the Mojave left behind.

The trees I'd seen weren't trees at all, but thick, black, stone columns that stretched to a ceiling far out of sight. From a gargantuan chasm off in the distance, a hungry, orange glow danced, the only light. I heard the loud grind of machinery but didn't see it anywhere.

A column loomed in front of us.

I slammed on the brakes, trying to skid away from it. I spun the wheel as hard as I could.

"Bishop!" Wyatt grasped my shoulder from behind, but I didn't have time to act.

The front of our car crumpled into the column, and we jerked catastrophically short on impact. Anya and I had been buckled in, but Wyatt launched forward and hit the seat with a hard thump.

Groaning, I sat up and glanced around.

"Who let you drive, Hoss?" Wyatt griped.

"Facility car pinged me and Anya as operators," I replied. "Blame Ling."

"The Designates are a bunch of reptilians," he muttered.

In the darkness beyond, gleaming, furious eyes shone with hatred like stark, burning coals. I shook my head and peered through the windshield again to get my bearings.

Darkness loomed, darker now that one of the headlights had smashed. I couldn't see the walls of the cavern, although I did see a deep chasm, burning with a hungry fire. The sounds of hidden machinery grew louder.

My focus centered on the creatures appearing from the gloom around us. One of them peered at us with a fiery, hateful glare. The horrifying, gorilla-shaped beast lumbered toward the car.

Its eyes appeared empty, hollow, mad.

"I do not like that," I informed my cadre.

"Agreed," Wyatt said.

It stood at least four meters high. Gray skin covered thick, knotted muscle; it must have weighed five or six hundred kilograms. Twisting, tattooed lines of script, unlike any writing I'd ever seen, had been inked into the tough skin. It wore a long loincloth, tattered and dirty, and brandished a vaguely hammer-shaped object the size of a small tree.

The elegant lines of writing caught at my gaze.

He doesn't look friendly, I linked, experimentally. As expected, the link felt clunky in my mind, more like a walkie-talkie. That meant we weren't connected to the Lattice, that we had only our available tech and Crown-links.

Bad news.

We are adrift in an unclassified sub-topia, Anya sent. I felt her exhaustion, even through the clunky link. *We are back to negative R thirty-two... thirty one—!*

"Do we have a beacon, *Preceptor?*" I didn't hold out any hope for that. The number of alternate realms the Facility had tagged with locater beacons remained relatively small.

"No beacon detected," Anya replied. "Although I shall leave one, if we have the opportunity."

"Fuck this." Wyatt opened the door and started to step from the backseat. I remembered that all his gear had been loaded into the trunk and hit the release.

Unfortunately, one of the lumbering creatures had reached the car.

Wyatt hurled himself back inside and pulled the door shut just before a massive fist caved it in.

"Okay," he admitted as the car slid a meter to the left. "Bad plan." He stared at me in the rearview mirror. "Yer the only one offensively geared, Hoss. I got the Tangler, but it's in the back."

"Right." I popped the knuckles on my right hand. "Naturally." I glanced into the mirror, as one of them shoved at the trunk, and we slid a few meters. "I don't know if my weapons will do much more than tickle something that size."

The entire world flickered back to the desert for an instant, all sunlit sand and open sky. Then, like changing stations on the radio, we plunged back into darkness.

I felt nauseated.

"We are at negative thirty-one. It is stabilizing." Anya's cool voice sounded calm. "Yet we are not fully immersed in the secondary topia."

I glanced at Wyatt; things had shifted toward the complex. If we sat thirty-one points below Rationality zero, we were more than a little adrift.

"I'd rather not be fully immersed."

Outside, more of the muscled brutes arrived, staring at us as if uncertain what we might be.

"How the hell did we get here?" Wyatt leaned forward and raised the Stetson's brim a bit. "Bishop's driving isn't *that* bad."

"We drove through another iteration of Irrational spikes, similar to those recorded before," Anya explained. "We somehow triggered the event."

"It had to be intentional," I spat. "A snare."

"L'shaea," one of the creatures grunted outside my window. It used the heavy length of wood it carried to lift my side of the car thirty centimeters or so, then dropped it.

"We can't stay here." I turned from Anya to Wyatt. "What about the vehicle's *Wraith*? Make the car vanish?"

"I'm pretty sure they know it's here, Hoss."

"This space is quite unstable," Anya stated again. "We might be able to force a change and shift ourselves back."

"That sounds simple," I muttered.

"If Wyatt can secure his equipment, together we can possibly create an axiomatic mean," she continued.

"You think?" The bearded barbarian considered her.

"With the appropriate calibration. This is not a natural event. We need to create a static zone where the axioms average to Rationality zero. With enough of an energetic remainder, this place will reject that ratio, and we will drift to Rational space."

"Huh." He scratched at his chin. "Maybe."

The car slid again with a second strike from one of the creatures. We stopped abruptly as the car struck the leg of another, who kicked the quarter panel.

At this rate, the *Legacy* would be undrivable soon.

"No time for maybe." I glanced at them. "Will that work?"

"I'm certain she's right about the instability, Hoss."

"It is our standard model," Anya replied. "Think about algorithmic averages."

"Yeah." Wyatt nodded, more certain. "If we can create Rationality zero with energy to spare, we'll separate like oil and water."

"Just like that?"

"It's complex, but we can do it." He paused. "Probably. I just need my gear."

"I have dampener grenades," I replied hopefully. "They create zones of Rationality."

"Not the same." I felt Anya's certainty. "In the airport, you altered Rationality to find your way back through. This topia is not stable and is much further from baseline."

"So I get to go outside." I peered through the windshield.

"Distract 'em. Just for a moment," Wyatt wheedled. "Once I get Rosie, it's all over."

I pulled a Stiletto and eased the door latch open, not quite disengaging it.

Copy that. I sighed. I toggled the *Adept* packet on and felt a burst of grace and preternatural speed like warm honey in my veins.

I honked the horn.

In an instant, the gray behemoths leapt back, startled by the cry of our odd steed. For a moment, they completely focused on the front of the car, trying to figure out what this meant.

I opened the door and sprung out. At the last possible second, I remembered the diaphanic emitter. I desperately hoped it would work.

Such things depended mostly on a matter of axiomatic divergences. The laws of reality could function drastically differently in alternate topias. I had no way to know if light even functioned the same way. What if it didn't and the emitter couldn't quite handle it? What if I burned out part of my Crown because light waves were a bit more truculent in this place?

Well, that would mean one of these gargantuan, Lord of the Rings rejects would likely put his fist through my head.

So I leapt, tucked, and rolled. The *Adept* kicked up more dexterity than plain ol' non-smoking Michael Bishop could ever dream of.

I engaged the emitter. Instantly a shadow of coolness fell across my skin. As I faded from sight, my own visual array resolved to black and white, as it always did when the *Wraith* initiated.

Hot damn, I linked, a wolf's grin on my face. *Now it's a party!*

The diaphanic emitter pulsed at the base of my skull, a cool, soothing throb. As per typical protocol, my Crown created a visual representation of 'me' that it relayed through my phaneric readouts. In this way, I perceived my own arms and legs, regardless of their current relationship to visible bandwidths of light.

Two of the creatures closing on me stopped, confused.

"Beh leii." The nearer one stared at his friend, his voice like stones grating together.

"Orris ruut bhaad." They peered again at the place I'd just been and sniffed at the still, sour air.

For a moment, the eldritch lines of runic script on their skin caught my attention. They seemed so elegant, as if penned by hands much smaller than these.

Anya, do we have any intel on these marks on their skin?

No, Michael. There are over seventeen thousand classifications of aberrations. Without access to the Lattice—

The first one muttered, taking an experimental swing in my direction with its club.

I stepped out of the way of its weapon, still mesmerized by the lines of glyph. I peered closer, trying to see what I could make out, when—

The creature's hide squirmed.

Um... My eyes widened.

It happened again, and I stared.

Something shifted beneath its skin, slithering between the muscle and the flesh like a thick serpent.

I watched in horror as it writhed along the behemoth's side before disappearing into its abdomen.

The one that sniffed the air turned its flat face toward me, and its eyes searched the darkness.

Oh. Oh God no.

Hoss? Wyatt glanced out the rear left window. *Problem?*

We may not fully understand what we're facing here. I took a few quick steps to the left, dismayed when one of them sniffed the air and slowly turned in my direction.

So rapt was I in the two behemoths near me that I'd lost track of the others, those nearer the car.

When one of them smashed his fist into the top of the sedan, Wyatt cursed loudly, "The hell!" *Bishop, a distraction is 'sposed to distract!*

Damnit. I turned my attention away from the beasts and the mystery of their wriggling flesh. *On it.* I aimed my Stiletto at the ground between the two closest to me. As one of the grunts stepped closer, I used my thumb to kick the weapon to its highest setting with the most focused field.

"Hey," I said conversationally.

Both of them stopped in place to stare about.

I took no chances with my moment. I pulled the trigger and the weapon warbled. An invisible bolt of kinetic force tore into the

151

ground between the two monsters with a low throbbing sound. My shot blew a hole the size of a beachball in the ground.

One of them roared as both leapt back from the hole. A third turned toward me, snarling as it sniffed at the air.

I spun without thought to fire at its chest.

The thing flew backward five meters. It lay on the ground and twitched.

The car suddenly became much less interesting to the creatures. They all watched, rapt, as an invisible kinetic explosion murdered one of their own.

One of them cried a hoarse, bellow that echoed through the cavern.

"LURRIK!" The word echoed in my skull. "KNAAG ROZZN!"

The things lost their minds. Two of them on the far side of the car lumbered in our direction, while a third bent over its fallen friend. The lot screamed and wailed, frantically searching for the bad-ass dealer of death who walked among them. One of them tipped his head back and screamed to the sky, beating its chest like a mutant gorilla.

Excellent distraction, Michael, Anya linked, once again maddeningly calm. *You likely just liquefied some internal organs.*

Your physics lessons are always appreciated, Anya. I modulated the second Stiletto as I unholstered it. This one would hit just as hard, but the focus of the force would be considerably wider, like getting hit with a Volkswagen rather than an explosive blade.

Just get them away from the car, Hoss.

Copy that, Alabama Slim.

I slunk to the side of one of the creatures, determined to be slow and cautious. The emitter might not mask sound in this bizarre place.

I count six remaining, Michael, Anya informed me.

Five. I slipped up behind one, the kinetic disruptor centimeters

152

from its skull. I fired, sending a sharp *siiiiuu* sound keening through the cavern.

Less than a second later, bits of brain and skull sprayed over one of its fellows, who roared in uncomprehending terror.

As the corpse fell, I saw the tendrils writhe within the body, madly squirming beneath the flesh.

That aside, there's something else here... something inside them. The link conveyed my revulsion.

Copy that, Bishop. Awe and disgust filled Wyatt's link. *I can see it in one over here. It's like thick cables running through them, just below their skin. It's—* He broke off, and I felt him retch. *It's... it's moving! Wriggling.*

Assets. Anya's crisp link came across almost curt. *These aberrations may be host bodies for some type of phage.* I felt her deliberately maintain calm as she linked. *Many Irrational species seek host bodies and—*

And they can go straight to hell. Wyatt recoiled at the thought. *You mean like a parasite?*

Exactly like that. My heart hammered against my ribs as I watched coils of tendril writhe within one of the corpses. Of all the fates that could befall an Asset, forced to be a host body for such unearthly horrors seemed like one of the more horrifying.

I felt quite vulnerable.

As quietly as possible, I stepped behind one of the other behemoths and aimed both pistols at the back of its head. I didn't know if it would stop the parasite...

I shrugged. Couldn't hurt.

The weapons sang, *siiiiuu siiiiuu.*

The monstrosity's skull cracked. It jerked twice from the force, then collapsed against the dark stone ground.

Bishop... I felt the warning in Wyatt's link. *We got five left, but they're all over there with you.*

Copy that. Now might be the time to grab your gear.

Yup. He flung the door open and ducked behind the far side of the *Legacy*. The movement caught the attention of one of the behemoths, which started to turn in his direction.

Nope. I took two quick steps to my right, aiming for that particular brute. Several more stood between us, and I couldn't get a square shot.

The beast cocked his head to see if something lurked on the far side of the car.

"Hey!" I cried, knowing none of them could see where I stood. "Let's look over here instead!"

I shot another of the creatures with my left-hand Stiletto and hit it squarely in the chest. The blow hurled the troll thing back over six yards where it crashed into one of the stone columns.

The remaining four roared their outrage. One of them, the smallest of the lot, stared around wildly before running off into the shadows.

They'll hear me the moment I shoot ol' Rosie. Wyatt opened the trunk and pulled out his gear. *I can crouch over here and get suited up. But the moment I fire up, I'm caught.*

I get it. I started to jog away from the remaining three creatures. *This should be easy. Our friends here aren't very bright. I can handle them all here in just a moment anyway.*

Seems like it, Wyatt linked. *As easily as you've put these guys down, I might as well wait before drawing attention to myself. I'll set the spikes when you're finished.*

That might be preferable, 423, Anya linked. *You will need the time to place them properly.* I felt a small twitch as Anya sent a patch. *This will help.*

Five glowing green indicators settled within my field of vision, widely scattered around us. These, I felt certain, showed exactly where Wyatt needed to fire. I needed to take care of business if Wyatt was going to place his algorithmic alterations in that pattern. He had quite a bit of space to cover.

Copy that, Anya. I felt Wyatt's grudging respect through my Crown.

I'll get them all over here, for a start. I powered the *Wraith* down where I stood, a good six meters from the nearest aberration.

Um, that's stupid, Wyatt opined.

The moment I faded into sight, the closest one snarled at me.

"Hey there, tubby." I fired once at the ground between us, leaving a hole nearly a meter across. "Look, I'm right here. All soft and pink and small." I grinned at it.

It roared and charged me.

I hadn't taken into account how fast the muscled creatures might be, due to their lumbering stride and immense size. But a charging gorilla can move scarily fast, as can a stampeding bison.

This thing put those two to shame.

It cleared the six meters in what felt like a step. Like the hammer of an angry god, it swung its maul-like fist down on me.

By sheer reflex, I leapt backward. Were it not for the grace and dexterity of the *Adept*, I would have been paste.

"AIIIIRI!" it roared, charging me again.

Ack! I frantically linked as I reengaged the *Wraith*. I raised both Stilettos and fired wildly. *Oh damn it, I—*

Michael! Anya linked, desperation woven through it.

The behemoth came crashing down at my feet, most of its skull blasted open.

I leapt backward, dodging away from the heavy corpse.

—ucking idiot! Wyatt yelled through the link. *Of all the batshit ideas!*

Hey, it worked. I sent him a weary sigh. *They're headed toward me.*

More aberrations incoming, Anya reported. *Seven degrees off functional northeast.* She inserted a small, pale blue marker over my display.

If I peered into the distance, I could just make out several lumbering shapes.

It's the same direction the other one ran off, Wyatt noted. *The little shit got reinforcements.*

155

Indeed, Anya linked, as concise as ever. *In addition, the more time passes, the more difficult our operation may become. I have concerns that we need to act as quickly as possible, while the realmwall remains weak and the topia remains in alignment.*

Right. Wyatt moved a meter around the side of the car. *Let's just end this, Bishop, and then we'll move on.*

The corpse of the one I'd killed caught my eye. Movement under its flesh made my skin crawl.

Involuntarily, I took one horrified step back. *Wyatt? Do you see this?* I took another step back from the corpse.

Asset Guthrie, Anya cut in. *I do not know how this topia intersects with ours, but further axiomatic drift is confirmed. Soon, we will need more than your equipment to return.*

Copy that. Wyatt glanced around to gauge the creature's movements. He shrugged the backpack portion of his gear onto his back and settled the crescent-shaped keyboard at his hip.

Um, you guys. I peered closer at the wriggling beneath the dead flesh. It positively writhed, far more intensely than before. It looked as if a nest of snakes lay just beneath the skin.

Not now, Hoss. Wyatt primed the business end of the Tangler, firing it up with a keening whine. He held it as one might hold a shotgun, with the keyboard within easy reach on his hip. He stepped over to one of Anya's markers, and I heard his gear whine a bit louder.

I really think—

In that moment the corpse before me exploded into a spray of warm, crimson viscera.

Shit—! I cried out in surprise and leaped backward as steaming globs of thick wetness struck me, covering my face and chest. I stumbled, and only the *Adept* kept me from landing on my ass.

The last two behemoths cried out with something like adulation. They fell prostrate, wailing in adoration.

What—? Wyatt's link went dead as he got a good look at what had happened.

I thought I might retch.

Sinewy blue-black tentacles, some masses of thin strands and others as thick as my wrist, burst from the corpse. I couldn't make out any center body, only hooked and fanged feelers. They ripped their way free from the creature's chest, tearing out from the mouth and nostrils.

"Oh," I mouthed, stumbling backward. "Oh God!"

With a wet, rending sound, they burst into the air, floating there through some power I couldn't name. They undulated, a grotesque testament to inhuman awfulness, a tangle of wet tendrils, repulsive in their thrashing grace.

Like a tide of turbulent malignancy, they fell on me.

2

Without thought or any active will of my own, the *Adept* kicked in.

The packet came installed with dozens of different combat routines, most of which involved tonfa, katana, and various knives. Oftentimes when I equipped it, I struck before I could even think, by reflexive instinct.

As the torrent of alien horror crashed down upon me, I leapt backward, springing into a crouch. Faster than the eye could track, I whipped up both hands and brought the Stiletto pistols to bear.

I frantically fired at the mass of tendrils and screamed.

The bursts from the weapon in my right hand drove straight through the mass, sliding between them like a needle into a mass of yarn.

My left Stiletto, however, had been calibrated with a very wide focus. Those shots punched into the greasy mass of squirming tentacles like extra-large cannonballs with a massive WHUB.

Some of the wriggling appendages under that onslaught flew away from the primary mass, only to continue their disgusting undulations.

Michael? Anya linked.

They can see me! Panic threaded through my link. *I don't know how, but they know exactly where I am!*

You're covered in a blood and guts, dumbass! Wyatt sounded exasperated, but I felt his mounting fear. *The gunk uncalibrated the* Wraith. *You're all flickery.*

Shit! I bit my lip. *I hate it when you're right.*

You must hate it an awful lot then. It's a burden being this brilliant.

I toggled the packet off and faded into full view. It would only take a few moments for the packet to reassess how much physical matter it needed to cloak, but...

Those could be a dangerous few moments.

Get to work, I shot back through the link, staring across the clearing.

Already on it.

From across the way, I heard the keening, high-pitched whir of Wyatt's Tangler. It built up power and made a loud **WHUF** as he shot the first spike into the stone at his feet. For briefest instant, a sphere of rippling energy silhouetted my large friend.

Spike one set, he drawled.

That's just awesome, I sarcastically linked as I continued to drive back the mass of squiggly horror. *Let's get this finished up.*

Michael, Anya warned. *Reinforcements have arrived.*

It would be handy if they all fell to their knees like their friends. Around us, the trollish brutes continued their prostrations, in awe of the tentacled creature.

Creatures. As in more than one.

Maybe.

Fuck, I found it impossible to tell. The main mass of tentacles began to break up into individual strands, each of which continued to writhe in the air like a serpent in the water.

No, Anya linked firmly. *In fact, they seem to be encouraging their comrades to rise.*

Not what I need right now. I toggled the Stiletto in my right hand so that its field focused wide, just like the other one. I fired the weapon and hurled four of the dark, mucous-slicked tendrils back.

Other tendrils, to my left, formed another body—a composite of individual lengths twisted together. Some held writhing hooks on the end, while others sprouted tiny maws or pods of ancient, mad eyes. The rotten, low-tide stench of it made me retch.

Second spike set. That same **WHUF** sound accompanied Wyatt's link. Again, a shimmering sphere of radiance briefly surrounded him, indicating the spike as active—for now.

It wouldn't remain so forever. Axiomatic programming

instructed the Tangler's tungsten alloy spikes to disintegrate after a certain period. Until they did, the spike would alter reality itself within its given range—just what we needed to get home.

"Fuck!"

Wyatt's sudden cry from behind one of the large columns drew my attention. I glanced over just in time to see one of the three-meter tall assholes chasing him, roaring.

It seemed as if the brutes had rejoined the fight.

That momentary lapse of attention cost me.

One of the tendrils, a thing the circumference of a garden hose, wrapped cunningly around my left ankle. A baleful eye sprouting from a pseudopod leered up at me.

"Oh God!" I kicked my leg, trying to break loose. The tendril dug in tighter as a response. As it pulled, I felt the wicked hooks on its underside shred my quasi-steel pant leg and cut into my flesh.

And… something whispered behind my mind. A faint echo of a tongue I didn't know, words that felt sharp, wicked, and alive.

"No, no, no!"

Panicking, I fired at the tendril again and again, blasting it into paste with a flurry of keening cries bursting from my weapons. The hooks still dug into my skin, not releasing even when the rest of it had been liquefied.

I whirled and aimed at the writhing, serpentine terrors that swarmed around us.

They're surrounding me, Wyatt linked. *I don't even have a mundane pistol!*

Gonna have to spike them. I dodged a swiping tentacle as I linked. *I know, it's not regs.*

Nothing about this is regs, Wyatt complained. *Simple dossier my ass!*

He wasn't wrong. I'd always found Wyatt's ass to be quite complicated.

"You can eat this!" Wyatt roared, accompanied by the *WHUF* of his device. I glanced up in time to see the one of the muscled behemoths stumble back, pawing at its chest where Wyatt had just sunk a spike.

"Hope you like it," he spat.

The head of the spike, the part I could see anyway, began to radiate a dull red light, gradually increasing to a brilliant white glow.

The behemoth screamed as Wyatt's spike altered the physics of heat, of thermodynamics itself.

He cooked the terrified brute alive.

That's horrifying, I noted

The Artisan *can be a bitch in combat,* Wyatt replied. *In the right person's hands.*

There are a total of eight of the large aberrations, Anya informed us. *At least four infected with the phage parasite.*

I don't like the way that sounds. The thrill of the *Adept* still coursed through my veins, augmented by whatever synthetic stimulant the Facility applied. Yet, even as I blasted another knot of the dark tendrils apart, I felt myself begin to slow. The packet truly hadn't been designed to run for more than a few minutes.

I've got the third spike placed now. I heard his device whine as Wyatt linked. *This will be over real fast.*

No. Anya's link felt curt in my mind. *Unfortunately not.*

What? I frowned at her through the link as I fired at one of the lumbering behemoths, bowling him over.

Current algorithmic alterations are not achieving their specified effect. Anya paused for a moment; I felt her mental calculations. *Something is bolstering local axioms.*

Is it, Anya? I linked with more than a bit of impatience, as I leveled a shot into the skull of one of the lumbering beasts. *Because that would be just superb.*

Emanations originating approximately two kilometers away are augmenting the natural properties of this place. Our current endeavor is futile.

Just what I wanted to hear, Wyatt linked sourly.

It is likely that altering those emanations will allow us to continue our operation, she clarified. *We just have to get there.*

Sounds like we have a new Locale One. I frowned. *Assuming we can get away from these jerks.*

Fine then, Wyatt grumbled. *At least that frees me up to deal with these assholes.* He punctuated his link with a **WHUF**, and I heard one of the mammoth freaks begin to scream.

Michael! Anya linked frantically.

I spun, Stilettos at the ready.

Tentacles, regrouped into a larger knot, swam right for me.

Their movement through the air entranced me, beautiful after a fashion. This group appeared thickest in the center, where the strands all intertwined. Five—no, six—with drooling maws all snapping and hissing. Other tentacles reached for me as well, reminding me of a nightmarish squid.

"Nope." I fired and fired and fired and fired, squeezing off a half dozen bolts of kinetic force that rippled through the air.

This time, they seemed to expect it. The tendrils responded as a fish might to a strong current, sliding up, then down, riding the force.

They simply slipped around my shots with no apparent effect.

"Oh shit!" I hurled myself to the left, desperately dodging the clumsy swing of one of the large-muscled monsters. I fired at *that* brute and knocked him backward.

Frantically, I glanced back over my shoulder to get a fix on the parasite.

Even more tendrils had wriggled into the mass. Now it appeared almost as large as when this mess started.

Michael! One of the gray figures apparently noticed Anya crouching in the *Legacy.* It slammed a fist into the car, causing the entire vehicle to slowly spin.

I can't!

The wriggling knot of horror undulated toward me, relaxed in its certainty. As it grew close, I felt the spidery touch of those

163

whispered words, caressing my thoughts. *Huuursushhh mmnemissshhh scoisssshhh...*

I couldn't help but shudder at their awfulness, as the alien logic trickled through my mind.

Hold up, Anya! Wyatt linked as he shot one of the ogrish louts squarely in the neck. It fell over, gurgling in agony as the large man stepped past it.

Yet Anya had no time. Her attacker punched the car again, shattering the reinforced glass of the passenger window. Even as it bled profusely, it grappled inside, grubby fingers reaching for her.

Get out! I linked as I fired on the tentacled awfulness again, this time striking it center mass. *Anya! The opposite side!*

As I linked, the parasite bore down on me, swimming unnaturally through the air. I turned, thinking to dodge behind one of the large stone columns...

Only to stop dead in my tracks.

Not two meters in front of me, one of the gray-skinned abominations waited, a sneer on its huge face. It held a crude stone axe, and unlike its counterparts, wore no clothing at all.

"Shhhalsss," it hissed, lunging toward me with inhuman speed. It swiped at my leg and scooped me off the ground as easily as if I were an infant.

I dropped both of my Stilettos as the seething fiend whipped me wildly around and flung me into the car.

I smashed into its side, face first.

Bishop! Wyatt's link echoed in my mind as if it had come from a thousand kilometers away.

Yup. I lay on the ground, my head a catastrophe of stunned pain. My back ached as if I'd filled my spine with molten glass, but I couldn't remember injuring it. *I'm Bishop. Bishop here.*

Anya! You gotta— His link suddenly cut off, and I heard a **WHUF** followed by a bestial roar of agony.

"Aaanya?" I slurred, remembering.

I reached up toward the car's side mirror and pulled myself

into a crouch, so I could peer through the window.

Across from me, on the passenger side of the car, one of the behemoths also peered in at her, red eyes burning with fury. Its head appeared to be covered in mange, its skin heavily scarred.

Our eyes met and it roared.

"Michael!" Anya, now in the back seat, whipped her head toward me. "Remain still!"

"What?" I blinked, trying to understand what she meant. "Why?"

The aberration reached its arm in again, as if it thought I might also be in the car. Its glass-sliced fingers scrabbled at the driver side window, trying to reach me. Quick as thought, Anya lunged forward, a white blur. She plunged one of her injectables into the gray, heavily muscled arm.

It didn't even flinch. I doubted it understood what happened.

"Viral mecha," I nodded drunkenly. "Perfect." Nasty safety protocols in all viral mecha ensured baseline humans couldn't task the technology to nefarious purposes.

The lumbering brute growled and jerked its arm back. It blinked down at the injection site, confused.

Moments later, a few hundred thousand viral mecha came online within the behemoth's body. Without a Crown sync, they initiated their defense variables. They began to rabidly devour the organic material of the creature's arm.

This process transformed minerals and base elements into fuel and raw materials for the rapid construction of more viral mecha programmed to continue the process.

In seconds, they would easily double their numbers. In minutes, they would consume the entire being, then self-terminate.

The behemoth screamed and waved its arm wildly, screeching as the mecha coursed through its veins. Its uncomprehending eyes grew wide, agonized. The bestial fiend staggered backward, arching its back. It shook its head, and its arm began to froth with silvery mist.

I scarcely noticed it.

My attention had been caught by the violently twisting tendrils writhing beneath the surface of the behemoth's flesh.

"Um," I said, intelligently conveying my point. I took a single step backward, agape, and my heart sank.

The gray abomination's neck and chest exploded, tentacled parasites desperately evacuating its corpse. Red blood and black viscera exploded over the passenger side of the car. The sinewy dread took to the air, just as its counterpart had, a floating knot of monstrous repugnance.

"Fuck. Me." I stared at the thing, my eyes wide. From behind, I heard the low growls of a few of the troll-like horrors, felt the mind-whispers of the first tentacled atrocity.

Anya's wide eyes met mine and, off behind me, I heard Wyatt curse violently.

My heart sank deep into my gut.

Things had just gotten much worse.

3

Michael! Anya's gaze darted to my right, surprised.

Taking her cue, I hurled myself left and again engaged the *Wraith.* The coolness of nigh-invisibility washed over me, as if I'd just stepped into a shadow.

I spun, just as one of the behemoths snatched at the place I'd been. Frantically I cast about, noting the horrors around us, while searching for my Stilettos.

Our situation did not inspire me.

I see three of the goons are still up and walking. I backed away from the car. *But at least two of them are infected.*

All three, Hoss. Wyatt stood with his back against one of the columns, the Tangler singing softly. *I'd have killed them, but I had concerns. You didn't seem to have much luck with squiggly.*

No. I eyed the thing hanging in the air on the other side of the car. *Killing the hosts doesn't improve matters.*

I didn't want to contribute to the problem, he continued. *That's when I came up with my genius plan.*

WHUF. His shot resounded through the clearing.

Genius, huh? I peered at the spike's landing place. One of the lumbering thugs stared down at the same spot. In less time than it took to blink, that spike pulsed with stunning brilliance, surrounding the large figure.

The light solidified, just a moment later. A silvery, mirrored dome encased the huge figure almost entirely.

Only one tightly muscled arm jutted out from the span of solidified light.

It fell to the ground, sliced cleanly by the field. Dark blood pooled beneath it.

It twitched.

423. Anya's link carried a healthy dose of horror. *You altered the axiomatic nature of space-time.*

Only an itsy bitsy little bit, Wyatt retorted. He fired again, and a second radiant burst solidified into a mirrored arch. This time, the half-bubble of light entirely encased his target. *Stasis fields. I'd been reading about the idea. Thinking on it for a bit now.*

Stasis— I felt a whisper of unbelief, of outrage in Anya's link. *Altering the nature of space-time is proscribed to Assets beneath third tier!*

Report me, Preceptor. Wyatt eased around the far side of the car in an attempt to get a clear shot at one of the goons. *The proscriptions apply within Rationality. What we have here's Protocol Delta-Four.*

Behind him, the second knot of undulating discord drifted his way, bobbing through the air in a blasphemous, impossible manner. Tentacles reached out, as if tasting the air, like the tongue of a serpent.

I don't see the Stilettos. I trotted past the spot where my face impacted the car and peered about. *I know they're here.*

They did you little good against the parasitical phage, Anya noted. *Your bladed weapons are still within the trunk.*

Of course! I smiled. *You're brilliant, Anya.*

Yes, she responded, confusion in her link. *My functional IQ is one hundred and fifty-three, although there are reasons to suspect that calculation. Have you not perused my dossier profile?*

From across the clearing, I heard Wyatt snort. *I'll keep these big boys busy.* He punctuated that idea with one last **WHUF**, which blossomed into a third silvery dome. *Even once created, I have to keep the algos current. The math is intense, just to keep them active.* He began to type rapidly on his crescent-shaped keyboard.

Keep them still, and I'll go after squiddy. I slid over to the trunk of the car, which Wyatt had left wide open. I toggled the *Wraith*, sliding back into visibility for just the scarcest moment.

I didn't want to knock the *Wraith* out of calibration by picking up extra mass—not again.

"Hey there," I conversationally snarked at the original tangle of tendrils. "Did you miss me?"

As one, the tentacles bent toward me, malicious eagerness in every movement. The entire mass wriggled for a moment, before gracefully arching through the air in my direction.

I picked up the katana, leaving the sheaths in the trunk.

Again, I engaged the *Wraith*, fading into cool shadows. The moment I felt the subtle *snick* of its engagement protocols, I re-engaged the *Adept* as well.

When I vanished, the mass of tentacles stopped in place. Its tendrils caressed the air, as if searching. The tangle on the opposite side of the car mirrored its actions.

Ssshhhhhrrrmmmmmsss... The sibilant whispers returned, a burbling darkness in my mind. *Hsssh... rrrrmmmmmkrrshsss.*

Is the parasite psionically active? Anya's link dripped with a mixture of wonder and revulsion. *Is it sentient?*

You hear it too, huh? I stepped around to one side of the creatures, eyeing them warily. With a katana in each hand, I knew I could get in a devastating first blow, but as soon as I did, they could blindly attack in my direction.

I needed my shot to count.

I've got the stasis fields stable, Wyatt reported. *I have to keep calibrating, so I'm out. But I can hold these three still.*

It's all me. I nodded, although no one saw me. *Okay.* Internally, I counted to three, reviewing melee protocols contained within the *Adept*.

I leapt at the writhing horrors.

For the first point-three seconds or so, my genius plan went exactly as expected.

Hidden beneath veils of bent light, I leapt and spun to the right, the *Adept* giving me some much-needed grace. I swung each katana almost without thought, the blades slicing keenly through the air.

I struck three of the slick tendrils in mid-leap; I severed a

169

fourth just as I landed. The rubbery flesh didn't slice easily, all corded muscle and sinew.

Still, Facility steel did the job.

Well, not steel. Electresium.

Whatever.

A few tendrils spouted gaping maws, teeth-lined things that snapped and drooled dark bile. Yet only a sibilant hiss issued from them, a sound of pure hatred.

Then the aberrations screamed.

No, that wasn't what happened, not truly.

The loathsome creatures screamed *in my mind*, the sensation like razorwire slicing between my teeth. It echoed like slivers of burning glass in my thoughts, as if something wicked and malicious dissected me from within.

I cried out and collapsed. Somewhere, over the music of the strip club, I heard Wyatt yelling for me.

I'm right here, asshole, I blearily thought. I tried to speak but couldn't.

Thought and sanity drifted away, smoke from my burning mind.

4

"Damn it, Bishop!" Wyatt sounded irritated. "Get your ass up!"

Crown Augment request detected. The Crown prompt felt slow in my mind, clunky. *Asset 108, you are currently designated* as **Legacy** *operator. Do you wish to allow Petrova, Anya to create connection 14-32dh?*

What? I didn't exactly have time to glance over my shoulder. I linked her, but it felt like moving bricks with my thoughts. *What augment, Anya?*

Allow the connection, Michael! I felt the slightly Russian bend to her words, even through the link. *Surrender operator status!*

Yes, I murkily sent. *I surrender operator status on the* Legacy.

Patrova, Anya has claimed operator status. A loud CLICK sounded behind my right ear, yet I scarcely noticed it through the mental agony. A river of razored edges poured through my mind as the aberrant things psionically screeched their fury.

One of the tentacles brushed against my arm, almost casually.

That caught my attention.

Shit! I recoiled at the touch of wet, tremulant flesh coiling around me. I pulled back but froze in place when I felt what the edges of those wicked hooks held hidden on its underside.

A second one brushed the side of my head, just as casually. Three more floated within my vision, hanging down over me. On the end of one serpentine limb, I saw a small cluster of cancerous polyps, one of which held a baleful, unnatural eye. The entire thing roiled with thick mucus, which smelled like the lurking rot of low tide.

I remained perfectly still, trying to assess.

If I jerked, those wicked barbs would dig in, or, worse, I could cause the creatures to go into some sort of frenzy. As it was, the tendril had only accidentally wrapped around me—I remained invisible beneath the *Wraith*.

It likely didn't know what it had.

I gritted my teeth against the fading onslaught of psionic anguish. Moving a centimeter at a time, I attempted to untangle myself.

Hoss? Wyatt's link held more concern than usual. *You done screamin'?*

It has me, I reported, matter-of fact. *One tentacle, at least. More are very close.*

I peeked around where I sprawled and found myself squarely beneath a knot of the abhorrent things. They wriggled there, strand after strand of undulating, unreasoning horror. On the ground around me, lay two severed tendrils, still writhing in their death throes.

How many of the blue-black miscreations lurked within this one knot? I couldn't even count them.

Remain still, Michael. Anya's link felt cool, calm.

Petrova, Anya has requisitioned two iterations of model 62d-Raiju-class drones. The *Legacy* augment buzzed in my mind, informing me only because I remained one of the potential operators. ***Initiating active sequence now.***

Anya, what—? I stopped mid-link, my breath caught as I realized her intentions.

Raiju ***drone AG-286f launching,*** the automated system within the *Legacy* droned in my thoughts. ***Active parameters engaged.***

"Oh fuck." No longer concerned about the tentacle on my arm, I hurled myself down, trying to get as flat as possible. I felt sharp hooks shred part of my suit, felt them wriggle and bite into my skin.

I didn't care in the least.

Raiju-class drones weren't part of my average dossier. Typically, they might be allocated along with large, long-gear types of equipment, such as the Tangler or the *Gatekeeper* packet. Those kinds of operations required vast, incomprehensible sums of energy. After all, creating wormholes or transforming carbon into silicon weren't standard bits of science. These minor miracles required more.

Thus, the need for the *Raiju*.

Quite simply, the miniscule *Raiju* gathered atomic energy from the surrounding area to power Facility equipment.

Anya now unleashed one of the drones that kept the *Legacy* running, since it sure as hell didn't use unleaded.

I doubted the Designates intended these tiny drones to be weaponized. Daring to peek upward, I watched the smooth silver marble sidle sharply through the air toward the knot of tangled, inhuman horror.

The tentacle around my arm tightened. The serrated hooks dug deeper, and I started to bleed. To my left, three other sinewy tendrils wriggled toward me eagerly.

They've found me, I linked.

Raiju *drone AG-876r launching,* the automated system within the *Legacy* informed me. ***Active parameters engaged.***

A second one? How many do you think you need, Anya? I winced as the tendril tightened. Another came closer, wriggling.

I have no idea. Four are available. Anya directed the drone straight toward the center of the mass clumped above me. *We shall know momentarily.*

AG-286f sailed directly toward the tendril-y center mass of the aberrations. Anya stopped the drone less than two centimeters from contact and engaged its acquisition protocols.

It burst with a violet light, emitting a wide field of energetic radiance around itself; about the size of a large beachball. It caught much of the central knot of creatures in that otherworldly glow.

It hummed and crackled as it built strength.

Watch it, Hoss, Wyatt linked, although he didn't need to warn me.

That energetic emanation shone and scintillated for a second while galvanic arcs sparked between the edge of the field and the small sphere within. They sparked faster and faster.

173

I ducked my head, averted my eyes.

When the burst came, the sound hammered my eardrums. I felt the heat of the flash but didn't feel the least bit tempted to peek. I didn't want my corneas burned away, after all.

Tentacle parts fell like sickening rain around me, splattering stringy mucous as they came.

Holy shit, Anya, Wyatt linked. *That's incredible!*

This time, no screams rent my mind—in fact, I didn't see even one tentacle that remained whole. Every piece of it caught within that glow had been atomically unified. The energies contained within, processed, and now stored within the sphere.

The sphere moved back toward the *Legacy*.

Now the second mass, Anya linked.

A second drone, AG-876r, zipped straight toward the remaining knot of tangled repugnance.

Too easy, Wyatt crowed. *Petrova, you may have invented a new offensive tactic!*

Doubtful. I felt her slight frown. *Raiju-class drones must dock quickly. I've processed data that claims they can become explosive and unstable.*

Explosive is a feature, darlin', not a drawback. I felt him grin.

This amount of atomic energy could be a serious danger, 423, she scolded. *This stratagem would never be allowed within Rationality.*

I won't rat you out, Petrova. I felt him snicker. *Besides, I've seen the specs. The Designates shift around the axiomatic coefficients for energy to store the damn things.*

So they aren't tiny, super-nuclear bombs? I asked.

No, not while stable and in their casings, Wyatt claimed. *The joules of force it would take to crack one of these suckers are unimaginable.*

I dunno, I chuckled as I watched, prepared to avert my eyes. *I'm pretty imaginative.*

Well, that's not even something worth considering. He shook his head. *This much energy would take out the Pacific Northwest, minimum.*

The drone made a beeline for the last clutch of tentacles, and I turned away.

But... nothing happened.

What? Get it, Anya! Wyatt's link only felt a bit nervous.

I glanced back.

I am attempting. I felt her brow furrow as the cluster darted away from the drone, moving at a speed I hadn't guessed possible.

It knows. I linked with dawning realization. *It knows enough to understand the drone is dangerous.*

Anya continued to reposition the drone, yet she couldn't catch the writhing aberrations. When the small sphere grew too close, the aggregation burst into a swarm of tendrils, each slithering off into a different direction before regrouping.

"Damnit." I cast about for my Stilettos. We'd gotten lucky once, but the second cluster thwarted Anya's attack.

Give me a moment, I linked. *If I can find my weapons, I can liquefy the individual strands. It's only when they're all together that things get tough.*

Or... A smile dawned on Wyatt's face.

Unnecessary, Michael. I felt just a whisper of smugness in Anya's link.

I glanced up. The tentacled parasite attempted to reform into one mass.

That gave Anya just the moment she needed.

The silver drone zipped up to the cluster and burst with violet shine, emitting energetic radiance around itself.

It hummed, crackling as it built strength.

I turned just before the MAWP pulsed against my eardrums and remained turned as the flash of heat pulsed against my skin.

I heard wet thumps as wriggling tendrils hit the ground.

Shit, Wyatt linked. *Not quite all of them this time.*

They tried to disentangle themselves, but the drone ignited first, Anya explained. *I see four individual tendrils which remain unaffected.*

Five, I corrected. *But they don't seem interested in a fight.* I watched as the tendrils squirmed away into the darkness of the cavern, taking different routes away from the *Legacy* and us.

They retreated, slithering off into the distance.

I don't like that, I linked. *What if they return with more?* I powered down my packets.

Yeah, you better run, assholes. I felt Wyatt's rebel grin. "We'll give you three steps toward the door!" he called.

Skynyrd? I sent. *So when we fight otherworldly tentacle monsters, it's time to quote Lynyrd Skynyrd?*

It's always time for Skynyrd, Hoss. I felt his grin. *Figgered you knew that by now.*

"Michael is right." Anya stepped out of the vehicle and peered off into the distance. "We have seen them return with reinforcements before. We should leave this area immediately and disengage the radiations sourced at Locale One. Once its emanations cease, we can proceed."

An icon appeared over my visual array, showing me the general direction we needed to go.

"We can't stay here much longer, regardless," Wyatt drawled. "These things require constant numeric input." He gestured at the three stasis fields. "Gotta remember, though, Rosie has about a five-hundred-meter range. Much further than that and the algorithms fail. The spike will straight-up vanish, and those fields'll drop."

"Letting the freaks loose, I assume?" I tilted my head at him.

"Space-time will regain its typical flow," he confirmed.

"The source of unnatural emanations is approximately two kilometers from our current location." Anya turned toward me, her face mostly shrouded in the darkness of the cavern.

"You truly think shutting them down will let us punch our way back into Rationality?" I raised an eyebrow.

"It is very possible that disrupting those emanations would allow us to return to Rationality."

"Possible?" I wanted a bit more.

"Probable, actually." She paused. "This source contains similar emanations to the ones recorded during the initial spike within the Mojave. I suspect whatever is creating these radiations is the source which pulled us here to begin with."

"It's better than any ideas I have," I admitted.

I toggled on my Crown's version of night vision and peered around for my Stilettos. The moment the optics initiated, the cavern seemed bright as day.

The Stilettos lay on the ground, one a few steps from me and the other five meters away. I walked over to pick them up.

I wished, and not for the first time, that I could use the optics while the *Wraith* was engaged. They certainly changed the game. I clicked them off.

"Might as well head that way, it's not as if we're driving home." Wyatt kicked at one of the *Legacy*'s tires. "Although Petrova might want to dock those drones first."

"I do," she replied. She leaned one hand against the side of the vehicle, her head twitching as she commanded the drone. "My understanding is that, if this device goes undocked for more than twelve-point-seven minutes, it has difficulty retaining its payload."

"I wondered, Petrova," Wyatt said, raising an eyebrow. "You *could* leave those here with the dead *Legacy*, or…"

"You would prefer I dock them within the housing of your equipment." She nodded. "It is sensible. We do not know what your energetic requirements might be while stranded here."

Her head twitched only slightly, and both drones veered toward Wyatt. Each of them emitted a sharp CLICK as they docked within his backpack.

"These stasis fields are burning a lot; I'll tell you that much." He gazed at me. "Which is why my vote is to get truckin'."

"Two klicks isn't far," I mused.

"There is no certainty our trek will be in a straight line," Anya noted. "There are tunnels that may make the journey further."

"Well, we have a direction." I centered the glowing marker over my visual array. "Two kilometers through dark caves."

"Looks like it," Wyatt agreed. "I'll let you know when we hit five hundred meters. I'll know when Rosie's spikes fail."

"I just hope we don't pick up a tail." I jerked my chin meaningfully at his stasis fields.

"Nothin' for it, Hoss." He chuckled as he clapped me on the back with his free hand. "We'll just have to see what comes, then blow it up."

"Keeping it fluid?" I shook my head.

"That's how it's done." He gestured around us. "We're off the map here!"

I grinned at my friend's idiocy, even as my heart sank just a bit.

Our cadre had gone further adrift than I'd ever been. Castaways in an unknown reality, we had no supplies, no conduit, and no communication back home.

We *were* off the map. Distinctly so.

I feared we might not find our way home.

The Alien Deep

Just as we prepared to set off through the caverns, Anya remembered one last detail.

"The *Legacy*. We cannot just leave it."

"We can't exactly drive away." Wyatt gestured at the crumbled front. "She's totaled."

"That is not what I mean."

When her head ticked the smallest bit, the *Legacy*'s system broke into my thoughts.

—*request detected*, the system was saying. *Asset 108, you are currently designated as one of the Legacy's potential operators. Do you wish to allow Petrova, Anya to initiate the Primary Protocols on this vehicle?*

"Ah." I glanced toward Wyatt. "She isn't talking about taking it, big guy. We just can't leave it."

"Oh," he responded. "Right."

Vehicles and equipment were actually covered under Protocol Alpha-Three, but the overall principle remained the same: No Facility Asset, weapons, or equipment were ever to be left behind, under any circumstances.

Even if it meant they had to be destroyed. Even if they had to be killed.

"We have no way to know who might encounter this equipment," Anya explained.

"No, I get it." Wyatt waved his free hand. "Do what you gotta. My fingers are goin' numb."

Clearance to initiate the Primary Protocol regarding vehicle class: Legacy. *Asset 108. Authorization code 020798361,* I sent.

Code received, Asset.

As we walked away into the darkness of the caverns, a brilliant magnesium white unfurled behind us, casting stark and sharp shadows before us. Some ordinance packet, hidden within the chassis, altered the axioms of heat and solidity, transforming the vehicle into little more than glowing slag.

I didn't look back, knowing just a glimpse of that intense light would ruin my night vision.

Instead, I kept my gaze ahead, and we strode forward.

Into the darkness.

2

"I think my optics are misqueing." I blinked and rubbed my eyes. The deeper we got into the dismal caverns, the more I noticed the degradation in visual acuity. It looked as if we slowly walked into a static-filled darkness.

"It's not just you, Hoss." Wyatt removed his hat, then shook his head. "Must be something about the axiomatic nature of this place." He put the Stetson back on his shaved pate.

"The wavelengths of infrared light are slightly different here," Anya responded.

"Well, I don't see why that's giving me a migraine." I rubbed my temples.

"The optic systems are a mixture of infrared radiation and a variance on night vision," she explained.

"That knowledge isn't helping much." I shifted my optics off, and then back on again.

"I mean," Anya explained patiently, "the infrared spectrum is not resonating within the same parameters as it does in Rationality. Therefore, the baseline settings within your Crown are misaligned."

"Do we have a fix?" I peered into the darkness, cycling back and forth between various optical settings. "This thing is worse than a hangover."

"Attempt fine alterations to your perceptual modes," she suggested. "The optic systems use the same network as visual indicators placed over your display."

"Yes, I'm completely qualified for that." I opened the dialog interface for my optics systems, blinking as it superimposed itself over the cavern walls. "There must be over a hundred settings for this thing."

"Does it look to you...?" Wyatt trailed off for a moment, confusion evident in his voice. "Is that wall moving?"

"It... it is." Dismissing the optics interface, I peered forward into the shadowy passage. Approximately thirty meters in front of us, something against the wall shifted, rippled. "Like it's wriggling."

"I don't like wriggling," Wyatt muttered. "There's been more than enough wriggling today."

"We've passed three other branches from this cavern just as favorable," Anya informed us. "If you have concerns, we could try a different path."

"You said this was the fastest way?" I stopped to glance back at her, squinting my eyes against the discomfort.

"It is impossible to say for certain." Her fingers twitched a touch. "It is my estimation this path will be the most efficient."

"If my head blows up, it doesn't matter," Wyatt grumbled.

Assets, make the following alterations to Optic Dialogue 452-I, Anya linked. *That should relieve any pain caused by the axiomatic differences.* She sent a patch with the relevant data.

I opened the dialogue again and quickly found the proper input. Within moments, my visual array resolved to a colorless but crystal-clear representation of the hallway.

"Oh God," Wyatt groaned as his own vision clarified. "We've upgraded from 'wriggling' to 'writhing.' What the hell *is* that?"

"I can't tell." I took a couple of steps closer and squinted down the passage. It bent slightly to the left as it continued forward, but the right wall appeared to undulate, fluttering slightly.

"I would like to reiterate that we could try another tunnel." Anya turned from Wyatt to me.

"Is it leaves? Moths?" I took a step forward.

Before Wyatt could respond, warbling chirps began, echoing down the passageway. First, only a few resonated toward us, but within moments it sounded as if hundreds, then thousands of creatures trilled and echoed in the passage ahead.

Nope, Wyatt linked. *I don't like that.*

You don't like anything.

I liked The Booby Trap.

I noticed. I glanced at Anya, watching the fingers on her right hand, which had already begun to twitch. The slow, mechanical movement indicated she trawled through her telemetry. She caught my gaze and gave the tiniest shake of her head.

Apparently, her readings didn't show anything *too* bizarre.

"Okay." I spoke softly, not taking my eyes from the rippling movement. "Here's the play."

"You're calling the plays now?" Wyatt muttered, only half-teasing.

"I'm going to slip forward. I'll keep the *Adept* toggled on and remain as quiet as possible."

"I doubt they'll hear you," Wyatt offered. "Over that awful screechin'. Fuck, *I* can barely hear you."

If it's nothing, I linked, *you'll know it. I'll stay in contact.*

It ain't nothin', Hoss.

If it's a threat, you'll both be out of range. Wyatt can always lay down a spike that will heat the atmosphere to cook... whatever the hell it is. I turned from him to Anya. *If there's any Irrational fuckery going on, Anya can link me before things get bad.*

If we fight, I'd have to stop fiddlin' with those stasis fields, Wyatt reminded me. *Those big ol' uglies would be free.*

If that happens, I imagine we'll have other problems.

This plan does not fall within protocol. Anya tilted her head as if trying to determine the best way forward. *Separating Assets is not conducive to maximum productivity.*

Putting all of your Assets in danger isn't wise either. I gave her a half shrug. *If you have a better idea, I'd love to hear it.*

Aside from one of the other passages, I do not. Anya gave the tiniest shake of her head, her brow furrowing.

I'd really prefer to remain on the most expedient path. I gestured at the cavern we walked through. *I'm ready to go home.*

Understood.

I'd just 'preciate whichever idea is the most rapidly functional.

Wyatt gestured at his other hand which still typed algorithmic computations at his hip. *There's only so long I can do this.*

This isn't outside our typical strategy where I pull point, so I'm going forward. I levied my gaze at him and then at her.

Typically, you engage the Wraith, Anya reminded me.

The Wraith *won't engage while my optics are active.* I shook my head. *But that doesn't matter. Wyatt has to keep fiddling with his equations or those stasis fields drop. You aren't exactly packing heat. If the three of us went together and there's trouble, we'd all be screwed.*

Brooks Brothers here is the only one with significant weaponry, Wyatt reasoned. *The dossier intended us to simply escort you to gather telemetry.*

I am aware we are undergeared for a topiatic incursion. That furrow on Anya's forehead grew deeper. *I simply hoped we might discover an alternative.*

You let me know if Rationality spikes. I nodded at her. *It'll be fine. I'll be careful.*

You are not known for taking care, she stated. *Yet, I do not see a better alternative.*

Just chill. I gave her the most charming grin I could muster. *This will be over in a moment.*

That does not inspire hope, she responded.

Turning from them, I slipped down the passage.

The *Adept* might have been constructed with preternatural grace and badass ninja flips in mind, but its base capabilities gave wider results. As I crept down the rough passage, silvery dexterity dripped through my veins, an inexplicable silkiness that guided my every movement.

Silently, I drew the Stilettos.

With every step, that incessant chirping became louder, nagging shrilly all around me. The closer I got to that darkened little bend in the passage, the more apparent my situation became.

I'd believed something undulated there, an entity that lurked along the edge of the hallway. Now that I saw more clearly, I realized the truth.

It wasn't some*thing*.

No, *thousands* of somethings perched there, insectine horrors the size of footballs. They looked like the bizarre result of a mating between a praying mantis and a cave cricket.

I shuddered.

They rubbed their sharp, serrated legs together behind them, sending that screeching, chirping cacophony into the passage. Then they undulated like a single organism, swarming over the wall of the cave.

Oh, hwurf, I sent, making certain the others felt my visceral nausea. *Check this out.* I sent a patch, a still image of the carpet of gargantuan insects.

That, roiling disgust came through Wyatt's link, *is exactly what I didn't want to see.*

Agreed. I arched my head closer, not exactly willing to take another step toward the insects. Most of them remained still on the wall, their only motion the slow, mesmerizing rubbing of their legs. That was what we took for leaves or wings—ten thousand pairs of insectine limbs, each playing their own part in a macabre symphony of dread.

I advise against further progression, Michael.

Advice taken. Even as I linked, however, I noticed something: a broken place within the wall, a crevice full of the creatures.

I took another step, trying to see.

Therefore, I assume you are returning?

A moment. I crouched. Perhaps if I got lower I could— *There's a crack in the wall,* I reported. *It's difficult to see, the optics make everything look black on black.*

What about it, Hoss?

I can't see within. I took a careful step to my left. *I'm enhancing my visual range.*

It took more time to report my action than it did to actually perform it. A minor shift of focus, similar to what I might make when peering at a distant object, let me zoom in on the fissure.

Deep. I enhanced my range again. *It looks as if they came out of this cleft. There's a floor right next to it that has a large clump of the insects. Beyond that, it just drops off. Optics can't read the bottom.*

Drops off? I felt Wyatt shudder. *Like into nothingness?*

I should at least be able to see the sides, but I don't. Even as I peeked I felt my attention drawn away from the cleft. I noted the shifting mass on the floor, a shapeless hump of insects which moved rapidly, eagerly.

I don't understand how this intel assists us, Anya linked.

I suppose it doesn't.

The mass moved again, rippling. The insects on that shifting clump didn't rub their legs together. Unlike their brethren, they didn't sit poised upon the wall, either. Instead, they frenzied. They wriggled and writhed in ecstatic fashion.

In that moment, I caught the scarcest glimpse of something beneath. A length of bone, attached to what appeared to be a ribcage. Dried blood and viscera had splattered against the stone of the ground.

Oh shit. I stumbled backward a step. *Oh, fuck me.*

Bishop? Wyatt's link felt sharp.

Just look at this, I linked as I stepped backward again. I took several quick images from my Crown and patched them.

They're eating. Wyatt's revulsion boiled in the link. *They're eating something.*

Return immediately, Michael. Anya's link held no room for argument. *Dossier specifications require you to regroup with the rest of your cadre.*

Agreed. I backed away from the mass of insectine repugnance, keeping my movements slow. If the creatures swarmed me, I didn't stand a chance.

I'm on my way now, I sent. *It seems as if Anya may have been correct after all. We may need to take a longer route.*

Great, Wyatt groused.

I do not think being correct is a negative thing, Michael.

Jesus Christ, Anya. I felt Wyatt's chuckle. *It's one thing to be right all the time; I just wish you didn't have to be so loud about it.*

3

A few minutes later, we found the nearest of the offshoot branches we'd passed. Little more than a crevice within the stone wall, it opened up considerably, shortly after the entrance, looming twice as tall as I stood.

"The marker is still accurate." Anya refreshed the light blue triangle over my visual array. "This is the general direction of the emanations' source."

"Is it centered downward?" I peered at the triangle as I rubbed my aching forehead. "As if it's in the ground?"

"I don't care. We can't get there soon enough," Wyatt muttered. "I didn't sign on for any long-distance hauls."

"I have been monitoring the emanations as we progress, Michael." Anya paused for a moment. "I am certain they are key to our return to Rationality."

"Good. Let's keep moving." I stepped through first, sheathing a single Stiletto.

The passageway carved around to our left and became quite narrow for a few steps. In the distance, I heard water drip.

We hadn't taken twenty steps before Wyatt exclaimed, "Five hundred meters!" He pulled his hand away from the keyboard, stretching out the tension. "Those spikes just underwent quantum dispersement."

"Is that the fancy way to say they vanished?"

"They're gone." He shook his hand. "I don't think I could've done that much longer."

"I don't know," I responded as I shook my half-closed hand up and down, mimicking his motion. "Seems like you're an expert."

Wyatt showed me a different hand gesture.

I chuckled and flashed it back.

Anya frowned. Slightly.

"So that's it?" I glanced back at him over my shoulder. "The mighty *Artisan* has allowed space-time to return to its normal course?"

"You don't get it, Hoss." Wyatt adjusted the Stetson on his head. "Temporal mechanics are a pretty big fucking deal. It's the reason *Gatekeeper* Assets require a Crown augment—the mathematics are brutal."

"Right..." I glanced at Anya. "But our *Preceptor* wasn't irritated with you because she worried you couldn't do the math."

"It's done." He gestured with one hand. "The fields are collapsed, and this reality didn't tear itself in two." He poked his head through a small archway, peered about, and moved on.

"So from the perspective of the assholes, what happened?" I followed right after him. "One instant we're there and the next we weren't?"

"In a nutshell." He adjusted his backpack. "There will need to be a lot more experimentation—"

"There will be no more experimentation," Anya asserted firmly. "Space-time is a key facet of Rationality. We are fortunate you did not generate a cascading series of aberrant vectors."

"I don't get it." I leaned one hand against the cool stone, as I gazed back at her. "Wyatt changes the axioms of reality all the time. He transforms one element to another or plays around with the energetics of gravity."

"Gravity isn't exactly a type of energy," Wyatt muttered as he stepped over a crack in the floor.

I glanced down as I passed. Like the cleft I'd seen near the insects, my optics couldn't find the bottom.

I shuddered.

"Aberrant vectors have been known to harm the axiomatic realmwall," Anya clarified. "We are proscribed from altering space-time in order to protect Rationality."

"That's the baseline of what we're *told*," Wyatt interjected. "Yet the *Gatekeeper* packet has been in use for thirty years. In all that time, we don't have one recorded instance of an aperture weakening the weave."

"Recorded or not, the mathematical certainty remains," the *Preceptor* argued. "Not to mention the fact that in the one hundred and fifty years the ARC-technology has existed, stasis fields have never been mathematically sanctified."

"Not by the Designates, maybe." Wyatt glanced back at her, as he ducked beneath a low archway. "That doesn't mean no one's run the numbers."

"You're saying you figured out how to do a stasis field… when?" I pushed past him, taking point again. "Do you practice dimensional mathematics while you work on stock cars?"

"'Course not," Wyatt huffed. "I've been following some of the research done by the Rook."

"The Rook?"

"Jonathan Crowe," Anya responded. "Asset 081. That Asset remains one of the most brilliant *Artisan* operators within the Facility."

"That's my guy." Wyatt pointed at her. "The man is a fucking artist. He uploads his personal data files to the Asset Archives. Sometimes when I have a few moments, I port a few to memory." He stepped over a large stone.

"Studious," I commented.

"Whether or not the axiomatic realmwall has ever truly been affected by aberrant vectors, other relevant concerns remain regarding space-time anomalies." Anya crouched a bit as she moved past a low spot.

"Like what, blondie?" Wyatt teased.

"Many cases exist where *Gatekeeper* Assets accidentally caught the attention of aetheric deviations from poorly chosen coefficients."

"Seriously?" I holstered the other Stiletto; it didn't seem as if I needed it.

"Michael, you have certainly been briefed regarding Construct Entity 234-B." Anya frowned.

"Construct Entity 234-B." I nodded, as if I totally understood her reference. "I see."

"You do not."

"Do you ever peruse the Asset Archives, Hoss?"

"I might." Something tickled at the back of my mind. "Temporal... splicers. That's what you mean, right?"

"Christ, Hoss." Wyatt shook his head, chuckling. "Temporal splicers? You sound like you're ten years old."

"Construct Entity 234-B is a ramification of improper space-time calibrations," Anya explained.

"I would have remembered it if we had a Lattice connection," I explained.

"It's not 'remembering' it if you have to flippin' look it up!" Wyatt yelled. "Long story short, sometimes the *Gatekeeper* Asset can mess up their portals. I've geared the thing; it's complex. If you flub it, you can create a time lapse between entering and exiting."

"What?" I stopped in place and turned to stare at him.

"Right." He nodded. "You step into an aperture, then step out about thirty seconds later, maybe forty-five. You experience it instantaneously, but it's not. That kind of misqueuing happens any time the Asset gets sloppy."

"That's..." I shook my head. "Where do you go for thirty seconds?"

"You don't." Wyatt waved one hand. "I once heard a story about someone exiting an aperture before they entered it!"

"Stories aside," Anya interjected, "there have been several recorded instances of Construct Entity 234-B entering Rationality during errors such as these. They seem drawn to incidents in space-time." Anya raised one eyebrow at Wyatt.

"So Wyatt could be drawing the attention of temporal splicers?"

"Asset Guthrie has no data regarding stasis fields. If he uses this algorithm while in Rational space—"

"There's a lot you don't realize, Anya." Wyatt shook his head.

"He's a *genius*, Anya," I sarcastically explained, with an exaggerated tap to my forehead. Then I ducked under a bulwark of stone before striding into an open, wide room in the cave.

"That." He pointed at me. "But also—"

Brilliant light flooded the cavern, followed by a loud BANG from off to our right. Instinctively, I jerked my head in that direction, staring directly into punishing light as if a small star burst to life in the cave.

Of course I didn't switch off my optics. Oh no.

That would have been smart.

Silent Gentlemen

Stunned, I stared straight into the punishing fury of brilliant light. Its rays stabbed me squarely in the brain. I yelped, swore, and then whipped my head sideways, rubbing at my eyes.

Bishop! Get down, you tit!

Agilely, I collapsed like a ragdoll onto the stone floor. As a panicked afterthought, I toggled the *Wraith*, and the cool shadows of invisibility fell around me.

"—can't say what caused it." The feminine, cut-glass British voice fell like a blade brushing across silk. She murmured from the direction of the light, just loud enough to be heard. "I need you to handle it. We have a timetable."

Blearily, I peered toward the voice as I wiped my eyes. From what I could make out, it seemed as if we'd stumbled on a place where the cavern widened considerably. In another five paces or so, my cadre-mates would have stepped out into the center of the open room. If we'd been here about a minute earlier, we'd have been standing in the open when that light came on.

"We'll do what we can, Ms. Thorne," a male voice replied. "We'll get it done."

"Dr. Thorne." She leveled an icy stare at the man. "And I'm certain you'll fulfill expectations. If Daisuke believed otherwise, you wouldn't be here." The tiniest hint of a bladed smile curled the edge of her voice. "Repair the resonator. Do it quickly."

A vague acknowledgment preceded a mechanical ratcheting sound.

Ambient Rationality levels dipping, Anya reported. *We are now holding stable at negative twenty-eight.*

I see four of them. Wyatt shuffled behind me, a mountain hidden in shadows. *Three men and that woman. At least two of the men are armed. Automatic rifles.*

Lovely, I groused. *Almost impossible to miss us at this range.*

Can you see any others from where you are? Wyatt paused. *And by that, I mean lying on the ground like an infant?*

I'd been just a few steps in front of my cadre. This meant I had a clear line of sight into the open cavern where the hostiles stood. Wyatt and Anya, on the other hand, remained hidden behind me in the crevice of stone.

Um... I don't think so. I blinked again, attempting to clear my vision. Gray blobs that might have been hat racks or human silhouettes danced before my eyes. *That light caught me with my optics on. It'll take a moment.*

"This thing's low on cryonics," the same male voice muttered ahead of me. As my vision clarified, I saw that he pried at the top of a meter-tall metallic cylinder, its dark base covered by a key panel. "Just like the other 'un."

"It is?" Thorne bit off the end of the word. The woman's hazel eyes crackled with unstated fury. Thin to the point of boniness, Dr. Thorne was nonetheless a striking woman with dark hair swept into a bun as precise as her accent.

"Yes." A loud bang, followed by clicks. "Absolutely."

"That's not possible," the woman responded. "We've checked the maths. The synergistics are spot on."

"I dunno what to tell you." The fair-haired man glanced over his shoulder at her, as he pushed his hand inside the device. "There are no cryonics here, Dr. Thorne. The math has to be wrong."

The woman stood quietly while he pulled out a small canister. With one deft motion he unscrewed the top. Dense steam wafted from the inside but nothing else. He gestured at it with one gauntleted arm.

"That doesn't make any sense," Thorne snarled as she stalked forward.

I'm moving closer. I pushed myself to a standing position, keeping my eyes on the targets. *We need more intel.*

Be exceedingly cautious. Rationality fluctuates around the

196

devices they wear, Anya reported.

On their wrists? Wyatt asked.

Correct. Her puzzlement felt sharp within the link. *As if there are dozens of minute changes in the axioms of physics happening within a tight field.*

Oh, good. That sounds completely normal and safe. I took a few steps closer until one of the men gestured back over his shoulder. Now that my vision had cleared, I saw a metal-and-glass wall a meter behind them. On the other side of that glass, a sinister light softly pulsed.

"I don't like it." Dr. Thorne peered down into the device. "That's the second resonator within the past thirty-six hours." She brushed her dark hair away from her face.

"You think it has to do with... our current project?" A dark-haired, tall man stood nearby, one of the machine guns in hand. "Awfully convenient timing."

"Anything is possible, Brooks." She crouched down next to the cylinder and pulled a small device from her hip. It emitted soft clicks when she punched the keys on the mechanism.

I slipped closer, trying to remain as silent as possible.

Brooks peered at Dr. Thorne while she and the fair-haired man tinkered with the cylindrical casing. Behind them, the fourth man paced, his automatic weapon at the ready. His beady eyes swept through the darkness of the caverns, alert.

"Look at this." Thorne stuffed her entire arm inside the device, grunting with the slight bit of effort. When she pulled her arm out, she held one finger up.

"That's the cryonics fluid." The blonde man remained crouched next to her. "Those canisters don't leak."

"Right." She stared at him. "Someone's been meddling with the resonators."

"Now that's just disturbing." Brooks glanced behind himself to the man who paced their perimeter. "You think it's one of ours?"

"Everyone in this station is one of ours." She glanced up at

197

him. "We assume. Ito says there's no way anyone else could even know we're here."

"Might be the Gentlemen." Brooks shook his head. "Never know what those spooky assholes are up to."

I stopped in place, my eyes wide.

Did I just hear that? Wyatt teased, yet I felt no smile through the link. These folks had just moved from 'individuals of possible interest' to 'likely reality terrorists,' all with one word.

Gentlemen.

You did, I confirmed. I ignored the headache from my optics and took a long look at the figures, making certain to get a clear image of each of them in my memory. *This little clan has encountered the Facility before. We're not dealing with garden-variety cultists here.*

There are garden-variety cultists? Wyatt's link felt weary.

Facility intel reported the term Silent Gentlemen originated from the fact that Assets don't often speak while on dossier—at least not while engaging Irrats—since our Crowns offered us the luxury to instantly link one another.

A handy tool.

From the perspective of an average Irrat, we appear mysteriously on the scene, often wearing black suits or uniforms. Then we go about the task of ruining their entire day. In complete silence. Utilizing well-coordinated attacks without saying a word.

Silent. Merciless. Wielding the laws of reality itself as our weapons.

The effect is chilling.

Like so many other secrets within the world, simply knowing of us as the Silent Gentlemen classified them as a certain kind of person, someone who escaped our intense interest, a dangerous person who was very likely to wield bizarre technology or summon faceless abominations from beyond the realm of reality.

This intel changes our situation, Anya linked, communicating the obvious. *While our previous goal focused upon our returning to Rationality, the discovery of reality terrorists while on dossier cannot be ignored.*

Agreed. I crept closer, a Stiletto in each hand. I knew from experience that, while beneath the *Wraith* I could slaughter two or three targets before my location became obvious, but this time I had a different idea. *I want to stay with them. Follow them back inside. See what I can discover.*

Absolutely not. Anya's link felt as if I had suggested throwing myself on a live hand grenade. *We have no intel about this location. Acting alone is completely reckless.*

It's not that reckless if we follow him, Wyatt reasoned. *As we just discussed, it's not uncommon for fancy pants here to pull point and scout ahead.*

"Edmund." Thorne stood and brushed off her pant leg, then moved toward the glass door. "I need you to run an errand. Go to subbasement three and bring up a new cryonics canister while John and I recalibrate."

"Yes, Dr. Thorne," the patrolling man responded. He turned toward the door just as Thorne placed her hand against a small control panel. A sickly light flickered from the device.

It's now. I picked up the pace and quietly trotted over to the door. *I'll follow this guy inside. He's supposed to bring something back, so I'll be able to return as well.*

Dangerous, Anya warned. *You will be cut off from any possible assistance. That hatch requires a biometric key, therefore we cannot follow.*

Relax. I can turn the glass in that door into oxygen, Wyatt responded. *If we absolutely need to get inside, we'll get inside.*

The door slid completely open with a sibilant hiss, and Edmund stepped through with a curt nod at Thorne. As the glass closed, Edmund stopped in place.

ACK! I halted just behind him on my toes and windmilled my arms. Another pace and I would have fallen over him.

Above the door, an angry light suddenly crackled, followed by a loud buzz. I glanced up, wondering what it might be. A furious shine, brilliant and warm, brushed against my skin.

"TWO BIO-SIGNATURES DETECTED," a mechanical voice informed us through some unseen speaker.

"What?" Edmund turned, his eyes wide. They flickered from side to side as if trying to catch something that teased at the corner of his vision.

Oh shit.

Hoss? Wyatt's worry bled through the link, but I ignored him. I had no way to know if my large friend had heard the voice, and I didn't feel as if I could take my attention from Edmund long enough to see if Thorne had.

Frantically, Edmund pushed himself back against one of the gunmetal walls. He swung his automatic rifle around to my left.

No time to waste.

I toggled the *Adept* the moment I realized what the man intended. With his back to the wall, he started frantically spraying the confined area with his weapon, trying to eradicate the second bio-signature.

I leapt.

No human could dodge automatic fire, even with my augmentations. At least not for long. Automatic weapons unleashed a ridiculous number of projectiles, all in the tiniest sliver of time.

The *Adept* carried me through the leap, giving me strength, dexterity, and speed unlike anything I possessed ungeared. Without thought, I spun sideways in midair, which carried me over Edmund's weapon fire.

He shot beneath me, snarling as he arced his weapon to one side.

"Edmund?" Thorne's voice came over the unseen speaker, mechanical and warbled.

I landed in a crouch and glanced to the side to see her speak into a small handheld device. "What is it?"

"There's another bio-signature!" he shouted, as if uncertain she would hear him. "Someone's in here with me!"

"It may be an error. I'll reinitiate the scan." She tapped on the screen of the device in her hand.

Michael?

So far, I'm green, I linked as that node of furious light began to crackle again. I turned toward the hallway in front of us and pumped my invisible legs. Perhaps I could exit the range of the scanning device.

BZZZZT! Again, that seeking shine filled the area, warm and soothing against my skin.

"TWO BIO-SIGNATURES DETECTED," the scanner informed us, like a jerk.

"Shit!" Edmund pushed himself back into the corner and began to spray the area with automatic fire again. "It's still in here!"

I cursed and hurled myself low beneath his spray of fire. As Edmund's shots went wide, I rolled sideways, holding my Stilettos forward.

Before Edmund finished his wild shots, I'd fired off three bursts of kinetic energy. Two narrow and sharp, while the final shot had been calibrated large, approximately the size of a cinderblock.

From the perspective of Thorne and her goons, something hurled Edmund back against the glass, his skull liquefied into scarlet, grisly death.

Thorne stared, horrified. After a moment, she brought that device back up to her mouth and said something I couldn't hear.

The same node that rested above the glass and metal door quickly shifted to a deep color I couldn't determine, as the *Wraith* only allowed me to see in grayscale. It began to pulse rapidly, an obvious warning that, perhaps, I should not have gotten out of bed.

"THIS IS A SITEWIDE NOTIFICATION," the mechanical voice informed me through the speaker. **"AN INTRUSION HAS BEEN DETECTED WITHIN ATRIFICIA 131. BRIGADE**

SIX PLEASE REPORT TO THE CAVERN BAYS."

We might be in trouble. I stared frantically down the passage-way behind me as I linked. I heard something, probably people deciding they needed to come this way and see how many bullets they could shoot into my face.

Trouble? Anya asked.

They know I'm here. I shook my head. *At least, they know something is here. They had some kind of scanner on the door.*

Sounds like you're sayin' the time for cleverness and quiet is over, Hoss?

It might be.

Behind me, the door hissed. Thorne had moved over to the biometric device to open it. Next to her, Brooks held a G36 in one hand and a grenade in the other. A third figure, the blonde, held no weapon, yet that bracer on his arm pulsed with a glow that throbbed like a migraine.

Oh good, Wyatt linked. *I gotta admit, I was gettin' pretty tired of sneakin' around.*

I took a deep breath, plotting how deep in the shit we actually stood. Three known hostiles just outside the door. One armed. An unknown number of hostiles to arrive on-site any moment.

Anya had no weaponry. Wyatt had the Tangler geared, which might be powerful but hadn't truly been intended for combat.

This could get bad.

"Brooks," Thorne ordered as the door opened.

"My pleasure." The smiling man stepped forward, preparing to lob the grenade into the small chamber.

I spun and brought the Stiletto in my left hand around. The moment Brooks tossed the explosive, I fired twice. Concussive force pulsed from my weapon hit like two invisible cannonballs. Brooks and his grenade both flew backward violently, while the other two hostiles crumpled to the side.

Hoss?

Yeah, I'm probably going to need your very special brand of help.

The grenade exploded, approximately twenty meters behind the fallen group. Since Thorne had already started to push herself up, the blast tossed her forward and left her sprawled on the floor.

While paying attention to her, I failed to notice John, the blond technician, approach. Like the lady, a bracer of leather and brass covered most of his right forearm. It held a half-dozen odd little devices, dials and diodes I saw even from a few steps away. Now, a pale nimbus of violent radiance burst from the device, a light that hurt to see.

Yet that glow reflected in John's gaze, reflected and reveled there. He turned those haunted eyes my way and his gaze rested squarely on the place where I stood.

He pointed. "Found one. Man-size and shape. Holding two weapons."

A sickly shine ignited upon the bracer on Thorne's wrist, a light that bent and shuddered as it shone. She pushed herself to her feet, her lip curling in a snarl of hatred.

Hoss?

I brought both my Stilettos up, intending one for John, the other for Thorne. I had no idea what strangeness those bracers wrought, yet I got the sinking sensation that I truly didn't want to know.

In that moment, Brooks shot me.

2

In my bizarre adventures, I experienced my fair share of reality-altering miracles. Thanks to Facility technology, I'd stepped through rifts in space-time, had horrific wounds knit a matter of minutes instead of days, and watched as physics itself got rewritten for the convenience of my fellow Assets.

Yet nothing in all that time had ever saved my somewhat snarky ass nearly as often as the quasi-steel woven into my suits.

Brooks knew what he was doing with the G36. The moment John pointed me out, he shot two quick, expertly aimed bursts.

I probably caught somewhere between eight and thirteen rounds, center body, the force of which hurled me back with an undignified, "GUUU-URK!"—something between a grunt and the sound an elephant might make when it vomits.

Pain exploded in my chest and shoulder. I felt like a musclebound luchador had pounded my chest with a ball peen hammer.

Michael! Anya's link hit my mind with almost the same amount of force as the bullets.

I heard her but found myself unable to respond. The suddenness of the pain catastrophically stunned me, and I fell backward onto the ground.

"There!" I couldn't identify the man's voice; it warbled in my mind. "Blood splatter! You see it?"

Hoss, I'm movin' on 'em.

I pushed myself to a seated position while my head spun. Frantically, I patted myself down trying to determine if the kinetic force of the bullets overwhelmed the quasi-steel. It didn't typically happen with a single bullet. With as many as I'd taken, however, the suit's weave might well be ruined.

Hit. I gaped at the blood on my hand, stunned. *I'm shot!*

Comin', Wyatt responded.

In that moment, Thorne hurled herself at me and spun into a dazzling kick. Her boot caught me straight in the face, and my nose exploded into a brilliant cacophony of pain and blood.

I fell back again, reeling. It felt like shards of red-hot glass shot through my face.

"Hello there." I felt her weight as she straddled my blood-splattered, partially visible chest. "I'd like to speak with you about my resonators."

When she punched, it felt like a garbage truck hit me in the face.

"Whu whoozzle?" I calmly elocuted.

"My resonators," she explained. "They keep failing, you see. Oddest thing. I've set them up myself, you know. I'm quite certain they were calibrated before."

I blinked, staring up at her stupidly. The shine of her bracer had encapsulated her entire body now, surrounding her in a wicked nimbus.

"If you're willing to talk, I'm willing to stop beating you bloody." She punctuated this idea with a backhand across my cheek that felt as if a gorilla had delivered it. She shrugged. "Or we can continue."

Packet designation: Wraith *is undergoing pattern loss.* The static-filled message in my Crown cut off the last portion of what Thorne said. *System requirements have been altered from standard settings. Viral mecha required.*

Shit. The autonomous systems within my mecha had reallocated them to damage control. A fine idea typically, except the *Wraith* needed a contingent of them to remain active.

"Otay!" I blabbered as blood ran from my nose. "We can tawk!"

Wraith *powering down.* No sooner did I hear the message than I felt those cool shadows vanish from around me. I watched as Thorne flickered between the soft grays the *Wraith* allowed me to see and the full-technicolor madwoman bathed in garish, crimson light.

She blinked, startled.

In that moment, Wyatt's gear fired with a **WHUF.**

Another man screamed.

I spun hard to my left, which knocked Thorne off balance. That instant of surprise proved enough for me to roll into a crouch and push myself to my feet.

"A Gentleman," she remarked coolly. Now, I saw the sharp scarlet light pulse around her, an eagerly burning aura of malignance. "We should have guessed." Behind her, Brooks fired his G36, but couldn't see either Wyatt or Anya.

"I heard you guessing." Noticing I'd dropped the Stilettos, I pulled the twin katana from my back. Thorne remained weaponless, I reasoned. Perhaps my blades would keep her—

She rushed me savagely, her fist high.

I couldn't help but gape at how freaking *fast* she moved, charging forward in a blur. Startled, I leapt backward and swung one sword as I scrambled.

I fucking *missed.*

My shoulder ached, a deep pain that made it difficult to hold the blade. I glanced down and saw blood seeping through my suit.

She charged again, whirling to her left.

I dove to one side and felt the air from her kick. If it weren't for the *Adept,* I would have eaten her boot.

"So, a spy as well as a saboteur." Thorne paused to give me a cat's smile. Then she stepped just out of reach of my blades.

Fast. So incredibly fast.

Impossible.

Anya, are you reading anything Irrational from in here?

"I'd love to know how you found us," Thorne said. "The timing is quite convenient."

I watched her warily. As fast as she moved, I couldn't let my guard down for an instant.

It is the technology she wears, Anya responded. *I am recording the specifics as she utilizes it.*

"Come now." Thorne tilted her head. "How can you possibly have any jurisdiction all the way out here? Any right?" She took a step closer, and I jerked my blades up into an active guard.

Behind her, the automatic weapon fired again. When my gaze flicked over her shoulder, she leapt at me again.

In an instant, Thorne closed the distance between us, swinging straight for my face. I ducked aside, but even with the *Adept,* not quite quickly enough. She caught my right shoulder with that strike, landing a punch a heavyweight boxer would have envied.

Pain shot through my wounded shoulder like a lance of fire. I cried out and dropped my katana.

She spun, swinging again.

This time, I brought up my left blade and caught her across the shoulder. Hot blood sprayed across my face.

Yet she didn't stop.

Thorne spun again, whipping her hand around for a strike.

I ducked but didn't dodge her second blow, which pummeled straight into my gut.

The breath exploded from my lungs, and I stumbled. Thorne hurled herself after and pinned me to the ground.

My katana skittered away.

"It doesn't have to be this way," Thorne hissed before giving me a backhand that would have shattered bricks. "Tell me how you found us."

"I..." I shook my muddled head, trying to focus. "I didn—"

"Liar," she spat. "You think I'm a fool?" She drew her arm back again, closing her hand into a fist.

WHUF. The characteristic chuff of Wyatt's gear was followed by its warbling keen.

Thorne wailed in agony and lurched. Her back bent into a bow as one of his spikes exploded through the right side of her chest, near the top.

Hot blood splattered across my face.

She peered down at the metal embedded in her and touched the bloody spike with trembling fingers. She blinked at me, her dark eyes wide.

"No…" Her voice wavered, cracked.

I rolled, spinning as quickly as possible to get out from beneath her. Frantically, I cast about for my blades and the Stilettos.

I didn't see either.

The head of that spike, still sticking out of Thorne's back, burst into a feral radiance. She screamed again, agony in that cry.

I felt the heat ripple outward from her.

"Somebody needs to learn not to pick on people weaker than she is." Wyatt stepped up behind her and gave me a toothy grin as he tapped keys on his device.

"Ass," I spat as I took a few staggering steps to my left.

"Not. Finished." Thorne stared at me, her eyes like frozen knives. Her trembling left hand fiddled with something at her belt, something brass and spherical.

Something that might have been a hand grenade.

Instinctively, I threw myself flat, grunting as I landed on my shot shoulder. Wyatt leapt back, not quite as agile.

Shadows and eldritch light exploded from her hand. For an instant, I saw through Thorne, through Wyatt, as a burning radiance shone through everything.

A splintering crack punctuated that awful light. I winced, and Thorne vanished into the weird luminescence.

Only traces of undulating smoke remained.

Wyatt and I gaped.

"She left a… a bowl." Wyatt tilted his head to point with the brim of his Stetson. The floor, right where Thorne stood, had a hole almost one full meter deep, a perfect hemisphere sheared from the metal.

What if I'd been a little bit closer? I regarded the depression with horror. Would I be carved in two?

"The spike!" Wyatt tapped a few keys and peered into the

holographic interface. He squinted and then shook his head.

"What about it?"

"She's gone," he sighed.

"Well, yeah." I gestured at the cratered floor.

"No. I mean she's more than five hundred meters away." He scowled. "Were she closer, I'd see the location on my array."

"So wherever she appeared… she doesn't have that spike with her?"

"Quantum dispersement, Hoss. It vanished."

"Fucking great. At least she'll still have the hole."

"Gentlemen?" Anya came up behind Wyatt. "Is this location secure?"

"Locale green," I replied as I pushed myself up. I prodded at my bleeding shoulder and winced.

"I did not realize the degree of your injury, Michael." Anya tilted her head, her brow furrowing.

"That lady knew what she was doing." I chuckled. "I think she broke my pretty face."

"She weighed, like, a buck-thirty, Hoss." Wyatt turned and peered down the hallway.

"She knew some kind of mutant Jeet Kune Do," I retorted, picking up my dropped weapons. "She came straight out of an old episode of Kung Fu Theater."

"You require an allotment of viral mecha, Michael." Anya dug in the squarish containers on her belt. "We cannot expect to advance with your current state of injury."

"This is the correct way?" Wyatt nodded down the passage. "I mean, I can see the marker, but we're certain?"

"I am." She gestured. "The source of the emanations is in this direction."

"Right." Wyatt turned from the mark to me and raised an eyebrow. "But it looks like it's below ground level."

"Affirmative." As she spoke, Anya handed me three small injectors. It took only a moment to apply them to the side of my

neck, and they sent coolness hissing into my bloodstream.

"So Locale One is ahead but also down a bit," Wyatt concluded.

"Looks about right," I grumbled as I took a glance at my suit. "Give me a sec, and we can move along."

Quasi-steel, as a textile, fascinated me. Each strand could bear far more strain than mere cloth or even actual steel. This wasn't simply some rare material; the components were constructed in extra-Rational Facility laboratories, designed to counteract sharp kinetic bursts. Quasi-steel could not be formulated within an environment that bowed to the traditional model of physics. Yet the material could be overwhelmed by kinetic force, like when Brooks decided to unload his weapon straight to my chest.

I reached beneath the jacket, unbuttoned the first button of my shirt, and gently prodded my wounded shoulder.

"Fucking ow." I winced.

"I did not realize you had actually been hit." Anya's eyes went a bit wide. "I assumed the blood belonged to one of the Irrationals."

"It's a through and through." I turned a bit so that she could see the ruined back shoulder of my suit. "Didn't hit bone or anything, didn't spin."

"Fortunate." She regarded me seriously.

"I feel well enough," I informed her. "The viral mecha immediately went to work on knitting protcins and dampening pain."

"Which powered down your active packets." She nodded. "I apologize for not providing enough mecha for your requirements. I am not typically responsible for allocation."

"It's fine." I gave her a half smile. "We managed to put them down."

"THIS IS A SITEWIDE NOTIFICATION," the mechanical voice reminded us through the crackling speaker. **"AN INTRUSION HAS BEEN DETECTED WITHIN ATRIFICIA**

131. BRIGADE SIX PLEASE REPORT TO THE CAVERN BAYS."

"We didn't put 'em all down," Wyatt growled. "I suspect we got incoming, any moment."

"Yeah." I spied one of my Stilettos and picked it up, groaning.

"We are not geared to engage a large force." Anya turned to me, her blue eyes slightly wider than usual.

"I'd wondered if you could use one of those G36s." I jerked my chin toward the fallen Brooks.

"I have no training with automatic weapons," she replied.

"It's kind of a point and click interface."

"You children don't need to worry." Wyatt grinned through his beard, a mad visage I found somewhat daunting.

"We don't, huh?" I raised an eyebrow.

"While you were getting beaten up by Barbie, I been thinkin'. Papa bear has it all figured out." He chuckled. "Never fear."

"Oh." My heart sank into my stomach. "Good."

Atrificia

Moments later, Anya and Wyatt waited in the shadows outside the Atrificia. They remained close, simply out of sight from the main hallway.

I crouched within, just beyond the place Thorne had straddled my chest and fed me her fists. Now that I'd geared enough mecha, the cool shadows of the *Wraith* lay across me.

I waited, unseen.

I hear them, I reported. *I can't see any targets yet; they're close, though.*

Just give me my mark, Hoss.

According to my Crown's system time, the first jackbooted thug turned the corner twenty-eight seconds later.

He poked his head around, then brought his weapon up. His beady eyes swept the corridor, taking in the blood and Brooks' body. Twice, his eyes brushed right over me. That cold gaze didn't stop, didn't hint that he saw me.

Difficult to clear an area when your target's practically invisible.

He stepped into the open, signaling his allies with two fingers like a professional soldier. Someone had seen fit to provide their dangerous thugs with proper equipment. He wore black riot gear, complete with helmet and every conceivable piece of body armor. He held his weapon at the ready, his eyes focused.

"Go, go, go!" one of the men chanted.

They're at eighteen meters, I reported. *Six hostiles.*

I show no unusual axiomatic readings, Anya reported.

I'd say we've got baseline humans here. Professionals though. I flicked my gaze across each of the men, searching for an identifying insignia or company badge.

I need a ten meter-mark, Hoss.

213

I know. I scowled at him over the link. *Not yet.*

Once all six men took position in the hallway, they quickly began to move toward me. Each kept their weapon pointed forward, focused.

Mark, I linked Wyatt just as one of the men passed his first spike.

Copy that, the barbarian replied.

Ignorant of their precarious position, the men rushed down the hallway. Mere moments later, a series of WHOMPS sounded in the corridor as Wyatt's silvery stasis domes popped up around their targets, encasing them.

Each of the men halted in their tracks, bound in a singular, interminable moment.

Clear, I sent. *All hostiles cleverly trapped by Alabamian ingenuity.*

Perfect. Wyatt's smug smile beamed over the link.

I would like to reiterate that stasis fields are outside of protocol, regardless of their utility. Anya crossed her arms over her tactical gear.

"I get it, *Preceptor.*" Wyatt strode into the Atrificia, fingers dancing along his keys. "We're outside Rational space. If nothing else, the Designates will appreciate the data they gain from my non-protocol dickering."

"I'm taking point." I slipped past one of the silvery hemispheres and slid through the walk space Wyatt had left. "Keep these guys still. I won't be long."

"No need to stray too far," Wyatt reminded me. "When I let the jackholes out, they'll have no idea we were here. They should keep moving away from us."

"Understood." I prodded gently at my shoulder, noticing most of the pain had entirely faded. It didn't seem to be completely reknit yet; that would take a bit more time.

Carefully, I stepped around the corner.

The inside of the Atrificia seemed to have been crafted of

gleaming metal and glass. The structure had been lifted right out of some fifties sci-fi flick.

I hurried down a few steps into a gleaming passage that ended in a *T*.

Halfway down the corridor, on my right, a metallic door had been set flush in the wall.

"Look at this," I muttered, considering. It held the same kind of bio-reader Thorne had activated before, but that wouldn't stop Wyatt if we needed inside. If my lumbering friend wanted, we'd walk right through.

This might be just the thing.

An empty room could be a good place for us to plan and reassess. Perhaps the alertness of our hosts might die down. I'd stay invisible, do a little recon, get the layout—

"No..." I popped the knuckles on my right hand. Bad idea.

The Designates had no idea what had happened to us. As far as their telemetry would show, we'd been in the *Legacy*, traveling down a lonesome highway. Abruptly, we flickered in and out of Rationality. They might have even received fragments of Anya's epic freak out as we drove between worlds.

We had vanished.

In most circumstances, holing up and gaining intel might be the smart play. But adrift in an alternate topiatic reality, the rules significantly changed. Without connectivity to the Lattice, my cadre had no way to know how long we'd been dimensional castaways. Real time had passed while we fought the tentacled horrors outside. It could have been hours, even days.

We might have been gone weeks or just seconds.

"Time is not on our side," I muttered. Turning, I crept further down the hallway, staying close to the wall.

You don't have to scout out the whole building, Wyatt reminded me. *If it's safe around the corner, we're ready to follow.*

Will confirm. I trotted over to the *T* where something on the wall caught my eye. *Give me a moment here.*

As I approached the hallway corner, the object came into view. A brass plaque that held a few lines of engraved text, first in English, then in Japanese kanji:

Sathantür
Research Station Garnath
Atrificia 131

Sathantür? Could that be the name of the reality we found ourselves adrift in? I felt confident that Garnath was the name of this structure.

"Nice to know," I muttered.

To my right, the passage extended several dozen meters before branching off again. Light flickered for a moment in that direction.

To my left, a smooth metallic door dominated the passage. A mundane elevator.

"Huh. Weird."

At the right of the doors, a sign attached to the wall read:

Admittance to sub-basements forbidden to personnel below Clearance 3. Proceed into the Atrificia at your own risk. Level seventeen quasi-radionics present. Please report to your supervisor if you experience hallucinations or difficulty sleeping after entering this area.

"Forbidden?" I scoffed. The elevator didn't seem to require a key or an access code. Exactly how forbidden could it be?

I turned, glancing at the triangular marker that showed the direction of the emanations. As Wyatt noted, the closer we drew to the marker, the more obviously it drifted below our feet.

Yup. We needed to go down a few floors.

I'm calling it clear, I linked, powering down the *Wraith* at the same time. *No one is here, and I may have found our way forward.*

Understood, Michael. We are en route.

For a moment, I examined the hallway behind me. The lights flickered again, as if there might be a poor electrical connection.

I took a step in that direction. Maybe I should have checked that out?

"Hey, Hoss." Wyatt held one hand up as he approached. "I see yer not getting yer ass handed to you."

"Not this time." I scowled at him.

"Good fer you, sport."

"I have, however, soundly defeated an elevator." I rapped on the door and pushed the button.

The door chimed merrily, in a way no dangerous door ever would, as it slid open.

"Weird." Wyatt eyed the doorway. "I have to admit, a mundane elevator in a dimension of murder-tentacles seems out of place."

"A *forbidden* elevator." I raised one eyebrow at them while tapping the small sign.

"Sounds dangerous." Wyatt flicked his gaze inside.

"We cannot possibly know the reasoning behind the classification." Anya glanced at the small sign and then stepped inside.

"Petrova, you rebel," Wyatt teased, raising the brim of his hat with one finger.

"If the device were truly dangerous, it would require an elevator key or a biometric reading to enter."

"See? That's what I thought." I gestured at Anya. "Thank you."

"I like that logic." Wyatt strode in, shrugging his pack higher up onto his back.

"Like a sign can hold us back." I followed and punched the solitary button on the panel with one extended finger.

The elevator shifted and then began to descend in jerks.

"We need some data." Anya brushed a golden lock away from her face. "If the area beyond is secure, I will take telemetrics."

"Not every danger shows up on telemetry." Wyatt raised an

eyebrow. "'Sides, you could take yer readings while we ride down."

"Are you worried, Anya?"

"I wish to share something. A suspicion." She glanced at me again. "I expect telemetry to become increasingly sub-Rational as we near Locale One."

Did I see a touch of nervousness in those blue eyes?

From a *Preceptor*? Surely not. Was that even possible?

The downward motion continued far longer than I expected. Just before we came to a jostling stop, the marker for our emanations' source shifted from its previously static position, a barely perceptible change considering the elevator's motion.

"Ground level," Wyatt snarked. "Otherworldly monstrosities, tentacled telepaths, and men's wear."

"I wish." I fingered the hole in my jacket, frowning.

With that happy little chime, the door slid open.

2

The vast cavern beyond the elevator surprised me, immense even at first glance. The doorway opened into a truly gargantuan space. Twisted plant growths dotted the walls. From those, a sickly, verdant glow oozed across the dark stone, bathing the space in unnatural light.

I stepped out of the elevator, marveling at the floor beneath my feet. Jet black, it had been polished to a mirror sheen. Even within this uncanny half-light, I easily saw my reflection within it.

"One moment." Anya followed me, her hands stretched out to her sides. Deftly, she began to pluck and pull with her delicate fingertips, manipulating an interface only she saw.

"Do we seem green?" Wyatt emerged, craning his head. He tapped at a couple of keys and his equipment emitted a whine. He struck a third key, and the timbre went up half an octave.

"I—" Anya moved her left hand down quickly, pinching at something and sliding it to the left. Her mouth tipped downward into the hint of a frown.

What is it? I came up next to her, even though I couldn't see what she saw.

Axiomatic strands are—she tilted her head—*curiously allocated within this cavern.*

Yeah? I glanced up at Wyatt, who shrugged.

I suspected they might be irregular, but... let me show you. Anya's eyes flicked from Wyatt to me.

I winced as the large packet hit me like a screwdriver stabbing into my brain. It consisted entirely of visual data and numerics.

"Damn, Anya." Wyatt shook his head and scowled. "You could warn a guy."

I immediately opened the packet. An executable auto-dialogue overlaid semi-transparent data across my vision. Hundreds of corded filaments unspooled across my visual array, stretching off

219

in all directions. Everything in existence had been tied together, wound about with threads of different colors and sizes. They stretched into infinity, passing into the ground, through us, and into the cavern roof above.

"Wow," I offered.

That is an example, a simplified approximation, of my visual interface for baseline Rationality. Each thread represents a local axiom. It is not factual in any way, simply the image my system interface creates.

I nodded and remembered the way her fingers twitched as if she played an invisible harp.

A single strand moves out of place to indicate a localized axiom has shifted. In this way, I can determine exactly how far a location varies from baseline Rationality. I can also ascertain which axiom has caused the disruption, since shifting one out of place warps the entire weave.

"It's just an approximation." Wyatt nodded. "Okay."

This is why Wyatt's gear is nicknamed the Tangler, I sent with realization. *Makes sense.*

Please initiate the second dialogue from the glyph in the upper left-hand corner of your visual array.

I found the glyph and triggered it with a thought. The strands all faded from view, replaced with a very different version of those filaments. Each one bent and stretched in wildly different directions.

"The hell?" Wyatt turned in place and stared at all of them. "So the fact that these strands have different positions indicates axiomatic differences?"

Many of the laws of physics here are identical to Rationality. Anya reached for one of the strands, plucking it like a violin string. *Here is the ratio by which matter bends space.* She pulled another. *This one involves the rate at which ferrous metals oxidize.*

So what's this, then? Wyatt gestured at a filament, approximately twenty times the diameter of the others. That thread pulsed a lurid, violent red and had dozens of other strands bound into it. It stretched out before us, running in the direction of the waypoint marker for Locale One.

The point of my quandry. Anya touched the strand but pulled her hand away quickly, as if it were hot. *I have no idea what it is. I've never seen anything like it.*

"That's unnerving." I swept my gaze along the scarlet strand, then met her eyes. "Could it be because we're in an alternate topia? Perhaps this is typical here?"

Unknown, Anya replied. *I could not perceive it directly when we entered the structure, but I inferred something irregular must exist. The strands above us all bend downward a few nanometers, pulled by the sheer force of this anomaly.*

"So what do we do?" Wyatt glanced from the strand to Anya. "Will this affect our gear? Alter the way Rosie does her math?" He gently patted the rivet gun.

It is quite possible your calculations will require more energetic input, 423. Anya leveled her gaze directly at him. *For this reason, I would advise using simpler algorithms while in proximity to the strand.*

"Understood, *Preceptor*." Wyatt nodded.

None of these strands affect the nature of light, Michael. At least, not beyond what we have already experienced. I expect the Wraith *will largely function as intended.*

"Good to know." I blinked, dismissing the visual of the strands. "And the *Adept*?"

As far as I can determine, our physical systems should continue to operate as they do within Rationality. The Adept *should function as usual.*

"Good." Wyatt edged further into the darkness. "If something's down here, I'd rather them not be able to see ninja-boy as he goes about getting his ass beat."

"I'd rather not see that too." I shook my head. "I mean, I'd rather them not—"

"The waypoint marker is directly in line with this unnatural strand." Anya indicated with a gesture. "I would appreciate the opportunity to read telemetry as we move, to learn as much as possible."

"Reasonable," Wyatt agreed.

"But this will slow our progress," Anya pointed out.

"Not a problem." My gaze drifted from her to Wyatt. "If our favorite hillbilly can stick with something fast and dirty, he's enough protection for you while you work. I can slip on the *Wraith* and peek ahead."

"Fast and dirty?" Wyatt teased. "You got any ideas there, Brooks Brothers? Please, do tell me how to use my equipment."

"Those thermogenerative spikes worked well back in the caves," I offered. "You cooked those things alive. Plus, it seemed as if you could fire them quickly."

"Always critiquing the artist." Wyatt sighed, as if put upon. "I create masterful works of scientific genius, and you just want me to shoot sharp, hot things."

"Fact." I flashed him a crooked smile. "Unless one of you has a better idea?"

"Please watch in all directions." Anya gazed off into the shadows. "We could just as easily be approached from one of the secondary caverns."

"Agreed." I nodded. "I'll be cautious."

"We'll give you a quick head start." Wyatt winked. "It'll give me a moment to do the computations required to treat the Tangler like it's basically a crossbow."

"With bolts heated to over three hundred degrees Celsius." I shot him a thumbs-up.

When I toggled the *Wraith,* the cloak of cool invisibility fell across me. The unnatural emerald light from the plants faded into a spectral, colorless glow.

I stepped into the alien shadows.

Each step echoed oddly, a fact which caused me to move with

extra care. Typically, the *Wraith* gave some amount of sound dampening, muffling small scuffs against the floor to better hide my movement. Yet here, my feet resounded clearly as they trod on that smooth surface.

I moved slowly, one ear canted.

Several moments passed as I ghosted through the uncanny half-light. Something about the room felt off to me; as if the space within had an unfamiliar texture. Moving through it inspired roiling gurgles in my stomach—not quite nausea, only close.

I paused for a moment, trying to shake the feeling. After a few deep breaths, I moved on.

It seems as if the passage gets a bit narrower up ahead. I broke into a trot, hoping to create a little distance from my cadre. *There's a large formation of stone, about seven meters high. The waypoint icon points between it and the wall.*

Understood, Hoss. We're starting to move now. Don't get lost.

I don't plan on it.

The stone jutted from the smooth cavern floor, surrounded by a small hill of scree and powdery soil. I pushed myself closer to the wall on the left, warily letting my gaze flick up the rock, searching for any signs of danger.

For a moment, I powered down the *Wraith* and toggled my optics. I figured if any otherworldly abominations lurked up there, I'd be able to see them in the infrared.

"Nope." The change in perception showed me other, small formations of stone scattered about, some of them nearly half as tall as this first one.

No horrific abominations lurked anywhere around.

I checked out the small hill with my optics. It's clean; you can pass safely. I paused. *I'm moving on.*

I slid forward, between the grouping of stones and the wall. I hadn't taken three strides before I heard a faint, chugging sound, echoing crookedly in the darkness.

I stopped in place, listening. Machinery?

Michael. The scarcest touch of warning colored Anya's link. *You are approaching a zone of slight axiomatic variations. It begins approximately sixty-five meters in front of you.*

In the direction of the waypoint marker?

Affirmative.

Any danger?

There is a variable of .23 from ambient Rationality within that area. Nothing serious, just a softening of axiomatic obduracy.

So physics is a bit fluid here? It might be slightly easier for some Irrat to alter stuff.

Affirmative. Note the interference we seek is emanating from approximately the same location.

That ain't right, Wyatt interjected. *That thing didn't read that far away earlier.*

True. Anya paused for a moment, and her head twitched as she performed calculations. *Yet accurate. I cannot say why the differential exists.*

I'm pushing forward, I informed them. *I won't engage any hostiles on my own.* I flicked on the *Wraith. Promise.*

The chugging sound became louder as I strode forward, sounding vaguely like a stuttering chainsaw trying to chew through a petrified corpse. As the noise became louder, an inexplicable unease settled over me, like warm grease running down my skin.

I felt my own pulse thrum in my temples. I wiped sweat from my brow as I studied the shadows before me. Wrong. They clustered, lurking around...

There's a structure up here.

A building? Wyatt sounded a touch distracted.

More like a device, like an engine.

Weird. Copy that.

I drew both Stilettos. As I shuffled forward, the innate wrongness of the construction became painfully apparent. It hurt my mind to look at it, even to consider looking at it. The darkness around it shifted as I grew closer, as if attempting to block my view.

I made out bits of the silhouette of that monolithic device, only half revealed. Even though I couldn't see any true details, , the sheer wrongness of the unearthly shape offended me.

I felt as if I gazed at something which should not be.

The machine had an insectine, organic feel to its curves, shapes which half-lurked in darkness. If I positioned my head just so, I could see the lower left side of it undulate. The machine moved like a living thing, breathing out fumes like mist in the shadows.

As I stared through those shadows, I made out figures moving around the device.

We have company. I flittered my gaze around the incomprehensible machine, snatching still shots as my Crown perceived them. I sent those images in a patch. Finally, I made certain to capture an image showing four silhouettes, graceful figures that moved around the base of the machine.

Interesting, Wyatt linked. *Just the four?*

So far. Hold on a moment. I'll get a better look.

I trotted forward and made my way to one of those ragged formations of stone. Once there, I crouched, trying to keep hidden. I took a breath and powered the *Wraith* down again.

Without the *Wraith*, color bled back into my vision. Again, that greenish light suffused the world, sickly and wan.

The moment my optics came back online, I toggled the controls to narrow the scope. This allowed me to squint to enhance my vision as if I used a pair of binoculars.

Well?

There's a few more than four. I flicked my gaze to the left, trying to peer through the darkness that surrounded the loathsome structure. *Six maybe? The entire area is hard to make out. It seems as if the machine is cloaked in a particularly dark smoke.*

Smoke? I felt Anya purse her lips. *I neither smell smoke nor detect combustion.*

It's not exactly smoke. I studied the shadowy darkness, watching as it wafted and whirled around the uncanny device. It reminded me of a cloud of ink left in the water by an octopus.

That misty twilight *moved*, as if it consciously chose to block my sight.

Regardless of what it is, I can't get a good view from my current location. I scowled, knowing they would feel it over the link. *I have to get closer.*

Regulations state that a single Asset should not approach a hostile location.

Christ, Anya. Wyatt's frustration bled through freely. *This entire place is a hostile location.* I felt the large man heave his shoulders as he sighed. *Although, Hoss, she ain't wrong.*

Unless you can use that turkey baster on your back to somehow make the two of you invisible, I don't see another way.

Huh, Wyatt mused. *I mean, you'd hafta alter the way light interacts with matter... a lot, like the* Wraith *does.*

I cannot imagine we have time to work out the mathematics on more experimental algorithms, Anya cut in.

I'll drop an Asset marker where I currently stand. I executed the command within my Crown, choosing a pulsing blue circle for my locale. *You can approach this location safely. I've visually cleared everything to this point.*

You're going on, then? Wyatt asked.

I am, I confirmed. I toggled the *Wraith* and watched as color drained from the world. *I won't engage any hostiles, at least not on purpose.*

I concur this is the most optimal choice, Anya linked. *I advise that you attempt to follow the emanations to their source.*

Copy that, I agreed. *It seems to have drifted down a bit more as I've approached. Just not as abrupt this time.*

We're on the move, Hoss.

I stalked on, sticking close to the shadows.

The more I examined the unnatural structure ahead of me, the more my stomach roiled with uncertain queasiness. It felt as if the shadowed machinery somehow sloped *downward* from me, into a vast and unnatural chasm. Vertigo swam through my body, forcing me to stop every few meters to regain my composure.

Until it *rippled*.

With a sound that began like the creaking of a falling tree and ended with metal grinding on metal, the structure in front of me... moved. Like some monstrous behemoth, it shifted to one side, as if rolling over in its sleep.

What. The. Hell? I gaped at the apparatus.

Hoss? What the hell happened? You square?

I'm green, I linked reflexively. *It's that contraption; the mechanism stirred. I still can't quite make out what it is.*

Terrifyin', from the sound of it. He paused. *Watch yerself.*

Yes, keep us apprised, Anya linked.

"Kasar Dhuun," a baritone voice opined from the shadows to my left. "Khabac Du Sava."

Slowly, I turned in that direction. After a moment, my vision adjusted to the pitch of the shadows. Two figures crouched, scarcely silhouetted against the ghastly light of the room, not ten steps from me.

"Sen dun Khabac." This quieter, feminine voice spoke urgently. The figure gestured toward the undulating machinery and made a curt slash with her hand. "Kava."

I sighed. If only my Crown had translation neuralware, this might be simpler. Supposedly, that enhancement would be included in our next update.

Of course, I doubted this language had terrestrial origins, rendering the question moot.

Still though.

"Dim Khadast. Dim Quavar." The baritone stood abruptly and threw both of his hands up. He stomped off in the direction of the uncanny structure.

"Risa Kab!" The smaller figure pleaded as she stood. She pursued him, desperation in her tone.

227

Quietly, I ghosted after them.

"Kara dun Khabiis!" The feminine figure put her hand on his shoulder, but he shrugged her off and continued forward.

I drew a bit closer. If anything, their drama would make a good cover for any noise I made.

As we stepped toward the chuffing machinery, I saw the couple more clearly. The skin of each graceful figure drank any available light, darker than pitch, darker than space. If not for the stark white robes they wore, they would be infinite sable, lost to the shadows. I stared at their smooth, hairless pates and the contrast of the simple robes with the darkest black I'd never imagined.

"Kavarri Din!" She whirled in front of him, again pleading. With her left hand, she gestured wildly before them.

"Kara," he said in a firm, almost consoling tone. He placed his hands on her shoulders. "Dul Kajani Kor. Sadhana. Hast Kava Vyriim. Hast Kava Thorne."

I stopped in place at the last syllable. Had I heard right? As in Dr. Thorne?

The male strode onward, the discussion ended. After a moment the woman followed, striding straight into those shifting shadows.

I trotted after, trying to keep them in sight.

We've made your marker, Hoss. Wyatt's link startled me. *You didn't get that far ahead of us.*

I'm following some natives. I sent them a couple of stills from my Crown. *I hope they'll lead to something that matters.*

Michael, Anya's link slipped in. *On those images, I see the… mist swirl behind them as they pass.*

Mist? Wyatt asked. *The shadow… stuff?*

If the substance swirls as you move through it, the Wraith *becomes less valuable.*

Right. I chewed my lip. *Thanks, Anya. I'll keep close on these two. Maybe it won't be as noticeable in their wake.*

"Kavatta." Another male voice sounded from ahead, stern and loud. "Risa, Kara. Jin Kavatta lo."

"Ki." The male I'd followed nodded, and the three moved deeper into the shadows.

Closer to the baffling, bizarre machine.

My initial impression of the metallic construct proved true. The plates looked every bit the chitin of some great insect. The device also bore a certain grace, a feline curve that ran along its side. Gears taller than I stood turned slowly, and exhaust pipes released sulfuric steam. Occasionally, brilliant sparks fired along its surface.

The marker for Locale One was almost underfoot.

The trio I followed stepped up to a small dais. The older gentlemen spoke to his companions, a muffled word.

Without touching the surface of the structure, an opening came into view, more an orifice than a door. One moment, it appeared as any other part of the construct. The next, an interior passage hissed open.

Oh man, I linked, certain of my next move.

Yeah? Wyatt felt a touch distracted. *'Sup, Hoss?*

Seems like I'm headed inside.

What?

As the three paced forward, I hurried toward the opening, not wanting to try the door myself. For all I knew it only opened due to weird, alien telepathy or by some genetic key code. Then, once they closed it, I'd be left on the outside.

If that happened, I'd never reach the marker, and we'd be stuck.

What choice did I have?

I slipped inside.

3

Within the device, the air smelled of ozone, like the wind after a storm.

Inside what?

Michael, please report.

I'm inside the structure. I stood against the wall of a narrow, rounded corridor, several steps behind those I'd followed. The gunmetal surface of the hall contained occasional accents in silver. The entire interior glowed with brilliant, crackling electric lights.

The robed figures strode forward purposefully.

That sounds brilliant, Hoss.

It's worse than you think, I informed him. *I feel jittery. The* Wraith *needs a rest.*

The organic structure burned with radiant light from brilliant orbs situated every one and a half meters. They simply hung in the air, attached to neither the ceiling nor the walls.

Don't know if you realize this, buddy, Wyatt drawled, *but without the* Wraith, *you ain't invisible no more.*

No, I get it. The jitters remained preferable to being seen. For now.

Michael, you stand twenty-three meters from the origin of the emanations. It appears to be somewhat below you.

Right. I gazed at the triangle marker down to my left and listened to the door close behind me. Now that I stood within the construct, my vertigo receded. *I'm uncertain of how I'll get out, but I've made it in.*

Leave another marker, Hoss?

At my current coordinates? I engaged my Crown and dropped a new token where I stood.

Right. That way, after you die of terminal stupidity, we might be able to find the way inside.

Ha. Ha. I scowled at him. *I'm moving forward.*

I eased down the corridor until I caught sight of a small group of figures.

"Kavak." The newest gentleman, the older one, spoke intently to his two companions. His voice rumbled deeper than the others and rang with the steel of authority.

"Savava." The female nodded abruptly and stepped through another door I hadn't noted at first.

I crept closer and captured stills of both men. Both bald with skin darker than anything I'd ever seen, they wore pristinely white robes. In fact, now that I examined them...

Check this out. I sent the images to my cadre, focusing upon the scripts embroidered around the hem of the sleeves. *Seem familiar?*

These symbols are stylistically identical to those we noted upon the large creatures we faced earlier.

Yup, Wyatt confirmed. *I still got those images in my Crown. Same icons.*

So perhaps these gentlemen are allied with our large friends, I mused. I remembered thinking those behemoths could never scrawl that script with those gargantuan fingers.

"You boys 'bout ready down here?" a male voice drawled from the side passage. "Gettin' pretty tired of waitin'."

Both men tensed; the older one couldn't quite hold back a scowl.

"Ree-dey," the younger man called toward the unseen voice. "Comb now." He walked through the door.

The older man stared after him for just a moment, fist clenched. Then he turned directly toward me and stalked straight for the doorway we'd just passed through.

Carefully, oh so carefully, I slipped out of the way and let him pass. The door opened, and he stamped through, fuming.

What was *that* all about?

"I gotta know when the next cycle's gonna be ready," the same male voice drawled. "How 'bout you and sweetness here head below and find out the particulars?"

Silent, I edged forward.

That entryway didn't lead into another passage but to an organically rounded chamber with metal lockers and a door on the opposite side.

Three light-complexioned men, dressed in riot gear like the professionals we'd seen before, sat at a wooden table in the corner. One, a lanky, appallingly pale man with a wild shock of hair and a bumper crop of freckles, stood and spoke pointedly to the two robed figures.

Did I... know him? I stared at the man, desperate to focus on anything other than the jitters from overusing the *Wraith*.

"Eet ees steel sleepinguh," the feminine figure responded. "For times."

In the background, one of the men at the table mocked her, exaggeratedly mouthing her words to one of his tablemates.

"There ain't more time," Lanky grunted. "We got problems here, big ones. Go down there, find out when the Parabola's cycle ends, and report back."

"Yas," the male said. "We well goo belo." He took the female's wrist and led her toward the opposite door.

The man nearest the door leaned to open it without leaving his seat or breaking his grinning sneer.

"Number six, reporting in," a voice buzzed mechanically at Lanky's hip. He snatched at the boxy device.

"Moshi moshi, Collins," the freckled man greeted, surprising me with Japanese. Then he leaned toward the door just as the bald female followed her companion through. And pushed it securely closed.

"Japanese? Someone's there, huh?" He waited a beat. "We clear?" the voice buzzed.

"We are now. Secure channel," Lanky responded. "The Kabs just went downstairs."

"We got nothin' on the Gentlemen, Firenzei." Confusion lay

233

heavy in those words. "I mean that. There's quite a bit of blood, even corpses. Brooks is dead. Edmund got his skull liquefied, and John got cooked alive."

"But no fucking Silent Gentlemen. No Assets. Not even one body?"

"I'm telling you, man. No sight of Thorne either. I wonder if they took her."

"Nobody takes Thorne anywhere." Firenzei chuckled darkly. "Take another look around; you'll find evidence she jaunted off."

At that, one of the men sitting in the room gave a little huff of laughter.

"She fucking went Earthside," hissed another, a slender man with a scar above his eye, turned to the fellow sitting next to him. "Left us here to rot."

"Boys," Firenzei warned. "Daddy's on the phone. Be quiet."

"You called it," the voice crackled over the box. "She took a huge divot out of the floor."

"It'd have been nice if she happened to take our Asset problem with her." Firenzei ran his free hand through his wild hair. "You sure you got nothin', Aaron? Not outside neither?"

"We haven't been too far outside," Aaron confirmed. "Those caves go on for miles. If the Gentlemen left, they could be anywhere out there."

"The Gentleman didn't fucking leave," Firenzei assured him. "The Gentlemen never fucking leave. We can't get comfortable thinkin' they're gone."

"Make the call." Aaron paused for a moment. "If Thorne lit outta here, it means you're the top runner."

"It does." Firenzei sighed, tapping his fingers against the wall in a fast sequence. "You sure you checked real good inside the Atrificia? There's no chance some fucking Asset slipped by?"

"No chance." The words crackled over the communicator. "Not unless they can turn invisible now."

"Don't assume," Firenzei muttered.

"If they're still on Sathantür, they're outside somewhere. I guarantee it."

"Then I guarantee I need you to peek around outside." He gestured to the men at the table, who began to mutter and stand up.

"How far outside?"

"Well, Collins, we sure as hell could stand to know exactly where they are." Firenzei pointed at the thin man with the scar, who nodded as he moved toward the door. "But here's the sweet bit. Even if you find them, you shouldn't engage."

"There's six of us, Chief." Aaron sounded certain. "I don't think we need to worry."

"Six monkeys in tactical vests against the Gentlemen?" Firenzei sneered.

"Hey, *we* ain't the monk—"

"Thorne wore one of her fucking reverberators. John too. He went down, hard from the sound of it. She had to run."

"Both of them wore one of those freaky siphon contraptions?"

"Um, yes. You think I don't know what the fuck I'm talking about?"

"That's not what I said."

"No, you tried to convince me you and five of your monkey-boys would be enough to take care of our Asset problem. I'm saying Thorne failed. You ain't gonna do better." He paused. "Recon only. Do not engage."

"Understood," Aaron replied. He sounded as if he might think Firenzei overreacted.

"Look, Aaron. I've sent the Kabs downstairs now. They'll let us know when the next cycle winds down. We've got plenty of Radonic Transmitters left, enough to get us all Earthside."

"I wondered about that."

"What I'm saying is, let's get your boys home, right? Once the next cycle terminates, we'll get the fuck off this rock. In the meantime, I just need to know we won't have any more surprises."

"Okay." Now Aaron's tone felt more solid. "I get it."

"Good man," Firenzei replied. "I'm going to take these boys to the Cliffside Bays. If our Assets took off for the caves, that's the next closest entrance."

As he spoke, the other men nodded and made general sounds of assent. The slender fellow picked up the automatic weapon he'd been cleaning and began to load.

"Got it," the words came scratchily over the box. "We're stepping outside now."

"Gotta move, boys." Firenzei stepped over to one of the lockers, opening it smoothly.

"Cliffside?" One of the men grunted. "You think they'd go that far?"

"I think I don't take risks with the Gentlemen." Firenzei pulled out a large weapons case, which appeared to be nothing more than a bulky leather briefcase. "All we have to do is make it one more cycle. Then we can light this fucking place up and say good riddance once and for all."

What did *that* mean?

Bishop, we got company. Wyatt's link startled me. *Couple of your pals in those white cloaks.*

Crap. I watched Firenzei gesture to his thugs, who followed him out into the original passageway. *I'm not exactly in a position to run back outside, Wyatt.*

If I have to engage, it won't be pretty. I can take these out, sure. But the moment I do, their screamin' will give us away.

I get it. I gritted my teeth. *I can't get there, man. Sorry.*

Understood. I felt the large man sigh. *Just wanted you to be aware.*

Our situation is green for the moment, Anya informed me.

"Let's get this done," one of the men grumbled as he walked past me. "I'm ready to go home."

I stood alone in the empty room. It took an act of will to not instantly toggle down the *Wraith*. After running it this long, I couldn't help but tremble, feeling as if I were strung out on diet pills and espresso. Making matters worse, I faced an important decision.

Wyatt and Anya weren't exactly geared for combat. Obviously, they'd both come through brilliantly so far, but we'd been pushing the odds.

I didn't care for that. Experience showed if we pushed the odds too long, they'd begin to push back.

Firenzei had proven to be a wealth of information, even in the brief moments of discussion I'd caught. More than anything, I wanted to follow him to the Cliffside Bays. I felt certain, if I spent enough time around the man, most of my questions would be answered.

Except that required continuous use of the *Wraith*. Driven by jitters, hyperactivity, and poor decision making, I'd eventually misstep. Or even face the more dire side effects of the *Wraith*. Our situation remained rather delicate. I truly felt as if I needed to give the packet a rest.

Tell me you're okay, I linked.

Do not over concern yourself, Michael. I felt Anya's cold calm. *The hostiles have not seen us.*

They haven't exactly been hostile yet, I pointed out.

They're still very close, Wyatt interjected. *However, our situation seems to have downgraded from 'fucking insane' to 'batshit crazy.'*

We are well in this moment. Anya paused. *Michael, you are considerably closer to the emanation point. Do you have any data to report?*

I have lots of data to report, I confirmed. Without realizing it, Anya had refocused me on Locale One. Despite Firenzei and all the weirdness, one fact remained:

We needed to get home.

Anything interesting, Hoss?

It's not vital this second. However, I haven't quite closed on Locale One. Which is what matters.

Correct, Michael.

So if you're safe enough, I'm pressing on. I'll inform you when I'm on site.

Inform us soon, Hoss. Wyatt's seriousness surprised me. *I'd rather not hafta cook anyone alive out here. We still ain't got a plan to get blondie and me inside.*

I hope we don't need to. I peered down the passage to make certain the thugs had moved on. *If I can patch Anya enough data, I hope she can direct me once I'm inside. Maybe I can shut this device down, and we can return to our entry point and punch our way home.*

Possible, she mused. *My readings show the realmwall suffered damage where we came through. If I can assist you to halt the emanations bolstering it, we may not need to enter at all.*

That's my hope. I gave her a small grin.

A reasonable plan, Michael. Contact us when you know more.

Will comply. I nodded.

As I severed the link, I turned toward the other door in the room. The triangle indicator blinked cheerily, pointing toward the source of the emanations.

It hung just a bit below my feet, several meters in front of me.

Downstairs. Firenzei had sent the Kabs below—obviously referring to the cloaked individuals. *Some kind of cycle, wasn't it?* He'd said something about a device that would allow him and his goons to go home. It didn't feel like a huge stretch to consider Anya's emanations might be involved.

After peeking back out into the empty hallway, I powered down the *Wraith*. Instantly, the sensation of hyper-jittery energy vanished, even as color bled back into my sight.

Stilettos drawn, I trotted toward the door.

238

4

The stairwell beyond lay wreathed in partial shadow, illuminated only by one of those floating orbs of radiance. Now that I didn't have to struggle with the colorless view of the *Wraith*, I saw the sphere burned an electric blue.

Heat brushed against me the moment I opened the door, but as I passed deeper, it only became more pronounced. Under my feet, the stone steps remained smooth, mirror-perfect black. I took care with each stride, noting again the twisted echo that came from the slightest scuff or misstep.

If I canted my head just so to listen, I occasionally heard a thick burble, a noise akin to boiling mud.

"*¿LLemviis nor an Twai?*" The phrase came from below, warbling and reflecting around me. The words felt graceful, fluid to my ear.

"K'sai." The light tones of the robed woman reached my ears. I quickly took a few more steps down and hoped their conversation would mask my echoing footfalls.

Ahead, the stairwell bled into a room. The chamber extended to my right, most of it around the corner. I couldn't see much of the space within.

According to my mapping overlay, I entered from functional east, in the southernmost corner. Dull light flickered on what I considered to be the southern wall and cast dim shadows against that dark surface.

"*Rev'anata.*" The first voice's musical tone captivated me. I felt certain this language must be different than the harsher one spoken by those in the white robes, but as I could understand neither, it scarcely mattered.

Carefully, I peered around the corner.

The entire chamber might have been constructed from one piece of smooth, volcanic glass. Its reflective surface caught and amplified every bit of available light, causing it to shine in the dark. The only source of true illumination in the room stood near the center, yet I couldn't see it well. Great stone columns, ringed in a reddish shine, cast stark shadows all around the alcove.

One of those columns, ten times as thick as my torso, lay directly between me and the origin of that luminescence.

I frowned, thinking. I really shouldn't engage the *Wraith* again, not this soon. Yet one important fact taunted me, forcing me to truly consider all my options.

Directly behind that stone pillar, in the center of the light, the blue triangular marker merrily twinkled. Whatever it might be, this also happened to be the source of our spectral emanations.

I needed a closer look.

Fuck.

Cautiously, I picked my way across the floor, choosing each step with care. The thick column provided a wide shadow for me to move within and kept me well out of sight from my two robed friends.

If that muffled conversation ended, I could trigger the *Wraith* in an instant. No reason to rely on technology when simple stealth would do.

They continued their discourse as I crept forward, musical, lilting speech followed by short phrases with lots of hard "ck" sounds. I paused, listening intently.

Nothing. Nothing I could make out, anyway. For the thousandth time, I wished my Crown came with translation firmware. After a moment, I gave up any attempt at understanding and focused on the chamber around me.

And paused, attention snagged.

Within a few steps I saw the odd pools. Crystalline growths surrounded them in a ring, scintillating violet structures approximately the diameter of a small barrel. The crystals jutted up out of the floor, none more than twenty centimeters high. A reddish-silver liquid burbled within the pool releasing shimmering waves of furious heat.

The first of these wells lay quite close to the shadow I used to hide. I crept up to the stone pillar itself, pressed against its coolness, and studied the boiling liquid.

Metal. It reminded me of a mudpot, boiling and burbling away. However, instead of volcanic fury and mud, the primary material seemed to be molten ore.

I crouched and squinted. Using my optics to enhance the image, I zoomed in as if I had binoculars.

"*Un'vala din,*" that sweet voice crooned from the opposite side of the column.

I ignored it as I took several images and stored them in my Crown. The small well resembled a tiny volcano. Its crystalline walls had pushed up through the obsidian of the floor, cracking and marring the surface. At the top, an unknown element boiled and burbled with unimaginable heat.

And yet, as I studied the formation with my optics, I saw even more I couldn't understand. Attached to the side of the well, tubular, gelatinous tendrils suckled on the crystalline formation.

What is it with tentacles today? I snorted, though these appeared completely different from the floating masses of murder tentacles I'd seen earlier.

The one I examined had three grotesque, arm-like organs latched to the outside of those amethystine stones. These appeared as ichor-covered parodies of human hands with five grasping phalanges. Where a person's wrist might be, the tentacles resolved into a singular membranous tube, colorless and clear. This vein looped and stretched out of my sight. Inhuman organs pulsed and writhed within, performing tasks I couldn't comprehend.

I turned away, revulsion boiling in my gut to match my suddenly aching head. After a couple of breaths, I examined the area further and noted even more amethystine volcanoes. They felt natural in this environment. The wriggling, suckling veins, however, inspired an elemental dread, a feeling of base disgust.

241

Pressing myself against the stone column, I slipped around the edge to better study the source of the emanations.

"Yvari Ness." The sibilant whisper echoed in the chamber.

As I peeked around the edge, I beheld the speaker for the first time.

I stared into that burning gaze and froze in place, eyes wide. The two Kabs stood with their backs to me, stark silhouettes against the bright orange light. Within the circle of pillars stood the largest of the crystalline wells—a structure approximately four steps wide and over a meter high.

Within, a figure of molten wrath loomed.

It stood at least four, maybe five meters tall, its body a dully glowing reddish-silver. Its head appeared somewhat like a malformed skull, covered with viscous, molten ore. The body stretched from within that well, comprised entirely of whatever unknown element boiled inside. It gazed down upon the Kabs, eyes shining with raw, crackling force.

The power of the creature terrified me for reasons I couldn't say. I didn't feel threatened by it, exactly, not like I had with the tentacular horrors of earlier. No, this particular awe felt akin to gazing upon a vast thunderstorm or visiting a city while a hurricane swept through the streets. It felt like staring at an ocean in storm or beholding the eye of a volcano.

I triggered the *Wraith*, specs be damned. The scene faded into monochrome as cool shadows settled around me.

"Ienrym Eaildrin Nie," the hulking shape informed them, its dulcet tones calming. It motioned, as if about to say more, then glanced sharply up.

Those hellish eyes bore directly into me. Or, at the place I crouched, invisible, on the other side of the pillar. I felt their touch like burning silk across my skin.

Shit! I linked, completely by mistake. I hurled myself back behind the pillar, hoping against desperate, unreasonable hope that the creature had failed to spot me.

It couldn't have seen me, after all, *couldn't* have. The *Wraith* functioned perfectly. The initial readouts on my visual array showed the packet in impeccable order.

I forcibly calmed my breath. My pulse felt like a hammer in my temples.

Hoss? I felt Wyatt's worry much more than his snark. *Here's where you tell me yer situation is green.*

Hold please, I linked as I slipped around to the other side of the column. After I made certain the *Wraith* remained toggled, I peeked cautiously around the edge.

The molten behemoth gestured toward me with one elongated, sinuous arm. A sphere of molten material broke off from the main mass, instantly forming a reflective globule. As if imbued with a will of its own, it darted out from the main body, straight toward my hiding place.

I whirled to keep that sphere within sight. Yet, instead of stopping where I crouched, the globe shot by. It came to an instantaneous halt approximately ten steps back in the direction of the stairs, over the upraised hand of a dark figure.

Its light shone across his features and made the truth plain. The third of the Kabs, the man I'd seen charge off into the caverns rather than speak with Firenzei, had returned.

"Kavast din!" The older man called to the other two figures. He moved his hand around and the hovering globe followed— allowing light from the molten sphere to shine further into the gloom. Squinting, he scanned the area.

When that light drifted across my form, I felt sick, certain I'd be caught. More than once, his gaze drifted across me.

Michael, I must insist upon an update.

Anya, I need to focus on what I'm doing. I'm safe for the moment.

The man took a few steps closer, again scanning in all directions. He seemed certain he might find something and stepped with exceeding caution.

I remained still as a stone, taking only the lightest and quietest of breaths. The *Wraith* did its best work when it had little to mask. If I simply remained still and silent, the packet would keep me hidden.

As the robed man drew closer, I took several stills from my visual array and saved them. I found it difficult to determine exactly why I felt him to be so much older than his two counterparts. Without significant hair on his head, I couldn't see a lot to make out the vagaries of age. With each step I searched for other small details, such as some faint wrinkles around his eyes or an overall slimness of his hands.

I finally realized it was his gait. The man strode with a kind of quiet grace, certainty in each step. I associated the way he moved with someone both cautious and wise. Therefore, he appeared older.

"Korvassi?" a feminine voice called out uncertainly from the other side of the pillar.

"Kavast din," the older man repeated solidly. He walked to the place where I'd previously crouched, the exact spot I suspected the molten monster might have glimpsed my shadowed form.

There he turned and strode straight toward me.

I pressed myself against the column as quickly and quietly as possible.

The robed figure stalked my way, eyes scanning left and right. That globe hovered over his outstretched hand, liquid, molten light. Without word or warning, he leapt, nimble and amazingly swift.

Little more than a blur, the Kab spun in mid-air, and connected his booted foot to the side of my invisible face with a swift, devastating kick.

He moved like poetry, like a song on the wind.

He hadn't even *looked* toward me when he struck.

"Aaarkk!" I stealthily grunted as the kick sent me stumbling sideways.

Without a pause, without a breath, the robed figure continued

244

his sinuous motion. He flawlessly leapt off his first foot as it landed and brought his other boot around to catch me with a second strike.

That dropped me. I collapsed to the ground, my bell thoroughly rung. Consciousness slipped away, like the setting sun.

Bishop? I jerked awake as Wyatt linked, his worry muffled as if through mud.

I tried to answer, but couldn't. Darkness seeped in around the edges of my mind.

Someone, someone incredibly far away, reached beneath my arms. Vaguely, I felt them hoist me. I fought for awareness, tried to drag my mind into focus.

I need a system report on Asset 108, Anya linked from the other side of the galaxy.

System recalibration in process, my Crown reported to us both. **Asset experienced disruption in consciousness. Booting primary plexus now.**

Oh.

OH!

Fuck.

That message meant my packets had all gone offline. With the *Wraith* powered down, they'd caught me easily.

"Kiva. Kiva!"

Rough hands lifted me to a standing position, then dragged me forward. I shook my head, trying to remember why someone had smashed cement blocks against my skull.

In front of me, orange luminescence burned in my blurry vision. I felt hot, as if I stood before a forge.

I blinked, trying to get a clear view.

Please respond, Michael.

I will, I promised. *Just gimme a sec.*

The people who held my arms muttered to each other in a harsh, unknown tongue. Their words bent strangely, warbling as if underwater.

"Hot." I closed my eyes against the heat. When I opened them, I saw the inside of the well. My captors held me a scarce half meter from the crystalline structure.

My bleariness burned away in the face of that terrible furnace. My focus sharpened into razor-sharp surety, as I recalled the skull-headed thing—

No. No creature loomed within the boiling fury.

Instead the thick liquid bubbling inside the well held a hint of deep crimson, so dark it scarcely gave off any light. Iridescent color spewed around the molten silver metal like an oil-slicked rainbow. Blue slid to aqua and green while yellow and pink glinted in my gaze. They coruscated in an ever-shifting sheen over the base silver, and a hellish red molten tone covered it all.

The Kabs wrestled me closer to the fury of that alien furnace.

"No—!" I struggled, assuming they meant to dunk me.

The room echoed eerily, sounding much, much larger than it appeared.

With a rumbling burble, the gurgles intensified and furious heat rolled over me. Sweat dripped from my skin and made my clothes cling as the liquid boiled.

"Stop!" I pulled against one of my captors.

A molten globule lurched up from the basin, startling me into silence. The amorphous blob of glowing metal twisted in the air before plopping back into the liquefied fire. Then it reached upward again...

...and formed into a crude, skeletal hand.

"Oh fuck, no!" I gaped as I jerked back with a gasp.

The skeletal hand reached up and molten silver ran down the slender appendage in slow, blueish rivulets. It twitched, reminding me of someone in the grips of a spasm.

"No," I repeated. The word fell from my lips like a lead weight.

More molten liquid rose, a deformed human skeleton that dripped with igneous sunlight. As I watched, the skull craned toward me with infernal motes of fury shining in the eye sockets. The creature possessed no jawbone, only the top portion of the skull and empty light in its eyes.

Yet, with sound echoing from beneath the world, it *spoke*.

"*¿LLemviis nor an Twai?*" The words echoed sharply, sibilant sounds that seemed rounded and edged all at once. They reverberated, echoing slantways through the air. A question, seemingly, but I had no way to answer.

Michael?

Patch incoming. I included all my sensory data from the last few moments and hurried it along, porting to their memory.

Shit, Wyatt elocuted.

"*¿LLemviis nor an Twai?*" the figure demanded again, dripping ribbons of molten silver. It leaned closer, its eyes wide.

Had they widened when I sent the patch, at that exact same moment?

Maybe.

"If you think I can understand what you're saying, you're mistaken." I struggled against the men holding me, wishing I could reach either my Stilettos or my blades.

"*Paach.*" The form spoke again, embers of crimson fury screaming in its eye sockets. "*Paach enkomig. Sheeet.*" It cocked its skull at me.

…It had repeated my link back to me, with Wyatt's response.

Without warning, it lunged forward, swift as a serpent.

"Fucking—!" I lurched away but found myself held fast.

Yet the thing hadn't been lurching at me at all.

It reached with those ungainly limbs, dripping molten metal. The skeleton's arm flew swiftly and uncannily true, stretching as it reached for its target.

The young woman.

She hadn't been one of the hands wresting me forward. Instead, she remained standing by the well as her two nefarious partners came and hauled the handsome off-worlder out of the shadows.

As the molten abomination reached for her, it flung a spray of melted ore in her direction. Those droplets sizzled where they touched her darker-than-midnight skin, and I smelled her flesh as it burned.

Her scream painted exquisite agony across the darkened room.

Gasping, I gazed up at the creature. It stood motionless in its basin and glared at us with eyes of elemental fury.

When I regarded the young woman, however, I gaped.

Her slender boots hung centimeters off the floor. She hovered, every muscle quivering. Tiny droplets of glowing silver sizzled on her face.

The drops moved of their own accord, branding angular patterns in her flesh.

We're comin' in, Hoss.

We are green, Michael. The patrol moved on.

Dunno how we'll get in yet, but you dropped that marker. We'll start there.

"No." I shook my head, the word a despairing whisper. *Fuck no. Remain.*

"*We main,*" the skull mimicked. "*Kno. We main.*"

An aura of crimson fury hung about the young woman, and her eyes burned with wrathful light. She turned toward me, those terrible eyes empty and desolate. They radiated white fury, a light that cast no shadow.

When she spoke, I *knew* her words made no sense, just like the creature's. This time, however, I understood. The words burned in my mind, keening a lost and terrible song.

MICHAEL BISHOP. YOU ARE A CATALYST OF THE ORDINAL STONE, FRACTURING 1309-971.

"I'm..." I canted my head at her, completely gobsmacked. "I'm a what now?"

THIS ATRIFICIA IS IN ALIGNMENT WITH YOUR FRACTURED SHARD. The woman paused, her head ticking slightly to one side. THIS CONFIGURATION IS AWAKENED. CURRENT STRANDS BEAR A NULL CHARGE AND ARE SEVERAL DEGREES ASYMMETRIC. PATTERN STRINGS HAVE BEEN REROUTED FOR NON-PRISTINE PURPOSES.

"I'm confused." I stood up straight and stared at the midnight-skinned woman. An aura of scarlet fury burned around her, and her eyes showed only the whites.

When I glanced to the two men holding me, I saw stern, devout faces. These guys were fanatics. I'd do well to remember that.

YOU ARE A CATALYST OF THE ORDINAL STONE. YOU BEAR THE CAPABILITY TO ALTER THE STATE OF THIS LOCALE. She paused. DO YOU ACCEPT THE CURRENT CONFIGURATION?

"Um, I guess?" I blinked, befuddled. "Can these guys let me go or what?" I glanced over my shoulder at one of my captors, the younger man.

DO YOU ACCEPT THAT WE ARE WITHIN ALIGNMENT?

"If that means your goons back down, then yes." I cleared my throat. "We are within alignment."

Instantly, the two men released me. I stumbled just a bit but caught myself.

THE SATHANTÜR CONFIGURATION IS WHOLE AND FUNCTIONING. WE ARE FULLY PREPARED TO BEGIN OPERATIONS.

"What operations?" I glanced from the spooky woman hanging

in the air back to the figure clad in molten ore. In the center of the well burned the blue triangle marker, the source of our alien emanations.

Right. I needed to stay on the ball here.

CURRENT REQUIREMENTS ARE OBVIOUS, she said, without a touch of scold in her echoing tone. STRANDS BEAR A NULL CHARGE AND ARE SEVERAL DEGREES ASYMMETRIC. PATTERN STRINGS HAVE BEEN REROUTED FOR NON-PRISTINE PURPOSES. BOTH SITUATIONS CREATE DANGEROUS INCONGRUITIES.

"You need help." I nodded, feeling as if I'd caught up at last. "I have no idea what most of that means, but words like 'non-pristine' and 'asymmetric' imply a problem."

WHILE ASYMMETRY EXISTS, THIS ATRIFICIA IS UNSTABLE. THE QUADRARY DICTUM STATES ALL ALIGNED CATALYSTS MUST STRIVE FOR SYMMETRY.

"Wait." I narrowed my eyes as I realized. "That would mean you expect assistance from 'Catalysts' who are 'in alignment'?" I turned from the woman to the lurking molten figure, feeling a bit duped.

TWO OTHER CATALYSTS ARE WITHIN THE ATRIFICIA. WE SHALL BRING THEM TO US AND DISCUSS NEEDED OPERATIONS.

"Two other…" It took me a moment, but the truth smacked me in the face at last. "You mean my cadre. There are two other Assets." I blinked. "You *did* hear our links."

YOU ARE EACH CATALYSTS OF THE ORDINAL

STONE, the young woman replied, as if that explained everything. INFORM THEM THEY SHALL NOT BE HARMED. WE ARE IN ALIGNMENT.

"Copy that," I responded, amazed. "I will... inform them."

The spooky levitating lady said nothing after that. I watched her for a long moment before opening a link.

Situation green.

A long pause followed. *Please apprise.*

Patch incoming, I responded. *I suggest you port this to memory immediately.*

Why do I have the feeling you're sending us nothing but trouble? Wyatt groused.

Because you're a God-damned genius, I responded, porting the data. *You understand how these situations tend to play out.*

Seconds later Wyatt opened the link again. *Damnit, Hoss.* I felt bone weariness in that link. *What have you gone and kicked up this time?*

I'm really not certain. I regarded the eerie woman and the molten behemoth which puppeted her.

For once, I really didn't have anything to say.

5

Less than ten minutes later, Anya and Wyatt stepped into the light of the well and its inhuman inhabitant. Other than to communicate our basic status, we kept the links to a minimum as the Kabs escorted them within.

My packet contained all the data needed to prove the molten skull-head could receive and understand our links.

Therefore, caution.

"Hey there, Hoss." Wyatt paced into the dull half-light and smiled. "You *sure* you wouldn't prefer hangin' out at The Booby Trap and drinkin' yer afternoon away? The ladies there are all kindsa friendly."

"Maybe I was mistaken about that. I'm just not accustomed to you being right." I shook my head. "You'll have to forgive me."

Anya ignored our quips and kept her eyes firmly focused on the form in the well. As she slowly walked forward, her fingers performed an undulating dance, twitching as she read telemetry.

"There." I stared up into the creature's burning eyes. "Now everybody is present and accounted for."

It remained silent, gazing back at me with hollow, ember filled orbs. That stare said nothing, indicated no human emotion. Before it, I felt like a speck, a mote of nothingness against infinity.

In that moment, I couldn't help but worry that Wyatt had been right.

Parabola

WYATT GUTHRIE. ANYA PETROVA. YOU ARE EACH A CATALYST OF THE ORDINAL STONE, FRACTURE 1309-971.

"I am uncertain what you mean." Anya turned from the igneous creature and regarded the floating woman calmly. "We have never been referred to in that fashion."

WE HAVE AN ALIGNMENT. The young woman tilted her head slightly as she studied Anya. Her eyes burned with the spectral light. THIS ATRIFICIA HAS AN ACCORD WITH YOUR FRAGMENTATION OF THE ORDINAL STONE.

"I took that to mean burny-face here thinks we're buddies," I confided to Wyatt.
"Yeah." He nodded, stoically regarding the woman. "I get it."

THIS CONFIGURATION IS AWAKENED. CURRENT STRANDS BEAR A NULL CHARGE AND ARE SEVERAL DEGREES ASYMMETRIC. PATTERN STRINGS HAVE BEEN REROUTED FOR NON-PRISTINE PURPOSES.

"When… 'she' said that before, I didn't quite get it." I turned from the woman to Anya. "But it seems as if things aren't exactly functional."
"Pattern strings." Anya peered at the woman. "That term is used by my equipment interface."

LOCAL PATTERN STRINGS HAVE BEEN REROUTED, the woman repeated. YOU MAY HAVE WITNESSED THIS

YOURSELF.

"The filaments within my interface are incorrectly aligned."
Anya brushed a strand of golden hair from her face. "Is that what
you refer to?"

THESE FORCES ARE BEING CHANNELED INTO AN
ALTERNATE PATH.

"Yeah, I'll bet." Wyatt crossed his arms and glanced toward
Anya and myself meaningfully.

"You will?" I shook my head, just a bit. "Do you know
something about this, Bubba?"

"Damn, you're dumb." My large friend chuckled.

"It's probably just that you're a genius," I snarked.

"I'll go ahead and walk you through it. If I go too fast, just say
so, and I'll use smaller words."

"Please." I gestured toward him. "Educate me."

"I know you're not a man for contemplatin' yer mission."
Wyatt guffawed. "But we're on this carnival ride because the
Facility found crazy-ass spikes in Rationality. Remember? The big
scary ripples that threatened the integrity of reality itself?"

"I remember." I watched the igneous creature regard us as we
spoke. How much of the conversation did it follow?

"So we head out searchin' for the source. As soon as we hit the
deep desert, Anya reads another spike. We get caught in its
energetic wake and deposited here in creepy-cave town."

"This is the energy source," Anya realized. "This is what
powered the spikes in Rationality. That is why I read the
emanations from this place."

"Gotta be." Wyatt nodded. "When it says 'forces are being
channeled into an alternate path'..." He gave a gentle kick at one
of the grotesque veins that suckled at the amethystine well.

"Do you know who is responsible for this?" I asked the figure directly. "We might be more 'in alignment' than I realized at first."

THEY ARE A VIRULENT SPECIES; A RACE OF PARASITES. The Kab woman stared at me, and her eyes burned with white flame. THEY CAME WITH THEIR SERVITORS AND BUILT THE PARABOLA. WITH THIS DEVICE, THEY ALTERED THE BASE NATURE OF THIS PLACE.

Wyatt met my gaze, and I knew we shared the same thought. 'Parasite' had a very specific association in our minds after our recent experiences with tentacular horrors.

"Parabola?" Anya tilted her head, a touch uncertain.

"Yeah." I nodded. "I forgot I haven't exactly shared all the secrets of my adventure with you. Hold on."

I assembled a patch, one comprised mostly of Firenzei's ramblings. I made certain to accentuate his discussions regarding 'the Parabola' and how they only needed to await the completion of a single cycle before they got off this rock.

"Here. This is what I meant earlier, when I linked that I had lots of data to report." I forwarded the link.

"Earthside," Wyatt mused as he perused the data. "Thorne didn't just teleport away, she shifted realities."

"They're traveling back and forth." I chewed on my lip.

"The energetic requirements to repeatedly breach the axiomatic realmwall would be..." Anya stared off into space for a moment and then shook her head. "Stunning."

"Do they have a purpose?" I regarded the hovering woman, trying not to be creeped out by her empty gaze. "Do you know why they're doing all this?"

THIS SPECIES IS WELL KNOWN FOR THEIR IMPERIALISTIC NATURE, the woman responded, her echoing words haunting. CURRENTLY, THEY HARVEST THE FORCE FROM THIS ATRIFICIA TO OPEN WEFTINGWAYS INTO A

SPECIFIC ALTERNATE REALITY.

"Into Rationality." Wyatt glanced from Anya to me. "Earth. Those squiggly shits are planning some kind of invasion."

"This place is a staging area," I agreed. "Those spikes were likely just them getting their equipment ramped up."

"Working with humans too," Wyatt growled. "Irrats."

"You said something about required operations?" I turned my gaze back to the Kab woman, the vessel for the Atrificia's voice. "Do these operations require destruction of the Parabola or the defeat of this parasitical species?"

THE DESTRUCTION OF THE PARABOLA, A TASK BEYOND THOSE WHO TEND TO THIS ATRIFICIA. The woman began to twitch, her back arching into a bow. YET ONCE IT IS DESTROYED, HARVESTING ESSENTIAL FORCE FROM THIS LOCATION SHALL BECOME IMPOSSIBLE.

"That sounds like something right up our alley." Wyatt turned to Anya. "'Course, if we destroy the mechanism the 'Rats use to go Earthside, we might find ourselves permanently adrift."

"Radonic Transmitters," I muttered, perusing the packet I'd sent. "That's what Firenzei said they needed to get the fuck off this rock."

THE RADONIC TRANSMITTERS ARE SMALL ORBS, POWERED BY THE FORCE HARVESTED FROM THIS LOCATION. CURRENTLY, SEVERAL GAIN HARMON-IZATION FROM THE PARABOLA ITSELF.

"On a cycle, I bet." I remembered Firenzei's assertion that 'once the next cycle terminated,' they could leave.

"That may be it, Hoss." Wyatt gave me a toothy grin. "First, steal their transmitters—and I'd bet they're exactly like the little

258

bronze doodad Thorne used to jump ship."

"I'd bet you're right," I agreed.

"Next," he continued, "blow their Parabola right the fuck up. Then skip town and leave 'em hangin'. Simple."

"Sounds like it." I eyed the eerie floating woman as my heart sank. "Maybe too simple."

"Can you direct us to the Parabola?" Anya stepped closer to the Kab. "If you do so, it is possible we can disable the device."

WE CAN PROVIDE MORE THAN THIS, ANYA PETROVA. The woman cocked her head as she spoke. ONCE YOU ARE PREPARED TO BEGIN THE OPERATION, WE WILL PROVIDE YOU WITH AN ESCORT TO THE PRECISE LOCATION OF THE MECHANISM.

"That's it then. Easy-peasy." Wyatt shrugged his shoulders and adjusted his Stetson. "That's all I need to know."

"Yeah." I turned from him to the igneous guardian. "Me too."

Yet some intuition nagged at me. I trusted the molten figure— it gave me no reason to believe it might have deceived us. In fact, the moment we'd begun to discuss our options, our situation had come into focus.

Clear, perfect focus. Our situation made sense.

That bothered me.

In my time with the Facility, I'd been on dozens and dozens of bizarre dossiers. I'd seen otherworldly horrors, witnessed mad humans summoning aberrations from the stark shadows outside reality.

I'd experienced wonders and horrors that beggared the imagination. Yet, now we had a clear direction, an obvious path. As Wyatt said, the situation had become simple.

In my experience, that's the way things always were...

Right before they went to hell.

2

"Kavasti." The night-skinned young woman, now released from the will of the igneous intellect, gestured for us to follow her down a narrow, winding passageway.

Over her left hand, a sphere of the molten metal floated, casting eerie light around us.

The entire hall gleamed subtly, every surface comprised of black, mirrored stone. Our shadows loomed stark behind us.

She gestured again, impatiently waving us onward.

"Yes. Forward." Wyatt rolled his eyes.

"Where else would we go?" I glanced at Wyatt, who wore the slightest smirk on his face.

We followed her through the winding passages for fifteen minutes, according to my system.

"There have been plenty of opportunities for us to wander into other openings," Anya noted. "This is a warren of corridors. We never would have found our way through them."

"I'm hopin' the Irrat assholes never found their way into this warren," Wyatt grumbled. "It's one thing if we have a secret passage through the place. It's another if we have to fight in here. There's no room."

I should be in front, I linked. *If anything does come along, it's up to Hillbilly Hank to take them out. I can't possibly aim past all three of you.*

Rosie will take care of it. Wyatt caressed the business end of the Tangler. *We'll be just fine.*

Before I could wittily retort, the Kab woman halted in place and traced her slender fingers along the smooth stone wall. She then leaned close to the surface and pressed her ear against its coolness.

"Kim lo gionva," she whispered and gestured at Wyatt.

"I completely understand what you're saying right now." He

nodded seriously. "I find your plan both brilliant and wise."

"There is something on the other side of that surface," Anya informed us. Her head twitched once, then again, as her right hand drifted higher. Her fingertips pulled and plucked at her interface as she read her data.

Interesting point, I linked to Wyatt. *Anya just told us her interface is largely metaphorical. Yet ol' magma-face really seems to speak her language.*

Didn't seem that metaphorical, did it? Wyatt asked. *Pattern strings and all.*

That's what I mean! I frowned. *Then there's that 'Ordinal Stone' bit. I mean, the Designates use an Ordinal slate to process data!*

I've opted to ignore the oddities of this place for now. Wyatt slid his gaze in my direction and raised an eyebrow. *It's a little too creepy. The Facility obviously had dealin's in this realm, but I can't imagine what that's all about.*

I'm surprised you don't think it's about reptilians. Maybe it's some Atlantean conspiracy?

We don't talk about Atlantean conspiracies. Wyatt pulled the Stetson low on his head. *At least not without the Illuminati findin' out about it.*

"Ambient Rationality is significantly modified approximately twenty-five meters in this direction." Anya gestured at the wall.

"We can't exactly phase through solid stone." I gently knocked at the surface, wishing I'd taken the *Spectre* instead of the *Wraith*.

"Kith!" the Kab hissed and grabbed my hand to stop the knocking. She shook her head violently.

"Sorry." I backed away from the wall. "It might help if you could actually give us some direction here."

"Ki'zaer Mud a'lib." She traced her fingers along the smoothness of the wall again. Her brow creased and she bit her lip, as if concentrating. Then she stopped and gave us a brief smile. "Karaza." She pushed on a small indentation.

With the slightest whisper of pressure, the stone swung outward, just a centimeter or two. A stream of white light shone into our narrow passage.

"Well, that's handy." Wyatt arched an eyebrow at Anya, then me.

"Kith!" the young woman hissed again, a syllable I assumed meant 'Shut your Facility hole!' She gestured meaningfully at the slender opening and pushed it just a touch wider.

"Ah." I nodded. "This might be a good time for someone to be invisible."

"Rationality remains altered in this location," Anya informed me.

"You usually give more information than that, Twitchy," Wyatt drawled.

"Typically my readings are static." She plucked with the fingers of her left hand as she spoke. "Oftentimes ambient Rationality is altered a few points or specifically weakened at a location."

"Here, I assume it's weird?" I gave her what I hoped was a wry smile. "Like the laws of physics are on fire or have become sentient snakes or something?"

"For reasons I cannot ascertain, the baseline axiomatic numerics continue to shift." She frowned, focusing upon her visual array. "Nothing fatal. It is not as if the air becomes unbreathable or the temperature fluctuates wildly. It is simply that physics grow more fluid as we continue onward."

"Well, that's both meaningless and terrifying." I nodded, slipping past her in the narrow corridor. "How's the nature of light? Is the *Wraith* going to explode or melt my face or something?"

"Not immediately, no." Anya gave me the tiniest hint of a nod. "I show only a seven percent probability of the *Wraith* creating cascading errors through your perceptual nodes."

"Wait." I halted in place. "You're serious?"

"It is quite unlikely initiating the packet will immediately terminate your visual array," she said, not at all soothingly. "I feel confident in my capability to inform you before that happens."

"Great." I gave her a wan smile. "That's just wonderful."

"I suggest not leaving the *Wraith* toggled longer than is absolutely necessary. As long as you do not over-rely on the packet, you should be fine."

"Understood." I stepped past her, hugging the wall to slip by Wyatt.

"Kiravista Dun lo," the Kab hissed as I approached. She gestured sharply through the crevice, as if I might not understand the need for secrecy.

"Kith!" I responded, half mockingly.

The woman's eyes grew wide, stunned.

I toggled the *Wraith* and faded from sight entirely.

"K'ora dama nun." She nodded her approval and pushed the wall a bit more.

As soon as the gap widened sufficiently, I slipped through. Static immediately crackled at the edge of my visual array.

Anya! I fought to keep the panic out of my link. *Tell me the* Wraith *is fine.*

You are well within functionality, Michael. I felt her certainty. *I will inform you if packet degradation begins.*

Good. I couldn't help but shake my head. *Because I don't want that.*

The broad passageway appeared easily wide enough for three or four Wyatts to walk abreast. Unlike the slender, obsidian corridor we'd slipped through, this portion of the Atrificia resembled the Cavern Bay doors. Metal and glass gleamed all around me, obviously newer construction.

So, do we assume the invading parasite is responsible for the sci-fi look? I peered to my left, as far down the passage as possible. The hallway in that direction terminated in a thick, stainless-steel door, complete with one of those annoying biometric readers.

I am uncertain what you mean, Michael. Anya paused. *It appears the fluidity in ambient Rationality originates from your right, functional north.*

Copy that. I turned right and ghosted down the hallway.

I assume Mr. Fancy Pants is referring to the differences we found in the structure, Wyatt linked. *Outside all stainless-steel and futuristic glass. Yet the deeper we went inside, the more it seemed like sculpted caverns of stone.*

My pants aren't that fancy. Ahead, the passageway turned to the right at a ninety-degree angle toward functional east. *But yes. I wonder if our parasitical invaders made the construction upgrades.*

I don't know that the Kabs have the technological mastery to create some of what we've seen, Wyatt mused. *It makes sense that squiggly might have been responsible.*

We don't know *squiggly is the parasite,* I realized. *Think about this: Remember how we noticed the script on the hem of the Kabs' robes? We saw the same symbols on the infected goons outside.*

Hey. I felt Wyatt's sudden confusion. *That's true! D'you think the goons used to be on the Kabs' side?*

Man, I don't even know. I peeked around the corner. *It's just something to think about.*

The passageway beyond stretched for approximately ten meters. Like the one I stood in, the construct displayed all the hallmarks of a 1950s sci-fi flick. Gleaming metal surfaces shone on all sides, only interrupted by panels of blipping lights and busy readout screens.

Also, two complete jerks stood at the end of the passage.

I mean, I assumed they were jerks. Just like the ones we'd encountered earlier, they wore black riot gear and held automatic weapons. They jerkily stood guarding a doorway comprised mostly of glass, a thick and imposing structure that menaced in its own right.

Each appeared ready, focused. Not men I should take lightly.

265

I've made contact, I informed my cadre. *Two jerks, guarding a door. About ten meters away.*

Jerks? Anya's link felt a bit confused.

They're obviously jerks, Anya, Wyatt explained, shaking his head. *I mean, they're guarding a door.*

Exactly. I nodded at my friend, over the link. *Thank you.*

The source of the variables in ambient Rationality is approximately fifteen meters from you, as of now. I would suggest this effect might be caused by the Parabola.

I assumed, I linked as I studied the men. *I suppose I need to take these guys out so we can continue.*

I would suggest haste, Michael, Anya linked. *I do not particularly like the most recent tele-axiomatic ping that the* Wraith *sent. I believe you should shut it down as soon as possible.*

Copy that. I sighed.

Hadn't I just been concerned nothing could ever be simple?

Whisper quiet, I drew the katana from their shoulder sheaths. Once clear, I toggled the *Adept,* delighting at the silvery alacrity that flowed, tingling, through my limbs.

The Adept *is active,* I linked. *If this will make my skin catch fire, please let me know.*

I will let you know if that is going to happen, Anya linked in full seriousness.

I chuckled to myself and shook my head. Then I sprinted into the hallway.

3

The *Wraith* did a bit more than simply alter the workings of light. While its photic veil and diaphanic emitter rendered me nearly invisible, other workings altered the nature of sound and muffle my movement. It wasn't *complete* silence, not by any stretch of the imagination, but it was a damned sight better than nothing.

I could easily race toward the two men without being heard.

That was, if the men were baseline humans.

"Hey," one of the men said as I darted forward. His eyes opened wide, burning brilliantly as he stared squarely at me. Around him, a shadowy nimbus began to take form. "HEY!"

Michael, I read fluctuations in ambient Rationality, four meters in front of you.

Fuck.

When I leapt, the *Adept* guided my every motion. I drifted through the air, poetry and swiftness and inhuman grace. Both of my blades already swung toward him, slicing through the air.

Yet the jerk moved *faster.*

He ducked low, easily dodging the space where my katana would have sliced through his neck. With one fluid movement, he rolled to the side and brought his automatic rifle up.

Shots barked at the same moment projectiles slammed into my calf and quadriceps.

FUCK! I linked. *Hit! I'm hit!*

Shit, Wyatt swore. *Okay, Hoss. Incoming.*

"What the hell?" The second man stared at his comrade, confusion splayed across his face.

"Shoot! Shoot, you idiot!"

"At what?"

I fell flat, my leg a burning fury of pain. I couldn't tell if the shots had actually torn through the quasi-steel, but even if the bullets hadn't pierced my slacks, they still hurt like a motherfucker.

Yet the *Wraith* remained powered up, as had the *Adept*. The mere fact that my packets hadn't undergone pattern loss implied I didn't currently suffer from a mecha shortage.

I might still be in this.

No sooner did I have the thought than rippling static trickled across my array again. It lasted a touch longer this time.

I decided not to push it. After all, this chump had seen me.

I powered down both packets. Then I pushed myself up, gingerly testing my leg as I hurled myself to the left. The original shooter, a pallid, bald man with a crown of tattoos around his head, fired again. His bullets tore into the metal floor a centimeter from my hair.

I pulled my Stilettos, panic burning in my veins. I didn't even remember how I'd calibrated them last time I'd used them, but I didn't care. I aimed both weapons in the general direction of the men and started firing.

Cries of pain drowned out the shattering of glass. Behind me, heavy footsteps pounded against the metal floor as a new party entered the fray.

I rolled wildly, bringing my weapons to bear.

"Hoss!" Wyatt stopped in place, waving his hands. "Easy, asshole!"

"Holy shit!" the bald man breathed.

I glanced back at where he'd fallen, only to see him frantically crabwalk through the bent metal and broken glass. The darkness had faded from around him, and he appeared legitimately frightened.

Good.

"Damnit," Wyatt swore. He stepped forward, his hands madly scrabbling at the keys on his hip. As I pushed myself to a standing position, the Tangler resounded with a loud **WHUF.**

"Michael." Anya appeared at my side. "Are you system

green?"

"I..." I tried to put weight on my right leg and found it able to support me. It hurt like a complete bastard, but it seemed the quasi-steel hadn't been breached. "I'm fine."

"What the fuck!" someone cried from the room in front of me.

I heard Wyatt's gear chuff again and turned in that direction.

The fierce Kab woman sprinted by me, that light sphere hovering just behind her. She didn't appear to be the least bit attentive to my potential injury.

Rude.

Nodding once more at Anya, I followed.

"Let's see what you think of this!" Wyatt sounded absolutely mad. The Tangler let out another *WHUF*, and I heard a deep voice scream.

The room beyond appeared nothing like what I expected. It appeared that the invaders had done quite a bit of remodeling to the Atrificia, creating a sterile, futuristic environment. In here, however, the typical obsidian of the construct had simply been overlaid, creating an amalgam of the two incongruent styles. While the floor remained volcanic glass, two of the walls held vast computer banks, showing readouts I didn't understand. The far wall appeared to be a great glass doorway, open to the night beyond. Several four-wheeled ATVs sat parked just beyond that egress.

In the center of the room, an organic crystalline structure pulsed, fed by nearly transparent veins that spooled down from the ceiling. These writhed and throbbed, grotesque and inhuman. Above them, an arched contour of liquid light burned in the air, slowly orbiting the crystal structure with silent menace.

Occasionally, brilliant sparks danced along that hemi-spherical surface, as if caught in the wake of its turning. These coalesced into even brighter arcs of multi-colored light, which crackled furiously with energies I couldn't imagine.

I stared at the thing. It looked decidedly surreal.

"Firenzei!" A man yelled wildly into a communication device affixed to the wall. "We're taking fire down at the Parabola Bay! We require backup!"

"Yeah," Wyatt spat, turning toward the man. "You do."

WHUF. He fired the spike straight into the man's chest, moving away before it took full effect.

That man screamed wildly as he died, cooked to death while yelling at Firenzei.

Fierce as Wyatt fought, it only took a moment to realize my friend stood vastly outnumbered. At a glance, I counted at least eleven of the riot-clad jerks waiting for him within the room. Now, even though he'd cooked a few of them alive, their initial bewilderment had begun to wear off.

"Over here!" one called to his comrades from behind a large bank of computer equipment. "Take cover, you idiots!"

Not today. I grinned, half-sprinting, half-hobbling over to a niche in the wall behind the bizarre device. From here, I could take aim and remain mostly unseen.

I raised the Stilettos and shot the first man squarely in the back of the head.

Much like Edmund earlier, that single shot liquefied the man's skull.

"Oh fuck!" One of his allies had been sprinting over to him, rallied by his call.

Then the man's skull had exploded, splattering red and gray all over the metallic bank of devices.

The thug froze in place, horrified.

"K'verta!" From my left, the young Kab woman leapt, her feet spinning. Her pristine robes blurred around her as her boot connected with the side of the gaping man's face and dropped him to the ground with a sickening crack.

"Nice." I nodded at the woman.

Michael. In those two syllables, Anya made me stop short. Something had gone wrong.

270

If this is the Parabola, it is a partially energetic construct.
Much of the device does not exist within this topiatic reality.

That's just great. I spun, diving behind a bank of computers.

Next to me, the graceful young woman gestured at one of the riot-geared men who ran up on us.

Her igneous sphere hurtled toward him with all the force of a meteorite slamming to Earth. In mid-air it elongated, becoming less globe-like, more akin to a flat blade.

It sliced into the man's neck, cooking the flesh even as it killed him.

"Wow!" I gaped at the young woman. "Remind me to never piss you off."

"Kirizin." She nodded, drawing the word into a hiss.

Can you spell the implications out for me, Anya?

I cannot even make out the full workings of the machine, she clarified. *It is quite difficult to say what the ramifications will be from its destruction.*

Copy that. I stepped out from behind the network of computers, my Stilettos blazing. With a series of *siiiiuu siiiiuu* singing through the air, I forced three of them back toward the large door and the nightscape beyond.

We mostly got this. Wyatt sounded positively chipper.

Lookie here. I dropped an orange indicator token over a man crouched behind the ATVs just outside. The bald man gestured frantically as he spoke with two of his allies, and even from here, I saw the dark nimbus hover around him.

I see. Wyatt grunted as he dodged a thug swinging the butt of a rifle at his face.

That's the Irrat who saw me in the hallway.

I have a second Irrational blip on my array. It appears to be in the corridor outside this room, at functional north 38 degrees, fourteen tack 537 by functional west 88 degrees, eighteen tack 372. It is moving in our direction.

What? Did we walk right past it? Irritation flooded Wyatt's link.

It only just appeared, Asset Guthrie. The target may be an Irrational human.

Fine. I drew my Stilettos and kept my gaze sharp. *I'd like a marker on the second Irrat, Anya.*

She said nothing, but a small green marker appeared, moving toward us.

Handle the first 'Rat and his buddies? The Tangler hummed as Wyatt geared up. *I'll play clean up in here, let you know if the second fella steps inside.*

You always take the easy chores, I teased. *Fine. Anya, I'm initiating my gear.*

I toggled both of my packets and faded into nigh-invisibility even as I felt ribbons of silvery grace tease through my limbs. Sure, my Irrational friend saw straight through the *Wraith,* but I imagined his baseline friends might have a more difficult time.

Understood, Michael. Anya sounded a touch distracted. *I will watch for pattern loss on your packets.*

I sprinted past Wyatt, dodging to one side as he swung the Tangler toward another hostile. Then I drew both of my katana and hurled myself toward the three men taking cover outside.

"Watch it!" Baldy scarcely had time to cry out before I leapt through the open door, swinging a katana directly at one of his allies' face.

My target started and blindly brought his pistol up in my vague direction.

In the end, he had no chance. Before the man understood what happened, I pushed my blade squarely through the left side of his chest.

His ballistics vest slowed the strike, but not nearly enough. He gaped stupidly, staring around, as if in death he might be able to catch sight of who had done him in. He whispered a single word, a bubble of blood on his lips.

He fell.

"Kris!" the soldier standing next to him cried out in a wail of terror and rage. He also brought up an automatic pistol but found no target to shoot.

Meanwhile, my darkly haloed amigo spun directly toward me. That veil of shadowed wrath swirled over him, and his eyes burned, frigid and unearthly. In an instant, the smoky darkness coalesced into something like a wispy, reptilian form that hovered over the man as an etheric cloak.

I continued my spin, letting my own inertia carry me forward.

The man mourning his companion must have heard a scuffed footstep or felt the wind from my spin. He brought his pistol around, aiming in my general direction, and fired three times.

I ducked and drove my second katana squarely into his gut.

He gurgled with agony, whirling his weapon to one side, and fired again, missing me cleanly.

The Irrat leapt then. He stood four or five strides away, yet somehow sprung near me, bounding the distance as easily as taking a single step.

"I see you!" he hissed, a serpentine sibilance cutting through his words. He swung his right hand high, swinging downward with a curved blade.

"Issithrk sees you, mortal!" The shadow-lizard's mouth moved with the words.

The mouth of the man beneath did not.

Interesting.

I leapt backward, away from his dying friend. That blade whispered as it sliced by my face, closer than my last shave.

I dropped one of my katana and stumbled, stunned at his wild attack.

The Irrat didn't let up for a second, swinging again even as he landed.

I rolled to one side, frantic to get out of his range.

He kept coming.

The whirling man's semi-automatic weapon, the one he'd

almost ventilated my skull with a few moments ago, still hung from his shoulder. He hadn't even reached for it.

Instead he bounced forward, light on his toes. That inhuman glow burned in his eyes, shedding an unclean light on my skin. An echo of that same piercing light created his transparent reptilian cloak.

"Cannot run." His wide, crazed eyes poured light. "Not from one who is touched. Not from the blessed."

The man's raptor hood preened like a shy high schooler given a compliment and raised a spiky head crest.

He drooled as he lunged forward another time, his blade whistling as he slashed back and forth through the air. Then, as if I hadn't even engaged the *Wraith,* as if the *Adept* didn't augment me at all, he leapt at me, wicked blade held high.

I swiped my remaining katana up, aiming for his arm.

He pulled the blow and rolled when he landed. His eyes bulged. His tongue lolled from his mouth, not quite imitating the motions of the shadowy reptile encasing his head.

More than an Irrat, some logical part of my mind registered. *An Irrat with a friend.*

I took another swing with my katana, watching how he capered lightly on his toes.

Predictably, he hopped to his left, easily dodging the blade.

I whipped my Stiletto up. As my Irrational foe dodged the katana, I fired quick bursts of kinetic energy squarely in his midsection.

WHUB-WHUB-WHUB.

This particular Stiletto still had a wide field. Three blasts of energy roughly the size of cannonballs struck him at nearly the same instant.

The Irrat didn't even have the breath to cry out. The force hurled him over thirty meters into the twilight. He landed in a heap beneath that alien sky.

He didn't move.

274

Dead?

"Better safe than sorry," I muttered.

I'd learned that lesson from Gideon DuMarque long ago. Otherwise, with my luck, I'd be right in the middle of dealing with other hostiles and this guy would leap back into the fray. It would happen at the worst possible moment, and I'd be screwed.

I scooped up my blade and toggled off my packets, trotting across the powdery soil in the direction he'd fallen.

Keeping both Stilettos aimed on him, I nudged his ribs with my foot.

No response.

Alright, I did a bit more than nudge.

Nothing.

"Okay." I nodded to myself, satisfied. "Good enough for me."

A screeching howl erupted from my left.

I whirled.

A ragged, reptilian figure, wrought from shadow and wind, hurled itself at me from the spot where I'd shot the Irrat. Its eyes burned with arctic fire.

"Oh, boy." I spun sideways, trying to keep the spectral-beast in sight.

It resembled an immense, humanoid reptile, with vibrant stripes of azure sparkling along its silvery scales and within its boggled chameleon eyes. It bounced its hunched form on three-toed feet and swiped at me with gangling arms, tipped with talons of living darkness.

"Ack!" I leapt backward and landed in a crouch.

On pure reflex, I brought my Stiletto up and fired squarely into its foul reptilian head. My shot rippled through it like sunlight through water.

The transparent, malignant thing remained untouched.

It drew back one of those serpentine limbs, swiping again as it leapt toward me. Those wicked claws had no difficulty striking their target.

I fell backward, rivers of pain burning through my chest. It missed the quasi-steel jacket altogether, instead shredding my shirt. Blood trickled from a dozen narrow slashes.

Michael? Anya abruptly linked. *Please report.*

I'm dealing with some class of Aetheric Deviation. I rolled to one side, as it leapt and came down right where I'd been. *The fucker just popped up out of nowhere.*

A Deviation? I felt her head twitch. *Non-physical?*

Quasi-physical. The Stilettos don't touch it.

Do you believe it to be native to this topia?

Allied creature. It gave that Irrat extra-human capabilities. I put down the man, but this ectoplasmic thing remained.

Troubling. She paused. *We are clear inside.*

I sure could use the hillbilly. If he can ground the Deviation, we're golden.

An Eidolonic Lock. She nodded in approval, likely pleased that Wyatt would be putting the Tangler to a Facility-approved purpose. *I will send Asset 423 right over.*

Copy that.

I triggered the *Adept* again, thinking any bit of speed and agility would help. Assuming the wretched thing had given its host the power to see right through the *Wraith,* I didn't bother activating the packet. It would be worse than useless.

As sweet agility traced its way through my veins, I rolled far to my left and sprang forward to draw the reptile's eye.

I didn't have to kill it; I only needed to stay alive until Wyatt showed.

"Hey there, asshole." I smirked at the pseudo-reptilian bane, watching carefully.

"CCCCcchhhhhhh," it hissed. Just like the Irrat, the filmy, not-quite-solid aberration hopped from one foot to the other and peered at me.

When it tensed its legs, propping itself up on the balls of each foot, I hurled myself sideways.

I landed on the other side of the dead Irrat and scrambled a couple of steps backward.

The ragged, shadowy form turned toward me, its back to the glass doors and the ATVs. It lurched forward a couple of short hops, a motion I mirrored, stepping back. The dusky abomination kept those alien eyes squarely on me, its mouth gaping open.

WHUF, WHUF, WHUF. Three of Wyatt's spikes stabbed into the alien grit beneath our feet, all near or around the spectral thing. It cocked its head and gaped at the spikes uncertainly.

Uniformly, the spikes began to pulse a shimmering green as Wyatt entered in algorithms.

"Hey, shithead." I waved one arm, drawing the abomination's attention again. "Right here, fucko."

Here's the field. Wyatt laid down a series of circles all across my visual array. They resembled a Venn diagram, each circle centered on one of the spikes.

Roughly in the middle, the gangling creature stood and hissed. It turned abruptly toward Wyatt, who had slipped up behind it.

Initiating Eidolonic Lock, he informed me, without even a glance at the reptile.

Understood. I drew both Stilettos.

The moment those spikes stopped pulsing, they bathed the area in a cool, sharp light that burst upward in three cylinders, none of the energy passing beyond the circles of Wyatt's radii.

The overlap caught the Deviation squarely in the center of its chest.

As the light began to flash again, Wyatt frantically worked his keys, altering the very nature of matter within the creature's body.

The seething thing screeched, wracked with agony. It trembled and spasmed caught in the grip of the *Artisan's* alchemy. Before my eyes, the ghastly reptile solidified, gathering about it the alien mass of this world.

Anytime, Hoss, Wyatt prompted, clear even over the racket the Deviation continued to make.

277

Copy that.

I brought both weapons up and aimed directly at the now-solid aberration. Without hesitation I fired each three, four times.

They didn't all hit; we didn't need them all to hit. My kinetic bursts tore into the rigid body of the reptilian obscenity, liquefying its form into quivering, syrupy plasma.

The screeches abruptly halted. Wyatt struck a few more keys, and the verdant glow faded.

A noxious, nauseating blob of mutilated flesh fell to the ground.

4

"Gross." Wyatt regarded the putrescent mass. "Worst piñata ever."

"I just love it when you're helpful." I turned back toward the enclosed chamber. "Come on. We have work to do."

We hadn't taken five steps before Wyatt stopped and gaped at the ATVs.

"We don't have time to go muddin'—or whatever it is you people do." I shook my head. "Get your head in the game."

"No, Bishop." His whispered voice caught me off guard. "Look."

It took me a moment, in all honesty. At first, I saw nothing where he pointed. But the longer I stared... A whisper of eldritch color burned in a halo around the vehicles, twinkling and flashing in an undulating fashion. That shine originated somewhere along the hand throttle, though I couldn't be more exact without getting closer.

"That's not bizarre or anything." I chewed my lip in thought.

The radiance writhed in the air. Its pattern reminded me of the gathering force inside the Atrificia as it hovered over the crystalline device.

"Remember what melty-face said about Radonic Transmitters?" Wyatt raised an eyebrow.

"I do," I responded.

"This means I get to check the ATVs for orbs, bud." Wyatt held out one hand, palm up as if to say 'obviously.' Without waiting for my response, he trotted over toward the parked vehicles.

Eleven late-model four-wheelers all sat parked together, lined up and ready to romp into the alien desert beyond.

As I stepped over to where Wyatt crouched, that unearthly glow sharpened, as if the energy grew stronger the closer I got to it.

Did it grow brighter the more I paid attention to it? Maybe.

"There." Wyatt gestured at a tangle of black wires wrapped all around a silver mounting bracket. The device had been welded onto the ATV and held a small brass globe securely against the vehicle.

"Just like Thorne's," I marveled. The device sat at the center of the undulating radiance, gathering it in. "So this is one of their Radonic Transmitters?"

"I might be forced to borrow an ATV after all." Wyatt gave me a cat's grin. "Sounds just awful."

"They might have to charge." I peered closer, noting the trigger switch on the side of the sphere. "But beyond that, they seem to be what we need."

"Lookit the back." Wyatt tapped the rack behind the driver's seat. Four canisters were stowed on the back of each ATV, secured with steel braces.

I studied the devices, and then glanced up at him.

"More of those resonators."

My forehead wrinkled.

He pushed his hat a little further up his head with a sigh. "The things Thorne said had been tampered with," he clarified.

"Oh."

"They have conduit cables runnin' off the left. Plugs into the side here." Wyatt raised an eyebrow. "Might work like batteries."

Gentlemen? Anya's link caught me off guard. *If you are finished outside, we should discuss how to deal with the Parabola.*

Copy that, Twitchy. Wyatt stood and shot me a sideways grin. *We located the Radonic Transmitters.*

You did? Her eyebrows raised slightly.

Wyatt did, I clarified. *It's looking more and more as if we might make it home.*

That is excellent.

I stepped inside and stopped in place, stunned.

280

A minor cataclysm had taken place inside the bay.

At first count, I saw nine corpses—four of which appeared to have had their throats slit by our Kab ally's shapeshifting sphere. Two men had been cooked to death, while another lay shattered, as if his flesh had been glass. Scorch marks scored the far wall, and two silvery stasis fields shimmered by the door. Flames covered one computer bank releasing black smoke to creep along the ceiling and eventually roll outside.

"Wow." I studied Wyatt and let out a low whistle. "You're really getting creative with that thing, aren't you?"

"Desperate times, Hoss." A cunning smile capered on his lips. "Don't worry, I'm keepin' a record of everything I'm tryin' out here. I'm interested in showing the Designates what can be done."

"Yeah." I shook my head as I took it all in.

The equipment Wyatt wore had a singular intention on dossier: to counter the reality-altering effects wielded by creatures from beyond our world. The lizard-lamentation outside had been just one example. Dozens of 'approved procedures' were in place to offset Irrational horrors.

After a taste of offense, Wyatt had thrown that philosophy to the wind. He hadn't simply reacted to Irrational hoo-doo; he'd brought the fight to these men.

The results lay all around me, in gory, glorious detail.

"These strategies are not in accordance with those typically approved by Designates." Anya arched one eyebrow at Wyatt. "Although that fact has little to do with their efficacy."

"Just getting the job done," Wyatt chuckled.

"Kerista Jur Jiddon." Our graceful ally walked into view from the hallway door. She gestured in that direction. "Eet's em-tea."

"Empty?" I smiled at her.

"It appears our friend has acquired a small amount of English," Anya informed us. "She has been watching me from the door as I take readings."

"What about that other Irrat, Anya?" Wyatt tapped a few keys on the crescent at his hip. "Fucker ever show back up?"

"He did not." Anya continued to pluck at the space in front of her but glanced back at him. "The second Irrat vanished from telemetry moments into the firefight."

"Smart man," Wyatt continued. "We handed those guys their assholes."

"We did... what?" Anya furrowed her brow.

"Nothing." I shook my head. "Other people's assholes aside, how are we doing in here?" I quirked up the edge of my mouth.

"It is troubling." Anya withdrew her fingers from her interface and turned toward us. "I have no doubt this device is the Parabola, which drains harmonic resonance from the local environment. It appears as if that energy is then stored in the resonators Thorne and her crew tended." Anya gestured off to her right. "An energetic distillation device is set up behind the Parabola."

"Stored? In those silvery canisters?" Wyatt clicked his tongue. "Told ya so."

"So they are making weird extra-dimensional batteries." I scratched my jaw. "There are several of them stowed on the ATVs outside."

"Based on what I have seen so far, I would guess our Irrationals have been siphoning and storing these resonances for some time." Anya turned from Wyatt to me. "Since they have the capability to breach the axiomatic realmwall and traverse realities at will, my guess is these resonators are intended for a second location."

"But we don't know exactly what they're for?" I stepped closer to the Parabola and peered up at that cacophony of weirding color.

"No way to know," Wyatt grumbled. "Best I can say, if invading monstrosities want the resonators, they can't be for anything good."

"I concur." Anya nodded. "I have therefore attempted to ascertain the simplest way to destroy the Parabola. Unfortunately, the problem seems to be far more complex than originally projected."

"How do you mean?" I glanced at her and then back at the spinning, dancing hues. "I mean, just look at the destruction in this room. It's obvious Captain Coveralls here can obliterate whatever he damn well pleases when he gets a mind to."

"The difficulty is in the energetic resolutions," she explained, her tone overly patient, as if speaking to a six year old. "Portions of this device exist in extra-Rational space. It is impossible to verify how much of the energetic payload is unstable or transdimensional. If we destroy the centrifuge for the harmonic resonances, the energetic potential exceeds any known manmade explosive."

"I don't like the sound of that," Wyatt muttered and rubbed at his ear just under his hat.

"We have the capacity to destabilize the energetic systems of the Parabola easily," Anya emphasized.

"Right." I popped the knuckles on my left hand as I thought. "We just risk blowing ourselves to bits."

"There are still preparations we can take." Anya glanced at Wyatt.

A miniscule tic of his head indicated he received a patch.

"What's this?" He sniffed.

"Those three markers show the preferred locations for three of your spikes. I also patched the energetic resonances required to destroy the device."

"Well, that seems simple enough." Wyatt tapped a few of his keys as he strode around the Parabola. "I can at least get the spikes placed."

WHUF. He fired the first, burying it within the dark stone of the floor.

"Before activating them, we need to discuss—" Anya stopped midsentence, her head whipping to the left.

A green indicator popped into being on my visual array as if appearing from nothingness, the missing second Irrat.

His physicality seems slightly adrift, just slightly out of phase...
She immediately began to pluck at the air.

Extra dimensional? Wyatt tapped at a few of his keys, and a
second **WHUF** echoed through the room.

Uncertain, Anya replied. She reached up with her left hand and
fiddled with a portion of her interface. Her brow furrowed as she
concentrated on what she saw.

The marker vanished.

I lost him. She turned toward me, bewildered.

I glanced at Wyatt and arched an eyebrow. *Temporal
displacement?*

Mebbe. He shrugged and started to input a series of numbers on
his keyboard while he walked around the Parabola. Another
WHUF announced his third spike.

As if toying with us, the marker appeared again. Anya didn't
say anything, but scowled slightly.

"Frensee." The slender Kab woman glanced from Anya to
Wyatt to me.

Maybe I'll just creep over there. I glanced sideward at Anya.
*Assuming I can avoid cascading errors setting my visual array on
fire?*

*This close to the Parabola, my readings indicate a forty-eight
percent chance of the emanations causing recurring energetic
remainders within your phaneric node.* She gave her head the
tiniest of shakes. *That said, as long as I monitor your system, you
should be able to toggle off the* Wraith *before that occurs.*

Perfect. I popped my neck. *Here I go.*

Cool shadows fell around me. The scintillating, multihued light
that danced within the room faded into a colorless glow.

I crept around the Parabola, ghosting my way back toward the
hallway.

The opening into the passageway proved difficult to find,
mostly thanks to a certain hillbilly gorilla and his stasis fields. Two

of the mirror-bright constructs sat squarely between the door and me, thoroughly blocking my sight. Still, I slipped past them, a Stiletto in each hand.

The marker remained consistent—a small green circle, several meters into the passageway. I turned down that hall and peered ahead of me, weapons raised.

When the marker vanished.

AGAIN.

God damn it! I turned back to the room, chewing on my lip. *Can't kill them if they won't stay still!*

I toggled the *Wraith* off.

Maybe we shouldn't worry about it, Wyatt linked. *If the Radonic Transmitters are affixed to the ATVs, then we could just hop on those bad boys and take off.* He eyed me as I walked closer.

And leave the Parabola? I shook my head, not quite following him. *I mean, I guess we can tell the Facility about it, maybe they can send a better prepared cadre?*

Rosie gives us a half-kilometer head start. Wyatt glanced from Anya to me. *We drive out on the ATVs and I trigger the spikes at five hundred meters out. If the energetic payload is too much...* He shrugged. *We bail. Trigger the Radonic Transmitters and go home.*

Except we just slaughtered all the Kabs. I glanced at the dark young woman nearby. *And remember, our molten amigo heard our links.*

I do not think that will be an issue, Anya replied. She stared up, her head craned back so she could get a full view of the Parabola. Her left hand arched around to the side of her face, and her fingers danced intently.

Yeah? Wyatt tapped absently at a few keys.

It is possible sabotaging the Parabola will result in an energetic payload comprising only local emanations. She brought her right hand up, pinching at her invisible interface. *Yes. I am fairly certain.*

Good enough for me! Wyatt gave me a cheesy smile. *I'm only*

285

interested in dimensions where NASCAR exists.

Assets! Anya's eyes went wide. *We have a localized spike in Rationality! I show—*

Before she could finish, the world trembled around us, just the tiniest bit. We *felt* his coming less than a second later, an alien fracturing that burrowed and warbled behind the mind.

A man crackled into existence, not five steps from us.

One instant, we stood with our Kab friend, peering at the unearthly device. In the next, he stood there, regarding us with cold eyes.

Lean but quite tall, he had unruly, fiery hair and wore thick, dark canvas pants. His shirt hung open to reveal a well-muscled physique and a holster strapped to his chest. Another hung around his waist.

Firenzei.

The man spit on the floor as he stalked toward us. If he thought anything odd about our presence or appearance, he didn't show it.

Again, I got the sneaking suspicion I'd seen the man somewhere before this alien nightmare.

"You." He pointed at the graceful Kab woman. "We need to have a word."

"Neww," she spat at him with a scowl.

"Oh, but we have some things to discuss." He took another step. "I think we know who's been fucking with our resonators, don't we?"

"Hey." I jerked my chin up at him. "Don't be rude. You have guests."

"Unwelcome ones." He gave a lurid grin. "Private property an' all."

"We're here on official business." I stared at him. "As you well know."

"Official business," the man muttered. He spat again. "A little outside your jurisdiction here, Asset. It'll prolly be better if you tottered off, back the way you came. Maybe there's a psychic on the telly you can go harass or some poor kid you can take from his fam."

The man's words hit me like a bulldozer. Little Bill Iverson flashed through my mind. I flinched internally, focused, and tried to remember how I knew the red-headed man.

"Officially, we are not outside our jurisdiction," Anya said in a crisp, succinct tone. "According to Facility sanctions and guidelines, actions of disruption and malfeasance originate from this location. We have—"

"Oh, Christ, won't you shut up?" The man gave us a condescending glower. "Yer trespassin'. Leave."

"You!" Wyatt bellowed. "You little shit-eater! What are you doing out here?"

With a start, I realized Firenzei's identity. I gaped at him as the second-hand memory washed over me. Firenzei had scrapped with Wyatt in The Booby Trap. I'd seen the whole escapade in Wyatt's patch. The man must have been on site, watching his movements at the bar.

The thought chilled me.

"Minding my own business," the man grinned at Wyatt. "Wondering why you folks aren't doing the same."

"I'm rememberin' what it felt like to hand you your ass." Wyatt straightened his hat.

"I wouldn't go thinking our last encounter has any merit, cowboy. I didn't try too awful hard, jus' checkin' out the competition."

My heartbeat shifted into high gear. How had he known where to find Wyatt? Had the parasites given him some kind of intel? Then my mind took the next step, and the icy fingers of fear trickled down my back.

What if this man *hosted* those ichorous, thrashing horrors? Wyatt wouldn't have known what he dealt with…

Could he have been infected? That woman, Jasmine, had been intimately close to him.

Shit.

"Now." The man took another step forward. "It's time for you to leave."

"Not happening." My eyes narrowed. I'd drawn my Stilettos, yet his guns still sat in their holsters. "Stand down and relinquish your weapons. The Facility shows leniency—"

"No." The man enunciated the word as if I were simple. "The Facility does no such thing. I know it. You know it. Leave. Now."

The Tangler hummed louder and at a higher pitch. I activated the *Adept*.

"You know we can't do that. Stand down, or I'm afraid—"

"Good." The man smirked and drew a long knife. "You *should* be afraid. If you'd like to go round up some friends, I'll allow it."

I decided.

Quicker than breath, I drew down on the man. The *Adept* packet guided my every move. I moved like quicksilver, faster than thought. Before he'd even stopped speaking, I'd brought both disruptors to bear on the man's face.

Michael!

The world trembled again, just a bit.

Firenzei vanished just as I fired.

Again, an alien crackling sensation burrowed and warbled within my mind. I whirled. Without a read on where the man might have vanished to—

—only to hear an unearthly, rending echo from behind me. I continued that spin, only to blink and reel back from a ribbon of ghastly light, which struck me squarely in the face, like a cinderblock.

The Kab woman screamed, a roiling gurgle.

Firenzei hadn't just teleported next to her; he'd appeared with that long blade already embedded inside her neck, running from side to side. His weapon shone with horrific, otherworldly radiance, a light so brilliant it glowed crimson through the woman's skin.

288

It screeched as he pulled it loose, sounding like the mangled metal of a car wreck. As soon as he pulled it free, blood splattered across the walls, and the Kab fell to the floor like a puppet with cut strings.

She twitched, gurgled, and then lay still.

The three of us stood, stunned.

"What the fuck was that?" Wyatt gaped at him.

"The light show? The Pauli exclusion principle." Firenzei met our gazes with flat, dead eyes. "It's that whole 'matter cannot occupy the same space' bullshit. Creates all kinds of weirdness."

With a flick of his wrist, Firenzei hurled his blade at Wyatt as we stood, gobsmacked.

Before I heard the blade strike, the world began that trembling undulation.

A wet slicing precluded a grunt from Wyatt, but I had no time.

Firenzei drew his pistols as I raced toward him, bringing my Stilettos to bear.

Wyatt hit the ground.

Asset Guthrie! Anya cried over the link.

I fired both weapons, snarling as I leapt at Firenzei.

Who vanished before my eyes.

That sharp, burrowing sensation returned, as if something tunneled through my mind every time Firenzei used his temporal gift. This time I ignored it and spun in place, both weapons held out. I toggled the *Wraith*, watching as color drained from the world.

Keep moving, if you can, I linked my cadre. *He probably can't teleport his knife inside you if he doesn't know where you are.*

His knife's already inside me, Hoss! Wyatt spat over the link.

How bad?

Just my leg, but fuck! Do you know how hard it is to stick a knife when you throw it?

"I asked you to leave all polite-like," Firenzei called from behind Wyatt's stasis fields. "You're the rude ones."

"We didn't exactly ask to be brought here," I countered, moving stealthily toward him.

"'Course not!" He chuckled. "Innocent Facility hounds. Just happen to stumble in on our little project."

I didn't respond, using the time he spent talking to sprint in his direction.

Firenzei proved no fool, however. The room about me began to tremble again, the tiny waver that occurred just before he leapt.

Shit! I peered around the edge of the stasis fields, just as that awful digging, clawing sensation began in my skull again. *Missed him.*

Behind the computers, Anya informed me.

I turned until I saw Firenzei's marker. But more, I heard voices, accompanied by heavy boots.

Reinforcements incoming, up the hall.

Asset Guthrie is somewhat secure. We've made it behind the Parabola.

It'll be a few before my mecha dull the pain, Hoss. It's all you 'til then.

Copy that.

Five short pistol bursts, each a few rounds, slammed into the room. One of those ricocheted off the floor less than a meter from me.

Firenzei peered out from behind the computers, a smirk on his lips.

"We were just discussing the possibility of invisible Facility fucks. Guess that means I'll be a bit liberal with my shots."

He does not realize where 423 and I are located. Anya's link felt like a scarce whisper. *He assumes we are all invisible.*

Firenzei fired again, randomly spraying bullets throughout the room. I saw him occasionally pop his head up to listen for a bit.

The man knew his way around a firefight.

I answered Firenzei with a fury of sharp bursts from my Stilettos, slamming cannonballs of raw force into this side of the

290

computer banks. When he ducked his head back, I sprinted, lest he triangulate my location based on my shots.

Just that moment, I realized I hauled ass straight toward a huge door, the one leading outside.

Where the ATVs sat, prepped for departure.

I turned and fired again, just to keep the man pinned down. In a few dozen steps, I'd be outside.

"Rudolfo!" someone called from behind me, on the far side of the room.

"Assets, three of them!" Firenzei called back.

Can you see how many we just picked up? I linked.

No, Wyatt came back wearily. *But I can probably move now, if it makes a difference.*

It might. I'm going to try to draw them outside. To the ATVs.

Yeah? I felt him raise an eyebrow. *Then what?*

What do you mean? I stepped through the glass door, my feet again sinking in the fine alien soil. *I never have a 'then what.' You know that!*

Right.

The twilight outside had deepened into a sullen evening, albeit an evening with a sky striped with unseen colors looming over it. The ATVs sat exactly where I'd left them, lined up as if ready to roar out into the night.

No keys though. It seemed as if these vehicles were equipped with a push button ignition. That...

That gave me an idea.

I trotted to the furthest one and pressed the ignition. It rumbled, but didn't start.

I did it again, this time giving it some gas on the throttle.

The ATV lurched and roared to rumbling life.

I repeated the process with the second one. No sooner did it start than I felt the world around me tremble, the harbinger of Firenzei's uncanny power.

Michael, he's on the move.

I bet. I smiled as I turned the throttle on the third ATV. *He thinks we're leaving.*

He appeared at the door, his weapons out front and blazing. His face twisted into a mask of elemental hatred.

I'd expected this, but I also expected he might not wish to shoot the canisters of weirding energy. That made them the perfect screen.

With the grace of the *Adept* trickling through my limbs, I hurled myself sideways, quick as thought. I landed in a crouch and brought my Stilettos up. I fired squarely at him, the *siiiiuu siiiiuu* of my weapons slicing the air as I clipped him. Force like a cannonball hurled the man backward into the bay.

"Shit! Oh, fuck me!" Firenzei cried.

Hoss, we're on the move, Wyatt's link felt urgent. *You've got another ten guys running up to join Firenzei.*

Can you hold them?

Stasis? Sure. I felt his wicked smile. *Although I can't confirm how the ice princess will feel about that.*

I will feel happy to survive this encounter, Anya clarified. *Even if I dislike the manner in which it is done.*

I'll take that as a 'go for it.'

No sooner did I receive the link than I heard the keening song of the Tangler, followed by a flurry of *WHUF*s.

"Oh, God damn it," Firenzei moaned, just out of my sight. "You Facility piece of shit!"

The men didn't even have time to cry out before I heard the WHOMP of closing stasis fields.

That stops them, not counting Firenzei, Wyatt reported. *I caught a few of them with a single field this time.*

Excellent. I peeked around the corner, trying to track where the red-headed shit-eater had gone.

You think so, except I have to keep doing all the mathematicals now. I heard Wyatt grunt. *Takes me outta the fight.*

We should take ourselves out of the fight. I edged closer. *Just get over here.* I moved forward again, searching for my new Irrat-of-interest.

No sooner had I sent the link than things began to tremble around me, just the tiniest bit.

Michael, Firenzei's moving!

I sprinted forward, Stilettos out in front of me. I hadn't exactly seen where Firenzei landed, but I knew if I could just catch him square with one shot, I could end this.

Yet the tremors came to a stop. Again, I felt that gnashing, tearing sensation somewhere in my skull. It felt as if some part of my very biology rebelled at Firenzei's talent.

I lost him, Anya reported. *He may be beyond my range.*

I don't care what the reason is, I linked as I flicked the Wraith off. I glanced back into the room where I saw my two cadre-members push past several silvery stasis fields. *We need to move. Now.*

A Body in Motion

As murderous stars gazed down from a crimson sky, I examined the small brass sphere affixed to the ATV. The switch that activated the device had been positioned squarely on top, easy to reach.

However, that didn't ease my mind.

As Wyatt limped outside, Anya just behind, the barbarian shot me a grin. "Parabola's rigged to blow. So you figgered these things out, Hoss?"

"It's the charge I worry about." I glanced up at him. "Firenzei said they needed to finish their cycle."

"Right. And our molten 'migo said the Parabola charged them, or some such."

"You have some concerns regarding their functionality?" Anya pursed her lips for moment, thinking. "We truly have no comprehension of these devices."

"That's it." I pointed at her. "What if they explode if they aren't charged properly?"

"What if they only take us halfway home?" Wyatt fiddled with his beard, even as his other hand continued to input stasis specifications. "Christ. They might leave us floating somewhere in the Maelstrom."

"I know I don't spend my weekends fixing up stock cars or anything," I teased, "but look at this. The canisters on back of the ATVs have some kind of connector leading to the Radonic Transmitter."

"I see it. Parallel circuit." Wyatt nodded. "Maybe they can draw off the canisters, if they need to."

"I don't believe we have time to figure out the specifics." I gazed at both of them. "Firenzei could return any moment. I say we take three of these out into the badlands. Once we're far enough away from teleporting motherfuckers, we can try to figure out the tech."

"Can one ever be far enough away from teleporting motherfuckers?" Wyatt mused with a grin.

"I have some concerns," Anya all but whispered. She stared the ATV, eyes just a bit wide.

"Is it how cool we're going to look?" I nodded at her as if I understood. "I get it. This is pretty bad ass."

"I have never driven a vehicle of this specification before." She blinked up at Wyatt. "I am uncertain how to modulate the craft's various gears without access to the Lattice."

"Ain't no gears, Twitchy." Wyatt threw one leg over the rumbling four-wheeler on the end. "All push button. All automatic."

"Perhaps I should ride behind one of you?"

"I don't think we can, *Preceptor*." I winced and gave her an apologetic smile. "When Thorne used her Radonic Transmitter, she took it with her. We might need one apiece."

"Perhaps the device is geared to whoever was riding upon the vehicle?" She arched one eyebrow.

"Can we risk that if we're wrong?" Wyatt sighed. "Anya, I'm sorry your upbringing in Sverdlovsk didn't involve completely awesome four-wheeling. But this is kid stuff. For throttle, twist your left grip. Pull the lever over your right grip to brake. Just steer in the direction you want to go. That's basically it."

"Understood." Her tone made it clear Anya felt quite uncomfortable. "But I was not raised in Sverdlovsk." Despite this, she stepped to one of the idling four wheelers and threw one white-clad leg across it.

She stared at me with wide eyes.

"Normally I would say Wyatt should take point. He has the most experience driving these things and will know what to avoid." I settled myself onto my own ATV. "But today he has to drive while doing math. So I propose I go first, and Anya hang in the middle."

Reasonable, Hoss, Wyatt linked as he revved his engine. *We doin' this?*

In answer I pushed my throttle and drove off into the crimson night. I heard my cadre's engines roar as they pulled forward, and we took off.

The sheer power of the ATV thrilled me, jetting into the infinite shadows of that weirding world. As we started up a small rise, I began to see outcrops of dark stone off to our left, along with what appeared to be alien pine scrub.

You good, Preceptor? I linked, attempting to keep it light.

I... am. She wavered just a touch, but I felt her focused intent. *It is different than I expected.*

I'm surprised at the power these things have, Wyatt linked. *I'd a guessed they'd be draggy, bein' automatics and all.*

We should probably stop soon. I glanced over my shoulder. *If you're going to blow the Parabola.*

Right. A white marker appeared on my visual array. *How 'bout there? On the edge of five-hundred meters.*

Copy that.

Wyatt followed Anya and me up the rise, keeping an eye on the rough terrain we'd just covered. After a moment, I found a flat space that held enough room for all three vehicles.

Once I pulled up onto it, I had a view back along the dusty path, down to the open door of the Atrificia.

The structure loomed far larger than I'd believed. An obsidian spire jutted into the sky, stretching distantly into the air. Silvery traces of unknown energy snaked along the surface of that pinnacle and danced there.

"'Purty." Wyatt pulled up next to me, steering his vehicle with one hand. With the other, he tapped on keys.

"Driving one handed?"

"Had to." He shrugged as Anya rolled up. "Remember, the moment I lay off, those stasis fields fall."

"Right, I know. But it can't be protocol." I rubbed my chin.

"Ha!" Wyatt shook his head. "There ain't no protocol out here."

"I have a question about that." Anya brushed red dust from her white field gear. "Regarding the order of operations."

"Yeah?" Wyatt arched an eyebrow. "*You* have a protocol question?"

"I imagine you cannot discharge the Parabola." She nodded at his tapping fingers. "You are currently in mid-algorithm. Certainly you cannot engage the spikes you left around the device."

"Yeah." Wyatt glanced back toward the Atrificia. "Right. I'm in the middle of holding the fields."

"Therefore, you are required to drop the stasis fields before initiating complete demolition." She cocked her head just a touch.

"That'll slaughter those idjits," Wyatt mused.

"Like shooting fish in a barrel." I ground my teeth. "Don't get me wrong, those guys weren't looking out for our best interest or anything."

"No, but..." Wyatt frowned. "Seems pretty shitty. Blowing the Parabola murders those fuckers. They don't have a chance."

"I can't think of any other possibility. Even if you release the fields, attempt to discharge the Parabola, then reengage the fields, you have no way of knowing if you can hit the mark."

"Impossible." Wyatt shook his head. "Doesn't mean I love it, though."

"Remember, you're the one who doesn't like to fight fair." I gave him a ghost of a smile with the tease. "Whatever gets you home, right?"

"These targets are enemy combatants." Anya's typically soft voice seemed even more reserved. "The Facility would not consider your conduct to be outside regulations, excepting the use of stasis fields."

"Bad luck for them." Wyatt turned from Anya to me and removed his fingers from the keyboard. He clenched his fist, then shook his hand. "These guys should have spent their day at The Booby Trap."

He stretched his fingers for a heartbeat while he read his visual array.

I peered back at the Atrificia, though I saw nothing.

"Stasis released," he informed us. The large man turned toward the Atrificia. He tapped a few of the targeting keys along the top of his crescent-shaped keyboard and then entered his remaining commands.

White light, as brilliant as the center of the sun, exploded from the Parabola Bay. It flickered, angry tongues of living luminescence lashing out at the landscape beyond before darting back into the structure.

Less than a second later, an atmospheric burst struck us, carrying the grit of this world in a singular burst of wind. The ground beneath our feet trembled, then stilled.

"Initiating optics." I squinted, performing the tic that allowed me to zoom in. As I examined the Atrificia, I noted the silvery ribbons of energy that had writhed around the top of its spire now flowed smoothly, elegantly. As if the turret somehow gathered radiance from the very sky to channel downward.

"Holy shit," Wyatt breathed. "There! Right by the bay door!"

I shifted my gaze downward and stopped when I realized what he meant.

"Jesus." I shook my head. "Guy doesn't give up."

There, just outside the bay door, stood Firenzei.

2

White light still flickered from the direction of the Parabola, outlining Firenzei as a stark silhouette. His hair waved in the wind whipping forth from the alien energies in the room.

"He's checking the ATVs," Wyatt realized. "Fuck. He's coming after us."

"He cannot know where we are," Anya reasoned. "If he did, he would simply use his Irrationality to reach us."

"I don't know that he's after *us*." I tapped the bronze globe mounted on my four-wheeler. "The transmitters are the only way home, after all."

As we watched, Firenzei hopped onto one of the vehicles, the one parked furthest from the magnesium-white flame. He fiddled with it for a moment and then began to pull forward.

"Okay." I gazed at my two compatriots. "We've blown the Parabola. Check. Done that."

"Now it remains to determine how the transmitters work," Anya said.

"Shouldn't be rocket science," Wyatt mused. "Thorn triggered hers mid-battle while shot through."

"The only possibility I have suggests one of us drive a short distance away and attempt to toggle their device." Anya shifted in her seat, and I thought the idea made her uncomfortable. "Assuming a lack of explosions, the other two will follow."

"That's your suggestion?" Wyatt let out a low whistle.

"It is." She paused. "I do not like this idea."

"We still have no way to know if it worked," Wyatt mused.

"No." Anya leveled her gaze at each of us. "It will be impossible to ascertain. If the device is triggered and the user vanishes, the remaining two have little choice but to follow suit."

"I'll do it." I pushed what I hoped was a jaunty grin past the beginnings of a headache. "Anya is required to read axiomatic statistics. Wyatt can alter those statistics with the Tangler." I shrugged. "Those two skills are vital for navigating extra-Rational space. I, on the other hand, am geared as a fight-monkey."

"I prefer to think of you as a suit-ninja," Wyatt teased.

"Regardless, with time, patience, and the energetic modules from the *Raiju* drone, you'll figure out all sorts of crazy shit. Together, the two of you stand a better chance of getting home without me."

"That is not how I would phrase our situation, Michael." Anya pursed her lips.

"You know what I mean."

"He ain't wrong." Wyatt scowled. "With those *Raiju* drones, the Tangler can go for years. There's been plenty of study cases where an *Artisan* makes tiny changes in ambient Rationality while adrift. Those can, with patience, be used to signal the Facility."

"Really?" The idea surprised me.

"Yup. Hell, Brooke once figured out a way to signal Substation 42 using tiny changes in magnetism. *Preceptors* figured out the source of Irrationality was a contained sub-topia and rescued her."

"Brooke?" I gave him a half-smile.

"Asset Walgrave." He waved a hand. "Anyway, point is Bishop ain't just tryin' to play noble hero."

"I am aware," Anya responded.

"We need to act." I nodded at Wyatt. "Now. I'm doing this. I'll pull over there, what, about a hundred meters?"

"That's as good as anything else," Wyatt grudgingly admitted.

"We did not agree to this scenario as a cadre," Anya protested. "I only offered it as a possibility. It is conceivable we can discern a less dangerous way to test the equipment."

"Not before he finds us." I pointed in Firenzei's direction. "We only went about half a klick; our tracks will be obvious."

"The atmospheric disturbance from the explosion likely interrupted those tracks," Anya countered.

Yet I saw the truth in her eyes. She knew what had to be done.

I nodded at her and twisted the throttle of my ATV. I steered further up the path, aiming squarely for a stone shelf.

There's a ledge up here; I'm pulling onto it, I informed them. *Best part is, if I die in a fiery explosion, the ledge should shelter you guys from some of the fallout.*

Always lookin' on the bright side, Hoss.

I wrestled the ATV around the scree on the shelf to get as far back as possible.

Okay, I'm in position. I let out a long breath. *Wish me luck.*

Before either of them had the chance to link back, I toggled the switch on the brass globe.

It clicked.

I toggled again.

Nothing.

Good luck, Wyatt linked. After a moment he asked, *You there, Hoss? Nothing exploded.*

Nothing happened at all, I replied, frowning. *It makes a clicking noise. That's it.*

Fuck me. I felt Wyatt's seething frustration.

Could it need more juice? I toggled the switch again. *I mean, we just blew up the power station! We can't exactly go back and charge them!*

Gentlemen, Anya's calm cool drifted through the link. *I have a suggestion.*

Oh yeah? Idly, I flipped the switch another time. Again, I failed to burst into a cacophony of fire and death.

I wanted to track our Irrat and his coordinates. It occurred to me that if Michael drifted across the realmwall, then Asset Guthrie and I would be without our... suit ninja. We might wish to know the Irrational's location.

Yeah? I couldn't help a smile. Anya had practically made a joke.

Although you cannot see him now, I obtained a brief glimpse of him. He piloted his vehicle in this direction, as if giving chase.

However, just after Michael left, I noticed a sharp up spike in axiomatic relativism.

Fucker's gone. Wyatt sounded a bit stunned. *I mean, he was just there.*

He initiated his device with his vehicle in motion, Anya clarified. *I watched as he pierced the veil.*

For a moment, both Wyatt and I sat silent, a rarity.

So we know it works, Wyatt clarified.

Only when it's in motion? I shrugged. *I don't see any reason why not?*

I suspect momentum is a factor, Anya reasoned. *Traversing the veil would take less energy if the vehicle is in motion.*

I'll buy that. Let's haul some ass. From below, I heard one of the ATV engines rev. *Hoss, there's a fairly clear path up this hill. Lead the way, same formation.*

I approximate Firenzei had been in motion thirty seconds before he initiated the device. He was traveling fifty kilometers per hour.

Roger that, I confirmed. I backed the four-wheeler to the path I'd driven up and throttled it. With a lurch and a roar, I shot up the hill.

I drove around a large outcrop of stone, noticing some small creature that skittered away from me into the shadows. As soon as I cleared the rock, I saw an uphill straightaway.

We're with you, Brooks Brothers. I felt the large man smirk. *Ready when you are.*

Initiating in three, I sent. *Two…*

I toggled the switch.

Just as before, the device clicked, solid in its casing.

I frowned…

The world around me burst into an azure flame.

Hoss? Wyatt's link warbled in my mind, sounding as if it came from far underwater or echoed through an infinite cavern. I felt that link like a tenuous, golden thread stretched between our minds.

Before it snapped.

For a moment, cold and darkness burned around me, sentient malevolence. I clung to the handlebars of the ATV and bit my lip against the onslaught. It felt as if I fell, as if the emptiness of that scarlet sky drifted away in a direction I couldn't name.

I heard screaming. A terrified, exuberant wail.

I wondered if it might be me.

Violent, sapphire explosions burst around me, each terrifically hot and close. Those bursts of eldritch fire burned against my skin, melting away parts of memory I held dear. The fires didn't burn me physically, yet somehow psychically scathed my mind.

I ducked closer to the ATV and then felt the tires hit as if I'd fallen from a great distance. Though clutching madly at the vehicle, I almost toppled off.

Then I drove through the vast wastes of the Mojave, tumbling wildly along.

"Yes!" I howled into the night air. "Fucking yes! Fucking take that!"

The front of the ATV wobbled, as I celebrated. Still, cerulean sparks burned brilliantly around me, igniting as if fireworks showed my way.

A snarling, warbling, shredding sound came from behind me. A quick glance over my shoulder showed the faint silhouette of Guthrie, riding his ATV through the sliding shadows of dimensions.

Like me, living cobalt fire surrounded him. Something about his shape, the way he appeared faded, an echo of himself, told me he hadn't quite made it through yet.

The Designate felt like frost-covered knives in my mind.

We require confirmation and access code check in. Ling frowned as she linked.

Yup. I grinned like a kid at Christmas. *It's us, Designate. I am Michael Bishop, 108.* I felt my Crown whir as it synced with the Lattice. *Authorization code 020798361. System green.*

305

We're through, Wyatt sent. *Dealing with Designates.*

I gave a thumbs-up.

You have been adrift for twenty-eight hours, Asset, Ling continued.

Twenty-eight?

Indeed. She paused. *We require a patch of all Asset activity from timestamp 6.21.1998/10:00:00.*

Understood. I opened the channel so my entire cadre would hear as well. *I'm pulling off over here so we can get sync'd and briefed.*

I slowed the ATV, glancing over my shoulder. Both Wyatt and Anya seemed secure. Ahead, I could pull off the little trail we found ourselves upon and get caught up.

As I slowed, an exuberant spark of turquoise luminosity exploded, a meter to my left.

Um... I veered away, startled, slowing even more. I'd assumed we were done with firebursts.

Michael! Anya's link came fraught with intensity. *Your device! Rationality is spiking around it again!*

Another burst of indigo embers dazzled me, and I felt a whisper of grasping cold brush against my face. I veered hard to the left, trying to pull away from it, and came to a complete stop.

A ringing cacophony of cobalt and sapphire pealed around me, exploding fire that felt as if it might burn away everything that had ever been. Its scintillating shine smoldered its way into me, feeding on my mind and sanity as if I were little more than tinder before it.

What the fuck? I madly linked. *Wyatt, Anya, are you—?*

Every surface around me thundered with impossible, eldritch flame.

I fucking screamed, wailed in absolute horror and agony. It felt as if that fire had a dark will, as if it sought to burrow into me.

Flashes of memory drifted into focus, burned away as I felt myself stretched, bent through directions of time I couldn't even comprehend.

306

Again I fell. Sadistic and malicious darkness grasped at me, fingers wrought from shadow.

I landed on the ATV, in badlands that stretched beneath a scarlet sky. I jounced along, nearly falling off. On the horizon, a sickly moon shone, painting the landscape with nightmarish light.

"What. The. Fuck!" I panted, staring all about me. I sat on the exact same trail my cadre and I had just left moments before.

"Okay." I breathed. "Think, Bishop."

Had I passed back through?

I stared around in horrified awe. This could be so much worse than the first time. Without Anya... Without Wyatt....

This is Michael Bishop, Asset 108. I am currently adrift. Please respond. I linked the standard phrase, hoping someone, anyone would pick it up.

Of course, if they did, that would mean I hadn't been the only one to get cast adrift a second time. I didn't know which possibility might be worse.

No response.

"Ohhh-kay." I sighed and gazed across the landscape. "What to do about this, now?"

I stepped off the ATV, wracking my brain. Common sense said maybe I should try the four-wheeler again, see if it had enough juice to punch back through.

But that could be a horrifying mistake. We truly didn't understand these radionic transmitters, after all. We'd literally just grabbed some Irrational technology and used it, in complete ignorance.

That hadn't worked out, not so far.

What if I tried the damn thing again but got stuck somewhere, trapped halfway between here and Rationality? I remembered the feel of those grasping shadows, the darkness that rested between home and this unearthly place. It didn't take too much imagination to fear being caught between the two.

Or, shit, somewhere else altogether. Another topiatic reality could be just as deadly if I weren't careful.

I needed to take stock. I needed to plan.

"I've got guns, swords, and smokes." I sighed. "I've got a nice suit with holes in it."

I paced.

"Fuck." I kicked a rock and then swore louder. "FUCK!"

Think. I needed to think.

The time-drift came to mind first. This place and Rationality had quite the temporal misstep. Ling said we'd been gone twenty-eight hours.

"But actually…" I reviewed the system time on my Crown. From the moment we'd veered here in the *Legacy*, my chronometer only recorded thirteen hours passing.

"More than double time," I muttered. That didn't inspire me. It meant, while I figured out what to do, time for my cadre zipped by more than twice as fast.

"So… what happened? Come on, Mikey." I popped the fingers on my right hand.

The most obvious answer lay in the idea that the Radonic Transmitters hadn't quite charged. It had been one of our primary concerns after all. We didn't understand the technology; we didn't even have the means to tell when the devices reached full power.

"So then where's Lumpy and Anya?" I gazed around, wondering if they'd managed to fall back through as well. After all, if the devices weren't functioning, they'd be stuck here with me.

"Fuck, Firenzei would be back," I growled. *This is Michael Bishop, Asset 108. I am currently adrift. Please respond,* I linked a second time, with next to no hope. I peered around the desolate landscape, searching for any signs.

Hell, what if they *had* come through but crashed? Or what if that hungry darkness leeched the life and memory from them as they passed through?

"No," I assured myself. "That didn't happen. You're alone."

It seemed as if only handsome Michael Bishop had won the fuck-you lottery for today.

I leaned back against one of the stone outcroppings and felt in my slacks for my cigarettes. All the shenanigans had crushed the pack, but I managed to salvage a few.

"There we go," I grunted. I popped a match with my thumbnail and lit it while I stared into the light of the twisted moon.

The smoke tasted like heaven.

I leaned there, lost, scrabbling for what to do.

Long, frustrating moments passed. I stared at the sky, considering all my options. Perhaps I should go back into the Atrificia? We had an 'alignment' with the thing inside, after all, and we'd destroyed the Parabola...

But perhaps I needed to look at the whole picture. The Kab woman had died, fairly horribly. The igneous being within might take issue with that. Also, I had no way to tell how the creature felt about us blowing up the entire Parabola Bay.

I paced, cursing.

Time drifted.

"Okay," I said, stabbing at the air with my second cigarette. "Let's play this out again." I paced back to the vehicle, my mind whirling.

At first the device hadn't activated. I remembered sitting right on that ledge, wanting to chew bullets.

"And then Anya saw Firenzei," I mused to myself. "We realized the ATVs had to be in motion—"

I stopped, mid-thought.

Had to be in motion.

"I slowed the vehicle, didn't I?" My voice cracked in excitement. I'd thought to pull over to the side and patch the Designate a timestamped packet of crazy. Then, as soon as I stopped...

"As soon as I stopped, I got hauled back here." A lazy smile tugged at the corner of my mouth.

Could it be that simple?

Obviously, keeping the vehicles in motion created all manner of concerns. With no concept of how long we could keep the ATVs moving forward, a million questions began to whirl through my mind. Did the transmitters only function for the ATVs and their riders? What happened if I leapt off? Did I perhaps have the taint of some strange emanation on my person that would drag me back here the moment the ATV stopped?

"I'm just not an 'answers' kind of guy," I muttered. All that mattered in this moment was to get back and let the Designates know I lived.

We'd figure out the rest afterward.

I turned and trotted back to the vehicle. Once there, I settled myself back onto the ATV. I lodged the remainder of my smoke between my lips, and hit the button.

The four-wheeler roared to life.

"Okay." I took a breath. "Let's do this again."

I cranked the throttle, listening to the vehicle roar. I glanced around one last time.

And thundered up the embankment.

I rounded the outcropping.

Passed the ledge.

When I hit the straightaway, I took a deep draw and tossed my cigarette away.

I toggled the transmitter.

CLICK.

Immediately, cerulean flame erupted in front of the four-wheeler, light so blue it screamed within my mind.

"C'mon." I throttled ahead faster as that hungry indigo fire blossomed around me. "Come. On."

In a turbulent crackle, another spark screamed into being, then another. They burned with the radiance of hateful, undying stars, with light that had shone across the worlds before mankind scampered down from the trees.

310

I had to say, the experience felt far less traumatic while the ATV roared beneath me.

With a final burst of sapphire radiance, I burst through the world again. Inhuman coldness caressed my face while azure flames burned at my thoughts and memories.

This time, I swore, I wouldn't stop.

3

"—uck you!" Wyatt's cry echoed from somewhere to my left, a direction that, momentarily, didn't make sense. The vast reaches of darkness between, that spaceless space, had left my mind muddied.

I landed, jolted. It felt as if I'd fallen from a height.

I require confirmation and access code check in, Ling linked, a bit desperately, I thought.

I am Michael Bishop, 108. Again, my Crown whirred as it synced with the Lattice. *Authorization code 020798361. System green.*

108, your cadre is currently under attack by a known and wanted Irrational. Our system shows the presence of Rudolfo Firenzei, an Irrat of interest.

Yeah. I bit my lip. *We've met.*

Patching his file to memory.

My Crown made an electrical twitch. For the scarcest instant, I saw a scarlet dataglyph.

When the packet synced to my memory, I knew the man, down to my bones. He'd fought in conflicts on three continents. He'd been renowned both as a decorated Soviet sniper and an Iraqi intelligence agent. He'd been in wars for the past twenty years. No baseline government understood the man's true capabilities.

He only took on targets others deemed impossible.

I had data on his service record, both official and classified Facility data.

Rudolfo Firenzei, Irrational 2187. Mercenary. Assassin. Maniac.

I knew everything about him.

My Crown stored the data in my memory as if I'd hunted the man my entire life. I had dozens of pictures and sub-dossiers at my fingertips. I felt as if I'd witnessed every conflict the man had ever been in, every contract he'd been known to take, and every false identity he'd used.

Rudolfo Firenzei held the distinction of being one of the most deadly Irrats I'd ever encountered.

The man had taken a truly odd path. Typically, when someone unfurled with crazy, reality-altering powers, they began to seek out otherworldly allies or collect all kinds of crazy, mystical gear. Instead, Firenzei had become a true professional. A problem solver. A cleaner. He understood tactics, weaponry, and patience.

Fuck.

Your cadre is over the next rise. The Designate placed two yellow triangles on my visual array. *Firenzei remains at a distance, keeping them penned in.*

Understood. I cranked the throttle and rushed toward the rise. Already my mind whirled with half-baked strategy.

An idea popped to life.

Designate, on a separate subject, have you processed the timestamped data from the rest of my cadre?

We have, Asset.

Please consider the tactics Wyatt Guthrie used while we were adrift. I understand their non-typical nature, but we're drastically undergeared out here. His capability to use offensive stasis saved our lives.

Asset Guthrie's algorithms are unlike anything allowed within Rationality. Function aside, these are far too costly and disruptive to consider, even in the present circumstances.

As stated, we are far under-geared. I pulled around a large boulder and then continued, *This dossier slated us for telemetry readings, yet we've already been far adrift and sieged a hostile installation.*

Yes, Ling responded, *so your cadre reported.*

Well, we still haven't even made Locale One. I twisted the throttle, surging ahead. *I request recalculation of the cost and disruption of Wyatt's algorithms, weighing that cost against the training, spec'ing, and equipping of the three Assets you're about to lose.*

A long pause echoed over my link, heavy with its silence. *Understood, 108.* Ling's link felt a touch impatient. *Yet while the sync remains active and the cadre remains within Rationality, I will determine the usage of stasis field algorithms. If you again find yourself adrift as the Asset with the sync, you will make your own determinations.*

I see. It was about as close to being told to go to hell that a Designate would ever get.

Now, Asset, please see to Firenzei.

Will comply.

4

I hadn't ridden the jouncing ATV another ten meters before Rachel Gardner's link touched my interface with a subtle whisper of her personality. A blend of snarky concern and professional aplomb, I sensed the *Caduceus* cared very deeply about her charges, while at the same time she didn't want anyone to realize she did.

Weird.

108, it concerns me that your cadre is severely under-supported on this dossier. She paused. *If I'd had any indication this mission would stray so far from its primary objective, I would've insisted on coming along.*

I'm also concerned. Aboard the ATV I twisted the throttle and hurtled over a small rise. *I just shared that fact with Designate Ling, actually.*

I spoke with the Designate earlier today. Her attention drifted away for a moment, as if she looked at something else.

You did? I peered out over the ridge line, trying to make out either Firenzei or my cadre. So far I didn't have visual, aside from the triangular markers given to me by the Designate.

I didn't like how far they'd roamed.

As the Caduceus *who will be responsible for stitching your reckless ass back together, I have received clearance to patch you an executable program. It's a little something of my own design and won't take up too much Crown space.* She paused again before continuing, *I'm loading it to the Lattice now and will patch directly to your ARC address in a moment.*

What does it do? I took a sharp right and bounced over a dry riverbed. As I throttled forward again, I peered past a small grove of Joshua trees and saltbush. While twilight drifted across the sky, the scant wind picked up, bearing the scent of sage and wisps of creosote. Even in the middle of all this excitement, I couldn't help

317

but notice the haunting beauty of this place.

It will activate when your axial implants indicate any kind of cascading error in your holotecture.

Oh. I nodded as if I understood. *I see.*

You don't. Somehow, she managed to send a scathing tone within her link. *How's this? When you do something stupid that will kill you, this executable will automatically initiate. Either you or your cadre will be capable of using it to burn viral mecha and save your idiot ass.*

Nice. I slowed as I pulled my vehicle around another curve in the dry riverbed. If I listened carefully, I thought I could hear the engines of the other ATVs. Beneath the triangular markers, the closest one's legend read, 1.7km.

It's an expensive process, mecha-wise, she continued. *Please limit foolish choices.*

You seem awfully certain I'm going to do something stupid, I commented. *I think the odds favor a quick little reconnaissance and then coming home.*

Right. She chuckled. *Never tell me the odds.*

Why not?

It's from— I actually felt her hold up a hand in mute frustration. *You know what? Never mind. When you get yourself in trouble, the executable is there. I've given one to every member of your cadre now, though I imagine you're the only one who will use it.*

Fair enough.

Rachel disconnected the link without another word, leaving me with wisps of her irritation.

5

Even though I kept a steady pace roaring across the desert like a bad ass, my cadre remained distant. They moved away from me as I rambled over salt and sand, and they moved about as quickly as I did.

I hadn't contacted them yet, which might have been dumb. I'd just kind of hoped to show up, ready to hand Firenzei a plate of fuck-off pie.

However, that'd never happen if they kept meandering across the Mojave.

I bet you guys missed me, I sent, shooting them a wry grin.

Michael! Anya sounded harried; I could feel her slight grimace. *Have you checked in with the Designate?*

All's well and system green, Preceptor. *Here's a marker over my locale.* I performed the mental twitch to show them my location.

Well, enough, Hoss, Wyatt grumbled. *But we have an Irrat assassin on our tail.*

The Designate has updated me. I intended to catch up with you lot and try to even the score.

We do need our suit ninja, Wyatt agreed wryly. *But I show you still over a kilometer and a half away!*

That's why I decided to reach out; I'm never going to catch you.

We can't exactly turn back now, Wyatt informed me. *We pulled behind a short mesa. We're finally out of his sight.*

If we turn around, he will be able to target us with his weapon again, Anya supplied.

I know. I bit my lip and thought frantically. They needed to be able to hide somewhere, somewhere completely safe from Irrational assholes. Our problem wasn't that I needed to kill Firenzei, after all. I just needed my cadre to be safe.

But out here in the wide desert, hiding places didn't come easily. They might have given him the slip for a moment, but I saw his marker on my visual array.

It gained on their current location.

Maybe we can start a large loop back around to you? Wyatt proposed. *We'd have to leave cover but it might work.*

No. You need more cover not less. I urged the ATV forward and hammered the throttle down. *Maybe we can get some kind of satellite map? I can offload one easily enough if we can just figure out a place for you to stop—*

My eyes went wide as I realized what I said.

Stop. They only needed to stop.

Michael?

I ignored her and peered intently at the two markers on my visual. While I possessed solid information on distance between them and myself, I struggled to figure out the distance between Firenzei and my cadre.

Okay. I have an idea.

Will it get us killed? I honestly couldn't tell if Wyatt actually meant the question.

Probably not, I linked confidently. *Are you certain you're out of sight?*

Absolutely, Anya instantly replied. *Every opportunity he has to fire his weapon, he does so. The fact that he is not firing currently means he cannot see us.*

Okay. I'm going to be the big amazing hero here. I need you to do exactly as I say.

That sounds unbelievable, Wyatt grumbled.

I want you to pull off to the side, somewhere off the main trail. I want you to stop your ATVs without turning off the engine. Make certain you leave them running.

Stop? Wyatt shook his head. *Hoss, that don't sound healthy.*

Remain stopped for precisely five minutes, I continued. *At the end of five minutes, I want you to take off again. By that time, I should be there, and if Firenzei is a problem we'll take care of it.*

Michael, that does not make sense, Anya stated.

You're wasting time, I practically snarled over the link. *I can't take the time to assemble a packet, and you're losing minutes searching for an explanation. I'm trying to save your lives here!*

Fair enough, Brooks Brothers. Wyatt sighed. *We'll pull over here.*

Remember, I linked urgently, *five minutes. Then get going again.*

Michael! Anya's link felt sharp in my mind. *We are experiencing extreme axiomatic fluctuation!*

I know. You're fine, I assured her, although, I supposed she might not be.

Hell, I'd been worried about getting caught between places. What if I'd just sent them to that fate?

I dismissed the thought. Not helpful.

Hang onto your ATVs, guys. I'll see you in five minutes.

Bishop, Wyatt linked, uncertainly, *you better know what the fuck—*

With that, my cadre faded from my Crown, cast adrift to Sathantür, just outside Garnath Research Station.

At least, so I hoped.

6

Firenzei kept right on truckin', just as I'd hoped. His flashing indicator passed right by the spot where Wyatt and Anya stopped their vehicles and left the world of men.

"That's right, asshole." I let out a breath, surprised that I'd been holding it. "Hit the road."

His marker did, in fact, continue on, completely oblivious to the fact that my cadre had gone.

Unfortunately, Firenzei wasn't the only oblivious one.

108, we have lost Assets Guthrie and Petrova from telemetry. The Designate's link held an unspoken request for intel. Concern, yes.

But pressing, too.

They operate the same kind of interdimensional four-wheeler I do, Designate. I pulled my ATV past an outcropping of stone. *I used that fact in dealing with Firenzei.*

You... did what?

I patched her my link-record of the last few minutes, along with my conclusions.

Reckless, she instantly responded. *You have no way to ascertain their safety. They might not have passed back across the realmwall.*

I considered that, I admitted. *But I've seen Firenzei in action. If the Irrat caught them, I have no doubt the assassin would have liquidated my cadre.*

Wyatt Guthrie has experience using the Tangler in hot zones, she tersely replied.

True, I responded. *But not the clearance to do everything he might require. Firenzei is a monster, Designate. I know you have his specs, but I've faced the man.*

We are aware of that, 108.

Mine is an elegant solution which didn't require under-

equipped Assets to engage a skilled assassin.

Thanks to your action, they are tech adrift and offline. Their system status reads as 'Asset is presumed lost.'

It's the only solution I saw.

We have yet to see if it is a solution, she responded. *Thank you for the update.*

I had nothing to say to that.

I watched as Firenzei's marker vanished and realized I'd left something out of my elegant solution. I should have asked Anya to drop a marker for me over their last locale. As it stood, I didn't know exactly where they'd stopped.

I turned my ATV, aiming for their approximate location. My vehicle roared and leapt over gully and stone, speeding beneath an infinite sheath of stars.

Slowly, I realized this whole situation still left us with a significant problem. The vehicles worked well enough, but how could we stop once we reached Locale One? The moment we lost momentum, the vehicles would again return to their home topia. I might engage the *Adept* and leap off. But Anya? Wyatt?

Unlikely.

As I pondered the problem, the Designate's wintergreen link whispered in my mind again.

108, I realized you had not been updated, Ling sent. *Moments after you first appeared on telemetry, Facility 67 created a package of all known and relevant data on Aberration 45171R.*

On what now? I frowned.

The Vyriim. The parasitic phage species you encountered.

Oh. I felt dumb. *Right. Squiddy.*

The Vyriim are a hyper-intelligent species that constantly seek to create new colonies, the Designate interjected coolly.

Right. Serious threat. Got it.

Assets Petrova and Guthrie received this packet, shortly after your vehicle initiated its return to the topia of Sathantür. We're porting now.

Thank you. I'd open it later. I didn't want to trawl through data as I roamed the desert. It appeared fairly large, with several images. I didn't need the whole thing ported to memory.

A scarlet dataglyph appeared in the upper left-hand corner of my visual array, pulsing brightly. Over the course of a minute or so the dataglyph slowly faded.

The moment it vanished, the intel pounced into my mind.

I winced at the size of the packet—far larger than I'd expected. The jarring sensation lasted only a moment however.

Also, please be aware a drone drop has been scheduled and is currently on route. You are to be resupplied with viral mecha for your current needs.

Thank you, Designate. I started to say something else, but my vehicle lurched, a violent wrench as the engine whined.

The ATV started to chug. Greenish smoke boiled out the back.

"Shit." I stared down at the device. For all I knew, the thing might explode with the fire and fury of a neutron star at any moment.

Or it might just be out of gas.

I drove on for another twenty meters or so, hoping the grinding from the engine might quit. When the verdant smoke grew darker and smelled like burnt oil, I made my choice.

I couldn't just stop the thing, after all. I had no wish to return to the fun-filled Atrificia.

"Just fucking great." I toggled the *Adept*. With silvery grace burning through me, I leapt off the ATV.

Without a driver, it sailed forward, hopping wildly over a large stone and into an ancient gullywash. The steering wheel spun sideways, and the vehicle careened around a small stand of Joshua trees, green smoke billowing.

It began to slow.

"C'mon." I eyed the vehicle. "It'd be a big help if maybe you didn't—"

As it slowed, azure starbursts sang around the vehicle,

screaming sapphire sparks. I shielded my eyes against the light as it gave one final furious flash, wailing with eldritch power.

The ATV vanished.

"That," I growled. "If you didn't do that."

I remained in place for a long moment, stewing. In less than thirty seconds I'd gone from a man in possession of a perfectly serviceable ride to a poor sap alone and all but lost in the desert.

"Shit," I repeated. I stood up from the badass crouch I'd landed in and glowered at the empty space where the vehicle had just been.

I sighed.

How far might it still be to where my cadre drifted through? More than a kilometer, I felt certain. Also, to add a shit topping to the piece of shit cheesecake, the sun had set. Soon, it would get cold.

"Nothing for it," I grumbled.

I could at least peruse my data. For a moment, I went ahead and considered just saving the whole thing to memory. That might be convenient, despite the size.

But I had time to kill. Also, the desert loomed before me, silent and dark. It might be good to have some company until Wyatt and Anya returned.

I began to walk, toggling the Adjunct within my Crown.

Good evening, 108. The chipper voice felt out of place with my rotten mood and this desolate landscape.

"Ugh." I frowned. I didn't feel up to the Adjunct's primary aspect with its sunny demeanor.

Adjunct, open saved aspects.

Will comply, 108, the cheery voice responded. *I have program 12A saved to your preferences.*

The Cap'n? I wrinkled my nose. *No, thank you.*

You have recently played aspect 78T as well.

James Thibodaux? It might be nice to interface with the data through the warm, syrupy accent of 78T. Dude was a hoot.

But no. I needed something warmer. More friendly.

Next, I sent.

F23 is a common choice of yours.

Paige? I smiled. That might be nice, out here in the desert. I took a breath, considering.

The night had already begun to chill, and Paige reminded me of warmer, happier times. I'd built the aspect based upon a lady I once knew—a *Gatekeeper* Asset. Elle Quirke had been a good friend and had met an awful end.

Yes. Initiate aspect F23.

Will comply, Asset. Paige's voice overlaid that of the base Adjunct, smooth and sweet. The input acted far more human than the base Adjunct. **I see we have a new data package here.**

We do. I walked past the dry creek bed and out onto the flats.

Looks like you're on foot, Mike. I could almost feel the Adjunct smile, which always creeped me out a bit. **Maybe you'd like someone to read it to you while you hoof it?**

That would be preferable. I nodded. *Let me focus on the road.*

Will comply, she chirruped. **Let me just open this package on up.**

Coppery memory burned into my mind, sliding through and past everything I knew. As if I'd catalogued the Vyriim my entire life, the data poured into me, molten and hot. It sat there, waiting to be perused.

Is there a lot in there?

Oh yes. It felt as if she pursed her lips. **We have everything. There are maps of topiatic territories. Check this out. Lots of dimensional topography.**

On the left side of my visual array, a small box appeared. Paige flipped through map after map in that field, just to give me an idea of the scope of the data.

Wow. I let out a low whistle. *Not exactly my specialty.*

Well, it wouldn't be, would it? She responded. **Mike, this is data assembled by Facility Arbiters. Hardly your pay grade.**

327

What all's in there? Does it all matter?

We have accounts where they took entire worlds, moving across the Myriad in an incomprehensible game of interdimensional chess. There's details about their psionic capabilities and some data regarding their means of infesting sapient organisms.

Sounds depressing. I glanced up, focusing on the wheeling stars.

This is serious, Paige insisted. **According to this, once the Vyriim have their sights on a world, they've never been thwarted—not as far as our records show.**

Never? I stepped over an outcropping of dun stone. *That's a large word.*

Mike, if they're truly invading, this is the largest incursion in a generation. I felt as if dark eyes regarded me. **God, the largest in centuries.**

"Fuck me," I muttered. My heart pounded in my chest.

In an instant, our problems had grown exponentially larger.

Aberration 45171R

Read it to me, I linked. *Let's hear it.*

I'll place the heading in the dialogue box. It isn't vital, but it might make things easier.

The maps vanished. A block of text replaced them, glowing blue on my visual array. It appeared to be general intel, followed by a stark warning:

———————

ABERRANT DESIGNATION: 45171R

TYPE: Physical Phage (HAZARD LEVEL THREE)

IRRATIONALITY VARIANT: Intelligent Psionic, Variant L-5

TOPIATIC LOCALITY: Varies, multiple localities along the Outer Umbral Arc.

RESTRICTION PARAMETERS: None known.

PHYSICAL DESCRIPTION: Serpentine, varying in width from .12 mm to individuals thicker than 125 cm and as much as 7.25 meters in length. They tend to form clutches of aberrants, clustering and twining together to act as one. Variants may be equipped with cycs, hook-shaped appendages, or any other organs to be used by whatever clutch they inhabit.

THIS ENTRY REFERS TO A RACE OF PARASITICAL AND INVASIVE ABERRANT CREATURES NOT FOUND WITHIN RATIONALITY. AS SUCH, SOME INFORMATION MAY BE MISCATALOGUED OR INCORRECT. ORDINAL OPERATIVES MAKING USE OF THIS INFORMATION ARE THEREFORE CAUTIONED TO TREAT THIS INFORMATION WITH SCRUTINY.

"Got it," I breathed into the chilly air.

Okay, she responded. ***Ordinal Arbiters report Aberration 45717R are known widely as Vyriim. They are primarily found along the Outer Umbral Arc, have been sighted from the Shadow Wells of the Abbomai to the desert vistas of the Dehichotegha peoples.***

"Wow." I shook my head. "Right into the alien topography, huh?"

More like alien topio-politics. There's all kinds of reports in here from different worlds, all with various viewpoints on 45717R.

"Really?" I reached into my jacket, hunting a cigarette. "Like what?"

You know I hate it when you smoke.

"Lay off." I grinned as I lit up. "Answer the question."

Well, for example, Arbiter 214 reports: The locals refer to the phage as 'The Night's Whisper,' as they believe it only comes in darkness.

The Night's Whisper? I rolled my eyes.

When they are asked the nature of the Whisper, the topic is universally met with revulsion and hand signs meant to ward evil. The leaders of these people take it for granted that the Whisper will come upon them every few years, burrowing into the living bodies of young men and women as they come of age. These are said to go mad and set out for the desert with no water or food.

"They just accept that shit?" I exhaled smoke. "What do they believe happens to the people taken?"

Further questioning leads to a cultural belief that these travel to a forbidden location, hidden among the sands. Here it is said that a temple of black jade rests beneath the world.

"Huh." I couldn't help but recall the Atrificia, hidden beneath Sathantür.

Once those afflicted with the Night's Whisper travel within, they are never seen again.

"Morbid," I opined. "Are they all like this?"

This is a typical example of cultural tales regarding 45717R. Common themes include the aberrants' horrific capability to burrow into living tissue and dwell within the host. Through means both physical and psionic, they come to control the individual, taking possession of all knowledge and memories.

"I've seen something like that." I shuddered. "I bet it's tactically handy."

They are the perfect assassins, the perfect agents of espionage.

"This warning says we've never seen them within Rationality?" I scrambled down to a small rock-strewn wash, then chose to walk along it.

Correct. The bulk of 45717R dwells within a cluster of topiatic realities centered on the Refting Dirge, realms where they control every sapient species.

"Every one." I shook my head. "That sounds implausible."

In many cases, these topias contain peoples which have been relocated from other worlds, entire races captured and enslaved by the psionic phage. Arbiter 712 estimates that, within these realms, trillions of sentient beings may be under 45717R's malefic control. Paige paused, as if waiting for me to respond. Yet the information boggled me.

Trillions.

How did one even stand against a foe like that? An enemy who could take on the body of a trusted friend? An enemy whose numbers comprised roughly three entire orders of magnitude greater the population of the planet?

"What records do we have of their armaments and strategies?"

The class of their technological advancement is typically

quite advanced; their tactics during war are brutal. When
45717R seeks to inhabit a world, it seems inevitable they do so.

"You're saying we can't defeat them?"

I'm not, Paige responded. *True as that may be, 45717R does*
not spread across the Myriad like a cancer. Their selection of
topias for occupation is very specific. Arbiter 817 gives us one of
several voice records which might assist.

"Okay." I took a drag. "Shoot."

Paige's tone shifted then, from a younger woman to a lady who
sounded as if she'd seen it all. The recording came crystal clear, as
if 817 stood right next to me:

The topiatic realm of Eredãs sat squarely within the Refting
Dirge for its entire existence, surrounded on all sides by worlds
held by 45717R for thousands of generations. This fact has been
noted and studied, with servitors of curious Archons occasionally
making inquiries. A peaceful culture flourished on Eredãs, one
which valued wisdom and curiosity.

For time out of mind, 45717R ignored the small world as if it
didn't exist. Then, for unfathomable reasons of their own, the
Weir-craft of Dhire Lith, Cirniel, and Fel Arasel ignited
weftingways into Eredãs.

That realm fell within days—

"Pause." I frowned and kicked at a stone.

What's up, Mike?

"You say there are several of these? Voice records?"

817 left fifteen voice records regarding her experiences with
45717R. She apparently believes them to be a great threat.

"Play me another." I took the last drag on my cigarette. "Some
other world."

Will comply.

The topiatic realm of Aelthien is a unique curiosity in this
regard. Located far outside the Dirge—indeed, outside the Outer
Umbral Arc—it would seem this primitive world should be far from
the attentions of 45717R.

Yet nothing could be further from the truth.

Aelthien is the home to several subraces of base sapiens, as typical for most worlds which contain sentience. Also expected is the worship of several different Archons, with living mythologies built around them. These worshipers have bound affinities with various elements or concepts.

Unexpected is the presence of 45717R, positioned upon floating outposts which hover above the surface of the world.

These beings do not attack the realm below, nor do they place their own among the populace. Any and all activities which some might view as hostile are avoided.

They simply wait.

No efforts have determine—

"I hate mysteries," I spat. "It sounds like all we have is a whole bunch of nothing. Just bullshit."

There is… something else, Paige offered, a bit reluctantly. **The official entry updated as we listened to 817's records.**

"Really." I arched an eyebrow.

I'll just place it on your visual array.

The box holding the entry headings emptied only to be replaced with different text. In stark white lettering it read:

ADDENDUM: It is a certainty that within Dossier # I63-1998, 45717R initiated events which directly affected Rationality. Specifically, 45717R ignited technology that damaged the R3 subset of Temporal Axioms, the L9 subset of Spatial Axioms, and the entire holoquantum spectrum of the Axiomatic Realmwall. Events are unfolding, and this entry will be updated accordingly.

"Oh man." I popped the knuckles on my left hand.

This is your current dossier designation?

"It is," I responded. "Things just keep getting better and better."

Mike, Paige linked, **this is too much. The Designates only have three Assets on dossier, don't they?**

"Yup. Three," I replied gloomily. "And we're in the middle of fuck all. No conduits. Extraction will be hard."

That's putting a kind face on it.

Hoss? The link burred in my Crown, sounding a bit disjointed. *Please confirm location so ass-kicking can commence.*

Slowly, one marker appeared on my visual array, followed by a second.

"Hey, Paige, hold on a sec."

Cool beans, Mike.

I pulled my attention away from the Adjunct, not liking what it had to say. It felt easier, thinking of it as the Adjunct. That way it remained a machine.

Because I trusted Paige. Well, I trusted Elle, the woman the Adjunct had been patterned after. If *Paige* thought we might be in too deep...

It confirmed everything I believed.

Drones, Glyphs, and the Age of Funk

Hey there, buddy. I sent Wyatt a rueful smile. *You enjoy visiting exciting and beautiful Sathantür?*

Beneath their markers, I saw 0.275km in a small legend. I grinned, impressed. I had little more than a quarter kilometer to go.

I'd made decent time.

That was some class-A motherfuckery right there, Bishop. Genuine irritation bled through his link.

Hey now. I chuckled. *Firenzei is gone. We're all safe.*

What did the Designate think of your stratagem, Michael? Even Anya sounded a bit annoyed.

We have discussed my elegant solution, I responded. *I'm glad you're both well.*

Reckless asshole, Wyatt grumbled. *I almost didn't make it back!*

Asset Guthrie's vehicle appears to be damaged, Anya informed me. *It is emitting vapors.*

Mine did that. I pulled myself out of the gully wash. *Green smoke?*

You called it, Wyatt admitted. *We throttled these things hard when fleeing Firenzei.*

They must not be charged enough to keep them running long, I reasoned. *I had to dive off before it stopped and pulled me driftways again.*

You what? Wyatt yelped.

When mine started smoking, I triggered the Adept. *Dove off the ATV. When it stopped, it fucked off back to its home topia.*

Did you not consider turning the vehicle off? Confusion wound through Anya's link.

I... I felt my cheeks burn. *You know, I didn't. I just remember-ed that whenever I stopped, it pulled me back.*

335

Christ, Bishop, Wyatt chuckled. *It's a switch.*

I was panicking at the time!

Oh God above, Paige interjected to me alone.

You stay out of this, I linked the Adjunct.

Why don't you stop panicking and rendezvous with us? We'll figure out what to do next, okay, Hoss?

I have another idea, Paige suggested, including all Assets in her link. **Mike is about 34 meters from the drop zone for Hornet-class drone YT-330t, which will happen in approximately three minutes. Perhaps the rendezvous can be scheduled for after the pick up?**

I winced.

Normally, this would have been a simple system message for all of us. However, I stood closest to the drop, therefore it made the most sense for me to be the pick-up man.

So *my* Adjunct had been tasked with providing the data.

I knew Wyatt's response immediately.

Mike? A wicked grin crept across his face. *Bishop, you runnin' simulations of pretty girls over your Adjunct while you're alone on the desert?*

What? I scowled. *No, I required the Adjunct to assist with data processing while I traversed the desert. That's all.*

So you don't have her walking around topless on your visual array?

No!

On my visual array, a ruby dataglyph appeared, approximately thirty meters away. I turned toward it.

Paige! Wyatt crowed. *That's what you named her, right?*

Michael, I did not know you still ran aspect F23. Anya's link felt odd, a concern I couldn't pinpoint.

Didn't you have an aspect specifically patterned after a French maid? I growled at Wyatt. *I don't think you have room to talk.*

Whatever. The large man chuckled. *I'm not one to deny a man his fantasies.*

I'm approaching the drone, I linked. *Maybe you can finish making fun of me after I bring you your much-needed meds.*

Ha! Wyatt actually laughed over the link. *Fair enough, Hoss.*

YT-330t proved to be a standard Facility drone. The winged robot resembled a metallic crossbreed between a jeweled wasp and a hyperactive dragonfly—if someone had blown the result up to the size of a dachshund and given it a pneumatic projector and a hold full of axiomatic spikes, limited-capacity, barbed grappling hooks, and God knew what else.

As Wyatt would say, these things didn't play fuck around.

The *Hornet* disengaged its *Wraith* as I approached, thus drifting into visibility. It peered up at me, eyes shining in the pale moonlight.

It flitted silver wings but didn't take off.

Let me access its cargo hold sequence, Paige cautioned.

Moments later I heard a quiet hiss. A silver panel on the chest of the drone slid open.

"These things creep me out," I admitted to Paige. "I can't help but think one could slaughter me if it had the mind to."

They're wicked little things, she agreed. ***But they're geared to ping an active Crown as a friendly—at least, when roaming like this.***

"That's good." I bent over and retrieved the small package.

No sooner did I have the mecha than the *Hornet* re-engaged its *Wraith.* I could still see it on my visual array, a simple white outline.

Its wings buzzed as it lifted off, speeding away.

Mecha achieved. I'm incoming.

We're here, Wyatt sent.

I'm a quarter klick away. I'll see you soon.

337

2

The first thing we decided, once we found each other again, was to sit put.

"Firenzei might double back," I reasoned. "Why don't we let the asshole get good and far in front of us? Then, we get in, get our readings, and get out."

Reasonable, Michael. Anya nodded. *I have already picked up some unusual activity from Locale One; remaining in place will help me determine the axiomatic means.*

"I can set up some perimeter spikes." Wyatt raised an eyebrow. "In case some motherfucker decides to teleport over and try to shoot us."

"Good idea." I pulled out the viral mecha from the drone drop, divvied up the spoils, and settled in.

An hour after Wyatt's ATV failed, we still waited.

Nothing. No Firenzei.

I think it's time to move. I stretched. *Dude's gone.*

But I have all these spikes laid out! Wyatt protested. *I wanted to watch him teleport into the middle of a fiery explosion.*

"Me too, buddy." I stood. "Just not in the cards."

Firenzei is not in operation anywhere on my telemetry. His range would seem to indicate we would read him before he targeted us.

You have an idea of his range? I raised an eyebrow.

I went over all the data we have, she replied. *His displacement is trackable.*

Huh. Wyatt stared at her. *Maybe we could do something with that.*

"I don't care if I ever see him again," I grumbled. "Let's move. We've got a Locale One to hit."

"I'm up. Let's get in, get out, and go home." Wyatt grinned at me.

I feel as if we have neglected something. Anya's link felt a touch distant. *That Irrational acted as if he knew you, Asset Guthrie.*

"Found 'im in the Booby Trap," Wyatt admitted. "I thought he was just some jackass." He spat into the dust.

"He did seem to be a jackass," I confirmed. "Good eye."

"We got into a bit of a scrap; he didn't pull anything Irrational though. Asshole must have been scoping me out."

"I know you're accustomed to weird dudes scoping you out in bars, but…" I hated to even mention it. "How did he know where to find you? Or who you were?"

"I don't know, Hoss."

"In that case, it is reasonable to assume they have identified all three of us," Anya noted. "Although I cannot say how."

Wyatt and I exchanged a dark glance. For a long moment, we stood in silence.

I sighed.

"There's no guessing, and it doesn't help." I stared up at the sky. "Time's tickin'."

"Roger that," Wyatt agreed. "Let's get going."

Traveling by foot, a long hour passed. Dark fell, swiftly growing deeper. We still walked, miles from anywhere. Anya all but crawled along so she could analyze her data. Wyatt's gear slowed him as well. Fortunately, I was practically high on viral mecha.

In fact, on that front, we were all feelin' fine.

After the drone drop, we'd acquired enough injectors for each of us to get four stims—and have several injectors left over. We each possessed different requirements, naturally. Wyatt received mecha that would augment the oxygen in his bloodstream as well as repair worn muscles from our long hike. I'd taken some of that myself, as well as a host of pain-killing VM. Also, I'd gotten another injector to help knit up the damage done to my back. By the time we'd reach Locale One, I should be nearly whole.

I'd probably learned more about viral mecha on this dossier than on all my others combined. Before, I hadn't cared to learn much about them, just 'inject this thing in your leg.'

Anya's experience with injectors played out quite differently.

The *Preceptor*-class viral mecha weren't as physical as ours. In fact, some of hers acted as slight toxins in a typical Asset's systems. Most involved an upgrade to her capability to process data, and some added extra memory capabilities through the mecha themselves.

Whatever her cocktail today, Anya seemed even more detached than usual. Her blue eyes vacant, her head twitched as she processed a huge amount of axiomatic data. She jerked as I watched, as if having small fits. As we walked along, she held her hands out, sometimes in front of her, sometimes to the side. Her fingers plucked at nothingness, as if the world had been constructed of some great string instrument only she saw.

We need to decrease speed twenty-seven percent, she linked, clipped and robotic. *Locale One is less than one-hundred meters away, up the mesa and around to our east. The area is not quite Rationality zero, so I need to do some quick analysis.*

You do what you need to, princess. Wyatt leaned against an outcropping. *My dogs are barkin'. I don't mind sitting a spell.*

Briefly, I glanced over the topographies in my Crown while Anya worked.

Five minutes later, she sighed. "This is going to take longer than I initially believed." While her right hand drifted down to her side, she turned to gaze at Wyatt and me. "There is an anomaly I cannot account for within the missile silo."

"Dangerous?" Wyatt pulled off one of his boots and massaged his foot.

"I do not think so." She glanced at him and her brow furrowed. "It appears as if some of the basic Facets of Rationality have been tampered with, yet only at this location. Even as I peruse the data, I cannot determine why this would be so."

"If it's not dangerous, are we ready to advance?" I popped the knuckles on my left hand.

"Unfortunately, no." Anya gazed at me, her eyes the blue of the summer sky. "I need to determine what is happening here and why. Telemetric readings are the entire purpose of our presence."

"If it's not dangerous, maybe I should go ahead?" I watched Wyatt put his boot back on. "It's not far, and I can toggle the *Wraith*."

"That sounds good to me," My large friend nodded. "But you're the one with the Designate sync in place. I know that makes you all 'in charge,' but maybe you should get clearance?"

"Smart," I agreed and stepped away from them.

"Super genius," Wyatt responded, tapping his temple.

I sighed and opened the dialogues on my visual array, selecting Designate Ling's crimson dataglyph. A dulcet tone pinged in my Crown.

Immediately, she inundated my mind, more intimate than any link.

108, she greeted me. *It appears you've almost made Locale One?*

Correct, Designate. First, I wanted your input on our next move. I toggled the sync port, making all my experiences of the last ten minutes immediately available for her.

The cool wash of her perused my Crown with fingers of silvery mint.

Preceptor *Petrova is correct. Her purpose is to process and record localized data.* She paused. *It is preferred that she continue her current task.*

I expected as much.

You should take point. Keep the Wraith *initiated and do not engage any unfriendly targets.*

Only fight friendly targets. I sent a wry smile. *Understood.*

We shall keep the sync on standby as you approach the loca-tion, she continued, as if she didn't realize how funny I was. *If you encounter anything unusual, initiate this connection first.*

Understood.

Hopefully, there won't be anything dangerous to report, Asset. She paused. *It is possible Petrova can learn everything we need to know here, and we can then plan for your extraction.*

Still no conduit? I truly didn't need to ask. We stood in the middle of a vast, empty nowhere.

A conduit to your current location is impossible, she confirmed. *However Asset 306, Liam Hunter, is standing by. We have a* Gatekeeper *conduit available in Barstow and Asset Hunter can extract you using an* Atlas-class *vehicle.*

No Facility helicopter? I teased.

The Atlas *is tactically outfitted, should you require additional firepower during your extraction,* she reminded me. *Resources are in position.*

Well, that's good. I nodded. *So Anya will stay here and continue her telemetric readings. I'll step ahead and provide a live link on Locale One.*

Exactly, Ling responded. *Hopefully, between these two actions, we shall determine all we need to know. In that instance, your extraction shall begin within the hour.*

Sounds good. I glanced back at the rest of my cadre. *I'll inform Petrova and Guthrie of our updated plan of action and then set out.*

Excellent, 108. She paused for just a moment before giving me the signoff I'd come to expect:

As always, we wish you well in the days ahead.

3

In the darkness, the old silo building loomed over me, almost as if it might fall over. A significant portion of its roof had been blown away. Holes gaped where the windows had been. The front door hung askew.

As I approached the structure, I saw a sign. I toggled my optics to read it properly:

WELCOME TO SITE 451.
Please have all clearance documents ready.

"I don't have those," I muttered. "I hope being nigh invisible is enough."

This is Locale One? Paige asked curiosity. ***Doesn't look like much.***

"Agreed." I studied the building again trying to notice anything at all out of sorts. "Of course, there's that ATV," I realized. I hadn't seen it at first, not with my optics switched off. Now as I approached, I realized the squat shape must be Firenzei's vehicle, parked off to one side.

I found our asshole, I linked my cadre. Moments later I sent them a small patch comprised of my current visual.

If I remember right, Wyatt drawled, *you're not supposed to poke that asshole by your lonesome.*

I'll leave all the asshole poking to you, hillbilly, I retorted. *Just keeping everyone apprised.*

Thank you, Michael, Anya responded in distant distraction. *I'm stepping inside.*

The single-story building had been abandoned long ago. So long that the shag carpet in the front room came right out of the Age of Funk. Dank, stale air wafted around me with each step, the musty scent all but overwhelming me.

Not what I'd expect, Paige interjected.

"Me neither."

At first blush, the ruined building appeared small. I, however, had uploaded the schematics to my Crown. Reviewing my dossier, I saw the building extended far back into the mesa. Several small laboratories as well as three launch tubes were included. According to the government, it hadn't seen active use in over twenty years.

The Facility had evidence to the contrary.

Anya, do you show any unexpected activity in here before I go inside?

I do not read anything. Anya's link held a confusion I'd never felt from her.

What do you mean?

Previously I had only perused the local telemetry with a wide field of focus. In response to your question, I focused that field to ascertain your safety.

I appreciate that, I responded.

There is nothing there. Her eyes widened.

Um. Wyatt spat and peered around. *So Locale One is at Rationality zero?*

No. She shook her head. *That is not it at all. I am not reading any Rationality levels, neither ambient nor artificial. No telemetry. No readings on the axiomatic weave.* Through her link I felt the fingers on her left hand twitch spastically, as if she reached for something not there. *There are no readings there at all.*

Not good, Hoss, Wyatt linked to me alone.

As much as we enjoyed teasing Anya, she provided invaluable data. Every cadre of Assets retained a *Preceptor* for a reason. Without her, we'd stumble about all but blind.

I always hate agreeing with you, I replied to Wyatt. To both, I sighed. *I'll engage the* Wraith *and scout ahead. Do you want me to patch my visual to one of you?*

Negative, Wyatt spat. *I'll set us a perimeter here, and Anya can keep trying to calibrate.*

If nothing changes, I will contact the Designate, Anya linked. *Dossier specifications may alter if I cannot take readings.*

Understood. I nodded in agreement. *I'll be back before I have to disengage my tech.*

Fifteen minutes. Copy that, Wyatt sent. *Be careful, Hoss.*

Cautiously, I walked inside. Detritus and shattered glass crunched beneath my feet. The interior of the building appeared as broken down as I'd expected. At one point, the front room had been a waiting area, complete with '70s style rounded, plastic chairs and a spot behind thick plexiglass for security personnel. Today I noted broken windows, an old couch someone dragged in, and a fine layer of dust covering everything. One of the walls featured a mural of spray-painted graffiti. Later, someone tried to cover the art with a flat whitewash. Over time, though, the graffiti bled through.

A dark, empty hallway next to the security window appeared to be the only way forward. Several old magazines lay scattered on the floor, but the hall quickly faded into blackness.

It gets dark pretty quickly. Engaging optics.

Copy that, Michael. Anya's voice sounded distant.

Our enhanced optics were a combination of night-vision and infrared. The Crown possessed the ability to read visual data, and it used both technologies to create an accurate picture of the world. It then used its connections to my visual cortex to provide the full picture, in the same way it added location markers or interface controls.

It also tended to give Assets a headache after a while. Like the *Wraith*, I couldn't keep it on for long.

Once my optics activated, the passageway didn't feel nearly as foreboding. It remained a mess, however. I crept forward, both Stilettos drawn. Broken bottles, folders of scattered papers, and stuffing from unfashionable cushions littered the floor.

I came to a doorway on one side and peered into an abandoned office. Remnants of a bookshelf and an old, broken desk remained,

347

nothing threatening.

Still, I kept my guard up. Without Anya's readings, an Irrat might lurk anywhere. Firenzei could jaunt in and have a bullet in my head, if I didn't take care.

This place seemed like an odd setup for some Irrat headquarters. Why leave all the debris? To make it seem abandoned? If so, they'd done a perfect job. The air smelled stale and dust covered everything.

Let me know if you see anything I miss, will you? I asked the Adjunct as I rubbed my achy head.

Will do, Mike.

I stepped into the small office and peered about. If someone had been here, I'd see a footprint in the dust on the matted carpet, a clean patch on the desk, some indication.

No. The room remained simply a mess. A mess no one had touched in years. I glanced around and nudged a pile of papers with my foot. A series of inspection records met my gaze, all faded ink and yellowed paper. I peered about; even the smallest detail out of place might matter.

You need to come back, Hoss. Anya's got news.

She's got me beat then. I kicked over the papers. *There's nothing here. Floor and furniture's all covered in dust. No one's touched anything in ages.*

I bet. Come on back, and we can account for that.

I turned, walked out of the musty ruin, and flipped off the *Wraith.* Color flooded into the world.

Hey. What's that? As Paige linked, she drew a circle around something on my visual array.

I turned back to see what I'd missed.

Next to the security booth, before the dust got so thick, a wooden post had been installed. At first glance, one might assume it assisted in holding up the gaping ceiling, just as a safety measure. Engraved on this side of the post, though, an angry series of glyphs burned, shedding a faint orange radiance.

348

I'd passed right by it on the way in, but approaching from this direction gave me an entirely new perspective.

"What are you?" I peered closer.

Scrutinizing the center symbol, it appeared somewhat like an Egyptian eye, only wider, rounder.

It stared as if it gazed on things it couldn't unsee.

Running analysis. It'll take some time, however. Lattice records show literally millions of Irrational symbols.

"I get it, Paige. Thanks."

I considered linking Anya but knew it to be of no use. After all, she'd already stated she couldn't read anything in the silo.

I stared at the symbol a moment longer, hoping to give the Designates a good representation. Then I placed my hand next to it, for a size comparison.

My hand tingled, instantly, as if falling asleep.

I gaped at the symbol when the air around me collapsed against itself.

BANG!

The loud sound washed over me, and I stumbled backward, only to fall against a curved surface.

What?

Hoss! Wyatt's link sounded muffled. *Are you alright?*

I... I stared around, somewhat gobsmacked.

A scarlet bubble encapsulated me, pulsing with a murderous crimson.

I don't know, I sent rapidly. *I think that—*

Before I finished my link, the bubble plummeted down through the floor. It carried me with it in a rapid fall that made my gorge rise.

An infinity of shadows swirled around me.

Then the bubble vanished and I fell.

I heard lamentations, the wails of inhuman mouths. Around me, epochs drifted and my mind scintillated.

I screamed, exactly in the fashion of a ten-year-old.

Doors Upon Doors

On my way down, I had the good fortune to clip my head on a rocky outcrop. I hissed in a quick breath, preparation for a burst of expletives when I smashed into the ground.

The hard landing knocked all the breath out of me.

For a moment my head swam, my clock thoroughly cleaned.

Fucking OW! I linked out of habit more than anything else, but the awful truth hit me immediately.

It felt like I'd linked into a large, empty room and heard only my own voice echo back.

Alone. Adrift.

"Paige?"

Nothing. Without the Lattice, the Adjunct had no connection to my Crown.

"Good. Absolutely wonderful." I pushed myself up and noted that, even though it felt as if I'd struck the ground with all the force of a falling dump truck, the ground here actually had a mossy, almost-but-not-quite soft texture. Just a little more padding than your average stone surface.

It hadn't helped much.

I tried to blink the stars away from my eyes. Adrift from Rationality, a terrifying pang of claustrophobia ran through me. Forcibly, I slowed my breathing and tried to relax my tightened muscles.

This is Michael Bishop, Asset 108. I am currently tech adrift. Please respond.

Nothingness. Only the empty, hollow echo of complete solitude answered me.

"Dammit," I grunted.

Of all the situations I could possibly stumble into, I hated this scenario the most.

As an Asset, I'd become accustomed to the constant connection to the rest of my cadre—or at least to a Designate on solo missions. Due to the existence of our Lattice and the Adjunct that helped us navigate it, Assets always felt an intimacy incomprehensible to baseline humanity.

Until one became severed from that link.

With a twitch, I switched my Crown's communication channels to manual. Like a walkie-talkie, this channel didn't need the Lattice.

This is Michael Bishop, Asset 108. I am present on reconnaissance and exploration of this topiatic locale. I am alive. This message has broadcast since [#system time] when I was located at [#system coordinates]. I continue my reconnaissance and await Facility contact.

"That might do." I spent a moment setting the general-purpose broadcast for any Assets who came within range, put it on repeat, muted the outflow on my end, and changed channels.

Now it would play endlessly. Anyone with a Crown would see the signal.

"That'll have to be enough." I sighed and pushed myself up to glance around.

Darkness covered everything except for a haunted, glowing haze, which hung like death shrouds in the air. It pulsed softly with an unearthly, saffron color—a hue my mind struggled to comprehend.

The mist swirled, and the air became heavy and hard to breathe. The hidden danger of my deep, gasping breaths became apparent.

"Fuck." I pulled my shirt over my mouth like a child trying to avoid a foul scent.

I had no means of knowing if the air here even contained oxygen. Breathing in glowing alien mist didn't strike me as the wisest of moves. However, I didn't exactly have Anya here to advise me on local atmospheric conditions.

"Okay, dingdong," I muttered from beneath my shirt, "think."

After a moment of paralysis, I realized it probably didn't matter. I'd fallen here. Whatever clever passage the Vyriim's servitors had contrived opened out somewhere distantly above this spot. I peered up, searching for handholds or some kind of climbing mechanism.

No such luck. The walls appeared smooth for the most part, although I saw a few outcroppings higher up.

A simple but elegant trap. I had no means to reach the door even if it were still open. The *Adept* might give me preternatural grace and dexterity beyond all reckoning, but it didn't matter if I couldn't climb up.

"Stuck." I glared at the shaft I'd fallen down.

I decided it unlikely that the atmosphere would be poisonous. The Vyriim had, after all, allied with human Irrats like Firenzei. Who knew how many were infested by the parasitical horrors, but I had to guess at least a few. The Vyriim wouldn't waste hosts in a topia where they couldn't breathe.

"Seems reasonable enough," I muttered to myself, knowing full well I grasped at straws.

As if to prove it to myself, I took several deep breaths.

I completely failed to collapse on the ground and writhe with seizures.

The atmosphere might be okay, yet I still found it difficult to breathe. To be honest, my head swam slightly. Now, I'd just taken a knock on the noggin, but...

"Better to be safe."

I selected the tiny, scarlet dataglyph and opened the internal dialogue of my Crown. Instantly, a ring of dataglyphs appeared on my visual array, each corresponding to a different firmware packet within my system.

Grumbling, I cycled through them, searching for the port to my physical statistics interface. I didn't commonly fiddle with my internals, preferring to leave that to a *Caduceus*. The vast sea of dataglyphs confused the hell out of me.

I found my metabolic indicators, as well as basic data regarding my blood pressure, white blood cell production, and respiration. That last one intrigued me, and I expanded the details. My visual array shifted to thirty different numeric indicators. Each displayed a meter to the side, color coded to show current status.

Nearly half of them had crept down to the yellow.

"Not good," I grumbled.

I couldn't know the nature of the mist. That made it nigh-impossible to calibrate my viral mecha against it. I mean, I could breathe, mostly, but that might not be enough.

To keep watch over it, I resized the dialogue and placed it in the upper left corner of my visual array. Then I pulled up the interface for my viral mecha. I rarely even peeked at their data, but today was one of those days. Fortunately, a good number of mecha went idle after they knitted up my earlier injuries.

Without a Designate or a *Caduceus*, I remained uncertain of what to tell them to do. Yes, I needed my oxygen levels moderated, but by how much? What rate of supplementation worked for the local axiomatic set up?

"Just impossible to know." I stood lost, helpless.

A few moments of study led me to recall type III mecha were typically geared to detoxify the system. I opened a small sub-frame which showed how many were available and tasked them to remove buildups of lactic acid in my muscles and carbon dioxide in my blood.

I quickly reviewed the system standard entries on hypoxia and wished for a moment that, just once, I'd actually taken the *Caduceus* module.

Mecha engaged, 108.

The Crown's response felt clunky and slow when disconnected from the Lattice, but for now I didn't mind.

Any voice provided more comfort than the silence of this place.

As a shot in the dark, I set several groups of type II mecha to produce oxygen. Typically, they augmented reflexes or manufactured hormones, but producing pure O_2 required far fewer resources than those tasks.

"Okay." I watched the system readouts for a moment. "That might be okay. I can adjust later if need be."

I pulled a Stiletto with my left hand. I'd never been the best southpaw shot, but I had no idea what the local axioms might do to my kinetic weapon. Since I didn't intend to discover my only weapon had become useless just as some gore-drenched abomination bore down on me, I drew a katana with the right.

Sharp pieces of steel tended to function almost everywhere.

I crept forward.

The spongy ground gave way to a pitted, metallic floor. The entire tunnel had been constructed of rusted iron or some other dark ore. Great plates of it had been fused together. While some places used precise welds, others held brackets and brassy pins.

The tunnel appeared octagonal at first, each plate fastened to the next at an unusual angle.

"But it's not." I ran my fingers along one thick plate and peered at the hall. The place tilted strangely, as if the world moved subtly beneath my feet, akin to the gentle roll of a ship but over more dimensions.

The nausea that resulted made counting difficult. I felt as if, unless I stared directly at a surface, it would shift.

"Seven," I stated.

Blinking, I immediately realized I'd miscounted. As the world bent and tipped, I couldn't track the sides of the hallway. I continually lost focus.

The sensation made me a touch dizzy.

I peered down the long, straight tunnel, but the mist proved problematic. Its spectral light obscured more than it revealed, and blanketed everything in a uniform, uneasy radiance.

I reached out and ran a hand along the wall as I walked. It both helped with my slight dizziness and made certain I tracked the hallway.

Very soon, the passageway branched off into several more tunnels.

"*Five* of them?" I peered at each, fairly certain of my reckoning. Yet each branch sat at right angles to the others. If true...

"There can't be a total of five passages," I muttered. "Not with those edges." Wary of the oddly shifting space, I counted again, noting the angle of the corners as best I could.

Five passages, all with right-angle corners. A patent impossibility, yet every corner I touched registered at roughly ninety degrees.

"Maybe I'm just delusional." I stopped for a moment and checked my oxygen levels. They appeared to be within parameters, but my Crown showed I'd overproduced monoamines and thyroid stimulating hormones.

Specific hormone levels lay far beyond my expertise. Still, I saw a few mecha available and clumsily allocated them to stabilize my baselines.

After a few moments of fiddling, I frowned.

"I can't do any good here." I closed the dialogues. None of the levels had hit yellow, so I felt fairly confident in leaving them.

For now.

I kept my hand on the wall as I turned down the first of the branches. After about ten strides I saw a hatch.

It loomed large, like the kind of door one might see in a noir bank-robbery flick. Not that I'd ever seen a vault set in the floor like this. Nor could I find an obvious handle.

The brushed steel and brass hatch gleamed, fully refined, unlike the not-quite-iron walls.

That caught me for a moment. It looked exactly like a thing I might expect to find in Rationality.

I peered around the edge of the hatch for any identifying

marks.

There.

"Sadhana Corporation," I mumbled. "Est. 1980." I nodded. Definitely produced in the Rational world and then brought here.

Still, no handle. Did it only open from the opposite side?

No sooner had I wondered than I heard a crushing, grinding sound down the passageway. It echoed hollowly and lurched into a whirring roar with clacks reminiscent of incredibly loud machinery.

Ignoring the inert hatch, I crept forward, wincing at the sound as I peered through the mist.

My initial assessment appeared to be correct.

Machinery sat all along the edge of the hallway. Turbines pulled at several convoluted systems of belts. I saw enough dials and needles to recreate the inside of one of the early Apollo rockets. Interestingly, I found no digital readouts, computer screens, or terminals. The outdated technology ran on steam that vented thickly into the room.

Soon the hallway ended at a slightly larger room. Here, clockwork machinery covered every wall.

I guessed different systems had been patched together over time. Grease dripped into shimmery pools on the floor and flowed down serial numbers and manufacturer stamps. Smoke and steam escaped from coughing valves, and the smell of burning oil hung in the air.

All of it remained very mundane: Rational technology brought into an Irrational world.

"Almost fifteen minutes." I scowled at the time. I'd been adrift now for a noticeable bit. Anya and Wyatt should realize something had gone wrong.

"Any moment now."

Unless the temporal drift stretched too wide. What if an hour here equaled a second back in Rationality? Temporal chasms weren't often that severe, but theoretically...

357

"It might take days for them to even notice." I paced, thinking about what I should do.

Gathering intel remained the best use of my time.

I turned down the second passage and walked through the citrine haze. Keeping my hand along the wall, I made certain I followed the path without veering.

The second tunnel opened up far sooner, and appeared to be older. Its walls held scattered, rusty pits all along its surface, far deeper than the ones I'd seen earlier.

"As if the passage itself is decades older, maybe a century." I made certain to get a good look at the battered walls, so my Crown would get a clear record of everything. "I don't know how that could be with interconnected passages."

Though this corridor housed far more machinery, these machines sat silent, dead as the grave. I didn't see any oil drips on the ground, and the air didn't smell of hot grease and steam. All the dials pointed slackly to one side, and none of the gears so much as twitched.

I did see another hatch, however.

This one sat in the center of the machine room and, though smaller than the first, it had been constructed in the exact same manner. Again I crouched, searching for a handle, a wheel, or a latch. I would have settled for a fucking doorbell had one suddenly shown up.

Nothing.

Nothing, save ironcast letters on the surface. I brushed away flakes of iron oxide.

"Sadhana, Est. 1980." I shook my head as I read. Those words struck me, here in a sideways, castaway reality.

I studied the wending corridor that stretched onward, trying to wrap my head around what I'd discovered. The hazy passageway continued after the machine room. Three more huge hatches waited, surrounded by glowing, eldritch mist.

Beyond, the hallway abruptly ended. A wall stood there, covered in machinery that appeared as if it had lain dead for many lifetimes.

"Damnit." I sighed and wondered if the corridors led anywhere at all. So far, each had been a no-go.

I headed back toward the nexus of passages and turned down hallway three.

2

I leaned against the pitted wall of hallway four—practically a replica of the first three—when the uncanny sensation of monster trucks and stock cars blossomed in my mind. Even more, I felt *him*, sensed his snarky smile and sarcastic wit. Just then, that half-broken link felt like a raft to a drowning man.

Hoss, I assume you're still vertical since you got that awful message runnin'. The scratchy words warbled, not as clear as a Lattice link.

Oh man! I laughed. *It always surprises me to be happy to hear from you, Wyatt.*

Had to come. I felt his grin over the link. *Figgered whatever kept ya must be something you wanted to selfishly have all to yerself.*

Like what?

Some Irrat hottie in this hole? Maybe a barrel of good whiskey?

Now you're dreaming. I grinned like a loon.

I have ambient data, Anya interrupted. *It is complex and will take a moment to compile all readings. Several axiomatic strands are far sub-Rational.*

I get it. I scowled. *Check out the atmospheric and gaseous subset. I'm convinced whatever we're breathing isn't quite right.*

Understood, Michael.

Oh man, Wyatt crowed. *You've just been having all sorts of fun, haven't you?*

Yeah, I responded. *I noticed oxygen was off right away. I know nothing about allocating mecha, but I've been fiddling with it anyway.*

Clear the line for a moment, and I will send standard directives for your viral mecha. Anya paused. *While I do not have the specifications of a* Caduceus, *I am aware how to use the mecha to maintain baseline metabolism.*

Wyatt and I linked our assent at the same time, *Clear/Understood.* The two links confused our Crowns' processing for a moment. Unlike a Lattice link, our secondary comms wouldn't temporally sequence our links and force them to make sense.

A series of high-pitched whines and seemingly random tones sang in my Crown. It warbled a long moment, and then I felt Anya connect like warm honey pouring into my mind.

Crown sync request detected. The prompt felt slow, clunky. **Asset 108, do you wish to allow Petrova, Anya, to create connection 01-012wk?**

Yes, I linked. *Allow connection.*

I pulled up my mecha interface and watched Anya set the parameters. She didn't fiddle around with the internal dialogues as much as I had; instead she went straight to the mecha command modules.

What are you doing? I asked as she pulled several of my currently active mecha into docility and then re-tasked large numbers of them using the command modules.

Viral mecha are, at their base, axiomatic engines, much like Wyatt's spikes. They allow for alteration of the basic laws of physics, only within a much smaller range.

Really? I cocked my head at that. I hadn't made much study of the technology; I'd just always assumed the VM were little more than nano-machines.

I lack the training to task them in the same way a Caduceus *might. Yet each mecha has a series of fundamental covenants programmed into it. These are fairly simple to access. One of the first codes is a command to maintain the body at its primary operating state.*

Okay, so that's just a setting? To do whatever the body requires in order to continue functioning?

It frees up the Caduceus *quite a bit. Once active, these viral mecha can choose to create extra oxygen, heal tissue, or modulate hormones, all based upon the Asset's requirements. They work much slower in this capacity but respond automatically to shifting conditions.*

So I didn't need to attempt to give them specific tasks?

All manner of specific tasks can be important, Anya pointed out. *In this instance, however, all you require is for the mecha to engage their fundamental covenants.*

Good to know. Another question occurred to me. *Do any of the local axioms interfere with our gear, Anya? I don't want to find out my disruptors don't work or the* Adept *actually slows me down.*

Your gear is fine, Michael, but Wyatt will have to recalibrate his baselines for the Tangler.

How far afield are you, stranger? Wyatt linked. *We gonna have to walk an hour to find you?*

An hour? My eyes narrowed. *How long have I been gone?*

According to our systems, Michael, you went adrift two hours, forty-eight minutes ago. Anya paused. *We would have been dispatched sooner, but the Designate wanted to put secondary protocols in place.*

Right, Wyatt cut in. *Easy enough to see why you didn't show. I'm only glad I didn't land on Rosie when I came through.*

Initial diagnostics seems to show no lasting damage to my systems either, Anya continued. *Although without the Lattice, my readings will be limited. We also lack deep telemetry and I cannot upload data on axiomatic weaving.* She paused. *I show your systems are undamaged, Michael.*

That's good. I'm not far. If you come forward, the passageway will split. I'll meet you there. I turned and headed back to the junction.

"Ha!" Wyatt gave me a big grin when I appeared through the mist. "Thought we'd lost you, Hoss."

"Not yet. So far, the most dangerous thing here is boredom."

The man came forward to give me a handshake that ended in

a crushing bear hug.

"The atmosphere might have eventually killed you." Anya didn't look directly at me, instead she read her visual array. "But not for another several hours."

"But my mecha have that handled now?" I popped a knuckle on my left hand.

"Affirmative." She met my gaze. "We could avoid breathing altogether if required."

"Here's where we stand." I turned back the way I'd come and gestured. "We've got antiquated machinery and dead ends down there. Also, I found hatches in the floor, but they don't open from this side."

"Sounds lovely." Wyatt grimaced. "If we're lucky, mebbe they're *all* dead ends, and we can be happy lil' castaways."

Anya's hands twitched, and she appeared distracted. I noticed her fingers moved a touch slower without the Lattice.

"If you want, I can patch you the layout of the areas I've covered." I smiled. "Then we can see if the next passage is different in any way. Maybe we can scout the last one together."

"Oh." She gave a slow nod. "I will not be able to get any readings from your patch, but please do send it."

I closed my eyes. Without the Lattice, patching data felt more difficult. The process took an onerous seven seconds. When I'd finished, I felt as if I'd been lifting weights with my gray matter.

"Let's move along." Wyatt calibrated his keys as he started to walk. "If Twitchy doesn't find anything along this hallway, we can always peek down the others."

We strolled through the strangeling amber mist, Wyatt and I on either side of Anya as she took her readings. We moved at a crawl that made molasses seem blisteringly hasty.

We found the first of the machines soon enough.

"Are they all like this?" Wyatt ran his finger along one of the greasy gears. "Last century, I mean?"

"Yep. All dials and gears. I haven't seen a computer screen or a keyboard anywhere."

"It might be indicative of strong axiomatic shifts in this area." Anya arched an eyebrow.

"Right." I nodded, though uncertain I understood. "So you think they might shift axioms often in here, and thus computer equipment might not be viable?"

"It is possible." Anya shrugged distractedly as her fingers plucked at the air. "There is no way to say."

"This one of your hatches?" Wyatt asked. He stood slightly ahead of us and tinkered with a shape wreathed in glowing mist. As I approached, I saw him trace a finger around its edge.

"It is." I crossed my arms and gave him a wry smile. "And you won't find a latch, either. It can't be opened from this side."

"Says you." He chuckled. "Good thing I don't care much about the impossible." He began to calibrate the Tangler, and it sang at a lower pitch than the tone I'd become accustomed to.

"One moment." Anya slid her left fingers closed, pinching at part of her interface. Then she pulled down while her other hand made a semi-circular motion.

"Got something, Petrova?" Wyatt squinted at her.

"Perhaps," she whispered.

"Oh good," he replied.

"Yes." The little spot between her eyes furrowed, and she blew a stray strand of golden hair from her face. "I read several sets of Principium Facets, just through this egress."

"Wait, a... full set?" I raised an eyebrow at Wyatt. Principium Facets referred to the twelve basic axiomatic readings most realities exhibited, data regarding gravity, thermodynamics, and properties of space-time. If Anya read a full Facet set beyond the hatch, it signified yet *another* topiatic reality hidden within.

Literally, a reality caught within this one, like Russian nesting dolls.

"No." She met my gaze. "*Several* sets of Facets. Some are closer than others, but I can perceive more than ten different sets of Facets, each within close proximity of this entryway."

"Ten..." Wyatt gaped. "What, just on the other side here?"

"Ten different topiatic realms?" I blinked, flabbergasted.

"Most are weak or distant," Anya admitted. "I read a singular, primary Facet set most prominently, but the more I narrow my focus, the more sets I discover." She favored me with a fleeting glance. "The realmwall of this new reality is quite fragile."

"Sounds like it," I admitted.

"It is highly possible I am reading a singular reality beyond this hatchway, but other, similar hatches are positioned on the other side, each with their own worlds," she reasoned. "Beyond that, I cannot say."

"So you think there might be a different topia behind each hatch?" I shook my head in wonder.

"Well, could you read *that* hatch?" Wyatt gestured ahead with the business end of the Tangler. "Maybe prove they're all like that?"

"Reasonable," she mused.

"Unless you wanna go back to the other tunnels my boy here found and poke around, I say we go forward." He quirked an eyebrow at Anya.

"I will take readings on the second egress," Anya replied. "From the data Michael provided, these tunnels seem quite similar. It is unlikely we would find significant differences if we backtrack."

Anya glided forward through the saffron haze. The next hatch lay only a few meters ahead, and she diligently set about reading her telemetry.

After less than a minute, she froze in place. Then her hands began to move more rapidly, eagerly.

"Anya?" I stepped over next to her. "So? Is it the same?"

"Again, I read one primary set of Facets," she replied. "Several other sets are located beyond the primary one. Most of these are different than the initial hatch."

"So, *another* dozen topiatic realms or so?" The idea boggled me.

"Indeed. It is quite difficult to sort the readings." She leveled her gaze at Wyatt and me. "Yet I have found something of note."

"Something positive?" I asked hopefully.

"Unlikely," Wyatt snorted and waved a hand. "They're all on fire. Or they're all full of six-eyed monstrosities."

"They are not," Anya assured us. "One set of Facets conforms to Rationality."

Wyatt and I simply gaped at her for a good long moment.

"By no means is Rationality the closest topiatic reality," Anya emphasized. "Yet it is a certainty that passing through this hatch will lead us closer to Rational space."

"Home," I breathed.

"Indeed." She raised one eyebrow. "Yet the topia just beyond this hatch is familiar as well."

"Say what now?" All the reality juggling had started to confuse me.

"The Facets of this reality align with those I read within Sathantür."

"What?" I blinked.

"If we pass through this hatch, we will return to Sathantür. The facets are exactly the same. Somewhere within that topia, a secondary egress connects to Rationality."

"That sounds too coincidental." I frowned.

"If Aberration 45717R is planning an invasion, this exit may be their method," she continued.

"That's all I need to hear." Wyatt grinned. "Let's get home." He moved to the hatch, his fingers tapping out algorithms I couldn't possibly track. He pulled the trigger to release a spike next to the hatch.

WHUF.

"Step back, katana boy. Dunno how this one will react to the Crown or some of your gear." He spat.

"Yeah?" I stepped back quickly, even though I expected I stood outside the range of his spike.

"Alters the nature of steel." He struck a few keys. "Fucks up the way quantum electrodynamics bind the iron and carbon."

"Huh," I responded from several steps away. "That's brilliant."

"It'll only be active for five minutes or so. Hopefully, that's enough. If not, I'll do it again."

Less than a minute later, the Sadhana-stamped door began to sag downward as if melting. The brass fittings and bolts remained unaffected, but the main structure of the door sank, as if made of taffy instead of iron.

Abruptly, a loud CRACK echoed down the passage, and I smelled scalded metal. The door collapsed inward, pouring down like fine black sand.

"I'm killing it." Wyatt struck a few of his keys. The spike pulsed once, an indigo shine. "Okay." He nodded. "We clear, Anya?"

"Indeed," Anya breathed with a glance over at Wyatt. "Ambient axioms have returned to their previous levels."

"I can scout ahead," I offered as I peered into the hatch.

"Below?" Wyatt suggested.

Unease washed over me as I tried to make sense of what I saw. Greasy, multicolored light shone there, its radiance eager, almost lustful.

"We have confirmation." Anya focused on the space before her. Her fingers moved more quickly. "It is Sathantür." She crouched down next to the hatch and peered over the edge into the unearthly light.

"Wellity well." Wyatt also crouched down and peeked in. He blinked and turned away. "Vertigo."

I understood exactly what he meant. The realm below sat at a ninety-degree angle to this one.

Wherever this hatch emerged, that world didn't consider itself to be 'down.' Our hatch opened on a wall, like a doorway. The dust from Wyatt's hatch melting episode had fallen in and gathered to one side.

I turned to Anya. "Readings?"

She nodded as her fingers twitched. "Sathantür is different here. Something at this locality is drastically altering physics."

"What kind of something?" I asked.

"Unknown." That tiny furrow between her eyes deepened. "I am not getting clear readings from out here. We will have to be very careful in our mecha calibrations."

"And you know how to do that." I turned to face her. "Right?"

"I have the same specifications as previously." Her fingers stopped for a moment and then started again. "There are easily a dozen small axiomatic conflicts, but I believe the mecha will be capable."

"Conflicts like what?" Wyatt asked as he secured his hat.

"Folic acid will break down. Serotonin seems to become an unbonding molecule. And there will be endocrine system issues." She glanced at us both. "I do not read nearly enough oxygen. I estimate that we cannot stay inside longer than seven hours, even with standard mecha covenant calibrations."

"Seven hours." I drew my disruptors. "I'm going to behave as if I understood the rest."

"Huh." As Wyatt shouldered the Tangler, he asked, "Will our gear function, Anya?"

"I am uncertain about Michael's disruptors." Her brow wrinkled. "They rely on null-point energy to create kinetic force." She gazed at me. "Some of the very basic forces are in flux." Her head twitched. "I am sending a packet for mecha specs." She turned to Wyatt. "I also cannot ascertain if you will experience your accustomed level of field control for similar reasons."

We both nodded slowly, applying her specifications.

"Understood." I turned to Wyatt. "You ready?"

The large man grinned. "Born to raise hell."

Together, we stepped into a world sideways to everything

we knew.

3

The avocado green carpet belonged somewhere in 1973. Gray particulates and brass fittings lay next to the hatch—all that remained of the door. The wood paneling caught my eye as well. Just as in the silo, the décor evoked a style from decades past.

"We all clear?" I kept my voice low, as I didn't want to attract attention. Immediately I began to cough.

Wyatt nodded.

Incoming mecha specs. Anya's blue eyes unfocused. *Give me a moment. I will determine the survivability rations of this area of Sathantür. We may need to make further alterations.*

Beyond the simple baseline covenants? I gave her a sideward glance.

Perhaps. Unknown.

A series of screaming whines and blips sang in my Crown. It chirped a long moment before Anya connected, flowing like sunlight into my mind.

Crown sync request detected. The slow prompt dragged through my mind. **Asset 108, do you wish to allow Petrova, Anya, to create connection 01-026wk?**

Yes, I linked. *Allow connection.*

My Crown filled with the high-pitched whines and clicks that calibrated the viral mecha, an annoying sound. I much preferred the way the Crown worked with the Lattice.

For a long moment I watched as she tinkered with the dialogues.

"It is not enough." Anya glanced down.

"Our current mecha supplies?" I exchanged worried glances with Wyatt.

"I still got a few here, Anya." Wyatt dug into one of the many pockets he kept filled with odd rambles of random detritus.

"I am in possession of the matrix numbers of every injectable we carry," Anya informed him. "Trust me when I say they have been accounted for."

"Well shit," he grumbled.

"So, given the baseline axioms in there, our physical requirements, and the injectables on hand, we don't truly have the resources we require," I clarified.

"Correct. The mecha are meant to supplement and augment your existing bodily processes. They will create the required oxygen, but they were not designed to keep your endocrine system functioning. They cannot alter axiomatic processes to such a vast degree for the time we require." She hesitated.

"Damn it." I sighed.

"We require a *Caduceus*. I apologize. We can survive for approximately four hours within this topiatic locality with current resources—almost half of my previous estimation. It is the best I can do."

"I'd like a countdown." Wyatt eyed her. "Something that adjusts and keeps our resource time up to date."

"Easily done." Anya's gaze went distant for a moment, and then the numerals appeared in the lower left corner of my visual array.

Four hours, three minutes. That was how much time our mecha would buy us in this realm. After that…

"Okay." I nodded at her. "Worst case scenario, we'll fall back into hatch-town."

"That's no better," Wyatt grumbled. "Twitchy here says Rationality is this way. Yer goin' backward that way."

"I know." I popped my knuckles as I thought. "I explored those hatch-filled hallways. There's nothing there. Those misty tunnels functioned like a foyer—" I stopped mid-sentence. My eyes widened.

"What is it?" Wyatt scratched at his beard.

"Wyatt." I turned to him. "I had a thought."

"Have another, then rub them together and see if they spark."

He gave me a wide grin, which fell when he saw the expression on my face.

"I know Anya patched you the phaneric record of our mission, even though you were drunk at the time."

"She did." He nodded affably. "But I wasn't drunk."

"Your blood alcohol level registered 0.18%." Anya blinked, confused. "I would most assuredly say you—"

"Whatcher point, Hoss?"

"I had a thought," I repeated. I'd already accessed the data in my Crown, though it came a bit slower without the Lattice. "The spikes of Irrationality. They *could* have rent the veil." I reviewed the visual of Anya's Fibonacci numbers. "But they *didn't*. Also, no Irrational after-echoes showed up."

"That's a fact." Wyatt shrugged. "So?"

"Well." I stared at them. "What if that's because those *were* the after-echoes? What if all we picked up were the remnants of some gargantuan event that didn't take place in the Rational world at all?"

"That's…" Wyatt paused to juggle numbers as he perused the data in his Crown. "A strange idea. What would be the point?"

"It'd have to be something incredible," I glanced up to indicate the topia we'd just dropped from, "if our spikes were just after echoes. How much energy do you think it would take to connect several topias together, like some kind of—"

"Like a goddamned trans-dimensional train station?" Wyatt's eyebrows shot up, somehow offended, as if he found the thought personally insulting. "Hoss, that's—"

"That's what we just stepped through, right? A hallway that contained dozens of doorways to different places? A nexus?"

"The theory does answer some questions regarding the lack of Irrational echoes," Anya mused. "There are known instances of large Irrational events creating harmonic reflections in nearby Rational space."

"I'm not the numbers man," I said with a glance to Wyatt and then Anya, "but I wager there's math that shows what would happen if a topia, say this one, were forced to make an incursion on another. And if each of those hatches has a different topia behind them..."

"Each fucking one of them." Wyatt adjusted his Stetson. "Damn it, Bishop, that's monstrous! Why would anyone have any cause for such a thing?"

"'The Vyriim are a hyper-intelligent species that constantly seek to create new colonies,'" Anya quoted the Designate back to us. She met each of our eyes. "Everything we know about them indicates their primary goal involves invasively spreading as far through the Myriad topias as possible." She gave the tiniest of shrugs. "Creating a realm to function as a waystation could fit that goal."

I had nothing to say to that. We stared at each other for a moment and pretended we weren't avoiding the topic of genius-level aberrations invading Rationality.

"Not for us to make that call." Wyatt cleared his throat. "If we don't get out of here, no one else will be able to either."

"Agreed," I said. "I'll take point."

"Don't slip off too far." Wyatt turned to Anya. "Can he use the *Wraith* in here without it melting his eyeballs or making his tongue explode?"

"I will check." Her gaze drifted off and she nodded slowly. "My readings indicate neither of those things would happen."

"I..." Wyatt took off his Stetson and ran his fingers across his closely shaven pate in frustration.

"I'm initiating the *Wraith*. Keep a good bead on my systems, please."

"Understood, Michael."

Coolness and shadows washed over my skin as I vanished from sight. I crept from the small room and padded down the hallway, soft green carpet beneath my feet.

The carpet and paneling weren't the only leftovers from the

era of funk. The halogen lights overhead revealed a hideous orange chair tucked off to the side. After approximately four meters, I found a door on the left with a small window and a brass plate.

Mr. Oglemeyer
Associate Director

As I read at the nameplate, a short, balding man strolled into view of the window. He shut another door. Had we been anywhere else, I'd have assumed he came from the director's private washroom. He wore khaki pants and a suit jacket that might have been at home in my closet.

Perfectly normal. Except...

Except he wore an old, battered gas mask, by the looks of it, from the Second World War. A small green tank hung at his side, and various tubes ran from the tank to the mask.

He sat at his desk and began to leaf through a manila folder full of papers.

I stood, entranced, and watched the man. He might have been in any office building in any city in the world. He would have passed for an insurance adjuster or an accountant.

Except.

He reminded me of an insect, wearing a gas mask as he worked. Apparently, whatever else might be going on, these folks had adapted to the local axioms well enough.

I have visual contact.

Armed? Irrat? Wyatt sent eagerly. He didn't exactly spoil for a fight; he just felt powerless and wanted something he could control.

Unarmed. Unless you count a business prospectus as a deadly weapon.

Michael, Anya linked. *Will the contact see us as we pass? Do we need to eliminate him?*

Well. I glanced down at the door. *We can slip by if we want,*

375

but he shouldn't be too difficult for us to take out if needed.

Perhaps we should hold our position. Anya's tentative link worried at me. *It would not do for us to engage the contact without more knowledge of the situation.*

I agree with Twitchy. I'd hate to have 'Rats swarm us while we focus on one guy.

Sure. I grinned. *Understood.*

I slipped down the hallway to two more offices, both with brass nameplates. Similar but empty rooms met my gaze. I decided they didn't warrant much attention.

I crept to the end of the hallway. A metallic door with an oily sheen sat squarely in front of me. To my right, a short hallway ended in another door. To my left, the door-studded hallway stretched into a corner.

There's a door at the end of the passage. I pressed my ear against it and listened. Shocking cold met my flesh, and I nearly jerked away.

Anyone home? Horrible tentacle monsters?

I pulled my ear from the door and glanced down the intersecting hallway, first right and then left.

Negative. Just as I linked, I heard rustling from behind a door to the left. *Check that. Potential contact.* I stepped close to the door and pressed my ear against it.

The door slammed into the side of my head and threw me back on my suited ass.

"Fuck me!" I cursed. My katana, previously held in my left hand, flew from my grasp and clattered on the floor.

Michael! We heard that!

Great. I turned and glanced up at the person who had come through the door.

She looked positively surreal.

Her hair had been styled meticulously, at least what I could see of it. Just like the man in the office, she wore a relic of a gas mask with large green lenses over her face. She had short hair and a figure to die for, all wrapped up in a power suit.

Unable to see me through the *Wraith*, her gaze dropped to my katana.

Shit.

4

Even though I couldn't make out the woman's eyes through the goggles of the mask, I imagined her wheels turning as she twisted her head to peer about.

She reached underneath her jacket to a holster.

I heard her raspy breath.

Wyatt. Get ready. I tensed. I had one chance to do this and be quiet about it.

Slowly, she wrapped her hand around her pistol. Drawing silently, she settled into a crouch and studied the corridor.

I struck, all grace and dexterity from the *Adept*.

Leaping, I swept her leg. As she went down, I lunged, hoping to silence her before she screamed. This could be over before she knew what happened, if things went my way—

Nope.

She struck far quicker than I expected. As she went down, her arm whirled toward me.

Fuck!

She managed to fire twice as she fell.

I tumbled sideways, dodging a third shot from her, then a fourth. Bullets tore into the ceiling and the wooden paneling, a thundering sound in the small space.

Excellent. Eagerness echoed through Wyatt's comm. *Let's rock.*

WHUF.

The woman tried to step back to get a wider shot on the entire hallway.

I caught her forehead, which I slammed into the door frame with a satisfying crunch.

The gun dropped from her unconscious fingers.

No sooner had I grabbed for it than someone else shot from inside the room.

I glanced up and saw four more people in business attire and creepy gas masks. One of them held an old, World War II-era machine gun, while another emptied his pistol into the air over my head.

Quickly, I grabbed my katana and threw my back against the wall, staying low.

We have four more. Two with guns that I can see, I linked.

Got Mr. Oglemeyer trapped in his room, Hoss.

We have no axiomatic disturbances yet. No data on Irrational capabilities, Anya chimed in.

Right. I glanced back through the door.

The two with guns advanced slowly, while another slipped out the back door.

Dammit. I had to move before he summoned reinforcements. *Advancing.* I spun into the room, low, silent, and invisible. As far as I saw, I'd entered a simple office. Boxy desks hunkered in neat rows, weighed down by reams of paper. Four clocks hung near a door on the far wall.

I let the men get a touch closer since they still couldn't see me.

The one with the pistol out in front trembled the smallest amount.

I've said it before: the *Wraith* combined with the *Adept* is a lethal setup. Unseen, I spun toward the first man and sliced with the katana. I opened his neck before he even knew what happened and turned to the second.

The figure only stood still for a moment. He turned from the slender woman on the ground to the empty hallway. Then he aimed the antiquated machine gun straight toward me.

It barked as he opened fire.

Target may be able to see past the Wraith, I linked as I rolled to the side and came up behind one of the desks.

What? Wyatt's incredulity made me smirk. *That's no fair!*

Agreed. I aimed my Stiletto and fired three quick shots.

One caught the gas-mask-wearing jerk in his side. He yelped

as he spun and fired off several more shots. One of the bullets hit my shoulder. I whirled from the impact and went down in a controlled fall behind the desk.

I'm hit. Shoulder.

Did the shot pierce the quasi-steel armor, Michael?

In and out. I thumbed my shoulder. *Still operational.*

Four more shots tore into the desk, showering splinters all around me.

From somewhere in the room, a gruff voice barked out commands in a tongue I didn't know.

Russian? Maybe. If I'd been connected to the Lattice, I could have patched it in for a translation.

Maybe Anya would know.

You still have mecha on standby, Michael. If you are wounded, I suggest tasking them for pain and tissue repair.

Copy that, Anya. I had untasked mecha? Hard to believe. *No time, though.*

The gruff voice cried out again, more urgently, and I heard surging movement.

I pushed up, aimed the pistol, and shot twice.

One blast punched through the gas mask. The other caught him in the neck. He fell.

The last man had disappeared. He, too, had run out the back door.

God dammit.

Michael, I am sending Asset Guthrie in. There are some peculiar readings out here. I will remain and try to make sense of them.

Be careful, Preceptor. I disengaged the *Wraith.*

"Clear?" Wyatt stepped into the room.

"They ran out on us." I pointed at the far door.

"I bet they have friends."

"I don't want to meet their friends."

"Let's get a handle on that." He walked over and shut the door.

Then he placed a spike on our side of it.

WHUF.

"Just in case?" I raised an eyebrow at him.

"Well." Wyatt's lips quirked deviously. "It's 'nother handy use for stasis spikes. Some 'Rat walks in and suddenly the doorway's blocked. No one will come this way for a bit."

"Huh." I raised an eyebrow in appreciation. "As long as you remain within five hundred meters?"

"Yup." He shrugged his equipment higher on his back. "If we're more than half a klick away, it won't matter much."

"And this definitely isn't you just experimenting while Anya's in the other room, right?"

"Never, Hoss." He gave me a sideward grin.

I prodded at my shoulder, wincing a bit at the jab of pain. Fumbling with my untasked mecha, I made adjustments to them as best I could.

Moments later, a thrum of soothing painkillers flushed into my veins. I blinked, a bit overwhelmed at the instantaneous change in sensation.

We have a target down, I linked, somewhat dreamily.

Down? Wyatt turned.

Injured but not dead. I jerked my chin toward the man who lay groaning on the floor.

Wyatt nodded once and walked toward the sprawled man. He kicked the machine gun, sending it clattering out of reach, and pulled the mask up, away from the man's face.

Unlike us, the figure had to actually *breathe* this awful atmosphere. He didn't have miraculous viral mecha to pick up the slack when trapped in a hostile topia.

"Mornin' buddy." Wyatt glanced over at the window and the sickening sky beyond. "Or evening. What-the-hell-ever."

"Who—?" Flecks of blood spattered the man's lips. He gasped a bit, as if having a hard time pulling breath.

"You don't know who we are?" Wyatt chuckled as he stared

382

down at the man. "You certain 'bout that?"

"I…" His panicked eyes went ever wider as his gaze flicked between Wyatt and me. He gasped again. "You're… them. Oh. Oh, God!" His voice broke as if he might start to cry.

"Here you go." Wyatt gave the man his friendliest smile and set the mask back over his mouth.

The Irrat gulped air, his eyes frantically passing between us.

"Now, we ain't *that* bad. Just searching for some answers is all." He glanced about. "Seems like there's only one poor sap left who can give us any."

"I… can't." The man's voice dropped to a reedy whisper. "No. No answers for you. They'll—" The man shut his mouth, as if he realized something.

"Well." I gave the man a dark glare. "You assume we won't do worse?" I glanced over my shoulder at the man whose throat I'd opened. "That is a dangerous assumption."

"I…" The man tried to get a grasp on himself. "You don't understand. They get *inside* people. If they find out I talked, I'll never be safe. My family—"

"You're working to harm a lot of other families here, I'll bet." I popped one of my knuckles. "We've gotta look at all sides here, friend."

"Yes." He shivered, then a scowl settled into his brow. "I know you'll do whatever you feel is necessary, **Michael Bishop**."

A chill ran down my back at the needles of ice in the man's voice. I blinked and staggered.

The world bent, warbled. The room smelled like rancid meat. *Hoss?*

You have a small spike in ambient Irrationality within that room, Anya stated to us both. *You are currently at negative one Rationality.*

"Hey!" Wyatt knocked the man in the side of the head. "Knock that shit off. You're not doing anything we haven't seen a thousand times before."

"Ignorant," the man spat. "You don't know what you dally with."

Yet the room settled down around me.

"Maybe not." I smiled, all charm. "But we can get along better than that."

"Man, we ain't even tried to kill you yet." Wyatt adjusted his hat. "We just have some questions."

"The answers are vast." The man's eyes drew to thin slits. "A monumental undertaking is at hand."

"You know, this is probably your last day on that task unless we give you a hand." I nudged at the man's side with my shoe. His clothing had turned dark and sticky with blood. "So whoever you're protecting won't be able to do much for you."

"The Unity wields power beyond any you can understand," the man sneered.

I glanced at Wyatt, long enough to see his brows knot up.

Unity? he linked, worriedly.

"But the Unity isn't here." I shrugged. "A Facility hospital might be better than dead."

The man laughed, a winding, meandering sound made all the stranger by the gas mask. It stretched on too long, a thin, reedy thing that heralded a broken mind.

Wyatt glanced sideward at me.

"I've known men who got reeducated. They came back all hollow. Dead inside. Broken." He coughed then, wet and raspy.

"But alive, right?' Wyatt queried.

"If you call that life." The man shook his head. "After you motherfuckers steal everything from them."

"Sounds like you have a choice." I responded. "Make it. You're boring me."

"Right." He turned toward me. "I'm dead here on the floor, or I go with a couple of black suits and get gentled. Then my gift is dead inside me, and I'm just another blind idiot." He coughed again and shook his head. "No. I'm a believer, asshole. I won't die.

I'll return to the Unity."

Watch it up here, Bishop. We have a zealot. He won't give us shit.

Agreed.

I found this to be the case fairly often. Sometimes, it felt like all Irrats were the same. Give some hillbilly reality-shaping powers, and it became a religious experience. I could only try to convince this one he wasn't among God's chosen.

"Oookay." I sighed. "Last chance, friend. We detected dangerously irregular readings in the Mojave Desert executed with extreme precision. They led us here. Do you have any information for us?"

Even though I couldn't see his face, I heard the smile in his voice. "Eat shit. You'll know soon enough. I'll die a free man, **Michael Bishop**."

Again, splinters of ice prickled along my flesh, a cold that burned. The room swam around me and dove straight down, as if I fell into a pit.

Hoss? Wyatt stepped closer, as if to grab me as I fell.

I groaned, vertigo making me retch. Shadowed infinities swirled around me, a darkness I couldn't name. I turned my head to shake the engulfing void away but stumbled.

Ambient Rationality has shifted downward four points, Assets. Anya's casual link might as well have related the time of day.

"Be still, **Wyatt Guthrie**," the masked man snarled.

My friend staggered, then fell. From his knees, the bear of a man lurched forward onto the Irrat, grunting as he landed.

Immediately, the masked man squirmed, trying to escape. The two grappled.

"Fucking horseshit!" Wyatt pulled the mask from the man's face and hurled it across the room. The glass goggles shattered against the wall.

Immediately upon breathing the air, the Irrat began to gasp.

"No!" he cried in rage. "You can't just—!"

The room stopped its maddening whirl. I shook my head and pushed myself up.

"Can't what, shithead?" Wyatt growled. "Can't defend myself from your bullshit?"

"I…" The man gasped, and I saw the whites of his eyes blossom red with blood. He trembled and collapsed into fits.

"You made the call, man." I nodded at the Irrat as he sank, twitching, to the ground. For a moment, I considered pulling my blade, ending his pain.

But a second glance told me his pain had already ended.

We're headed back, Anya. I glanced at my system time. Three hours forty-eight minutes remained.

Copy that, Michael.

I wrinkled my nose. I hated the way the secondary comm made her link feel so heavy and slow.

I can feel your irritation, she informed me. *Please hurry. I have some new data.*

Copy that.

When Wyatt and I stepped back into the hallway, Anya's blue eyes gazed into distant nothingness. She stood in front of the oil-slick door, a vibrant cobalt now that I could see it without the *Wraith*. Her left arm stretched toward it, two fingers pinched closed.

"My guess is you found the way home," Wyatt said confidently. "Through that door, the Facets of Rationality are shining for our lovely, twitchy *Preceptor*."

"After a fashion," Anya replied, "yes. The Facets of Rationality do lie in this direction."

"Well, hot damn!" Wyatt chuckled. "Let's ramble home!"

"Those Facets do not lie directly through the door." She fixed him with one arched eyebrow. "Yet this is the path."

"That's good." I studied the door. "So why aren't we going through?"

"It is a similar situation to what Asset Guthrie and I uncovered in the missile silo," she informed me. "Someone has built a new technology. The door is axiomatically bound."

"It is?" Wyatt frowned. "Iiiinteresting."

"I'm lost." Obviously, I'd missed something. "What?"

"The blue door." She rested her hand against it. "I picked up unusual readings in this spot. I thought they might originate behind the door, but actually, someone altered the way mass and motion function in the space of this doorway."

"Door no open-y if motion no work-y." Wyatt made expansive hand gestures.

"Okay, I get it." I glowered at him. "So it's some kind of axiomatic… lock?"

"After a fashion." Anya turned her head, twitching just a bit. "It is the same type of alteration we discovered before."

"Before?"

"Hoss, we dug deeper into things at the missile silo while you traipsed around here."

"We could not even see where you passed through at first. Asset Guthrie only made it possible by noticing oddities while using his equipment."

"You didn't even need me to help you find it this time, princess," Wyatt teased. "Next thing you know, you'll be taking up the katana and the Tangler yourself."

"No." She stared at him, a bit incredulous. "I do not have the requisite Crown slots. The *Preceptor* packet is a permanent installation—"

"Christ, Anya!" He laughed. "This never gets old."

"So we couldn't see the trap because some Irrat tampered with the laws of physics." I stared at each of them, still not following. "Big deal. Irrats alter axioms all the time."

"And when the little shits move on, Rationality again holds sway. Things shift back to baseline." Wyatt gave me a wink. "Naw, Bishop. This is different. Someone tampered with reality, hid the trigger, and it remained that way, even after they vacated."

"I see."

"This is the second recorded implementation of that type," Anya continued. "Only this one does not manipulate light. It alters a subset of the axioms of motion."

"I get it," I cut in. "Do you know what's behind the door?"

"Undefined." She shook her head. "Fortunately, I can read the statistics Asset 423 needs to alter in order to alleviate the situation."

"Of course you can." I smiled at her and then gave Wyatt a glance. "Shall we see what's important enough to keep this door closed?"

He grinned and powered up Rosie. "Seems reasonable."

I watched the miniscule head twitch as Anya patched him the required data. Moments later, he found the ideal spot for his spike, fired one into the floor, and began madly mathematicising on his keyboard.

When the spike pulsed a soft, emerald light, Wyatt glanced up at me. "Clear."

"Copy that." I reached for the door handle and found it still cool. As it turned I whispered to the others, "Let's be careful. Our last two doors have led to different topias."

"It's like an Irrat travel agency." Wyatt chuckled. "Maybe we can collect souvenirs."

"I already have a bullet hole in my shoulder. That's enough for me." I pushed at the door. It swung slowly, ominously inward.

I nodded at Wyatt, then Anya, and stepped into the room.

Invasive Species

The room's overwhelming, horrific scent made me gag, and I stumbled backward a step. The place absolutely radiated an earthy, sour aroma reminiscent of low tide.

"Any strange readings, Anya?" The shirt I'd yanked over my face muffled my voice.

"No." Anya stepped up next to me while her fingers plucked and twitched. "Nothing new. The axioms remain the same."

"Good to know."

I partially opened the door and took a cautious step. Inside, I found twisted shadows and murmurs in the darkness. Reaching behind me, I opened the door completely, letting the light of the hallway splash into the room.

Shadows of tall, cylindrical structures loomed, scattered across the large space. Some gave off the faintest bit of light.

"Oh, oh God!" Wyatt waved a hand in the air, as if he could fan the nauseating odor away.

If anyone had been inside, they would have known about our intrusion the moment we cracked the door.

As I hadn't been greeted by gunfire already, I felt relatively safe.

"I'm switching to optics." I accessed the infra- and ultra-spectrums through my Crown. As the data synced with my visual cortex, I blinked to get the room in focus.

It appeared we stood inside a gigantic metal dodecahedron. The entire floor comprised a single side of the shape, while the walls and ceiling made up the other eleven.

"Understood." Wyatt powered the Tangler back up, sending an eerie whine echoing around the chamber.

The three of us crept inside.

After a moment, the shadowed cylinders became far easier to

make out. Metallic, dark, and uniform in size, they stretched upward, vanishing in a tangle of wires and cables near the ceiling. Yet, toward the center of the room, several panels shone with a weak inner light.

"Look at these." I studied the closest column, realizing it had a thick glass door set in one side.

"Look at *this*." Wyatt shuffled toward a wall.

He peered intently at a large mechanical structure. A bank of terminals took up much of the space, CRT monitors with green displays, mostly. Several different panels had been fit with traditional keyboards, although another input device had also been installed. A glowing sphere had been affixed to one screen, with several keys gleaming on its surface.

I stared, steadfastly ignoring my headache.

Along the bottom, fastened to the wall with a series of copper brackets, I saw something I didn't expect. There, several silvery canisters, the same ones that previously had been charged by the Radonic Transmitters, sat nestled in the shadows.

"Pretty fucking interesting," Wyatt whispered.

"What's that?" I pointed, still several steps away. Some kind of ideogram had been set into the surface of the panels with a series of differently sized straight lines connecting twenty or so spheres.

"No idea," Wyatt muttered. "Anya, can you take a quick reading?"

"I already am," she responded coolly. The *Preceptor* took a few steps toward the large gunmetal casing at the edge of the chamber. After less than three seconds, the tiniest frown pulled at her mouth.

"Is it monsters?" I whispered. "I hate it when it's monsters."

"It is an interface connected to an engine buried within the wall." She glanced at Wyatt. "It is not unlike your equipment in several ways."

"Really?" Wyatt scratched at his beard.

"An educated guess might claim this engine is constructed to traverse axiomatic coordinates." She tilted her head. "This is my supposition, at any rate. It is designed to weaken realmwalls and alter local ambient emanations."

"It's a dimensional... taxi?"

"Not by *altering* axioms. It is more akin to traveling to localities based upon the axioms of that reality."

"Using axioms like longitude and latitude?" The idea excited me. We knew the specifications for home quite well, after all.

"I would guess this device capable of creating a rather large field," she went on. "Perhaps the size of this entire chamber."

"So you think they regularly move chambers like this one through space-time?" I asked.

"Such a device might make the Vyriim's goals simpler."

"Do you know how to operate the thing?"

"No. I do not." She traced one hand along the device, and a screen lit with soft crimson light. "Although if one discerned the manner..."

"Do you hear that?" Wyatt asked in a sharp whisper. "It sounds like wet breathing."

I hadn't heard it, but now that he brought it to my attention, I did. It sounded like the great inhale of some huge creature looming in the darkness.

"It's like a bellows." I glanced up.

My optics had a hard time keeping focus, but it sounded like the noise came from in front of us. The more I strained, however, the more my visual readout jumped and glitched.

"Can you see anything?" Wyatt sounded irritated.

"Optics aren't working well. Maybe another vault door, across the room?" I swore. "Must be some kind of interference. I'm altering my parameters."

No sooner had I begun cycling through the Crown's settings than I saw it—a darker, somewhat circular area on the floor, hidden in the gloom.

A pool of liquid?

From the way it shifted and bubbled, it might be.

Wyatt walked around one of the cylinders that clustered the edge of the pool of burbling murk, running his hand along the metal surface. As he passed, he shielded his eyes with his hand and peered into the soft, greenish glow.

"It's—" His eyes went wide. "There's a person in there!"

"The fuck you say." I frowned.

Anya and I stepped around together.

Sure enough, a female figure floated in the urine-colored goo filling the vat. From below, that greenish light illuminated her naked form. Tubes ran into her nose, ears, and several points on her arms.

Anya took her readings. "I cannot say what all this is, but—"

"I can." I heard the terror in my whisper. "Look. In the liquid."

As one, we all peered into the metallic cylinder.

Wyatt and Anya saw what I'd seen at the exact same moment. I saw the cold horror drift into Wyatt's eyes just as Anya's breath caught.

"Oh. Oh, fuck me!" Wyatt's tone held the heavy weariness of despair. I watched his shoulders deflate.

Inside the cylinder, swimming in the goo, I saw dozens, hundreds of pitch-black larvae, the largest no bigger than an earthworm. They undulated in the liquid. Some wound around each other to form impossible bodies before releasing to join up with others.

As I watched, a thick strand swam out of the woman's nose.

"The Vyriim." I shook my head, a dreamlike dread creeping over me. "Maybe some kind of incubator?"

"Confirmed." Anya nodded. "This is almost certainly the larval state of Aberration 45171R."

"That's bad news." I turned toward Anya, who studied the writhing larvae. "The idea of a container of larval Vyriim, all in a room designed to traverse different realities, disturbs me."

"Kinda drives home the whole 'invasive species' angle, don't it?" Wyatt paced to another of the cylinders.

"We saw how large these things can get. The idea that one of them breaks through to Rationality is horrific, but hundreds?" I peered closer at the larvae. "Truly monstrous."

"Well, it ain't *a* container," Wyatt informed me. "It's container*s*. There are people in several of these."

"It's like a fucking nursery." I turned toward him. "If Anya is correct, they can just send this entire room wherever they want, setting these infected people loose in the population. It's a damn invasion!"

"Yes." Anya faced me. "That is not an assumption, Michael. Every piece of tactical data we have on the Vyriim state that colonization is their primary goal. They have never been encountered in these numbers so close to Rationality." She shrugged. "I think their plan is apparent."

All logic pointed in the same direction. There had to be hundreds of the creatures in a single cylinder. Positioned this close to Rationality, this wasn't just a simple incursion.

More like the first volley in all-out war.

"Seems there's only one place where humans would be the vessel of choice," Wyatt responded.

"Not humans." I heard the trace of alarm in Anya's tone.

"What?" I turned toward her, my hand on one of my katana.

"I read a local spike, sub-Rational." I watched as she brought her left hand up, pulling at nothingness. The furrow between her eyes grew deeper.

"Where, Anya?" I nodded at Wyatt, who began tapping on keys.

"It is small, but—" Anya glanced behind me, her eyes wide. "Oh, Michael."

I turned to gaze at the woman adrift in the thick liquid. Her black hair floated around her, and her eyes blinked open.

Open, aware, and filled with an alien blackness.

She screamed.

2

The muffled sound rippled into expanding bubbles within the liquid. It echoed through me, a haunting cry that hunted me, stalked me through dark places in my shadowed mind.

I gaped, lost.

The woman had huge, dark eyes, no white within them. Only madness dwelt there.

"Not humans, not anymore," Anya repeated. "These are Irrationals. The Vyriim have infected Irrational targets."

"Do we have local telemetry?" Wyatt growled.

"Rationality negative two." Anya turned to me. "That is from the ambient Rationality. We were already sub-Rational." She paused. "Negative three."

The world around us rippled and undulated like a serpent. Dizziness gripped me, a nausea that rippled from the center of my being.

"Fuck!" Wyatt yelped and hurled himself to one side.

A dark tentacle of shadow and talons writhed out of the gloom. I spun and saw its source, the shrouded pool at the center of the room. The eyeless, knotted strands of corded tendrils ended with wicked hooks and small, hungry suckers. They glistened with unknown ichor.

The large man stumbled backward in a blind panic.

"Wyatt!" I headed toward the center of the room as I pulled both katana off my back.

My sidekick fell against another of the cylinders. Within it floated a naked Asian man with hauntingly pale skin. The moment Wyatt slammed against his small chamber, the man's eyes opened. Like the woman's, they were orbs of haunted midnight.

The man's mouth opened in a feral cry that bubbled through the liquid and sliced at my mind. Lonely, forsaken vastness lurked within that wail, an emptiness that filled me with despair.

As I drew closer, I saw tubes ran from the cylinders. They stretched across the ceiling, then dropped into the foul-smelling pool.

Immediately, another pair of hungry tendrils appeared in the darkness. They whipped around as if tasting the air.

I leapt forward and swung with one of my blades.

Nothing. They'd disappeared back into the shadows.

"What. The. Fuck?" I spun on one heel, tracking Anya in an instant.

"Multiple Irrational targets," she continued. "Each being in these devices is a snarl in Rationality."

"Lovely." Wyatt pounded a few keys, his eyes reflecting the greenish light of the columns. "Damned 'Rats." The Tangler began to whine.

Behind me, an explosion of viscous bubbles burst from what I had only suspected might be a pool of murk. It gurgled as if something beneath suddenly began to thrash.

Ssssshhhhhhmmmmmsssss... Just as before, the Vyriim buzzed in my mind like whispering hornets. Their sibilant murmurs reminded me of the whispers of the long mad.

"They know we're here." I turned to face the pool.

"I hear 'em," Wyatt confirmed.

"Negative five, gentlemen." Anya's voice grew tight.

Within her glass and metallic device, the dark-haired woman still screamed; gurgling cries of anger and horror echoed through the thick liquid. I kept expecting her to break forth or to use some fell power against us.

I glanced at Anya, then at the Irrats.

"Can we shut her up?" Wyatt peered at the dials and switches at the base of the woman's cylinder even as he watched the shadows.

"We have no way to know what these do, Asset Guthrie." Anya checked her readings. "For all we know—"

Blindingly fast, one of the cold, hooked tentacles swiped at us

396

from the brine.

I leapt back and swung both katana but missed. As I watched that tentacle, a second swiped at my leg. Boney hooks tore through the fabric of my quasi-steel slacks.

"Fuck!" I cried and rolled away, even as it tried to curl around my leg. *Engaging the* Wraith. I'd already begun the process as I linked.

"Oh, fuck this." The high-pitched whine of the Tangler amped up.

Wyatt tapped so intently he didn't see the shadowy tendril looming behind him.

I lunged again for the place in the darkness where the tentacle had just been.

Again nothing.

My leg throbbed in agony where those hooks carved into the meat, sending an icy sensation straight to my bones. My heart thundered as I wondered if those wicked teeth had somehow injected me with larvae.

No time. I ignored my wound, instead glancing around for the next tentacle.

Hhhhhshhhh mrrrrrrrsssss. I felt the aberration laughing, mocking us, like knives in my mind.

The woman still raged. That scream changed in pitch, from fury to primordial fear.

I didn't even turn around. I had eyes only for those strands of coiled darkness. I watched, my blades held high.

"I'll stop 'er," Wyatt snarled.

"Will you?" I stepped sideways. "What's she doing?"

"Pissing me off," he grumbled. "I dunno, Hoss, but it ain't good. That screamin' gets under my skin."

Ambient Rationality has dropped another two points, Anya informed us. *The Irrational is certainly responsible.*

"Jus' a sec." He tapped keys. "I can shut 'er up, but you'll wanna move, Anya."

WHUF. WHUF.

Before me, the sludge in the pool rippled sinuously, gurgling and bubbling. A tentacle whorled up to show an inhuman cluster of eyes. They blinked, gazing outward balefully.

Behind my mind, those whispers grew louder.

"If you're doing something, you should wrap it up," I hissed. "I'd love for you to be available when the murder-tentacles decide to attack."

Wyatt continued keying something up, his fingers flying. As he worked, the woman's screams grew louder, changing into wails of agony.

"Jus' a sec," he repeated.

I focused on the burbling pool, knowing I likely didn't want to see what Wyatt unleashed. While the Tangler hadn't been intended for offensive use, he could make blood boil, reduce the water in living cells to absolute zero, or force bones into a gaseous state. Such options were never pretty.

I didn't need to watch.

The woman's scream choked off, liquid and wet. The sound ended suddenly with a final gurgling gasp.

"There," Wyatt spat. "Done."

As the woman's strangled cries silenced, however, I saw the briny pool ripple. The muttering in the back of my mind shattered into angry shards.

Wyatt, that may not have been—

I hadn't even finished my link when the Vyriim exploded from the brine. It splashed globules of stinking filth across us. Grotesqueness dragged itself from the pool and swam into the air, an immense, vaguely squid-shaped mass of bundled, graceful tentacles.

Wordless madness screamed in my mind.

With less than a thought, I had the *Adept* in play. I tumbled across the floor, aiming to be directly beneath the bundled mass. Perhaps if I struck at its center with my blades—

398

But it had already moved, arcing through the air like some terrible denizen of the deep ocean. A few tentacles broke off to form smaller clusters, swarming before they rejoined the whole. The creatures surrounded us in a cloud, a thunderstorm of ichorous fury. Their menacing whispers harried us, sharp and spiteful.

With an urgent intensity, that storm bore down on Wyatt, dozens of hungry, writhing tendrils.

He didn't have a chance.

"Stay back, assholes!" He ducked, dodging a grasping tendril, only to hurl himself sideways to avoid another. Wyatt tapped madly at his crescent-shaped keyboard, almost unconsciously gearing up his spikes.

I watched in horror as one tentacle wrapped around his waist and two more grabbed a leg.

You can fuck right off! Fury and unreasoning panic echoed through his link. The Tangler whirred.

WHUF, WHUF, WHUF. One of the spikes flew wild and pierced the side of another glass-and-metal cylinder. A second tore into one of the canisters against the far wall, which immediately began to seep fluorescing blue fluid.

Wyatt! I sprinted toward him, katana out.

My friend cursed and spun, squirming free of one of the Vyriim that grasped at him. But the vile things obviously knew full well who had attacked the Irrat woman, as another clutch of them swarmed from the opposite side of the room, eagerly wriggling and writhing.

Using every bit of fluid grace the *Adept* would grant me, I vaulted forward and swung the katana. With one strike, I severed a knot of the slime-coated creatures, which mentally screamed as they fell around me, squirming on the floor.

This act sprayed me with their sticky ichor, the scent making me retch.

Michael!

Anya's warning came just in time, as I managed to duck a

second group of the aberrations.

I hurled myself to the left, slipping a bit in the gore from the sliced and dying Vyriim.

That one tiny slip proved to be one microsecond too long. The clutch of glistening black tendrils fell on Wyatt, grasping both arms and a leg.

Oh shi— Wyatt's link thrummed with primal terror and mental anguish.

The barbed tentacles shredded both clothing and flesh.

In an instant, that miscreation swam back toward the pool of bubbling brine, dragging Wyatt along as he bled.

I felt the adrenaline in his body, the agony of the hooks, and the terror of death.

No, no, no! Still beneath the *Wraith*, I leapt forward, blades flashing. I couldn't possibly reach the tentacles that held Wyatt, but I had to try. I sliced through a small cluster of the serpentine filth, my blades cutting cleanly.

A yellowish ichor splashed the floor, and the severed tentacles continued to writhe, undulating where they lay. They screamed in my mind. Those wriggling parts spasmed, hungry tendrils seeking.

It seemed like the aberrations had sensed me through the *Wraith* in the past, though I still had no idea how that could even be possible. Now, however, the ichor-coated lamentations lashed out blindly, even though their filth covered me.

Instead, they focused on Anya.

Like a nightmarish cuttlefish, they swarmed toward her, appendages writhing.

No! I spun toward it, slicing as I came.

Three more of the rubbery tentacles fell before my blade, spraying a mist of otherworldly viscera.

I'd swung again when Anya screamed, sending shards of ice through my Crown, cutting me to the quick.

Michael! The link carried with it shock and sensation. I felt the fiery pain as gore-coated hooks dug into her, as they shredded part of her white tactical gear and the skin on her arms and legs.

The awareness crushed me, and I suffered a horrified realization. The hooks had a terrible purpose: They removed any barrier between the creature and any orifices it could use to claim a body as its own.

It all happened so quickly. My connection to my friends was so intimate. I experienced their pain and fear as smaller tendrils sought ingress to their bodies. I felt Wyatt's panicked link as a slender strand snaked its way up his leg—

No. No! No! Nooo!

It slid around his more… intimate areas, seeking only a means of ingress.

I lunged forward in an attempt to reach the tentacles that held him, but the entire tangle moved. It again swam back toward the pool of slime, hauling him along.

In a shining moment of clarity, I realized what would happen. It would retreat into the brine, dragging my friends with it into those murky depths.

They would be truly lost.

I only had a moment to think. Anya and Wyatt were across the room from each other; I couldn't get to both of them. Every time I struck with my blades, more tentacles sprouted in their place. No, I needed something different—

Frantically, I scoured through my pockets, my mind whirling.

My hand came to rest on the cool disk of the Tabula Rasa—the one I'd grabbed in the airport.

"Fuck yes." I'd completely forgotten I had it.

A last-ditch device, the Tabula Rasa banished all matter, leaving a spherical void in its place. The device created an unstable axiomatic field, and then vented the matter into the aetheric tides.

It could destroy this entire room, Vyriim and imprisoned Irrats alike.

Of course, if I wasn't careful, it'd slaughter us just as easily. The thought of being adrift in the aetheric tides didn't exactly appeal.

"Mich—"

The Vyriim had Anya in the air when her cry cut wetly off with a strangled gurgle.

As it carried her toward the pool, the Vyriim forced one of its thick, greasy tentacles down her throat, suffocating her. She gagged around the invading filth as tears streamed down her face.

It savaged her, forcing its way into her body.

Anya squirmed, helpless.

I couldn't look away, stunned at the sight.

"Fuck this." I shook my head.

I'd rather us *all* be dead than hosts for these monsters.

My fingers grasped the small disk of the Tabula Rasa and pulled it out, while I watched the slithering aberrations. I pulled the silver lever along one side and began twisting dials.

I knew I wouldn't get the settings exactly right; I couldn't possibly judge distance perfectly in this gloom.

"No time for exact," I growled to myself. My breath came fast, my limbs felt full of lead, and my head pounded with my thundering pulse.

I sprinted, desperate.

I only had one chance.

3

As the device began to heat in my hand, I leapt toward the main body of the monstrosity. The undulating tendrils had all gathered together, squirming and slithering. I reached the gigantic clutch just before it slithered into the pool.

Three of the tentacles curled toward me, as if unconsciously sensing my presence.

I stepped carefully, dodging one's casual swipe.

It missed.

I tried not to retch as I pushed as deeply into the mucous-laden knot as I could. The rot of low tide combined with the sensation of dozens of tentacles slithering against me had bile rising in my throat.

I buried my arm to the shoulder before I triggered the Rasa.

I felt the hard CLICK as the device engaged.

Tabula Rasa initiated, my Crown reported. *Please retreat to a safe distance.*

"You think?" I cried. With revulsion burning in my blood, I yanked at my arm.

For a terrifying moment, it stuck.

I yanked again.

"Oh, fuck me!" The second I'd touched the strands they'd wrapped themselves around my arm and sank tiny barbs into my jacket. I pulled again but to no avail. The Vyriim's barbs bit into my flesh.

Your current position is within the specified radius, my Crown calmly reported.

"I know!" I pulled again, true terror setting in. The Vyriim held more than my jacket, it seemed. The tiny barbed hooks had nestled so that, with each pull, they burrowed deeper.

Well.

"Okay, Bishop." I grit my teeth, knowing what I needed to do.

I took a deep breath.

And pulled one last time, using all my strength.

I tore free, shredding portions of my inner arm. Strips of pure agony burned through me.

"Fucking OW!" I screamed as the hooks shredded my flesh. Frantic and bloody, I stumbled away from the horror.

I didn't even know what radius the device had been set for, as I couldn't exactly make out the dials in the misty gloom.

It didn't matter, not really.

I turned. Settling into the grace granted by the *Adept*, I sprinted, terror spiking in my mind.

The Rasa could take the entire room for all I knew, but that would be better, far better than—

An ululating scream of rage thundered around me. A pulse of energetic fury washed over everything, hurling me forward.

"Uurck!" I wisely opined as my entire body tumbled, ass over Crown, through the air. I landed hard, knocking all the wind from me in a painful burst.

I glanced over my shoulder. The abomination hung in the air, a nightmare of impossibility. Its many tendrils thrashed about, wildly seeking. From its center, a point of brilliant white, phosphorescent magnesium blossomed to fill my vision. That light radiated, burning away reality itself.

The Tabula Rasa obliterated everything in a sphere around it.

I had to turn away before it burned my eyes. With the maddened, primal ramble of an ape fleeing nuclear fire, I scrambled from that hellish glow.

Too large, my senseless, frantic thought screamed. *I set it too large. It will swallow us—*

An explosion.

Sickening, unnatural cold.

The field collapsed.

In an instant, the air in the room crashed in the vacuum, and dragged me backward like a rag doll. A loud peal of sound rumbled in my bones.

"ACK!" My head struck the stone floor, and pain blossomed sharply in my skull. I slumped forward. The dark curtain of unconsciousness slipped around me, soft and inviting.

"No…" I tried to push myself up, tried to bite my tongue in the hopes that pain would keep me awake. I couldn't though. Lead ran through my veins, my mind drifted, dreamlike…

Bishop, Michael. 108. The Crown prompt, Rachel Gardener's recorded voice, felt clunky and heavy in my mind. ***Shall we initiate autonomous medical protocols?***

"Yes." My tongue sat like a stone in my mouth. "Initiate."

Will comply, Not-Rachel responded. ***Now initiating type III emergency protocols.*** The commands whirred in my Crown, but they seemed impossibly far away.

However, I had to admit, I preferred the recording to Rachel's actual bedside manner.

Altering operating parameters and rerouting viral mecha.

My heart nearly exploded as adrenaline poured through my system. I lurched upward and gasped, eyes wide.

Writhing appendages covered the ground. Dying strands had been left, sliced neatly when the body of the aberration ceased to exist.

I heard Anya, gagging and retching. When I turned, I saw her on all fours, sicking up a good half meter of tentacle.

"Anya!" I pushed myself to my feet and stumbled toward her.

The blonde woman gagged again, vomiting more tentacle on the ground.

It still wriggled.

Tell me you're green, Preceptor. I knelt next to her as she gagged again.

Michael. She collapsed forward, exhausted. *My systems show I shall recover.* She hurked up long strands of yellow slime.

A wide frenzy of static and emotion burst over our comms. Not words exactly but a panicky mix of pain and terror laced with horrified bewilderment. The scarlet sensation roiled over me, a thing of lizard-brained furor.

Wyatt? I stood, searching for the bear of a man. I found him on the other side of the pool, dragging himself out. Dark ichor sluiced from his body as he collapsed on the ground.

He appeared pale, sickly. He trembled.

Come on, buddy. I trotted over to him, my heart in my chest. *We gotta move along.*

Hoss. I felt his searing pain, his heart hammering furiously in his chest.

Violet-black tentacles still wrapped around his legs and face, twitching even though they'd been severed from the main body.

He shook his head, as if trying to shake off the one wrapped around his neck and skull. Blood ran in crimson rivulets down his wan face, stark against his features.

Coiled around him, the tentacle spasmed, and Wyatt sucked in a quick breath.

"It's got its hooks all in me," he said calmly. "All along my face and cheeks. Forehead too."

"Okay," I responded, attempting to match his calm. "How can I help?"

"Do you have any type I mecha left?" The sinuous tendril twitched again, and Wyatt grimaced. "I'm out, but I'll need the pain dampening."

"Yeah." I patted at my pockets, feeling around. After a moment I found the injectors. "I still have three."

"Give." He extended a hand, nodding gently.

When I handed them over, he injected two right away into his leg.

We waited for a moment, Wyatt breathing deeply as the painkilling mecha activated.

Local axioms have returned to baseline parameters, Anya reported. *Also the Tabula Rasa seems to have destroyed a great deal of the systems here. The Irrationals in these containers are dead.*

Copy that, Anya. I stared as Wyatt carefully pried one of the severed tentacles off his face. Every few moments, the tendrils twitched reflexively, pulling at the barbs embedded in his flesh.

"Damn it." He winced at their wriggling movement and gritted his teeth. Every time they rippled, fresh blood ran down his face.

"I'm gonna have to just yank it off," Wyatt growled. "Feels like they're barbed. And in too deeply."

"You might be right." I nodded, remembering how I'd had to shred my arm, pulling it free from the slime-covered, knotted repugnance.

"Well." He gritted his teeth. He took a deep breath and grasped the tendril firmly at the top.

"Man, are you sure?" I peered closer as he wriggled a finger under the dripping tendril. Those barbs clung to his flesh.

"Yeah, Hoss." He sighed. "I gotta."

With one fierce pull, he tore the dead Vyriim loose from his flesh. Blood splattered outward from the motion, thick and crimson. Wyatt screamed, a roar of fury as pain overwhelmed the viral mecha.

The left side of his face was a ruin, the flesh like pounded, raw hamburger. Part of his nose had been entirely peeled, and in one spot I saw through his cheek entirely.

He dropped like a stone.

Wyatt! Horrified, I fell to my knees next to him.

He hurled the dead tendril in his hand against the hard ground, cursing.

"Wyatt?"

"Fucking damnit!" he railed. "That asshole got me, Hoss. I can't see, not outta this eye."

He turned toward me, and my heart fell to somewhere around my knees.

Wyatt's left eye had been completely shredded. A thick, white drool of liquid left a trail on his cheek, mixed in with far too much blood.

Fuck. I gaped at him, completely lost for words. *Wyatt, I—*

"Gone, ain't it?" He groped at his empty socket, cursing and raging. He struggled to stand, failing at first. "It's fucking gone!"

"I got you, man." I stood myself, pulling him up. "We'll get you home. The Facility—"

"Cocksuckers," he raged. "Fucking monsters."

Steady now, he marched over to where he'd hurled the wriggling tendril, his every motion burning with wrath. He brought one heavy boot down on the tendril in disgust and cold hate. He stomped, again and again.

It squelched to pulpy liquid beneath his foot.

"I'll kill every body-stealing, uncle-fucking one of them," he seethed. "I will cook their children alive and laugh while I do it."

"Yeah, man." I nodded. "We will. Not just you. You and me."

"Mother-fucker!" His voice cracked with rage and despair. He pawed at his empty socket again. "Oh, God. God damnit, Bishop!"

Wyatt Guthrie sank back to his knees, trembling with a righteous fervor unlike anything I'd ever seen from him. His head sank into his hands, and he bawled, wracked with such fury and lamentation the feeling bled into my Crown, storming through my mind.

I watched the best friend I'd ever had, my own rage an echo of his.

For once, I had no idea what to do.

4

Michael. Anya slipped up behind me as I dealt with our *Artisan.* She held something out to me.

What's this? I took the petite tube and studied it closely. It appeared to be small with two injector ports.

It was nothing like any mecha I'd ever taken.

A Preceptor-*class augmentation injector,* she explained to me alone. *It is useful when attempting to clear the pathways between the telemetric nodes and their interfaces with the nervous system.*

Okay? I shook my head and gestured at Wyatt. *I don't understand how that helps us.*

Those mecha are calibrated toward Preceptor *modules only.* She tilted her head at me. *Engaging them with a typical Asset Crown causes a temporary sense of euphoria, along with a general numbing of physical sensation.*

You... I gaped at her in disbelief. *You think we should drug him?*

We do not currently possess access or clearance to all the viral mecha we might require, Anya explained. *I have examined the damage to my systems as well as accounted for our current supplies. I am unlikely to require that injector. This path allows us to task other mecha to achieve different goals.*

I glanced down at the silvery blue injector in my hand and then studied Wyatt. The man still trembled as he gingerly poked at the grotesque wound on his face.

If you're certain we understand the effects? I linked.

The injector will create a somewhat soporific effect with a bit of euphoria. It will leave him feeling numb. It is similar to a narcotic in some ways, except the Designates will need to manually purge these mecha from his Crown.

Okay. I nodded. *You might be right.*

I knelt next to the large man and put my hand on his back.

Then I opened my other hand front of him to show what I held.

"This is a little something I got from Anya," I explained. "She thought it might help you out."

"Is it an eye?" The bitterness that seethed in his words contained a touch of his sarcastic laughter as well. "That would be fucking helpful."

"It's *Preceptor* mecha. Specified to their modules."

"Oh, Christ." Wyatt shook his head. "You're trying to get me high. I've seen what those things do."

"Definitely not." I chuckled just a little. "But we're low on resources. If Anya's mecha can help modulate pain, then I think we might need to try it."

"I'm in shock," Wyatt nodded. "I don't need to be no fancy *Caduceus* to guess that."

"Your baseline Crown protocols defend against shock," I responded. "I believe it's extremely low blood pressure."

"Oh. Okay." He reached out and took the injector, craning his head toward Anya.

"This thing intra-muscular? Or do I need a vein?"

"Place it on the right side of the neck," Anya answered. "The mecha will find the vein, even if you happen to miss."

"Copy that," Wyatt sighed. He held the injector to the side of his neck, wincing just a bit as it hissed.

"Okay, so what do we have?" I stood up, wiping the Vyriim viscera from my face and chest. "You said you'd been examining our supplies?"

"I would like to examine our current system status in detail." Anya's prompt hit my Crown.

Crown sync request detected, the prompt reported, slow and clunky. ***Asset 108, do you wish to allow Petrova, Anya to create connection 01-027wk?***

I acknowledged the connection and waited. While Anya tinkered around in my Crown settings, I opted not to watch the specifics.

Oh... Oh man, Bishop. Wyatt blinked at me. *Remind me to smuggle some of Anya's injectors home.*

I don't think that's the best idea, buddy.

I am sending calibrations for each of you, settings for your viral mecha. Anya's link sounded... weary, exhausted in a way I'd never heard from her. *These suggestions for tissue regeneration and pain management will bring us as close to status green as possible.*

I heard the whir as the packet hit my Crown. Accessing the data caused it to blossom into a field of data within my array.

Dismay seeped through my veins, brackish and bitter.

This gears almost everything I have toward pain management and system maintenance. I stared at Anya. *Is that right?*

I lack the Caduceus *module, Michael, but your injuries are significant. You have a deep slice across your back from the event in the airport lavatory. You have been shot through the shoulder. During the encounter at the* Legacy, *one of those creatures smashed your head into a car.*

I've had better days, I agreed.

Those are only your *injuries.* She met my gaze. *423 and I have sustained several ourselves.*

Anya. Wyatt groaned in agony as he sat up. He held a handkerchief against the side of his bleeding face. *These settings—*

Will not restore your loss, Wyatt. She gagged again and turned away from us. She bent over, retching wetly.

No. That's not what I mean. He shook his head. *You're suggesting we recalibrate the viral mecha we need to survive in this place.* He waved one hand. *We still need oxygen and metabolic augmentations. Our mecha are tasked with basic axiomatic alterations just to survive the next few hours.*

"Yes." She sat up and wiped her mouth. Her voice sounded positively dainty in the cavernous room. "These settings will reduce us from three hours, twenty-three operational minutes to fifty-three operational minutes."

411

"This doesn't sound like a *good* plan." I raised one eyebrow at her.

"However, during that time we will be pain free and capable of near optimal operational standards." She gazed at each of us. "If we ignite the remaining mecha reserves now, we can continue our dossier easily."

"And if we don't, we'll be limpin' along, waiting to get picked off." Wyatt tied a second handkerchief over his eye. "Fuck me if that's not grim."

"Correct." She nodded. "We are not in a position to engage enemies as we are. Not at all."

"Anya, do you have a reading on the exact location of the Principium Facets?" I asked hopefully. "The ones for Rationality?"

"Too many Facet radionics emanate from this location to be certain," she explained. "This room in particular is filled with them. Yet, I can estimate we should be within forty minutes or so from those emanations."

"Tight." I grimaced. "Thirteen minutes to spare."

"Possible, though." Wyatt cleared his throat. "Twitchy here has more than enough readings to satisfy the Designates. If we can get back to Rationality, that's end game."

"We will conserve energy further by not utilizing the comm," Anya continued. "It is the best we can do." She gazed from Wyatt to me.

"We *could* go back." I let the words hang in the air for a long moment before I spoke again. "We didn't need to task our mecha so intently back in the hallway with the vault doors. Perhaps we can find another path that leads to Rationality."

"I'd wager my right eye the intel we need is on *this* side of the hatch." Wyatt wore a goofy smile, the byproduct of narcotic biochems in his bloodstream. "'Sides, for all we know, every one of those hatches fucking sucked. Maybe this one is the only one with Rational Facets within it."

"*Every* one? That's a bit of a stretch."

412

"Anya needs to get all the readings she can," he retorted, somewhat dreamily. "Also, we wasted an awful lot of eyes coming this direction."

"Our life expectancy…" Anya's gaze went distant, but then she focused on me, "will not increase by a great deal on the far side of that hatch. We might gain time, but no one knows where we are. We would die just as certainly. "

"Dammit." I shook my head. "You guys have it. The best choice is the crazy one."

We stood there in silence and half-darkness, listening to the chugging of unearthly technology grinding away in some other chamber.

I clumsily input the appropriate alterations to my viral mecha.

Initiate mecha alterations, Asset?

Yes, I replied. *Initiate changes.*

The burning pain where the tentacles struck me faded into numbness, along with my other injuries.

"So we survive." I gazed at the other two.

"At least for another fifty-three minutes," Wyatt chuffed.

"I'll grab one last phaneric record of the room," I said. "Any small scrap of information might be what saves our collective asses here." Furthermore, anything recorded by my visual could be accessed by the Designates, provided we regained contact with the Lattice.

Always better to have more intel.

First I stepped over to the cylinders. They'd all gone dark after the Tabula Rasa went off, presumably due to the destruction of some key piece of technology. Peering through the darkened glass, I saw the young woman floating there, dead. Tiny filaments of violet-black tendrils floated at the top of the thick liquid, hundreds of the Vyriim larvae.

In fact, every strand in the room seemed to be dead or dying.

The Tabula Rasa had worked just as intended. The parts of the creature caught in the blast radius simply ceased to be, as the

413

device obliterated everything within range. A shallow bowl sat where part of the floor had been carved into nonexistence. Another sliced cleanly through the wall Wyatt had examined, the one which contained Anya's supposed 'axiomatic taxi' and the Radonic Transmitters.

Pity.

"Room's clear." My voice echoed in the gloom. I let my vision drift through the various spectra of light but couldn't see anything moving except for us.

"I'll take your word for it," Wyatt grumbled. "My optics are all wonky." He adjusted the handkerchief tied around his head, stanching the bleeding with another one. He stood then and shouldered the Tangler. When he stepped to the edge of the pool, I heard his gear start to whine.

"Wyatt?"

"Let's make certain no more squiggly motherfuckers can have their happy birthday in here." He fired one spike, then a second into the pool, his fingers gleefully keying in some destructive spite.

"There might be dozens of these rooms, Wyatt." Anya sounded so tired.

"I don't care. I get to have this one, at least."

"According to our intel, the Vyriim invade a topia in swarms of tens of thousands," she mused. "Destroying this one pool is not remotely enough to halt their actions."

"Well, they can't use *this* one." Wyatt pressed one final key. "We should move though. I bet this stuff smells even worse while boiling."

Even as he spoke, the first bubbles began to roil within the goo.

"Ugh. Roger that." I picked up one of my katana from where I'd apparently dropped it and checked that I still had both disruptors. "There's another door on the far side of the room—one of those bank vault doodads. I glimpsed it when I saved everyone from their horrifying fates."

Save me faster next time, yeah? Wyatt's playful grin tugged at me over the link, and I couldn't help but chuckle.

He amazed me. We had no concept of how to get ourselves home, much less stop thousands of alien aberrations from invading our world. I knew the cocktail of viral mecha cloaked his pain, but the fact that he could still tease, even with his eye ripped out...

Wyatt hadn't been defeated. Even in the face of physical disfigurement, one hour left to live, and the invasion of our world, he was still himself, still refused to stay down.

That was who he was.

Who we were.

Temporal Anomaly

"Tokyo, Japan."

"What?" I turned around to see Wyatt tracing one finger along a brass plaque fixed to the outside of the vault.

I'd stepped outside the alien nursery first but hadn't bothered to examine the door itself.

"Tokyo, Japan. Ryuu Tower." He shrugged. "I don't know what it means, I'm just readin'."

"I'm surprised you can read." I studied the plaque.

"Is it possible Tokyo represents the incursion point?" Anya squinted at the sign and then turned her blue eyes to us. "Perhaps the equipment inside had been intended to shift the chamber and the breeding pool to Japan?"

"Scarcely matters now," I growled. "Although I suppose we couldn't have exactly used the device, not without trafficking aberrant horrors into Rationality with us."

The area beyond the nursery seemed more like a warren of small rooms than a hallway. The first three doorways chugged and whirred with odd engines, devices constructed of gunmetal gears and sprockets that shone lazurite blue tucked away within.

"What's all this shit?" Wyatt slurred just a bit. "Just more Irrational garbage?"

"We dunno, Wyatt."

"Should I break it?" He tapped at a couple of keys. "I'm good at breaking."

"These devices may power the constructs in the previous room. They may also be the cause of the odd axiomatic changes to this area of Sathantür," Anya mused, her fingers twitching.

We crept further, slipping through the shadowed chambers. I took point, both katana drawn. Anya daintily paced along, taking careful readings with each step.

417

Wyatt giggled drunkenly at a joke he didn't share.

"This place reminds me far more of an old office than a hideout for Irrational terrorists or a breeding ground for human-incubated aberrations," I whispered. "It's surreal how ordinary everything is."

"'Cept for that," Wyatt mumbled and gestured. "'Nother damn vault door."

I hadn't seen it. I'd been focused on the chamber ahead, where a set of double doors loomed in front of us. Wyatt, however, had noted another of the Sadhana doors snugly set into the wall.

Above it, shining as if it had been installed yesterday, sat a brass plaque that read:

Dhire Lith

"What language is that, Anya?" I remembered then I'd forgotten to tell her about the Russian I'd overheard.

"Hmm." She peered at the letters. "None I know. We can analyze it if we contact the Lattice again, but otherwise, I cannot say."

"When." I put my hand on her slight shoulder. "When we contact the Lattice."

"Yes." She blinked up at me. "Of course."

"Thing is, I don't think that's home." Wyatt leaned one hand against the wall.

"I've never heard of anything like it." I shook my head.

"But it's another pool, isn't it?" He turned his head toward Anya. "You can read the stats right through that door, I know you can."

"I can, Asset Guthrie." Her reserved tone sounded a bit more so than usual. "And yes. Behind that entryway the axiomatic statistics are practically identical to what we found before."

"Fucking good." He began to tap on his keys, his brow furrowed. "What I wanted to hear."

"Woah there," I placed one hand on his shoulder, my tone easy and smooth. "I don't know if we should start a fight with every puddle of monsters we come across."

"I think you might be wrong, Bishop." Wyatt gave me a sharp grin. "I think these motherfuckers deserve to boil alive in their shitty lagoons."

We only have forty-seven minutes, I reminded him in a private link between us. *I don't know how many more fights Anya can handle.*

Wyatt stared at me a long moment, that spark of fury in his one good eye.

He sighed.

"You asshole." He shook his head but stopped initiating his gear. "Fucking guilt trips."

"I'll buy you a beer later, after we get home."

"You'll buy me a whiskey at The Booby Trap. Or three."

"Deal." I chuckled.

We took a step into the next room, the one that held a double door at its far end. To our left, a long expanse of glass showed a vista I never could have imagined.

"Fucking terrifying." Wyatt peered through the window. He stared for a good long time, blinking slowly.

I wondered exactly how much of a buzz Anya's injector had given him.

The sky appeared more bruised violet than black, with only a blurry smear of visible stars. The desolate wasteland around us gleamed under a low-hung moon as it shone with an orange and sickly light.

It gave me nausea just to look at it.

The bent sky writhed and bled. It was... *wrong*. Fundamentally broken.

"Crimson, earlier." I looked at the other two. "Right? The sky was a bright red."

"I don't even want to know why," Wyatt grumbled.

419

At the end of the chamber sat another set of double doors. Normal doors, just like any one might encounter in an office.

"One moment." Anya busied herself taking readings. Her head twitched once, then again. She glanced up at us. "Safe enough. Still no axiomatic fluctuations."

I nodded at Wyatt and cracked open the door.

No one.

Worktables with unfamiliar gear and a shelf with binders of notes waited within. The laboratory appeared quite sterile with metallic surfaces and white walls.

"Hmm." Anya's fingers twitched. "Zero. But..." She tilted her head, as if she listened to echoes. "I have traces of Irrational activity. I cannot do a weave analysis without the Lattice. If I could, I believe it would show Rationality is often altered in this room."

A chart on the wall caught my eye, a series of numbers along one side that spiraled into a symmetrical curve. A record of data analysis?

"Anya," I said in a quiet but excited voice. I'd found something... something familiar. "Look here."

She stepped to me, her eyes distant. As she gazed at the chart, I watched recognition blossom in her eyes.

"Fibonacci numbers."

"What?" Wyatt asked in a slur.

"Remember? While you enjoyed yourself at The Booby Trap, our *Preceptor* noticed something in the packet. Whatever Irrat tech created the spikes in Irrationality, it did so in waves of Fibonacci numbers."

"Right!" He brightened as he remembered.

"Here," she muttered. "Whatever they were working on, they did it here."

"Did they?" I peered at the papers Anya studied.

"These formulae are complex." She leaned closer, her eyes narrow. "But yes, I believe these calculations are the ones utilized during the creation of our Irrational spikes."

"So." I scowled. "Their fuckery reached not only through this reality, but also the one we passed through to get here. Those were the echoes registered by Facility 17."

"You are thinking about it wrong, Michael. I do not think this was a separate topia at the time." She turned to me. "Does the architecture of this place seem anything like the inside of the missile silo, what little of it you saw?"

"Oh." My eyes went wide. "Some of it does." I thought of the thick shag carpets and the office décor.

"Refer to the blueprints," she requested.

I pulled up the dossier and found the schematics on the silo.

"Oh," I breathed. "It's the exact same building." I identified the lab we stood in, as well as the hallways and rooms we'd passed through.

"That's impossible." Wyatt perused the same schematics. "So 'Rats just plucked a building out of Rationality and left it here?"

"Something like that." I noticed the data matched on every point. "The interior is slightly different from the schematic, but yeah, architecturally it's identical."

"This is axiomatic weaving at an unprecedented level." Anya picked one of the binders and paged through it. "With this technology, the Vyriim could create conduits into any point of Rationality. The desert in Nevada was a test—"

"What the fuck is *this*?" Wyatt poked at a set of Polaroid pictures pinned to a cork board.

"What?" I leaned closer. Above the pictures, the words, "Remember the Unity!" had been printed in big, blocky letters. Below them, scrawled in slightly smaller ones, "We've already won!"

"Those images." Anya peered closer. "Are those corpses?"

"It looks like it." I peered closer, studying the bodies in the photos. They all appeared to hang from a shadowed ceiling, suspended by tendrils that coursed into their flesh or down their throats. Below them, a basin of ichor bubbled, and tentacles writhed within.

"Maybe what they did to some enemy?" Wyatt turned to me. "After some great victory?"

"Maybe." I traced my finger along one of the pictures. Tentacles tunneled into the flesh of a young woman's neck and back, and a thick one ran squarely into her mouth. She stared into the camera, her eyes glazed over in a blissful, narcotic haze.

Two men opened the door on the far side of the room, startling us.

"Told you to leave." Even though I couldn't see Firenzei's face through the gas mask, I recognized his shock of red hair. Bloodstains covered his side, and he held a sawed-off shotgun.

"Asshole," Wyatt growled.

"I told you we couldn't leave." I narrowed my eyes at Firenzei.

"Well, you are now thoroughly," he grinned, "outside your jurisdiction. I'm afraid you need to come with us."

"You should be afraid." I gave him a tight smile. "If you'd like to go round up some friends, I'll allow it."

The smile fell from his face as he swung the shotgun toward me.

"My friends are already here, Bishop."

2

I engaged the *Wraith* only a moment before he opened fire. Wyatt hurled himself to one side, Anya ducked behind a whirring mechanism.

Around me, cool shadows drifted close as I faded from sight.

"Kill them," Firenzei spat. "These assholes mucked up Garnath Station."

The other gas-mask wearing man, a fierce looking fuck in a leather jacket, ran to the side of the room and flipped up a metal table.

My eyes widened as I realized his plan.

He opened fire. His gun barked as Wyatt and Anya hit the ground.

Already the world trembled around me, my visual thrown off by whatever Irrational fuckery Firenzei used.

The lean man had vanished, crackling out of existence.

Immediately, that familiar burrowing sensation began to crawl through my mind. It felt as if, simply by using his power, Firenzei offended physics itself. His eldritch weirdness writhed like a maggot eating its way through my brain.

With a shimmer of greasy light, Firenzei appeared atop Wyatt, spinning uncannily fast. The Irrat swung down with the butt of his gun and struck Wyatt where his eye had once been.

"Fu—luck!" Wyatt screamed and stumbled backward, fighting to remain upright.

For an awful moment, I thought Wyatt would drop. I knew he wasn't quite up to spec, even with Anya's injector buzzing in his mind, but I needed him up and on it. I didn't want to handle Firenzei alone.

The world pitched in a nauseating tremble, and the red-haired jerk disappeared again.

"Dirty asshole!" Wyatt cried. "You won't do that twice, you

shit-eating little fuck!"

WHUF. WHUF. WHUF.

The bark of an automatic weapon caught my attention as the second man began to spray the room.

I toggled the *Adept*, leaped over his wild shots, and fired back. *The second guy is just pinning us down,* I reported. *Firenzei intends his buddy to hold us here so he can take us out himself.*

I planted stasis fields. Wyatt's link wobbled a bit. *I'll patch you both their location and radius. They won't last long, but they'll stop his ass cold if he hits one.*

As Wyatt patched the location of his spikes, they blossomed into yellow fields on my visual.

What's the trigger, Wyatt? I peered around the room. No sight of Firenzei.

Yet.

Um… more than one pound of matter that doesn't currently exist in the field or matter that travels faster than 150 meters per second. That'll set 'em off.

Matter but not kinetic force? I raised an eyebrow. *Smart.* Maybe my buddy wasn't high off his ass.

Brilliant, in fact, he replied.

Assets, Anya primly linked, *I identified a pattern in Firenzei's leaps.*

Really? I fired my Stilettos in the direction of leather-jacketed man, trying to keep him down. The left issued wider, basketball-sized blasts, while the right remained calibrated for tight shots.

It is not perfect, but I have been running analysis since we first encountered him. I think we can predict his motion with some accuracy.

That's amazing, Twitchy, Wyatt responded.

I am sending you both a patch.

A large patch, full of numerical analysis, hit my system. My head jerked slightly at the sheer amount of data, ported straight to memory.

I knew Firenzei's pattern, saw it clear as day.

Holy shit, Wyatt linked. *It's a geometrical alignment. He always leaps along certain angles.*

I can't believe he plans *that.* I fired my Stilettos again, putting dents in the metallic table our enemy used for cover. *Maybe it's something about the direction in which his power bends space?*

We have no way to know the distance of a given leap, Anya pointed out. *Tracking the angle is simple enough, but he may teleport two meters or twenty.*

So far he's made pretty large jumps, I sent. *But if I could get him to fight in close quarters and he holds true to form, we might have him.*

That's a lot of ifs, Hoss.

A burst of shots barked from across the room and triggered one of Wyatt's fields. With a WHOMP! sound, the silvery half-dome blossomed between Wyatt and the shooter. The bullet halted in place.

Anya, I linked, *have you done any analysis on the predictability—?*

The room trembled madly again. I held my pistols out, slowly turning to try to catch where the asshole landed.

"Hello, bitch." With a sneer Firenzei slammed his gun against Anya's temple.

She cried out, a wail of surprise and pain. As she staggered, his fist met her squarely in the face. He followed it with a second punch.

"Hey, asshole," I called, hoping to distract Firenzei. Invisibly, I ran toward him, the Stilettos held out in front of me. I didn't dare fire with Anya so close, but if I had a shot...

Firenzei gave a wolfish smile in my general direction. He wrapped an arm around Anya's waist and held her against him tightly.

The world quivered again, beginning to shudder even as I screamed. I fired, trusting my mecha and the *Adept* to protect

Anya. I didn't think I'd hit her. Even if I did, that might be better than letting him—

They both vanished.

"DAMNIT!" I roared, as the tunneling, serpentine sensation burrowed through my mind.

Gone. Anya—

"You dumb fucks did *not!*" Wyatt yelled, enraged. He stood and fired a spike into the metal table the other Irrat had used for cover. His fingers danced madly against the keys, and his eyes glinted with a feral, terrible gleam. In less than a second, that spike glowed white hot, shining with a malefic umbra.

The table sagged around his spike, molten.

The man screamed. He hurled himself backward, but I saw his mask had melted against his face. Just being *close* to Wyatt's spike had probably ruined the only thing keeping him alive in this awful place.

Anya? I linked. *Do you know where he took you?*

No response.

"We'll find her." I stepped over to Wyatt. "She's got to be close. I don't think he can teleport kilometers away."

"He's comin'," Wyatt responded with a snarl. As the room began to quiver, he tapped a couple of his keys, and the Tangler whined.

Firenzei appeared within the corridor we had originally come down. In his left hand, he held a fire extinguisher.

"Boys," he said conversationally. He threw the extinguisher toward Wyatt.

I spun toward him. Thanks to the Stilettos' specialized mecha, I fired faster than thought.

In the same breath, his pistol barked.

The canister exploded.

I couldn't say whether he'd hit it or I had.

White, foamy powder exploded into the room, coating everything.

Including me.

Immediately, the extra matter began to uncalibrate the *Wraith*.

That retardant burst had startled me, freezing me in place for a moment, which proved to be a moment I didn't have. I jerked my guns up and fired, but the asshole had already jaunted away.

Shit. The Wraith *ain't doing you any good now, Hoss. Yer flickery again.*

Acknowledged. I disengaged my gear, scowling. *He's too fucking fast. I have the* Adept *geared, and I still couldn't catch him.*

Yeah, Wyatt spat.

We gotta get out of here. Find where he's got Anya.

"Far door?" Wyatt gestured.

I nodded and ran across the room to where the burnt man wailed. Most of the skin on his face had melted into the rubber and glass of the mask. He screeched in agony.

"Cowaards!" he raged in a thick Russian accent as he swung his empty firearm at me. "Facking cowaards!"

"You gotta chill, man." I struck him once behind the ear.

He dropped like a stone.

On the move, Wyatt's fingers madly scrambled on the keys.

"What are we doing?" I smiled, not loving how far his pupils had dilated.

Recalibrating.

As I received Wyatt's link, the room drifted around me a bit, spinning.

What? Those spikes back there?

"These three spikes were to be stasis fields, but if we're moving on…" He paused to tap three keys, and a burst of intense heat came from behind us. "They can just mimic that last spike and wreck some havoc."

"You mean—?" I glanced over my shoulder, immediately squinting against the brilliant umbra of furious light raging within the room. Instantly, the shag carpet caught fire. "Why?" I turned

427

to him, raising both hands. "Why are we starting random fires?"

"Fuggin' fuck these people," he responded.

"Damn it." I threw the door open as the room caught fire. The passage beyond stretched into shadows.

"We're not done." Firenzei stood at the end of the hallway. He raised an automatic pistol.

WHUF. Wyatt's spike came at the exact same time as the thunder from the gun. Instantly, his stasis field turned silver in front of us.

Fuck. I gaped at him, amazed. *That was fast.*

Yup. He glanced to the left. *Side door.*

Right. I opened the metallic door and peered into the darkness within.

Michael, Wyatt, Anya linked weakly. *My previous packet held an executable sequence. It should help you track Firenzei in live-time.*

Oh! I see it, I linked back as I initiated the executable. It whirred in my mind. *Are you green,* Preceptor?

No, she replied. *I will drop a token over my current location.*

A sky-blue triangle appeared over my visual array. Beneath it, tiny numbers indicated Anya was sixty meters down the hall.

We're on our way, darlin'. Wyatt grit his teeth. *Just hang on.*

Darling? Anya wrinkled her nose over the link.

Our Artisan *is enjoying his cocktail of mecha,* I reminded her. We pushed on, down the narrow corridor.

The new section of Irrational awfulness devolved into a labyrinth of cubicles. The first and only door we came to opened into a wide room, an office-themed hellscape.

You are getting further away, Anya reported.

Firenzei blocked the other path. I responded. *We can't exactly go back, Anya. Wyatt started a fire.*

He did what? Confusion swam over the link. *Why?*

He might be high off his ass from that injectable. It could also be a hillbilly thing. I glanced at my friend. *They like to start fires.*

"Born to raise hell," Wyatt agreed and gave me a wide smile.

In that instant, the world began to jitter and palpitate around us again.

Wyatt shot me a glare, and I nodded and peered into the shadowy room.

WHUF. WHUF. WHUF.

The room stopped its wild gyrations. Instead I felt that slithering sensation within my skull.

"There we are," Firenzei quietly snarked from our left. "Two little Gentlemen, lost and all alone."

I turned toward the sound but saw nothing aside from cubicles and broken desks. However, as I peered into the darkness, Anya's executable whirred in my mind.

Irrational source located. Calibrating anomaly.

Over my visual, three red lines drifted into alignment. One of them showed vertical, one showed horizontal, and the other estimated distance.

The three crossed just behind a thick square pillar, approximately eight steps away.

"You here to surrender?" Wyatt's drawl held more than a touch of smugness. "I'm certain we can go easy on you."

"No, oh no. Not at all," Firenzei chuckled. "I'm here to clean up a pest problem."

As they spoke, the executable began engaging angles and probabilities based upon what we knew of Firenzei's Irrational nature. Four white lines showed the most likely angles of the man's next teleportive jaunt. They stretched out over my visual, plain as day.

One of these reached out to Firenzei's left, toward the door we came in. Another two went behind him, stretching at oblong angles.

The last led almost directly behind Wyatt.

"You... um... you think so?" My friend shook his head and slowly keyed in his algorithms. "You've had a time of it so far."

"Let me rectify that." The room began to tremble again.

I scrambled to make some calculations from Anya's lines. If this asshole had truly come to finish business, then only one line of possibility would accomplish that.

I leapt.

The jerk had uncalibrated the *Wraith*, true enough. But the fire retardant didn't affect the *Adept*.

In the space of a breath, quicker than I fully realized, I turned and raised my blade. The *Adept* had pronounced judgment before I consciously realized what happened, before Firenzei even appeared.

Firenzei crackled into being two steps to my left, behind Wyatt, and raised his gun toward my friend's head. He positively leered, his red hair a halo of demonic fury.

My katana already whispered in the air.

"NO!" Firenzei screamed. A scarlet blossom of blood spattered against the wall.

The gun fell.

Part of his hand dropped to the floor, thumb attached.

He had me. Wyatt stared at me, shaken. *Oh God, Bishop.*

"Oh, Oh God!" Firenzei screamed at me, furious. "Oh, motherfucker! You piece of shit," he raged.

For a moment, his eyes were all I saw. They burned through me, aflame with shock and malice and hate. Around him, the world spasmed, and he vanished—

—only to appear just to my left. Before Anya's program had time to compile his new location, Firenzei punched me in the face, just as he'd done to Anya.

He hit me twice and then once in the throat.

My nose cracked, and I stumbled backward. Agonizing stars burst in my vision.

Reeling, I struggled to remain upright but failed.

WHUF.

Grunts followed, then the sounds of a scuffle.

Michael? Anya linked. *You are not getting any closer.*

Busy getting my ass beat. I pushed myself up and shook my head.

Wyatt dropped the business end of the Tangler to trail behind him, attached to its backpack by three sturdy cables. The large man stomped after the Irrat, not even utilizing his gear.

Wyatt?

The *Artisan* growled and swung his meaty fist at Firenzei, knocking the lean man backward through a cubicle.

"Didn't get to finish our business from the bar," Wyatt muttered, staring down at the Irrat. "I prefer it this way, honestly."

"Do you?" Firenzei reached for a second pistol at his hip, struggling to draw it with his left hand.

But I'd already drawn down on him. My Stiletto sang low-toned warbles as I fired a wide burst into the Irrat, catching him square. If only I'd calibrated the weapon tighter, that shot would have punched straight through him.

Instead, force the size of a beach ball slammed Firenzei right in the chest. It hurled him, head over heels, and he landed in an unceremonious heap.

Hey there, Hoss. Wyatt gave me a quick thumbs up as he stomped toward Firenzei. *You show up for the beat down?*

I did. I drew my other Stiletto, this time making certain to dial both down to a very tight field.

The room began to quaver, a mad frenzy.

Fuck no. Wyatt broke into a sprint, dragging his gear along behind him.

Firenzei pushed himself up, wiping at his face with his wounded hand. He glared pure, elemental hatred at us.

Wyatt's expression matched his.

"Wait 'til you see what I did to her," Firenzei crooned. "If you find her in time, that is."

I stopped in place, bringing my weapons up.

Wyatt kept running as the room undulated around us...

And Firenzei disappeared.

Irrational source lost.

"Damn it!" Wyatt raged. "Piece of inhuman shit!"

"Just grab your gear and watch." I spun slowly, taking in the room. "When he reappears, the executable will begin tracking him again."

We stood for a long moment, surveying the room. The nauseating sensation of squirming grubs burrowing into my mind slowly faded.

Wyatt sighed.

"I think he had enough, Hoss." He shot me a rueful grin. "We were just too much."

"Then we have other things to deal with," I responded, holstering my weapons. "Are you okay?"

"Sweet as peaches." He chuckled. "S'all good."

"Are you in an altered state?" I frowned at him. "Between setting things on fire for no reason and pulling off gunslinger moves with the Tangler, I can't tell anymore."

"I'm alright, Hoss." He nodded. "Yeah, I'm feelin' Anya's lil' gift, but I'm on the job."

"You called her darlin'." I chuckled.

"Did I?" He shook his head. "That don't sound right."

Anya? We're on our way. I sent the link as we walked toward the far door of the room. I hoped it led us back in her general direction.

We needed to hurry if we were going to find our way home.

Thirty-eight minutes and ten seconds remained.

3

There is a trap. Anya sent the weary link as we entered a hallway that led us on an arc, where her marker blinked twelve meters away.

A trap? Wyatt blinked rapidly. *Like a trap door?*

Unless I am mistaken, I saw several kilograms of plastic explosive on this side of the door. Logic dictates that Firenzei intended for it to go off if you found me.

Asshole doesn't know we can talk through the link. Wyatt nodded. *He left it in case ambushing us didn't get the job done.*

From this side, it appears to be strictly Rational technology. I can easily patch Asset Guthrie the physical location of the device. As long as he uses that, he should be able to focus one of his spikes into a field to nullify the explosive.

Understood, he replied.

I worried about her. She hadn't been completely honest. Just behind her link trickled whispers of pain.

Hold one moment while I patch Asset Guthrie the specs he will require.

Wyatt twitched from the size of the patch. He shook his head, then smiled.

"There's not too much to this." He gave me sideward glance. "If we alter the axioms around the door, we can change the requirements for combustion."

"Easy enough," I agreed.

WHUF. He placed one in the center of the hallway and walked over to the side door. ***WHUF.***

Okay, I linked to Anya, *he set the spikes. Are we ready?* I paid very close attention, trying to determine how badly she'd been hurt. *Do we have anything else we need to worry about?*

All clear. She took a moment to respond. *Local readings are stable, although we remain far below Rationality zero.*

"This'll be a breeze." Wyatt peered down at his keyboard, angling his head to see with his one good eye.

"Are we green, Asset?" I hoped I could keep him professional if I chose my words carefully.

"Yeah. I mean, yeah, er, yes." He chewed his lip. "The real issue's not stopping *all* chemical combustion. I mean, we need to combust glucose and oxygen to keep our big brains going."

"Right," I agreed, eyeing my friend. "Just get it done."

Less than thirty seconds later, one of the spikes pulsed a deep magenta.

Wyatt struck one more key.

"Alright." He reached out for the door handle. "In we go."

I peered into the room. Shadows clung to the walls. I brushed more of the white flame-retardant powder from my body as I stepped inside. The room appeared to be little more than storage space. Next to the door, though, I saw the explosives Anya warned us about.

They completely failed to explode and blow us to smithereens.

As I walked further inside, they continued to do so.

Seems clear in here, I linked. *There's another door on the far side.*

Yup, Wyatt linked back. *Go on, I've got yer six.*

I strode ahead of him, slipped to the next door, and listened at it.

Nothing.

I cracked it open and peeked through. Beyond, I saw ragged green carpet. A light flickered overhead as if about to go out, a—

Anya.

She crouched on the floor in a small pool of blood.

I sighed in relief.

Until she coughed. Flecks of blood dotted her hand.

In the dim light, her fair hair seemed angelic. Tears had worn trails down her face.

He'd beaten her—more than the quick punches we'd seen. Her

face blossomed with bruises already, and one eye had swollen shut. The top part of her shirt had been violently ripped, showing far more than Facility regs.

It scarcely remained decent.

"Anya?" I stepped closer.

Blood stained her leg. Not her leg—her knee. She'd torn her shirtsleeve and used it as a makeshift bandage, but she'd bled a lot.

The asshole had brought her here, beaten her, shot her kneecap, and came back to taunt us.

She'd lain here in agony, in the near-dark, as she waited for our timer to run out.

I cannot walk alone, she stated matter-of-factly, though she trembled. *I will have to lean on you, but all my gear is still operational.*

"We can do that." Rage boiled in my blood.

"All my potential mecha are tasked, Michael." She coughed again, her voice rough. "I cannot dampen any more pain." She paused, her next words little more than a whisper. "I tried. I tried while he—"

"No. I'm here now. I'm just happy you're alive."

"As am I." Her whispered words sounded broken, lost in this room.

"Let's get you up." I reached down and wrapped an arm around her.

She pushed up but cried out in pain.

I froze.

"Stop!" Tears traced down Anya's face. "Hurts."

She's injured. Asshole shot her kneecap, I linked to Wyatt as she again struggled to stand.

Fuck, Hoss. Wyatt's bubbling anger matched my own.

Front of her shirt's ripped. She's been crying.

I'm glad you took most a' his hand off. I'm glad. Motherfucker needs a beat-down.

"My right leg is fine." Anya hissed in pain as she adjusted her

435

weight. "If you can support me on the left, we can move." She smiled briefly, a smile that broke my heart.

This was what it had taken. We stood adrift in an alien world, and she'd been beaten, abused. An Irrat had shattered her kneecap and taunted us about it.

All this before I saw her beautiful smile.

"I have you," I whispered. I put an arm around her, surprised at how light she felt.

I started to say something more, but an ominous sound rumbled through the room like a giant engine. It grumbled, grinding like a transmission slipping past several gears.

What? I glanced at her questioningly.

"That is the second time." She jerked her chin at a wooden door across the room. "It sounded a little louder last time."

"Any readings?"

"The Facets of Rationality are in the same direction," she said. "We are not far, although I am picking up a lot of principle interference."

Wyatt, I'm moving into the next room.

What? Why? he asked in a distant, slightly dreamy tone.

Wyatt, we gotta move.

Oh, okay. Copy that.

I'm leaving Anya here for the moment. She can't walk without help.

He said nothing, but I felt his dark scowl over the link.

Slowly, I limped Anya toward the door. When we got there, I leaned her slender form against the wall.

Pale. She looked so pale.

"I'm headed in first, just to poke about. Wyatt will run back point. He'll be along in a moment."

Understood. She nodded. Her wan face seemed so tired, and I thought she might cry again.

I didn't want to leave her, not now. I'd never seen Anya like this, not a single moment where she wasn't in complete control.

Firenzei had beaten her right to her edge. It hadn't even taken him long to do it.

I won't be far. I opened the door and glanced at the ever-ticking clock.

Thirty-two minutes remained.

Unimaginable Force

The long hallway beyond the cubicle room had been carpeted in thick, red shag while the walls remained dark wood paneling. The lights overhead flickered, more than a few burnt out. The hallway smelled wet, vaguely moldy. I couldn't help but blink as I walked along, a raging headache pounding in my skull.

This passage opens out into a hallway with a T at the far end, I linked. *I don't love it down here, something seems off.*

Off? Wyatt responded.

I got a headache the moment I strolled down this way. It only gets worse as I push on.

We're clear here. I'm with Anya. You scout us out but don't waste any time.

Copy that.

I triggered the *Wraith* again, hoping it'd had time to recalibrate. Firenzei's attack had added matter to the veil, making me visible until the packet adjusted, typically a few moments at Rationality zero.

Cool shadows drifted around me, and I faded from sight.

I slipped down the hallway.

I'd only taken a few steps when I heard that grumbling, grinding sound again. It shook the hallway so violently I halted in place, pressing myself against the wall.

Just as suddenly, it faded.

That wasn't you, right? Wyatt's forehead wrinkled as his eyebrows raised.

Anya said those tremors have been happening. Stronger this way, though. I paused.

And you're over there all alone. I felt his scowl. *Weird headaches, gargantuan noises. I don't like it.*

I took a few more steps, eyes trained on the hallway. The walls within the T ahead appeared slightly curved.

I'll come back. We seem clear.

I think you'd better. I don't like us being separated in this shitopia.

Moments later, the three of us crept down the hallway together.

"I'll take point," the barbarian gruffly said. The Tangler whined softly as he moved ahead, entering inputs.

"Yeah?" I raised an eyebrow at him.

"I'm fine," he grumbled. He tapped two keys, as if punctuating his point.

I had no doubt he'd keyed up some nastiness in case we made contact.

"Got you." I wrapped an arm snugly around Anya. "Go slow if you have to."

"There is no time for going slow," she responded. "Space is diffracted here."

"Space?" Wyatt scowled. "Isn't... isn't diffraction something light and sound do?"

"Typically." Anya winced as we moved. "Yet due to whatever Irrationality happened here, space is behaving as if diffracted. It is miscuing within our perceptual nodes."

"Is this why my head is starting to kill me?" Wyatt asked. "I mean, I'm still feelin' a bit high from earlier, but this headache is a buzz kill."

"Affirmative." Anya hissed in a breath as we stepped forward. "There is little we can do, I am afraid. All mecha resources are utilized."

We slipped down the passage, Wyatt just ahead. When we came to the T, he turned and regarded us.

"Not straight hallways," he muttered. "Look, both veer off, toward..." He glanced at Anya.

"Functional east," she supplied.

"It's as if they go in a circle." I nodded.

"Interesting enough," Wyatt remarked. "Although, I'm far

more interested in what *that* is." He pointed to the left hand hallway, just past some insipid office art.

A circular fixture, some sort of metallic apparatus, had been set into the wall.

"I might have an idea what it is." I raised an eyebrow at him.

"I'm hopin' I do too." He grinned wolfishly at me. "Let's check it out."

We hadn't taken five steps before the shape came fully into view. Immediately, I recognized it as another of the vault doors, this one wide and round.

"Sadhana," I mused, tracing my fingers along the inscription. "Wonder if that means anything."

"It's the ACME of trans-dimensional doors?" Wyatt grinned.

"Well, we wanted a way out," I admitted.

"Not this way, I'd bet." Wyatt squinted as he read the small brass plate next to the first door. "Second Circle, Ætern." He tapped it with one finger. "Familiar to anyone?"

"No," Anya said, her voice small.

"It's not Tokyo," I responded. "More's the pity."

"There are others." Anya pointed down the curved hallway, her fingers twitching gently.

"I'm only interested in one reality." Wyatt sighed. "Any news on that one?"

"I read no Facets of Rationality behind this door."

"Moving on then," Wyatt responded. He shrugged, hoisting his backpack higher onto his back, and crept forward.

"Din Modar," he read the next plate and glanced back over his shoulder. "I plan on strollin' on unless limpy here says different."

Carry on. We both felt the agony in Anya's link. *We are close.*

My head pounded, as if every heartbeat pushed an ice pick into my skull. The hallway went on and on. Some of the names sounded simply nonsensical: The Nimjemen Remnant, Ar'Ghosa, Lucimiir. Others were more descriptive, such as The Last City of Man and The Labyrinth of Isowyr. One label read The Starsailed

City of Mür, which I found intriguing.

"Well now!" Wyatt's tone turned jovial. "Lookie here."

Another door stood before us, completely unlike the vault doors along the walls. This one appeared newer than the rest of the office, constructed from stainless steel.

"Listen." Wyatt leaned closely, pressing one ear to the cool metal. "It's that rumbling sound, only quieter."

Before I got two steps from the door, I heard it, a grumbling, growling sound. The floor vibrated with it, like the purr of a gargantuan feline.

"I'm going in," I said. "You two stay here while I poke about with the *Wraith*."

"You best be fast, Hoss." Wyatt chewed his lip. "We ain't playin' fuck around here."

"I get that," I hissed. "But Anya's half crippled and you're high off your ass. I'll poke in and—"

The door opened. A cacophony of grinding metal rolled over us.

A young man stood there, dressed in a white coat, rubber apron, gloves, and gas mask. He held an engraved iron box in his left hand, which vibrated and steamed with glowing green mist. For a moment, he gaped at the three of us. The smell of burning oil and hot metal wafted from behind him while steam and smoke billowed forth.

"*C-chert poberi!*" he cried, stammering in his shock. He stumbled backward, the door closing behind him while he continued to yell.

"Well, fuck," I muttered. "There goes any surprise."

I leapt forward and hurled open the door before any Irrat weirdos could levy a response to our presence. The room appeared huge. I couldn't see the far walls through the steam. It washed over me, as well as the scent of hot grease. Machines the size of houses chugged all around us, sinister things wrought from gunmetal, gears, and wildly screeching flywheels. Several small pedestals sat before these devices, their tops shimmering sapphire blue through the misty shadows. Silhouettes of many men moved frantically among the machines, some of them pushing carts piled with various cogs and sprockets.

As soon as one saw me, he yelled something unintelligible. Russian again?

Maybe.

Three of them ran, wildly sprinting for a vault door on the other side of the room. One of the men barked something, a growl of a word I couldn't make out.

Two stayed behind, obviously furious at the men who ran.

"*Mu'dak!*" one of the remaining men cried.

Here's where everything is. I sent my cadre a small patch including my visual of the room's layout. *I don't think these guys want a fight.*

One of them stood and wrenched at a gigantic gear. At first tug, it wouldn't budge, but in a moment it began to grind with screeching complaint. A loud horn sounded, followed by a scratchy recording of someone speaking in a language I couldn't understand.

The man who'd pushed those hulking carts ran over to help the lever-man push. After the gear moved a few centimeters, something whirred deep within.

The world trembled.

What the fuck was that? Wyatt spoke as succinctly as ever.

A large dip in Irrationality. A twenty-three point shift and back. It happened all in a matter of milliseconds.

It's the machinery in here, I conveyed. *They did it.*

Maybe you need to focus on finding a door, Hoss, Wyatt mused. *Although, one of those boys might know exactly where to point you.*

Copy that. The big lug nailed it. Our countdown read twenty-eight minutes exactly; we had no time to waste.

I shrugged. *Maybe it's time to capture a friend.*

We clear to enter?

Probably, I responded. *They aren't on the offensive.*

Roger that.

Another set of the men off to my left realized I wasn't one of their own. They backed away slowly into a small alcove in one of the machines. In just a moment, they vanished entirely into steam.

They certainly recognized me—what I was, at any rate.

These guys seemed terrified of Assets and probably the Facility in general. If that held true, perhaps I could threaten one of them to show us the way home.

Now to personify the big, scary Silent Gentleman…

Katana drawn, I sprinted through the steam, toward the men at the gear-lever. Covered in blood, my own and Firenzei's, I must have resembled a madman. Further, I still had white fire retardant smeared in my hair and clothes. As I charged across the room, I held both swords over my head and screamed.

Before me, the three men still struggled to budge the gigantic gear. A yellow mist chugged from their device.

One of them waved at the other two frantically. *"Vot blin zasranec!"*

Another turned to me and clenched his fists. Behind his antiquated gas mask, I saw nothing of his face.

"Hold on there." I held my katana at the ready but didn't directly brandish them. "Can any of you speak English?"

"Gavareetye pazhalooysta myedleeney?" one asked, backing away.

"No," another replied gutturally. "We are no speak."

"Sounds as if maybe you do." I nodded at the man. Through his gasmask, I just made out an aging face and dark eyes.

"You no come this place," the man continued. "You not welcome."

Overhead, those speakers sounded again, calling out repetitive phrases I didn't recognize. However, at the end of the broadcast, one word jumped out at me, clear as day. A name.

Rudolfo Firenzei.

"I know I'm not welcome. Maybe you can help me leave." I gestured at the vault door, the one his fellows fled through. "Earth. I fucking know you have one of those doors, somewhere. Where is it?"

"Maybe you be going and fucking mother," a second man said.

"Not nice." I toggled the *Wraith* twice so I flickered momentarily from view.

The one closest to me took a small step back.

It's always nice to show Irrats you can pull some strangeness all your own.

"Maybe I'll kill you all." I bared my teeth in a grin, then turned my head to one side and popped my neck. "Unless you help me leave."

"No," the first man responded, his eyes black within the mask. "You are the dying, I think."

Michael. I felt the sharp warning in Anya's link. *Rationality just spiked two points in your vicinity in the last five seconds.*

I see why, I linked.

The man who spoke took a step toward me, his hand wreathed in a black miasma of boiling shadows. He slashed downward abruptly.

Between us, five sharp lines of darkness rent the air. Each burbled and roiled, frothing in space.

I smelled rot, the foulness of things long dead.

Two more points, Michael.

Thank you, Anya. I stepped back and brought my katana into a guard.

Necrotic ichor oozed from the slashes, burbling forth like malignant fonts of elemental obscenity. A seething whir howled, like the drone of a gigantic insect.

"You see!" one of the men cried, a wild laugh lurking on the edge of his lips. "You see last time!" He backed away, as did

445

another man. They left me with the dark-shrouded Irrat, as they retreated into shadows and steam.

In that moment, alien repugnance lurched into the room, birthed through the drooling tear in the fabric of the world.

Fucking great. My katana already in motion, I leapt forward.

I hadn't seen the thing's head or really made out its true shape, not yet. And I couldn't tell what incomprehensible powers it might have.

But.

When a crazy Russian is cackling about slaughtering you while otherworldly miscreations ooze into your reality, one does not wait for confirmation.

One acts.

My blade clacked against something hard, as if striking porcelain. The carapace buckled, the aberration writhing away from the keen edge.

I swung with my second, but my enemy undulated backward, rolling up into a tall, manlike figure.

Hoss? Wyatt gamboled into my mind. *What is it?*

A… hornet? I took a step back, confused. *A man?*

The dark, insectine shape loomed from its full height. Venomous eyes gazed down on me, multifaceted planes radiating alien fury. Four sets of hairy, multi-jointed legs sprouted from the creature, each ending in chitinous pincers. Sickly, malformed wings sprouted from its back, blurring with speed to produce the droning noise I'd heard. It leapt upward, not quite able to fly, but carried further by those abhorrent wings.

WASP-PERSON! It was all I had time to link.

What is your status, Michael?

Not good!

I swung my katana as I stumbled backward into the steam, attempting to keep the thing at bay.

Much of its body still dripped with the dark putrescence oozing through the rent veil, but the substance boiled away into reeking vapor.

It screeched at me, its insectine mouth opening wider than I thought possible. Thick mucus drooled onto the floor as its wings buzzed angrily.

I didn't bother to hide my disgusted expression.

It leapt, swiping at me with razor sharp pincers.

"Fuck!" I heroically cried as it dove through the air. Those wicked claws all around, I lurched sideways.

The insect turned, eyes glinting with inhuman hunger.

Fast. Ridiculously so. Also, I got the feeling those pincers could peel my skin away, like an over-ripe tomato.

I had to change the game.

Daring a glance at our surroundings, I dove behind one of the metal carts. Flipping it, glass beakers and metal instruments crashed to the floor. I toggled the *Adept* and thrilled at the silvery grace that swam through my veins.

The aberration hurled itself toward me, sickly wings droning. With its misshapen form, they didn't seem to grant true flight. Instead, its leaps were remarkably powerful, as the wings carried a good portion of its weight.

I swung the katana, swift as thought.

The hornet-strosity dropped, slamming into the cart. Both careened into me, pushing us all back three or four meters.

Comin', Hoss, Wyatt drawled through the link. *Drop me a marker.*

Will comply. I made the mental tic, and my Crown whirred.

Then I peered over the edge of the table.

The creature hissed and swiped wildly at me, jagged pincers grasping madly.

I leaped to my left, cursing at the near miss.

"Come. On!" I cried to the Russian man, who cackled in delight. "Just help us leave. I don't want this to get ugly."

"Ugly now," he called. "Too late for you!"

I glanced over my shoulder at the man and saw wicked hatred

447

gleaming in his eyes. Between us, those undulating slashes of midnight shadow still oozed with living pustulence.

From that primal ichor, a second shape fell to the floor, quivering and twitching. It shivered and spasmed, birthed from some unimaginable darkness.

My heart sank to somewhere below my feet.

The thing stretched its wings as it pushed itself up, shaking the stinking plasmatic fluid from its nightmarish body. Ooze steamed in the air, radiating away into foul mist.

Behind it, a third abomination screeched its way into the world.

"Okay," I said to myself. "Fuck this."

I toggled the *Wraith* and stood as I faded from sight. Sheathing the katana, I drew my Stilettos, one in each hand. I took a few quick steps to my left, not wanting to be in the same spot where the bug saw me disappear.

The insectine horror, all savage claw and horrific shrieks, fell on me anyway.

Even with the blessings of the *Adept*, keeping ahead of the grotesquery felt almost impossible. As the waspish-thing hurled itself at me, I dove backward again, slinging my weapons forward.

It followed me, step for step, without missing a beat.

"What the hell?" I screamed, firing squarely at it. My Stilettos keened a high *siiiiuu siiiiuu* as kinetic force tore into the wasp creature, splattering yellow, stinking filth all over my shirt.

The malific nightmare shrieked in incoherent rage and swiped at me with one of its wicked pincers. It caught me across the face, and scarlet agony tore through my cheek.

I roared, fury and pain exploding from my chest. Swift as the *Adept* might be, this thing matched me move for move.

Somehow.

I feinted to one side, then dodged behind one of the pedestals positioned around the room. Brilliant shone over me, yet the *Wraith* cloaked me.

But no. My foe's head tilted, following me.

Holy shit.

The fucker could *see* me.

"You die!" the Russian cackled again, losing himself in a fit of maddened glee.

The second creature now stood on its arthropod legs, misshapen wings droning. It stared squarely at me, those multifaceted eyes gleaming with otherworldly light. It hissed, a hateful promise in a tongue I couldn't know.

I powered down the *Wraith* and faded into view. If the packet didn't help me, then I should conserve the resources. The idea that these horrors saw right through its protection didn't inspire me.

In that moment, I didn't think things could get any worse.

"Stay back!" I fired in the general direction of the second monstrosity, trying to keep it at bay. My kinetic shots made the mist swirl around them.

As I yelled, the room around me spasmed, trembling, nauseating. My eyes went wide with realization.

"Damnit," I swore, searching around for the teleporting asshole. This had to be the worst possible timing.

Hoss... Wyatt's link warned me. *We got issues.*

You're telling me. I aimed at the closest mutant yellow-jacket and fired burst after burst, intent on finishing this quickly. Those spasms could only mean one possible thing.

Firenzei had arrived.

2

He's over here, Wyatt sent. *Engaging.*

In the distance, I heard a mad flurry of **WHUF**s.

I screamed as I fired, a wordless howl of rage. I closed in on the hornet-strosity. I didn't let up but pounded shot after shot of kinetic fury into the inhuman carapace.

Those shots drove it backward several steps, splattering me with thick mucus once they finally cracked through the insect's tough shell.

It fell back, skittering away from my shots even as it gurgled and spat.

I leapt forward, bringing one of my Stilettos up toward its head—

—when the second malignance leapt at me from the side, shredding part of my shirt with those fiendish talons.

"No!" I twisted, bringing the Stiletto in my left hand down on the buggy asshole.

It grasped me around the waist, mandibles snapping.

Surely a shot this close would end the thing. Surely—

But it swiped at me, smashing into my bicep with one of those multi-jointed legs.

Pain ran through my arm like an electric shock, and I dropped the pistol.

Wings blurring, the aberration leapt straight up, dragging me into the steamy air. It slammed me into the ceiling, smashing my head squarely into a metal strut.

With a savage twist, it spun its abdomen down toward me.

As we started to fall, I saw the stinger: a quarter-meter long, barbed hook of edged spite.

It stabbed me, burying the stinger deep into my stomach.

I screamed.

The hateful thing bore me to the ground, smashing my broken

body against the floor.

It stung me again, stabbing into my stomach a second time. It burned like fire, like shards of poisoned glass. I gagged on bile.

"Oh, oh FUCK!" I wailed. I reached for its face, for its eyes. I had to make it stop, had to—

It stung my gut and groin three more times.

I howled in agony, thrashing, scrambling madly. Around the edges of my vision, the darkness of unconsciousness closed in on me.

"No…" I tried to push myself up, patting at my body, frantically trying to examine my wounds.

Bishop, Michael. 108, my Crown prompted, Rachel Gardner's recorded voice a clunky whisper in my mind. ***Shall we initiate autonomous medical protocols?***

"Yes." I spat blood as the hornet-strosity scuttled off me. *Fuck. Please.*

"Stupid." The gas-mask wearing man strode over to where I lay twitching in a paroxysm of torment. He spat in my face.

Will comply, Rachel's executable responded. ***Now initiating type III emergency resuscitation and priority one pain dampening protocols.*** The commands whirred in my Crown but seemed impossibly far away.

Asset 108 has suffered terminal damage, the voice reported. ***Rerouting all viral mecha operating parameters.***

Adrenaline and Facility-produced hormones poured through my veins. I *felt* the tell-tale warmth of the mecha doing their work: altering the axioms of reality within my body. Every bit as powerful as Wyatt's spikes, the mecha altered physics itself to begin immediately, miraculously, knitting my body.

"God," I groaned, my hand on my stomach. "Oh you motherfucker."

After a moment, the pain all but ceased, even though I had five or six gut wounds. A golden, narcotic glow replaced the sensation.

Recommend immediate evacuation to Asset Emergency Ser-

vices, Rachel's voice stated. ***System integrity is critically damaged.***

I blinked, trying to track what happened. I'd been cataclysmically wounded. Warily, I moved just a few centimeters to see if I would collapse from the pain.

No. Just now the mecha blocked that sensation.

Thankfully.

In the lower left-hand corner of my visual array I saw the counter, the one that told us how long our available mecha would keep us alive in this topia. That number blurred, rushing downward.

It stopped at nineteen minutes and forty-five seconds.

What?" I spat in disbelief. I realized what had happened, but it seemed so, so…

Unfair.

After burning those mecha on Rachel's executable, I didn't have nearly the resources I'd held previously. I'd almost died, of course.

I guess I'd bought nineteen whole minutes of life.

WHUF. WHUF. WHUF.

Spikes whizzed by, two of them tearing into the wasp that stung me. They cracked as they punched into its carapace.

The thing screeched, savage rage echoing even above the whirrs and whines of the machinery. Foul-smelling smoke began to pour off its body.

Hoss?!

"Who now?" The sadistic Russian turned toward Wyatt, his hand still bubbling with shadows.

I searched about. If any of his friends remained, I didn't see them.

But I did see one of my Stilettos.

More of the insectine monstrosities scurried out of the wounds the man carved in space. As he gestured, screaming furiously, two took off in the direction of Wyatt's spikes, their wings droning a malefic buzz.

I frantically grabbed at my pistol, wincing at the movement. It didn't exactly *hurt*, but I could just imagine the damage to my internals.

No time to worry now.

"Hey!" I yelled, trying to catch the man's attention. "Here, shithead!"

"Not yet?" He turned with a snarl. "You want more of—"

I aimed and shot the motherfucker in the head. His skull exploded, riven into pieces by furious kinetic force.

His body stood for a moment, unaware some badass had just blown its fucking head off. After a heartbeat, it fell, first to its knees, and then completely over. That aura of boiling midnight faded from around his hand.

The slashes he'd rent in reality vanished, crackling and hissing as they drifted away like smoke in the wind.

The singular hornet-asshole I could see screamed frantically, thrashing about as its carapace dribbled down its form, steaming and smoking as it dissolved. The bug raged and raved, its legs and wings and head dissolving into steaming, reeking gore.

"Hoss," Wyatt panted, staring around wildly. "We gotta go, bud."

"No shit." I coughed, spitting up the remnants of my own bile. "My counter's almost done."

"Firenzei's staying back," he scowled. "Motherfucker's been toying with us. The executable is struggling."

"How so?"

"He's shooting from outside the range of our program," Wyatt panted. "Can't pick him up."

Gentlemen, Anya linked. *I show 423 has arrived at your marker, Michael?*

He's here. I blinked, somewhat dizzy. The mecha certainly continued to work overtime just to keep me upright and conscious, so I truly couldn't complain.

454

Saved his ass is what happened, Wyatt smiled.

Here is my marker. She dropped a blue triangle over our visual array. Below it her distance, 102m, glowed in sky-blue.

Copy that, Anya, Wyatt straightened his Stetson. *We'll be right there.*

"It may take me a sec." I coughed. "And I know I don't have a sec."

"You'll wanna hurry." Wyatt gave me a sideward grin. "While you played pest control and I fended off the teleporting sharpshooter, Anya actually did something important."

"Oh yeah?" I coughed again. "What's that?"

"She found our vault door, buddy." He chuckled.

"Oh." I shook my dizzy head and stumbled forward. The world seemed too white. I couldn't find the words. "She did?"

"Complete with the Facets of Rationality shining just on the other side." He glanced back over his shoulder. "Comin' up on endgame, Bishop. Keep it together."

"I am. I mean, I still have both my eyes," I teased. "I'm more together than you are, man."

"You *need* both eyes, just to keep up with *all this,*" he shot back playfully. "'Sides, you know the Facility will fix me up. I'll get some kind of nuclear laser eye or maybe—"

From behind us, several rapid gunshots barked. They echoed, like a chime ringing the doom of the world. A harbinger.

A blossom of blood, crimson.

A snarl of curses.

A cry of pain.

"Guthrie?" I spun, my eyes wide.

"I..." Wyatt stared at me. His hand touched his chest and dripped with blood. He stumbled.

The mountain of a man fell.

3

I whirled, toggling the *Wraith.*

Behind us, I saw only one of the great, building-sized engines grumbling along, chuffing out yellow steam.

I had a good idea what direction the shot must have come from, but no...

I saw nothing.

Bishop, Michael. 108. Rachel Gardener's prompt slid into my mind. *The executable for Asset 423, Guthrie, Wyatt is not receiving input from its host.*

"Not what I wanted to hear." I crouched next to Wyatt, still searching for the shooter.

Firenzei. It couldn't be anyone else.

Asset 423, Guthrie, Wyatt, is not responding to his system initiative. Shall we initiate autonomous resuscitation and pain blocking protocols?

I stared down at Guthrie and hissed through my teeth. The shot had been square, entering and then exiting the right side of his chest. I'd imagined he'd been hit several times, but only one pierced his quasi-steel.

The blood screamed scarlet. Some of it frothed from his mouth.

"Wyatt," I barked. "Say something for me, pal."

"Who's the lady?" He moaned. "I hear—"

Yes. I grit my teeth, knowing full well initiating the executable would devour his resources. *If the situation is critical.*

Asset 423 has suffered terminal damage, the voice reported. *Cardiac and respiratory systems will fail in less than one minute.*

Initiate protocols!

Will comply.

Another shot fired, this one tore into the floor.

I turned again with a glance up toward that gargantuan, chugging machine. I toggled my optics, zooming my vision closer to the device.

Recommend immediate evacuation to Asset Emergency Services, Rachel's voice repeated. **System integrity is critically damaged.**

"I get it," I muttered. "I've got about eighteen minutes left myself."

Not that it mattered, in all honesty. Wyatt stood a full two meters tall, layered with muscle. The pack strapped to his back added to his mass. Even before my own injuries, I would have had a difficult time moving him.

That immediate evacuation didn't seem possible.

I flitted my gaze about, searching for any sign of Firenzei. The man's qualifications as a sharpshooter had been well documented in his dossier. If I didn't figure out something, he'd just pick us—

Anya's executable whirred in my mind.

Irrational source located. Calibrating anomaly.

Over my visual, those three red lines drifted into alignment.

Firenzei had made his way about three quarters to the top of one of the machines, where he nestled against a steam pipe. I saw his fiery shock of hair as well as the wicked scope of his weapon, glinting as he aimed it through the steam.

I pulled both Stilettos, then took a long moment to aim. Beneath the *Wraith*, I had the luxury of caution.

Not that I'd hit him—not at this range. The kinetic disruptors hadn't really been built for distance.

I fired, sending a half dozen sharp *siiiiuu siiiiuu* sounds keening through the room.

"Fuck," I snarled, even though I'd expected to miss. My closest shot hit the steam pipe above Firenzei, punching a hole in the metal.

He leapt back into the shadows.

Irrational source lost.

Hoss. The link felt faint, like a shadow of the man. *That cart, man. Can you flip it over?*

I stared at the cart, the one I'd used to hide from the asshole hornet monsters. The various bits of machinery and tools it held lay scattered around the floor.

"I can."

"Might make a nice conveyance for my huge ass."

"It might." I flipped it upright and then pushed it over to him.

"I assume, as I'm breathin', you set my mecha to work," he drawled as he patted his chest. "Fuck, that hurts."

"I did. Rachel's toy. I bet it kicks your counter down, though."

"Only a lot." He nodded.

"Can you crawl inside the cart?" I couldn't keep the hope from my tone. I might not be able to lift the man, but I could sure as hell *push* him.

"I *think* I can." He rolled, then coughed, spitting out an alarming amount of blood. "I assume I'm hurt a fair bit worse than these little mecha are letting on."

"You are. The prompt threw around words like 'critical' and 'terminal.'"

"Fucking figures." He lurched forward, hissing in pain. "Scoot it closer; I'll roll onto it."

I did just that, and Wyatt grunted, slowly flopping onto the cart.

The world around us began to tremble, blurring and warbling as Firenzei used his Irrational gift.

Wyatt shot me a glance.

I nodded.

We needed to move. If we could get deeper into the steam, perhaps it would provide cover.

"'Bout a hundred meters," he drawled. "She ain't far. We get there, we get out. Maybe grab a conduit to Facility Prime."

Wyatt situated himself, grunting.

"We can try." I pushed the cart forward just a bit. "I've got seventeen minutes on my counter."

"Sixteen minutes fifteen." He coughed. "You'd better fucking hustle."

4

Firenzei kept firing as we sprinted through the mist. The jerk had decided to stay back, relying on his sniper rifle and our unfamiliarity with the compound.

That might have been smart. As I recalled, the last time he'd appeared, a handsome genius had chopped his hand in two.

There, Hoss, Wyatt dropped a marker over a narrow path between two of the chugging engines.

I might not have seen it, in all honesty, due to the thick, rolling steam within.

Got it. I wheeled the cart wildly to the left and ducked my head as Firenzei fired again.

We dodged behind those whirring, grease-spitting engines, our eyes watering from the acrid mist as we passed. The whole time, I kept a close track on Anya's marker, tracking how far we needed to go.

Bullets sang against the machinery. Apparently the mist didn't do Firenzei any favors.

Anya, Wyatt sent, *it'd be nice if you'd figgered out that door. We're coming in fast.*

I have not, she linked succinctly. *It is exactly like the vault doors we have encountered this far, seemingly impossible to open from without.*

Lovely. Wyatt coughed wetly and began tapping at a few of his keys. *Fortunately, I have just the thing.*

It took less than a minute to melt through the last one, I reminded him. *I'm certain it's fine.*

We rounded a corner and found ourselves running alongside a wall lined with the stalwart doors. Each held a brass nameplate I made a point to peek at them as we went by:

Calyptia, the Radiant.

The Wastes of Sijil.

The Ulüm Driftlands.

The Cacaphonie Meanders.

The Shard of Corsün.

Not a one familiar and each set me ill at ease. As Assets of the Facility, we'd trained in the cosmology of the Myriad.

We therefore understood the truth.

Existence comprised of Rationality and the howling chaos of the Maelstrom. Yes, other realities existed, but they appeared like bubbles in a savage, storming ocean before vanishing forever.

Yet... if other realities were as transient as I'd always understood, why create doors? Why give them fancy-ass nameplates?

As I ran, unnatural machinery gurgled and spat on both sides of us. The steam coated my skin in sticky, gummy sweat, and I briefly wondered how long a baseline human would survive breathing the stuff.

Without care, my mecha would run dry. Then I'd find out.

Wyatt's Tangler cried a whining song I recognized well. He tapped a few more keys, preparing something.

"We're good, Hoss," he gurgled. He gave me a thumbs up and grinned widely.

Yet I saw the utter exhaustion in his eyes.

When Anya's indicator read 15m, she came into view, leaning against the wall of the room. One of those odd pedestals sat squarely next to the vault door, blue numerics shining from its top surface.

Pale. Her leg had started to bleed again.

What—? She gaped at us careening wildly toward her. *What are you doing?*

Long story. I heaved Wyatt to a stop.

Incoming patch, Twitchy, Wyatt replied. *Our past fifteen minutes. It explains the hurry.*

I watched her head tic as she received the packet.

I see, she responded. *Our egress has become vital.* She turned toward the vault door with a gesture.

To its side, a brass plate read: **Manhattan, New York. One Ito Plaza.**

"Hot damn." A broad smile lit my face. The moment we stepped into Rationality, the Designates would modulate our mecha. The *Caduceus*-class Assets could step in.

Our survivability would increase exponentially.

I have the proper algorithms, Wyatt linked. *Just like the others, this door is a steel composite. I can melt our way through it.* Without waiting for a response, Wyatt fired a spike squarely into the center of the vault door.

Careful, Anya. I pulled the cart up next to her. *Do you need help moving back a bit? Wyatt said earlier these spikes might affect our Crowns.*

I remember, she replied. *He is altering the manner in which quantum electrodynamics bind the iron and carbon.*

Rather well, I might add. He snickered.

Immediately, the thick vault door began to sag downward, as if melting. The brass fittings and bolts remained unaffected, just as before.

The resulting *CRACK* echoed, resounding loudly through the room. The door drooped like melting rubber before pouring down as a fine, black sand.

"Go!" Wyatt cackled. "Yah, Hoss!" He slapped the side of the cart.

I grinned and pushed the cart a bit slower as Anya grasped the side. She visibly kept her weight on her good leg.

We pushed through.

5

Thick, clammy air washed over us as we strode into the dusky murk of the next room. Occasionally, a drifting bit of emerald light shone through those sinister shadows.

It stank. The entire room reeked of the sour rot of low tide. My heart sank in iron dismay.

This wasn't home at all.

Um. Wyatt glanced up at me. *Is your death counter still going, Hoss?*

It is. I scowled. *Fifteen minutes.*

No axiomatic alterations have taken place. Anya stared at us, her eyes wide. *We are still adrift.*

Fucking what? Wyatt pulled his hat from his head. *It said Manhattan!*

It did, I confirmed.

That can't be right! Every fucking time we step through those doors, we end up in some other cock-sucking murder-verse!

Not every time. I gazed at them, apologetically. *Remember leaving the last breeding room? The one with the well in the center of it?* I gestured at the door behind us. *As we left, we saw a placard that said Tokyo.*

We didn't exactly go to or from Tokyo, Wyatt admitted.

This is the location I have been tracking on telemetry, Anya informed us. She stepped forward. Her hands outstretched, she gestured toward a bank of terminals. *These are active. They are calibrated with the Facets of Rationality as directive settings.*

The setup appeared exactly like the mechanisms in the dodecahedral Tokyo room. Terminals flickered all along the wall, ancient CRT monitors with green displays. Workstations had been fit with traditional keyboards, many of which appeared to be well used.

Look. Over there. I dropped a marker, centering it approximately thirty meters to our functional southeast. Shrouded in shadows, I just made out the columns that stretched from the floor to the shadows above. Some of them gleamed with haunting viridian light.

Initiate yer optics, Wyatt drawled. *Then you'll see the shit we're in.*

I did. Immediately, devices came into sharp focus. I saw the relays along their metallic undersides, as well as the thick cables running into them from the ceiling.

I also saw the human figures drifting within.

Fucking lovely, Wyatt snarled. *There's another septic tank o' monsters over here.* He dropped a marker of his own.

Yes. I could see the pit now. Just as in the Tokyo room, it appeared that columns of unconscious humans circled the lagoon.

I only have one more eye, Wyatt groused.

We can be more cautious this time, Anya reasoned. *Perhaps we can slip right by them.*

Perhaps we can turn this thing on without waking them? Wyatt turned back toward the machine. *Bein' as it's set for Rationality and all.*

Coffee cup. I picked it up from where it sat next to one of the keyboards. *Still warm.*

There are more of the Radonic Transmitters here, Anya informed us. She studied them, the fingers of her left hand twitching. *These are fully charged.*

They're ready to go. Wyatt pushed himself upward, slowly. He took a deep breath. *They're taking off. That's why you read the Principal Facets here.*

I gave him a quick, questioning glance as he rose. I knew the mecha worked quickly, literally altering reality inside our bodies. But I didn't think he should be up so soon after being shot in the lung.

He gave me a tremulous thumbs up.

Maybe it's just a matter of triggering the device. I took a couple of steps closer. *Remember? We thought the entire Tokyo room might be a transport.*

I reached out with one hand and touched the keyboard.

"Ti cho ebanuti?!" a voice barked from the darkness. A dark-haired man moved over to us, clad in the gasmask and gloved attire so popular in these parts.

When he saw us, he stopped in place.

Let me. Anya stepped forward, holding both her hands out in a non-threatening gesture. Rough and fluid Russian danced off her tongue as she gestured to Wyatt, myself, and then the room.

"No." He shook his head violently. When Anya said something else, a long ramble of Russian bolted from his lips.

I only made out the word *"Pizdetz."* Yet the man's angry expression it said all.

Anya responded, her words obviously a question.

The man made a gesture of fierce negation.

For an interminable time, the two debated back and forth.

Anya? Wyatt linked. *Time's tickin'.*

Patch, Anya warned the exact same moment she sent it. She directed it straight to memory, an intimate act she'd normally discuss with us first.

I appreciated it in this instance. Time slipped away, after all.

The patch didn't take up much room; I barely felt it hit. Yet the moment it did, I understood everything.

The memory came from Anya's perspective. It felt exactly as if I'd been the one conversing with the man.

"We need assistance. We have injured." I held one of Anya's hands up, attempting to calm the man. *"We would like to find our way back to Rationality."* I paused for just a moment. *"Earth. We need to return to Earth."*

"No." The man smirked and shook his head. *"We were told there were Gentlemen within the compound. Enemies will find no assistance from me."*

"We truly mean no harm," Anya reasoned. *"We are not here by our own wishes, and we simply require help to leave in peace."*

"You don't exactly appear as if you're looking for peace." The man glared at each of us. I watched him take note of our many wounds. *"You look absolutely fucked up."*

"We know our reality is close." I met the man's gaze. *"If you help us get home, there will be no trouble. That would be best, would it not?"*

"Trouble?" The man laughed, making a gesture of negation. *"Your deaths will be no trouble."*

"My companions will agree to pass in peace if you help us." I furrowed Anya's brow. *"If you do not, I cannot say what will happen."*

"I can say what will happen," the man chuckled darkly. *"Do you know what this room is?"*

"We have been in one similar," I replied.

"So you've seen a Broodwell?" The man's eyes gleamed painfully bright. *"Impossible. You never would have survived the terrible power of the Unity."*

"We destroyed it." My words came as a quiet hiss. *"My friend did."* I tilted Anya's head toward the stunningly sexy figure standing behind her.

"I doubt that very seriously." The man shook his head, as if speaking to a child.

"Please." I took a breath. *"I would much rather work together to create a positive outcome."*

"The outcome is certain," the man rambled. *"Soon the stars shall shift, and the great dance of worlds will commence again. Then these gears will be turned, and we shall finish the Work we have started here."*

"What work is that?" Anya couldn't help but dig for more information, even now.

"The Unity shall come to the realms of men," the man positively cackled. *"Every man, woman, and child shall be blessed with*

468

its touch. This is the Holy Work you attempt to impede."

"That was not our stated goal." I gazed into the man's crazed eyes. "We simply wish to return to our home."

"You shall not." The man chuckled. "You shall die here, and I shall be happy to watch it."

Fuck, Wyatt sent.

I nodded.

We'd been correct—this location was being prepared to launch. Just like the Tokyo room, the entire chamber had been constructed with the means to traverse reality.

Unfortunately, this guy's mind had already been made up. Exactly like the man we'd interrogated earlier, he worshiped the terrible Unity we knew nothing about.

A zealot.

I recalled the other man's ramblings, tried to piece together some small scrap of data that might matter here.

No. Nothing interesting aside from their fanatical fury. I felt certain they'd seek to serve their Unity far beyond any acts of self-preservation.

Hmm. But did I *know* that?

Anya said something else to the man in Russian, gesturing to add emphasis. This time, he only laughed, a hollow sound behind that gas mask.

"Alright, fuckface." I stepped toward him, my disruptor rising to the forehead of his mask. "Maybe this will help you decide?"

"No." He laughed again, stepping forward. He sank to his knees. "No." Slowly, he reached for the end of my weapon.

Knowing he lacked the specialized mecha in his bloodstream that the pistol utilized, I watched, curious.

When he grasped it, he pulled the barrel to his forehead, his eyes on mine. He spat several words at me in Russian.

"It is no use, Michael." Anya sounded defeated. "He does not care for his own life. He is a part of the Unity. He will not be threatened."

"That seems apparent." I frowned.

Few things in my line of work caused more difficulty than zealots. They didn't care about their own safety, didn't have the same kinds of concerns most men held. Typically, the only thing they cared about—

My breath caught in realization.

I turned and gazed at Wyatt.

My barbarian friend stared down at the man, who knelt with dark fire in his eyes.

I pulled my gun free, holstered it, and nodded at Wyatt. I strolled over to him, as if I didn't have a care in the entire world.

Anya, I need you to translate.

Understood. I picked up on the scarce trace of confusion in her link.

I stood next to Wyatt, my gaze on the kneeling man. I made my eyes iron hard.

"You know who we are," I opened, letting Anya translate.

"Gentlemen." The man spat the word as if he tasted something filthy.

"You know what we do." I cocked my head at the man. "We destroy. We find filth like you, and we purge it from existence."

The man said nothing, simply stared up at me with pity and disdain. I paused for a moment, letting his eyes drink me in. Meanwhile, I accessed my viral mecha dialogues, poking until I saw *Specialized Mecha*. Once there, I found the contingent of mecha that only existed to sync my nervous system with the Stiletto disruptors.

They hadn't been tapped for my health and upkeep; they simply wouldn't work that way.

I sent the termination command to the mecha docking station.

"You're willing to die." I paused. "That's fine. I understand. We're willing to die."

Anya translated with just a touch of incomprehension.

108, Bishop, Michael. Do you wish to ignite mecha subset 152-J, Stiletto-class?

Proceed, I responded. *Reroute available resources, according to standard protocols.*

Will comply. Available energy output will increase by 1139%.

"On the other hand, you don't have the ability to do any true harm to the Facility." I smiled at the man. "There, I'm one up on you."

Anya translated.

"Tell what mean." The jerk gaped at me.

I turned to Wyatt and, as casually as plucking an apple, pulled the *Raiju*-class drones from the housing on his equipment. The silver spheres snicked loudly as they came free.

WARNING. **Raiju** *improperly docked. Please follow Facility protocols regarding this device. Improper handling could initiate catastrophic failure.*

"Hoss?" Wyatt turned toward me, stunned. "Whatcha doin'?"

Initiating catastrophic failure. I gave him a nod. *If you haven't already, I suggest you toggle your optics off.*

I toggled the *Adept.* Silvery quickness and sparkling agility twinkled and caroused in my bloodstream.

"I have here the capability to destroy this entire compound." I held the *Raiju* where our kneeling friend could see them. "Not just this room and not just this breeding pit. I can destroy every sludge-filled cesspool these slimy motherfuckers have on-site."

The man blanched as Anya translated. She certainly seemed nervous as she spoke, something I hoped would lend me a bit of weight.

His eyes practically popped through his mask. Yet he said nothing.

"How many deaths would that be?" I mused. "Tens of thousands? Hundreds of thousands?" I glanced at Wyatt. "Practically genocide, right?"

"*Bred sivoy kobyly!*" the man snarled as Anya translated my words. "You a lie!"

"He does not believe you, Michael." She shook her head. "I do not think you can bluff him."

"I agree." I gazed at her in serious contemplation. I turned back to the man. "The problem is he's put us in a corner. The only option he's left us is how to die." I raised one eyebrow. "That's why I'm not bluffing. Tell him."

She spoke, and I kept my hard gaze on the man. Racing behind my mind, I ran every possible scenario I could conceive. Wyatt had insisted the drones weren't tiny, super-nuclear bombs, at least not while stable and in their casings. No, the casing would have to be opened. He had claimed that the joules of force it would take to actually crack one of these bad boys open to be unimaginable.

I considered my Stilettos, weighing the force their specialized mecha could burn.

We'd see.

"You a lie," the man repeated. "You filling of shit."

"I thought you'd say so," I responded. "But my friend already told you." I nodded toward Anya. "I took out the last Brooding Well we came across. I'm happy to take out the rest."

Without waiting for a response, I spun in place toward the ruined vault door. I hurled both of the *Raiju* into the room beyond, then dropped my hands to the Stilettos in my holsters.

The *Adept* sang in my bloodstream, a silvery susurrus of electric alacrity. I pulled both pistols in a blur, swifter than wind, swifter than thought.

The packet tracked my shots, worked out angles and distances. My Crown knew the exactitudes of my targets before my eyes even marked them.

I fired each Stiletto, sending a cascading, anguished torrent of tones from the weapons. The barrels cracked in my hands as a raw hurricane of kinetic force focused itself down to something the approximate circumference of a pencil.

I'd never burned my Stiletto mecha like this, not once. But

from what I understood of the energy outputs—

I hit.

Both times.

Each shot sent one of the *Raiju* spinning out into the room beyond. The first struck so squarely that the drone sailed high, lodging into one of the chugging, grumbling engines in the room. The second cut through the air like a comet, slamming into one of the devices directly across from the vault door.

I only had to watch for a moment. The first of the *Raiju* pulsed an angry violet, like a star shining over the chamber of yellow mist. With a sound like the cracking of deep lake ice, its casing shattered into dust.

Raiju *drone AG-876r has suffered terminal damage. Protocol 17-R engaging.*

Its violet light swelled to the size of a basketball. It pulsed there, furious and brilliant to gaze on. Before I turned away, it CRACKED loudly, bursting with a searing flash of light.

In that instant, it surged in size, now up to a large beachball. It burned there, amethyst energy crinkling and sparking as it drank in matter around it.

That energetic emanation shone and scintillated for a moment. Galvanic arcs sparked between the edge of the field and the small sphere within.

They gamboled, they capered.

Faster and faster.

I eyed Wyatt and Anya, silent truth hanging between us.

Our earlier discussion had mostly regarded whether or not it was *possible* for the device to explode. Now, with the casing shattered, the outcome wasn't in question. The *Raiju* would attempt to hold itself together—for a brief while.

During this time, it would digest the matter around it and use that energy to enhance its own shielding capabilities.

Until those capabilities failed. Which they would. Catastrophically.

At which time, the device would explode with the fury of a small star.

Maelstrom

Oh fuck, you're stupid, Hoss! Oh you dumb motherfucker!

I gazed down at the pistols I held. Both of the Stilettos' barrels had exploded, furling outward like flowers.

I threw them to the ground, where they lay, still smoking. Without their specialized mecha, they were little more than paperweights.

Drone AG-286f is also critically damaged, Anya reported. *Its casing is not completely shattered however. It remains at two percent resilience.*

The first drone blared out a sharp warning siren, or at least a recording of one. Just the sound of it raised my hackles and made my pulse race.

"What is it?" The man on his knees gaped at that wrathful light reflected in the eyes of his gas mask.

The siren gave me an idea. I didn't know how the thing projected sound, but the fact that it *could* might come in useful.

"What you do?" The kneeling man stared up at me frantically. He looked like a man who had seen the secret and unknowable face of God.

"Exactly what I said I would." Before he could respond, I opened the link.

Raiju *drone AG-876r. Can you receive input commands?* This might be tricky. I could easily imagine such a dangerous device only receiving input from someone with Designate clearance. Then again, once the device suffered a catastrophic failure, I imagined the Designates would allow *anyone* to try to take control of it, simply to shut the damn thing off.

Command capability limited, Asset. The words felt scratchy in my mind, like steel wool. ***Verification code?***

Asset 108. Authorization code 020798361. System... um, green.

475

Welcome, Asset. The system greeting slid as brisk as cool spring water into my mind, a sharp contrast to the siren.

System command: Play all system warnings audibly. This will assist with evacuation.

Will comply.

It did comply, immediately.

"RAIJU DRONE AG-876R HAS SUFFERED TERMINAL DAMAGE!" it screeched. "PROTOCOL 17-R ENGAGING. PLEASE CLEAR ALL NON-FACILITY PERSONNEL FROM THE AREA! ESTIMATED EFFECT RADIUS: 978 KILOMETERS."

I leveled my gaze at the kneeling man. I couldn't make out his full expression, what with the gas mask, yet his wide, terrified eyes told me much.

"Anya," I said solemnly. "Will you please translate the system message for our friend?"

Yes, Michael, she replied. Her large blue eyes appeared luminous. *Although I imagine he already understands.*

What the hell are you thinkin'? Wyatt exclaimed.

What? I raised an eyebrow at him. *We're dead in minutes, Wyatt. This demented shit has no intention of taking us home.*

Well, he linked, gesturing at the futility, *I mean we could have tried to jury-rig the room's devices ourselves.*

We still have that option. I smiled at him. *I stand by my work. That's why the drones are outside the room.*

Oh. He considered for a moment.

Besides, I thought this was the plan, I linked.

You thought genocide was the plan?

I ignored the link. I tried not to think about the word *genocide.* Instead, I sent him a small patch, my memory of him.

"I'll kill every body-stealing, uncle-fucking one of them," he seethed. *"I will cook their children alive and laugh while I do it."*

"Yeah, man." I nodded. *"We will. Not just you. You and me."*

"Heh." He shook his head. "Okay. You got me. Asshole."

"You stop now," the man pleaded. He gestured out the vault door. "Make stop."

"Well!" I barked a laugh. "Too late. You made your choice." I paused as Anya translated. "*You* chose this, man. You could have peaceably taken us home. But you chose our deaths."

I reached into my pocket, fumbling for a cigarette. My hand trembled, just the tiniest bit.

I needed to play this straight.

"No," the man babbled as he shook his head. "I no understand."

"It can't stop. That opportunity is gone." I gestured at the furious luminescence that flickered hateful light into the room. "You have a new choice now. A different choice."

There. I pulled a smoke out and lit it.

Oh yes.

Much better.

"No, no, no." The man practically wept as Anya translated my words.

"You're not listening." I stepped forward, pulling a katana from my back.

"They fucking kill you." Now he did begin to cry, tears of rage on his cheeks. "You do not know."

"Listen. To. Me." I held the blade of my katana out and tapped his gas mask. "Should I just destroy this? Would you like to die here on the floor? Or do you want a chance to serve the Unity?"

"You a lying," he spat, just as soon as Anya finished translating.

"I'm not." I pointed at the far side of the room, directly at the ichor-filled Broodwell, hidden by shadows. "You see, friend, you still have an opportunity to serve those disgusting monstrosities you worship."

Outside the room, a loud CRACK came again, along with

another emanation of violent luminescence. It lit the room like a strobe light, brilliant and stark.

"RAIJU DRONE AG–876R HAS SUFFERED TERMINAL DAMAGE!" the drone wailed from outside. I stared at the man as it continued, not wishing to offset the drama of the drone's message.

"What you mean?" The man stood, his hands clenching and unclenching at his side.

I felt more than half certain he prepared to leap over and strangle me to death.

"The moment *you* decided we three should die here," I said as I gestured at my cadre, "I decided to do that!" I pointed at the warbling drone. "Because of your choice, I've killed every Brooding Well within a thousand kilometers of this place. Sathantür will never be the same."

"You are fucking," the man raged, trembling. "You are asshole being fucked!"

"You aren't listening," I growled. "There's *one* Well that could still be saved." I gestured into the shadows. "Only one. This one."

Anya translated, and I watched the man's face. It took him a long a few seconds but realization dawned.

"Right," I said, nodding. "Either all of them die or one of them survives. Just like before, it's your choice." I shrugged and took a drag on my smoke.

"You." His brow furrowed as he thought. "You let me save?"

"I'd let you take *us* home." I gestured to the corner. "And those with us."

Dangerous, Michael, Anya warned. Through her link, her leg throbbed.

"They sleeper." He pushed himself to a standing position and glanced over his shoulder. "The stars not straight."

"I don't give a single fuck." I leveled my gaze at him. "You can take us home or we can all die. That's the choice."

He stared at me for a long moment as Anya translated. Cold

calculation burned in those eyes.

"You dog fucks. You eat shit like baby shits." He bobbed his head. Once. "But yes, I take."

"Then you should get started," I growled at the man.

He stepped over to one of the keyboards and scanned the readouts. He adjusted a dial, and I heard it click. Then he began to madly tap on one of the keyboards.

"Earth," I called to the man's back, and Anya translated. "You take us anywhere else, and I'll kill the ones in this Well too."

Smooth, Wyatt admitted. *Now as long as he doesn't drive the lot of us into a star or something.*

The Designates will not be pleased, Anya noted.

Let me get us home, I responded. *One disaster at a time.*

Dude's got seven minutes, by my counter at least. He better fucking hurry.

What's your counter at, Anya? I kept my gaze on the mad Russian.

I have adjusted my mecha to a similar timeline as yours. Anya leveled her gaze at me. *To assist in pain moderation.*

You burned mecha for pain? And dropped your countdown? I shook my head. *Why?*

Without backup I am unlikely to return to Rationality. This way I can enjoy slightly less pain. She shrugged. *I felt I should suffer as little as possible.*

As we traded links, the zealot began to babble at Anya. He gestured wildly at the systems in front of us before pointing at the vault door.

He says the system is not designed to run without a door. He has concerns about quantum tunneling and emanation shields.

I can handle that, Wyatt responded.

Slowly, the large man stepped over to the pile of sand which had once been the rounded door. His fingers ticked thoughtfully away at his keys.

"We'll fix the door." I pointed at the readouts. "How soon?"

"Soon." He nodded.

"Make this work," I told him.

The man glared at me over his shoulder. In all my life, I'd never seen so much hatred in one look.

He turned back to the screens, muttering to himself. He typed on the keyboard and took a sip of his coffee.

What's he saying?

He is worried he cannot do this alone, Anya linked. *It seems he expected to have an assistant when they performed the dimensional shift.*

He'll have to figure it out, I responded. *If he wants to save his fucking Unity.*

Unless you have another Tabula Rasa, I do not know how you would follow through, Michael. She glanced toward me. *With your threats.*

She appeared tired, so tired. She leaned against the wall, keeping as much weight off her knee as possible.

Maybe you should sit on Wyatt's cart? I moved it over to her and wedged it between the wall and a workstation.

Thank you. Slowly, she sat, wincing a bit.

Lady's got a point, Wyatt linked. *What's your follow through, here?*

Oh, I've got nothing, I told them. *Best case scenario I have is to go get the second drone and throw it in the Well before it goes critical.*

I see, Anya sighed. *Well, he believes you. Or seems to. That will have to be enough.*

I can seal this door with a stasis field, Wyatt linked. *Unless one of you has a better idea?*

Go for it. I gave him a thumbs up and took the last drag on my cigarette. *It's better than anything I could do.*

WHUF. A silvery dome sprouted over the doorway, blocking it against the outside.

The Russian saw this and stared for a moment. Then he shook

his head and muttered again. He stepped away from the consoles and started to walk into the shadows of the room.

"Um, where are you going?" I asked, and Anya repeated for him.

"Charts," she responded for the man. "Specifically charts of the Milky Way Galaxy. Apparently, stars have much to do with this device."

"Don't play fuck around," Wyatt called to the zealot. "We're watching."

Anya attempted to translate, and the man adjusted his gas mask, grumbling to himself. A moment later he stalked back over to where we stood, papers beneath one arm. With no ceremony, he thrust a large pipe wrench into my hands.

"Here go, cowboy." He shook his head at me in disdain. He returned to the cabinet of screens and keyboards and crouched. In that position, he adjusted something on the top of one of the Radonic Transmitters.

"What's this?" I asked Anya as if she knew.

She relayed my question, to which the man responded a bit mockingly.

"He says it is a wrench." She raised an eyebrow. "He also says you should help him, as he needs to turn one of the gears below the terminals."

"Fine." I took the few steps over to where the man pointed and put my back into the wrench. It turned, and I pulled until I couldn't go further. "Can you ask him how much longer this will take? Time is of the essence."

"Soon." The man replied to Anya's translation. "Minutes. Don't be bitch."

"He can't help it," Wyatt muttered. "Not for as long as I've known him."

"Again." The man pointed to the wrench as he input numbers. He held the charts open on his lap.

"I already did it." I pulled as if to show him, and the wrench easily turned further.

I sighed.

The man rolled his eyes at me.

I turned the wrench until it stopped.

Along the far wall, a series of red lights flickered for just a moment. Our masked friend took note of this and cackled.

"You be seeing." He shot me a dark glare. "You all be finished soon."

I don't like the way he phrased that, Hoss, Wyatt linked. *I notice we don't have much of a plan past 'return to Rationality.'*

I'm thinking about that. I watched as the Russian entered a series of figures beneath a readout titled **Second Horizon**. A quick bit of mental math proved my suspicions.

Fibonacci numbers.

The thing is, we aren't really ready for a fight, Wyatt continued. *What if Petrov here drops us in the middle of fifty guys with Uzis?*

Is that the man's name? Anya turned to me. *Petrov?*

"You go again." The man gestured at me.

I didn't bother to complain that the wrench couldn't go any further. It easily did. This time, however, a solid SNICK ran up my arms as the wrench locked into a slot.

Those red lights all flared on, scarlet eyes at the corner of the room.

"You look now!" The zealot pointed at one of his screens. "It start."

Something certainly had. Long strings of Cyrillic characters moved across the screen, each separated by ellipses.

The room shook, as if loosened from its planar moors by a minor earthquake. I heard the hiss of gas being released, a soft whispering from somewhere in the machinery.

The dodecahedral room *turned*, just the smallest list. The Russian laughed giddily at this and scrambled over to the side of his equipment.

There, he shrugged on a harness, one with a thick, nylon line clamped to its front.

Um, Anya? I gestured toward the Russian. *Why do you suppose he's wearing that?*

Before she answered, the entire room abruptly tilted upward, about fifty degrees. The wrench, which I'd left on the floor, skittered off to one side.

As did Anya in the cart.

Michael! She clung to the side of the rolling trolley, her eyes wide.

"Got you!" I grabbed at the side of the cart, dropping the katana I held. It clattered as it slid along the floor.

I grasped at a nearby iron pole and swung her toward me.

"Fuck!" Wyatt stumbled and fell.

"What do?" The Russian clung to the side of his systems bank as he angrily called to us. "That!" He pointed.

He gestured directly at Wyatt's stasis field, which remained firmly in place. It appeared different than the other fields the barbarian had created, slightly less rounded on top. Also, I occasionally saw a flash of lurid scarlet run through the construct.

The whole thing pulsed angrily. A whining cry warbled from the field as it bent and twisted.

The axioms of your field interfere with our transport. Anya held onto the cart with one hand and used the other to read telemetry. *It anchored a portion of the room within space-time.*

"He said he needed something over the door!" Wyatt snarled out loud.

My readings show it has become unstable. She paused. *If it explodes, the energy released will be terminal.*

"It stop!" The Russian sounded somewhat frantic.

The ruby lights, which he'd previously been pleased to see, began to dim and dance at the edges of the room.

"Fine!" Wyatt cried out. He slid down the angled floor until he rested one foot against what had previously been the wall. He frantically began to key in algorithmic changes, preparing to kill his stasis field.

With a loud BANG, the field sizzled away into nothingness. Orange smoke and the scent of burnt Cyprus wafted up.

Like a rubber band snapping back with eager force, the entire room cart-wheeled sideward, returning the floor to its previous position. All three of us went bumbling hard to one side.

For a moment, I couldn't track where I'd fallen.

"We good?" I called, glancing about.

In the instant after my tumble, I happened to glance squarely through the vault door at the room we had left behind.

Toward the ceiling, drone AG-876r began its failure in earnest. Its violet sphere had now grown to larger than an automobile, cackling and thundering with malicious, hateful shine.

In its awful and unholy light, a slender silhouette stood near the opening to the vault door. He crouched and plucked the second drone, AG-286f, from the rubble.

Anya's executable whirred in my mind.

Irrational source located. Calibrating anomaly.

Over my visual, three red lines burned over the man's location.

Firenzei glared at me, indigo light reflecting off his gas mask's eyes. He glanced up at the bruised radiance that scorched the room, then back toward me.

Violently, a different kind of tremble ran through the room. This one seemed less like an actual movement of the chamber and more like my mind had been twisted. It felt as if space itself writhed, rebelling against an egregious affront.

Anya's executable provided nine or ten white lines—too many possible vectors to track.

"We are not good." I crab walked backward. "We need to move. Now!"

Firenzei vanished, drone AG-286f in hand.

In that exact same moment, I began to feel a nauseous gurgling in my mind, a feeling as if rotten maggots tunneled their way into my brain.

"Fuck!" Wyatt swore from the far side of the room, obviously understanding the implications of the sensation.

"What is?" the Russian spat, irritation plain in his tone. "Be stopping!"

I pushed myself to my feet, drew my remaining katana, and stared around warily. After the other one had slid away, I hadn't yet—

"Michael Bishop." Firenzei stood near the door, grasping the handle of a pipe. "I wonder if you dropped something?" He hefted the silvery drone in his other, maimed hand.

"I must have," I spat. "Weird too. You'd think a man with both his thumbs would be more careful."

His eyes went flat, murderous.

Anya's executable whirred in my mind.

Irrational source located. Calibrating anomaly.

Drone AG-286f's casing is at one percent resilience, Michael.

It's definitely gonna go. Fuck me, Wyatt cursed.

Right now, the only place it's going is Rationality, I snarled through the link. *That's bad news.*

As the unnatural turbines within the room began to whir, Firenzei leapt toward me, pulling a pistol with his good hand.

I stood stunned for only a moment—all he needed.

The man swung his weapon down to pistol-whip me.

I dodged and swung toward him. With the fluid grace of the *Adept*, I hoped to have gutted him before he had the opportunity to say another word.

Not fast enough.

Firenzei lunged for me, firing three times. He missed each shot.

In the darkness behind me, I heard the glass shatter and the gurgle of liquid.

The Russian yelled something, but I didn't understand.

I dodged left.

Firenzei matched me. He leapt forward, stretching out his one empty hand.

Where had the drone gone?

"Oh, Bishop," he grunted. "You are going to *love* this."

I swung on him, again missing.

Firenzei's fingers clasped the front of my shirt and swung me around. The beginning of the tremulous harbinger that came with his power twanged at me.

Suddenly, darkness. Spiteful cold.

For an eternal instant, frigidness clawed into the center of me. I couldn't catch my breath. I fell, my back exploding into pain.

—*op!* I caught the tail end of Wyatt's link, as if I'd been out of range.

Which I apparently had.

Firenzei had simply used his temporal prowess, same as on Anya. He'd pulled me driftways with him, throwing me off balance.

We appeared across the room, a meter off the floor. While I floundered, he knew exactly where we'd be and what to expect. He slammed me to the ground without interference.

Stunned, I dropped my sword.

"Let's end this discussion," Firenzei spat. He brought his face centimeters from mine and pulled his mask aside.

I smelled his fetid breath.

"It go now!" the Russian called.

A rapid clicking began somewhere in the shadows.

In that moment, the moorings of reality released the chamber. Colorless thunder rumbled in my bones, a sound that pealed ominously through every memory I ever owned.

The room quivered, teetering as if it spun like a top on some impossibly tiny point.

Reality fell away.

While Firenzei pummeled me in the face, we tumbled sideways. We gamboled and jounced, spinning through infinite space and shapeless time.

The room screeched as it ripped its way through reality itself.

2

My mind bled, stretched thin. My teeth felt as if they wriggled loose, moving of their own accord.

It had to do with the open vault door. I didn't know this logically; I *felt* it. An infinity of black emptiness lay beyond, watching us, hungry.

Firenzei and I wrestled far from the door, maybe thirty meters. Yet even from here, alien desire beckoned from that pitch emptiness.

I rolled to one side, the motion slow as if I rolled through taffy.

Firenzei held me, wrestling me back beneath him, his face bent, unnatural. His eyes shone with madness and rage.

"We keep talking about who should be afraid, you and I." His leer went wide as he trembled with fury. "I thought perhaps we should settle it once and for all." He retched, the sound gurgling deep in his chest.

Animal panic sent a burst of adrenaline through me, burning in my veins. I worked one hand free, but Firenzei proved stronger.

He punched me once. As he went for the second strike, I blocked, knocking the pistol from his good hand.

He heaved, gagging.

My eyes went wide as he vomited thick strings of mucus onto my chest, filth that reeked of low tide.

The tiny strands came first.

I screamed, reared my head forward, and bashed him in the nose.

Firenzei wailed, but the alien repugnance did not stop wriggling forth. Tentacles not much thicker than a hair wriggled around his eyeballs and reached for my face.

When I saw the tendril slither from his nostril, the thing as thick around as my pinky, terror clutched at my heart.

I screa—

Nothingness, then. The dark eternity of the void whispered through the open doorway. It cackled, it beckoned. It grasped me with cold, undying fingers.

I felt my mind adrift in darkling dreams.

—ndless shadows lurked in the space beyond, peeling my mind into them. Consciousness unraveled, thin as thread, and spooled me outside, out the door and into the boiling midnight beyond.

I burned. The light of heaven burned within me.

"Bishop," Wyatt said, speaking from infinitely far away.

I saw he possessed three mouths, each opening one upon the other, cascading forth secrets I didn't care to know.

"Wyatt?" I shook my head and stared into darkness that laughed at me, scorning me for my infinite smallness.

"There's a city," he said. I didn't see him point as much as I felt it, a gesture that bubbled through me like dark and viscous tar. "It's forever. The people within it are forever."

I turned in the direction he indicated and saw it, a city wrought from light and incomprehensible pain. As I regarded it, its history swirled around me, events like sand borne upon an endless and sapient wind.

"What did they do?" I shook my head, feeling thin and wan. The beauty of the city hurt my eyes, astounded me with truths given terrible form.

"They were never noble." Wyatt cackled, as if he'd made a joke. "Everything they touched melted, rotted away. They were more madmen than gods. Once Cæstre fell—

I was what fell. I spun and twisted as I hurled through the pale shadow of space.

I screamed, frantically attempting escape. Even in my adrenaline-fueled horror, I couldn't push Firenzei off me. He forced me to watch as the hungry aberrations squirmed toward my eyes, my ears, my nose.

He retched again, gagging their slime forth. The thick ichor drooled over my face, into my mouth.

490

I completely lost it, animal instinct and primal fury taking over. My mind absolutely broke as I screamed, thrashed, and vomited.

The sensation of the small tentacles twisting and oozing into my body sundered all human logic.

Madness reigned.

I'd never stopped screaming, but as their warm wetness drooled down my ears and nostrils, my cries became so loud my voice cracked and I could scream no more.

Pain unlike anything I'd ever known blossomed. I felt the serpentine movement in my sinuses, heard the wetness of the tentacles in my ears.

I watched, powerless, as one of the creatures beheld me with a single, alien eye. That tentacle wriggled before me and then forced its way into my mouth—

Space bent as we cast ourselves along the wending corridors of existence. My mind buckled with unreality.

—yramids of black stone stretched far overhead, almost blotting out the crimson sun. The people who milled about below appeared to be carved from amber and labored to bring more of those basalt stones.

Those pyramids spoke, I knew. One, the blade. The second, the chalice. They whispered words that created time.

I knew, somehow, once my entire mind had been drawn into the shadows, I would be able to understand.

"Michael." Anya's voice rang like a bell, like music echoing in an empty room. "Look at them. They live their entire lives in devout worship."

I gazed at her, trying to see past the aura of living flame that surrounded her. We'd both had that fire. But it had been taken. The Ordinal—

"We are between," she explained. "I assume the vault door would have shielded our minds from the ravages of traveling between worlds."

"These people." I stared below, their minds laid bare before

me. I saw simple lives, good lives. People watched over by something so terrible they never need know fear.

They were people, shapes, notes played on a divine flute.

"Far from Rationality," she confirmed. "But they are an old race. They were brought here by one who sang the very stars."

"I..." Something troubled me. I smelled a brackish, earthy scent, like the rot of low tide. "Anya, I think I'm in trouble. I hurt."

She gazed at me, her eyes burning sapphires. They stretched through time itself, bending light until she could see.

She gasped.

"Oh, Michael." She reached for me. "I did not know. I have been here—"

Reality crashed around me again. The vision faded, and I found myself choking on Vyriim.

I couldn't breathe, couldn't think. The knobby protrusion of its slick eyeball burned, scraping as it violated my throat.

Hoss—? The word carried confusion, a disoriented ache.

With a blindingly painful burst of wet, gruesome agony somewhere at the base of my spine, I experienced the Vyriim in a way I never could have dreamt.

My entire body lurched upward, my back drawn into a bow of paralyzing misery and torment.

Wordless, sharp sensations drifted through my mind. Thoughts felt like concepts, primal ideas from before the Earth turned.

Space, shaped differently than I'd ever known, created directions my mind couldn't accept as reality. Ideas I didn't have enough senses to perceive blew through me. I learned the ancient and secret names for what they did, names forgotten ten-thousand years before man stumbled out of the jungles.

Unity.

The Vyriim were one. One organism. In the same way the hairs on my body might appear to be different things but were really just a part of me, the Vyriim had a single, ancient mind, a driven mind, insatiable.

They didn't plan to invade like carrion crows, and they weren't our predators.

No, the Vyriim were moths, seeking the mad, undulating darkness that beat like a heart between all worlds. And when that darkness began to seep into a world—

"No!" The feminine cry came from the depths of eternity.

I felt as if I should care about that sound but didn't. Couldn't. It seemed petty, small. As lyrical words moved through my mind, an incredible peace fell over me, a happiness I had no name for.

Unity.

My life had been a shadow, a whisper striving to be a song. Compared to this glorious oneness—

Screaming.

Like a pane of glass, existence shattered around me. Burning shards of slivered fire crackled in my mind.

"What?" I mourned, stunned. I stared around, then at myself. For a moment, I didn't understand why I had a body. Why it mattered. Wasn't I part of them? Why did I even need this greasy, disgusting shape?

"No. No, no, no…"

I reached for them in my mind, tried to feel where the Unity had been.

Gone.

I wailed despair and horror and animal fury.

I saw Firenzei's face. He reeled backward, screaming and gagging. Violet ichor sprayed as he gagged. Sliced in half, tentacles violently writhed, seeped with gore.

"Naaarrrgh!" he cried and fell off me, his body convulsing wildly.

Michael? That word made sense to me, although I couldn't say why. *Please confirm you are system green?*

I gaped at Firenzei.

Something had sliced us apart, something wickedly sharp.

His mouth hung open, and a mass of writhing, severed tentacles poured from his body.

He gagged, spitting up a thick piece of undulating Vyriim.

I blinked and shook my head. I'd been the *same thing* as this man. An instant ago I'd known him better than I knew myself, as if we'd truly been one.

A stranger's voice swam between my thoughts.

Anya, is he okay?

I cannot say. The reply felt like a woman, and for a moment I thought how strange there should be male and female. It seemed like an abomination to live that way, split in twain and not in blissful Unity.

Anya, her face splattered with blood and her hair like a wild Amazon's, hobbled forward. She held a gleaming blade in her left hand.

My katana, I realized. Had she used it? Had Anya attacked Firenzei?

A symphony of agony blared in my body, and I began to retch. Thick pieces of rubbery Vyriim wriggled as they squirmed from my gorge. Vomiting thick mucus, I fell onto my knees.

Frantically, I rolled to the side while I retched writhing tentacles. I pulled them from my ears and nose, the horror assaulting my mind.

Anya screamed. Not through the link, but in actuality.

I heard the fear and fury in her voice.

"NO, NO, NO, NO!" With one smooth slice, she severed one of the creatures I'd sicked up. It had still been whole, writhing.

Thick, liquid warmth splattered me, but I didn't care. I shook my head and searched for Firenzei.

There. As the room spun through space and non-space alike, Firenzei crawled away. He moved a mask over his face, his glare filled with elemental hatred.

"Anya," I croaked weakly.

She turned toward Firenzei but not before that savage trembling began to take the room. I saw three white lines—the executable's determinations of his angles—stretch out away from him.

Now, Anya! Wyatt linked. *Hit the motherfucker!*

Anya swung the blade, but far too slowly and far too late. As reality quavered around us, Firenzei's strange and terrible power took hold.

The man vanished.

3

"He's still here." I crawled to my feet, my knees shaking. As I scooped up the katana Anya dropped, I peered into the darkness.

Where else would he be, Hoss?

"We be almosting. Stop soon," the Russian called, apparently still working at the consoles. "Ready, you."

Around us, the room tilted maniacally, spinning sideways in a meandering yaw that made me ill. Still, I kept my gaze focused on the murky gloom of the chamber.

"Hey. Here he comes!" Wyatt called as Firenzei's sickly tremor thrummed through the room again. It roiled in my mind, a sickly nausea.

I spun in place, my eyes casting about for the lean Irrat. Steaming pipes and gear-driven madness blocked much of my view. He could be anywhere in this shadowed chamber.

"Michael!" Anya cried from behind me, where she stood by one of the greasy iron pipes.

I whirled.

Firenzei lurked behind her, his weapon beneath her chin. He held her arm pinned between her shoulder blades. The Irrat glared at me, feral eyes aflame with malice.

"Fucking asshole," he spat at me. "You think the Unity can be stopped?" He laughed. "They'll have me back. I'm one of theirs now, Bishop."

Anya's executable whirred in my mind.

Irrational source located. Calibrating anomaly. I watched as red lines designated the Irrat's location.

"She's the only leverage you got, southpaw." I hobbled closer. "Shoot her and I'll slice your balls off. I'll feed them to you before you vanish on me again." I gestured with my katana, trying not to notice I'd brought a sword to a gun fight.

"They wanted your pathetic asses alive," he crowed. "All of

you. Why do you think I haven't slaughtered you yet?"

"Ineptitude?" I snarked. "Your parents were siblings?"

"Well, this bitch interrupted my Union," he growled. "So maybe she doesn't get taken alive." I heard the sepulchral clack of his weapon as he cocked it.

"That wise, friend?" I held up one hand. "Seems—"

He wrenched Anya's arm up until she gasped. Then he pressed his pistol into the hollow of her neck.

I leapt forward, the truth screaming in my brain. *Too slow, too fucking slow—*

WHUF.

"AARRGH!" Firenzei roared as he stumbled forward. He spat blood and spun half around as Anya lunged away from him.

A silvery spike jutted from his right shoulder.

The executable whirred as it calibrated the possible angles Firenzei might jaunt off to. I couldn't help but notice one of those shining white lines led him directly behind me.

I tensed with that rotten burrowing in my mind. It writhed and gnawed at me like a maggot eating its way through a corpse.

In the distance, an explosion like cannon fire in my bones rang through the room. Simultaneously, a loud CRACK burst, crashing over us with a searing flash of light.

Raiju *drone AG-286f has suffered terminal damage. Protocol 17-R engaging.*

Hoss? Wyatt's link warned.

"Oh, shit," I breathed. Still, I had no time to even glance toward the failing drone.

As Firenzei's form crackled out of existence, I whirled. Quick as thought, I sliced directly behind myself, into the center of the glowing white line from Anya's executable.

For an instant, I worried I might be wrong. If the Irrat jaunted to any other spot—

Firenzei appeared, gurgling and screaming even as the world trembled. I *felt* him teleport onto my blade, felt the steel whir and tremble.

He spewed blood and his eyes went wide.

My katana jutted out of the center of his chest and through his back. It crackled with horrific, otherworldly radiance. That light sang, so brilliant it glowed crimson through Firenzei's skin.

His eyes bulged as he glared stupidly at me.

"Know what that light is?" I hissed, pushing the blade deeper. Due to the weirdling energies, it screeched, like metal against stone.

A crimson bubble burst on his lips.

"It's called the Pauli exclusion principle," I snarled, staring down at him. "It's that whole 'matter cannot occupy the same space' bullshit. Creates all kinds of crazy mumbo jumbo." I took a step closer, shoving the blade further in. It felt as if I pushed through coarse, heavy clay instead of human flesh, and the light streaming from his chest shone brighter.

He tried to speak again but couldn't. For the scarcest instant, the world trembled about me, and I thought he might try to teleport away.

I jerked my arm up.

That awful light all but incandesced as the blade rose, eldritch plasma sawing through bone and the thick flesh of his shoulder and neck. Firenzei's hot blood splattered against my face.

His dead eyes glared at me.

His corpse fell to the floor.

"What you do?" I heard the mad Russian behind me, caterwauling with unbent rage. "You a lying shit dog!"

Bishop, Wyatt's link warned. *More trouble.*

"What?" I tuned toward the Russian, staggering against the impossible tilt of the room.

"You say you work with me, rat fuck." The man gestured violently into the darkness behind me, those shadows which shrouded the Vyriim's foul lagoon. "You play stupid tricks."

I didn't need to turn around to understand. In the background,

499

furious indigo light boiled and spat. The stark shadows it cast around me were sharp, wrathful things. That light made dire promises.

As if on cue, I heard the device in my Crown.

Raiju *drone AG-286f has suffered terminal damage. Protocol 17-R engaging. Please clear all non-Facility personnel from area. Estimated effect radius: 745 kilometers.*

I cast my gaze over my shoulder as I shielded my eyes from that vengeful radiance. The violet sphere burned in the shadows, molten plasma surrounded by hateful arcs of energy.

The scornful light scalded my retinas. I toggled my optics off.

"You it stop now!" I heard the implied threat in his words, even though he barely spoke my tongue.

"Okay!" I shot the man an annoyed glare. "I don't want to have my flesh melted either, alright?"

The Russian gibbered at me, something I felt certain I didn't want to understand.

Talk to him, I linked to Anya.

I will make certain he knows who brought the device inside, she responded.

I shambled toward the fractured drone, without a single amazing idea. It'd been a long fucking day, and I'd had the snot beaten out of me eleven different ways.

Try as I might, I had nothing.

This is the moment I actually need a genius, I linked Wyatt as I stepped between the cylinders of glass and mad technology. Inside them, naked Irrats floated in urine-colored ichor, tiny parasites squirming around their noses and eyes.

I bet it's already too hot to touch, Wyatt lamented.

It's about softball size. I eyed the violet sphere of hatred. *And I can already feel the heat of the thing.*

I can't use a stasis field, he groused. *That got the room stuck last time.*

Maybe we need to be stuck, I realized. *We're tumbling through the Maelstrom, headed straight toward Rationality. We're carrying a drone that's about to explode.*

I've already considered it. He blew out a long breath. *Stasis is hard and requires a fixed point in space-time to center on. The Tangler can't really find that fixed point as we Tokyo-drift through the Maelstrom. I tried.*

Fuck. I glanced behind me. *What about moving it? Through the door?*

Okay, he agreed amiably. *How? Can't touch it.*

Shift gravity? I grasped at straws. *Make it fall? I don't fucking know.*

Even as we brainstormed Anya's discussion deteriorated into a violent argument in rapid-fire Russian.

Michael, we have a problem, Anya linked. *Our friend believes you intended deception from the start. He thinks you are currently attacking the Broodwell.*

I don't speak Stupid, Anya. I stepped closer to the crackling, cackling sphere. *Convince him.*

"I be showing!" the Russian roared, his words hollow behind the mask.

I glanced over, just in time to see him grab an antiquated iron lever and furiously yank it down, using all his weight.

A loud CLUNK reverberated in the room.

He pushed his chair to his left, madly typing on a cube-shaped device that pulsed green. Lightning, verdant and silver-swift, exploded from the ceiling to my right. In its brilliance, wicked machinery showed.

I glimpsed metal structures and darkness that curved like the tail of a scorpion.

That galvanic fury wailed and screeched in demonic delight. The savage lightning bolt sang as it pummeled the dark liquid surface below it.

The Vyriim pool began to roil, rippling and boiling beneath the onslaught.

501

"You fucked my mother this time!" the man screamed.

What? Wyatt linked. *That isn't even...*

What is that asshole doing? I gaped at the pool, my heart sinking.

Waking up the sewer monsters? Wyatt snarled.

"He isn't," I breathed. "He said they slept, that stars needed to be in position." I turned to stare. *Anya, do you have telemetry?*

No. Impossible to be certain in the Maelstrom, Michael. She paused. *Yet I believe his screens show us as close to Rationality. The drone is failing, and we are—*

As if to accentuate Anya's words, colorless thunder rumbled in my bones. That sound grumbled, echoing ominously through memory, through forgotten dreams. The room quivered, slowed, as if the universe burned around us, as if all existence turned on a singular moment in time.

Reality and physics fell onto us. Odd dreaminess hung over my mind like an opiate, then faded.

Anya? I blinked, hoping for an update. That sensation reminded me an awful lot of the moment the Russian first activated his interdimensional chamber of fun.

Rationality. Every nuance of her quivered in my brain, her wide eyes, her madly twitching fingers. *Almost. Thirty points sub-Rational and rising rapidly. We have seconds.*

"You liar and we die! Now you die too!"

The Vyriim pool burst with a flash of that same argent-emerald lightning. The color sang through the madly boiling liquid. The thick, tendrils running from the murk into the glass cylinders with the naked Irrats pulsed.

One Irrat twitched, as if jolted with electricity.

Then another.

And another.

Another.

I stepped backward, clutching my katana.

One of the Irrats blinked and opened her eyes. They held no

whites, those eyes. Meeting her gaze, only an abyss stared back.

The mad Russian awakened them all.

My cadre had been nearly beaten to death more times than I could count. Now several dozen Vyriim-infected Irrats stirred in their incubators while a catastrophically terminal drone raged and screamed its violently violet light.

Rationality zero, Michael.

Yeah.

I'd never felt Anya so close to despair.

Incursion

The moment we touched reality, I felt her. Designate Ling slipped into my mind like ice and razors.

We require confirmation and access code check in.

It's us, Designate.

Us? The Designate arched an eyebrow.

The room shuddered, as if vast metal latches seized hold of space and secured us in place. Instantly, the sensation of drifting ceased.

The former drone raged, violet hatred taken form.

We had to stop it, whatever the cost. Wyatt's stasis might hold the explosion at bay, but the Designate had said—

My eyes widened as I recalled exactly what the Designate had said.

"Wyatt! Come help!" I took a stumbling step backward.

We require confirmation and access code.

Michael Bishop, 108, I frantically linked. My Crown whirred as it synced with the Lattice. *Authorization code 020798361.*

System... orange. Situation red.

Orange? Red?

It's pretty bad here, Designate.

Initiating sync.

I had mere seconds before the sync. Ling had specifically told me that stasis fields within Rationality were right out. She said that when the sync was online, she'd make the calls regarding stasis fields. She'd said that if we found ourselves adrift, I could make the call.

Well, we'd been adrift. And the sync hadn't come online yet.

"Hoss?" Wyatt wheezed as he stumbled up next to me.

"As the Asset with a Designate sync, I am unofficially Asset-in-command. That applies even if the sync is offline."

505

"It… does." Wyatt blinked. "Technically true."

"Fucking do it." I pointed at the violently quavering drone. "Initiate a stasis field immediately. Here, over that drone, within Rationality."

"You—?" Wyatt stared at me, gaping.

"You're saving the lives of millions, Asset. Do it!"

After a second, Wyatt realized what I'd done.

Taken responsibility.

Designate Ling might never authorize a stasis field, but then… she didn't have to.

"Yes, sir!" He grinned while his fingers danced madly.

I selected Designate Ling's sync the exact same millisecond the scarlet dataglyph appeared on my visual array. As I heard the dulcet tone in my mind, I scrambled to create a patch: my memories from the moment I'd first drifted into the Vyriim's topia all the way to this one, including the command I'd just given Wyatt.

The moment Ling synced in my mind, I sent her the entire patch.

WHUF.

I breathed, relaxing tension I hadn't known I'd held. Wyatt's silvery dome blossomed over the drone—

And immediately turned a sickly green. It shuddered, roiling in place. The construct whined, keening alarmingly.

What? I whirled toward him. *What is that? What's happening?*

It's a lot of energy, Hoss. He began tapping inputs. *I think I got it.*

Don't think. Have it. I clapped him on the back.

Says the man who couldn't understand the first thing about a stasis field, Wyatt grumbled. *Doing what I can here.*

Asset Bishop, Ling linked, *due to the severity of your situation, we have tapped Asset Gardener. We are going to authorize a system-wide acceleration on your Crown's processing capabilities for seven seconds.*

Yes. My mouth formed a tight smile. That small blessing would give me room to actually speak with the Designate. The next few seconds would have the processing space of minutes within my Crown. *Thank you.*

I felt the acceleration's mental twitch when she augmented my Crown's processing via the Lattice. In the same moment, she sent me a patch. Compiled to be small, the thing felt quite dense.

Knowledge poured like molten quicksilver into me. Facts flowed faster than thought, deeper than memory.

We'd arrived in New York City.

The system showed us in the upper stories of a building named One Ito Plaza.

Help was on the way.

In a fraction of a second, I saw Ling's entire plan. I understood it and my place in it.

We are currently assembling resources, 108, Ling linked. I felt how distracted she was. *Hold your position. Remain functional. Your extraction is on the way.*

Copy that, Designate.

We will discuss some of the choices you've made once we complete our extraction.

I didn't like the sound of that. Before I could respond, however, I received another link, swift and complete.

I'm reviewing all available mecha, Rachel Gardener linked us as a group. *You won't be using quite so much to breathe and remain upright now that you're home. You should get a considerable boost for the next few moments.*

Thank you, Caduceus, I replied.

Keep your cadre alive and whole, 108, Ling re-stated the priority she had sent in the patch. *It wouldn't do for all your sacrifices to be for nothing.*

Yes, Designate. I started to snark a bit, but a something else snagged my attention.

Wailing, dire and spectral, echoed across the room.

507

Michael! Anya linked. *Hostiles are entering the chamber.*

Hostiles are already within the chamber, I spat.

The dozens of Irrats within the tanks came more and more alert. The young woman who met my gaze still seemed only half lucid, but I had no doubt she'd be awake and terrifying soon. Bubbles drifted up as the topaz-colored ooze began to drain from the bottom of her tank.

Automatic fire barked from behind me, and I heard deep voices curse. I turned and saw Anya had grabbed Firenzei's automatic pistol and now fired through the vault doorway at the chamber beyond.

That idea gave me pause. Wherever we'd fetched up, this room held to the same dodecahedral dimensions as the original—doors and all. The whole design had been planned meticulously.

I can hold the door for now, Anya continued. *Firenzei possessed several magazines and more than one pistol.*

I'm going to determine the threat level within the room. I turned away from her. *Link me the instant you require assistance.*

Will comply.

The wailing began again, and this time I noted its source. One of the Irrats stood in a tank almost completely emptied of amber ichor. It had drained through two small holes at the bottom of the glass—holes that appeared to have been shot there by Firenzei in his mad attempts to murder me.

Naked, the dark-skinned man screamed at the glass, his cry forsaken and lost. He roared a formless word, the name of something faceless and mad.

The glass shattered before the power of that eldritch cry.

"Nope. Not today." I moved forward. We might be minutes away from a couple dozen naked Irrats kicking our asses, but I felt certain I could handle this single guy.

I toggled the *Adept* and the *Wraith.*

As the shards sailed outward, the young man stepped from his technological coffin.

I spun, all grace and silvery swiftness.

He glared at the space where I'd just stood and spoke again, a bitter word that soured the souls of men. As he called, the concrete floor shattered into slivers.

Shadowed and hidden, I whirled toward him, death unseen. My lone katana whispered toward his neck.

A blend of Facility-wrought steel and electresium tasted the young man, slicing swift and clean. I pulled back as I sliced his throat, then twirled around for another strike.

His chest exploded. Strands of thin aberrations pulsed outward, each tendril as thick as my thumb. They wriggled frantically, attempting to wrest themselves from the Irrat's corpse.

The body fell.

I stumbled back, stunned. I'd *known* what those cylinders were, witnessed the Vyriim using them to infest their hosts.

But seeing them... seeing this...

Hey, Mike, we have an incoming patch from Designate Ling—addressed to the entire cadre, the Adjunct, still shaped by the aspect of Paige, chirped in my mind.

Paige? I felt stunned. *Hon, you can't be here!*

Why ever not? she asked with an indignant huff.

I couldn't explain why not, not exactly. I liked Paige as she was—innocent mostly. Sweet. I didn't *want* her aspect touched by horrifying tentacle monsters from beyond reality.

Adjunct, initiate aspect 12A, Cap'n Stern.

Will comply, Mike, Paige muttered sullenly.

The Vyriim knotted together and one of the strands hissed.

I couldn't help but notice their size as they tried to writhe free of the body. Were they young? Is that why they were so small?

Perhaps.

The Designate's patch hit my Crown like a runaway train. Data and objectives, like swift and molten stars, burned their way into me.

You two got that? I thrust forward, driving a few of the strands back into the young man's fallen body.

They're coming to extract us, Wyatt confirmed. *Primary objective: escape with Anya's pretty head in one piece. It's the data they want, I'm certain.*

Affirmative. I nodded as I leapt to my left, scarcely dodging more probing tentacles.

The Vyriim could *see* me.

I disengaged the *Wraith.*

Also, it seems our local Caduceus *is modulating our mecha,* Anya poked in. *Now that we no longer require them for simple survival, we should notice an increase in performance.*

"I also see I'm prohibited from any stasis fields until further notice," Wyatt grumbled. He stepped closer to me, firing into the corpse with a *WHUF.* "That's fine. Just fine."

With three keytaps, an azure burst of incomprehensible cold erupted from the spike, a surge that stiffened my skin. In a second, the corpse froze into one solid mass—including half the strands of the still-squirming Vyriim.

Wyatt kicked at the trapped strands, shattering them like ice. In the shadows of my mind, I felt the creatures' psionic screams as they snapped into shards.

Hey, punk. Cap'n Stern flowed into my mind, grizzled and tough. He sounded exactly like the fictional character I'd patterned him after. *Remember when Firenzei shot into the darkness while beating you like a little bitch? Remember what you heard?*

Glass, I realized. *I heard him destroy one of the containers. Like this one.*

You think it's the only one? Because if so, you're an idiot.

Frantically, I glanced around. If any of the Irrats were already free, we needed them put down quickly. Otherwise, they'd ruin our day.

Anya, you green? I couldn't see her anymore but occasionally heard her shoot. *Is the door secure?*

Secure, Michael. Weariness made her limbs heavy. *The door is held; the hostiles have pulled back. The Russian has vanished into the darkness. Presumably he is hiding.*

Keep me apprised, I told her, then addressed Wyatt. *So, we probably aren't alone in here.* I stepped forward. *Firenzei shattered some of those containers while trying to murder your personal hero.*

Oh no! Rowdy Roddy Piper? I felt the horror in Wyatt's link.

Come on. I crept past the Broodwell, watching the burbling pool with unease. Behind us, Wyatt's stasis field flickered violet rage. *These other assholes will be free any moment now.*

Unless they aren't, he sent, his nervous unease palpable. *I mean, they're stuck right now.*

Good point.

I didn't need him to spell out his thoughts, unsavory as they were. The Irrats remained helpless after all, at least for the moment. A spike would make certain they stayed that way. Wyatt could freeze the blood in their veins or transmute the calcium in their bones into helium.

He'd slaughter them before they had an opportunity to twitch.

We eased past the gurgling ichor. Along the other wall, two more rows of the technological sarcophagi loomed, each filled with the silhouette of an Irrat. A few moved drunkenly, as if not quite in control of themselves yet.

This is one of the reasons Artisan *Assets aren't typically offensively geared,* Wyatt linked. *The possibilities are gruesome. Atrocities become simple.*

I realized that, indirectly, Wyatt sought guidance. I'd already taken command responsibility once, after all. And in that alternate reality, he'd killed targets just like these in the first Broodwell.

But here? In Rationality?

Lay the spikes, I linked. *You can leave them inactive for now. Patch locations and area of effect to me.*

And if we need 'em, I can light 'em all up at once. He nodded. **WHUF. WHUF. WHUF.** He paused, as if considering, then,

WHUF. WHUF. WHUF.

Six azure circles appeared on my visual array.

There! I placed a marker to our left, near the corner.

Another vault door sat, cunningly wrought into the wall. Next to it, three glass containers lay in ruins, shattered. Two contained motionless, slumped bodies. I couldn't say if they were dead, but they were definitely bleeding.

The body of a raven-haired young woman lay on the floor.

Careful. I stepped forward, katana at the ready. *We don't know—*

She coughed violently, retching up a thin length of alien tendril. Thick mucus came with the writhing worm, followed by another pencil-thin tentacle.

We crept up close to the slender figure. Wyatt stomped on the undulating Vyriim, squishing them beneath his boot.

She's coughing it up, Wyatt linked. He pecked at a few of his keys, keeping the Tangler aimed at the nude woman's head. The device sang softly, a weirdling song.

Doesn't mean she's not deadly. I turned back toward the woman. "Hey." I peered at the intricate tattoo on her back and shoulder. "Can you hear us?"

"What." It wasn't actually a question. She stared up at me, blue eyes wet.

Beautiful, I thought.

She retched again, bringing up another tendril.

Wyatt stomped it.

"What the fuck is happening?" The young woman slowly pushed herself up, seemingly unconcerned at her lack of clothing.

"We thought you might enlighten us," I responded.

"You people—" She froze, staring at Wyatt. "*You.*"

For a long moment he stared back, shocked.

"Hey there." My barbarian friend finally gave her a surprised grin. "Don't I know you from one of the worst days of my life?"

"It *is* you," she whispered. "Fucking Gentlemen."

512

"The worst what now?" I turned from the woman to Wyatt.

"You aren't here to save me, I'll bet." She coughed a wet gurgle that brought up thick yellow mucus. It stank of low tide and bile.

"Well." I stared at the woman—the Irrat? I didn't know what to think. She'd been in the tube, and our working theory indicated the Vyriim were using Irrats as hosts.

I felt as if I'd lost control somewhere.

"Are we?" I gaped at Wyatt. "Here... to save her?" The large man obviously had intel I didn't.

If we can, he linked. *If she'll let us. She's good people.*

Well, of course we can. We can just knock her ass out if we have to. I shrugged and holstered my katana. *What's the deal?*

"You don't get it." He adjusted his hat, frowning. "She's good people," he repeated.

"You..." I stared at the nude woman and then my friend. "Is this some kind of Firenzei thing? Are you collecting all the wrong kinds of friends?"

"What's the deal with you even being here?" Wyatt asked her, sounding legitimately concerned.

"Just another example of you folk screwing over the little guy." She shrugged and flapped her hand irritably. "Girl. Whatever. You get it."

"That's not really telling us what the deal is," Wyatt observed.

"Garret can fuck himself in his Ass-hat ass. *That's* the deal!" The young woman coughed again, even as she snapped at Wyatt, "Dude double crossed me. Left me to rot with these Sadhana apes." She paused. "Taught me all I need to know about you people."

"This place is..." I took a step forward as I searched for the right words, "horrifically dangerous. Maybe you should come with us."

"We're talking here," the young woman snarled at me. "Maybe you should step back."

513

"We don't have time for this," I fumed, waving my arm. "We can *make* you come peaceably."

Behind us, I heard gunfire as Anya held the door.

Bishop. Wyatt's link carried a soft warning.

"Can you." She gave me a stark, bitter smile. It cut like the wind in winter.

"We can," I confirmed.

"How about you make a saving throw, Ass-hat?"

"What?" I blinked, confused both by the young woman's words and her rapid transformation.

In an instant, her eyes burned ice and ember blue, bluer than the sky in summer. That dark hair lifted, flowing around her, teased by an unnatural and spectral wind.

Something screamed, something dark and terrible. For a moment, I felt caught in a hurricane, an endless storm of wind and lamentation.

Her eyes.

Inhuman. Terrifying.

Irrational.

"Elizabeth," Wyatt cautioned, "you can't—"

"It's Liz," she snarled at him, her words echoing through wind-filled caverns. "And I've had about enough of being told what I can't do!"

An azure symbol burned in front of her for the briefest instant, a sign in some ancient and forgotten tongue. With the fury of a wrathful god, a sharp and savage tempest pummeled into me, a strike like a wayward comet. I didn't even have time to blink before I found myself hurled backward, ass over ankles.

I landed on the far side of the Broodwell, slamming into the ground.

I crumpled like a puppet.

Violet light washed over me, sharp and stark. I found myself blinking at it, mesmerized by that discordant shine.

The shine of Wyatt's stasis field flickered faster.

514

After an eternal moment, I pushed myself up.

Wyatt?

I got it here, Bishop. I know the lady. I'll be right back.

I'll check on Anya, then. I turned, wondering how he had come to know an Irrat?

Mid-thought, I found myself face to face with an imprisoned woman, still within her mechanical incubator. That dark gaze glared at me, raw hatred in her eyes. She pounded one naked fist against the glass.

"Oh. Um, hey." I took a quick sidestep, keeping my eyes on hers.

I couldn't help but notice one stark fact.

The amber ichor had drained almost entirely from the container. The nude Irrat, along with several of her companions, appeared to be completely aware.

Awake.

Filled with a dark and terrible fury.

With a sibilant hiss and wrathful verdant light, the cylindrical incubators began to open.

Extraction

You'd better fall the fuck back, Asset, Stern barked in my mind.

Yeah. I watched as three more of the incubators opened. Billowing steam pooled out from the devices as naked forms stumbled forth.

I bravely ran away.

We had one overriding objective after all: remain whole and functional. At this point in the game we weren't fit to take on a squadron of Irrats by ourselves. We just needed to hold out. When the extraction team arrived, we'd gain the help we'd need to make away with the data we'd worked so hard to gather.

I toggled both the *Wraith* and the *Adept.* As cool shadows settled over me, I began to move back toward the same door we'd entered by, the one Anya held. Behind me, Wyatt's stasis field pulsed, throbbing and thrumming.

My mind scrambled. *That* remained our greatest threat, even though it seemed handled for now.

I hoped.

We had no way of knowing how long the stasis field might hold the drone. This singular question mattered more than any other, but I couldn't lend it any attention.

I knew what we needed to do.

This is a wait out the clock kind of deal, I linked my cadre. *Our primary objective is to stay alive.*

Three new hostiles have arrived outside this door. I heard Anya fire more shots. *However, they remain deterred.*

I'm on my way, Anya.

Understood.

What about you, Guthrie? I leapt past Firenzei's dead body. *Did you deal with your lady friend over there?*

WHUF. WHUF. The echoing sound of the Tangler answered me.

Moments later, Wyatt linked, *Situation handled, Bishop. Yer not gonna have to worry about that particular Irrat again.*

Good man, I congratulated him. *For a moment there, I worried you'd insist we rescue an Irrat.*

That young lady is far beyond my ability to rescue, Wyatt replied. *But the issue's resolved.*

Good, I replied.

However, I do have something like two dozen hostiles stumbling out of their glass coffins over here.

Use those spikes. Keep yourself safe.

Any suggestions?

Before I could respond, a shadowy figure fell on me.

He lunged from my left. Fast. Faster than I could track with my eye, even running the *Adept*.

Michael!

Lines of agonizing fire sliced across my upper arm. With one swipe, the shambling figure disintegrated part of my quasi-steel suit, rending the flesh beneath.

"Fuck!" I threw myself backward, stunned at the sudden pain. "How do you assholes keep finding me?" I reached for the lone katana strapped to my back, but stumbled backward over Firenzei's corpse.

As I sprawled to the ground, I glanced up to behold the entirety of the figure.

Certainly, a human silhouette remained within, yet that form stood so deep inside a shroud of shadows I couldn't make out any details or features. Darkness flickered around it, almost as if alight. It reminded me exactly of how a flame might appear burning around a human body, but this fire crackled with darkness, a pyre blacker than the most lonesome and empty night.

That malefic shadow had touched me.

The thing held no weapon. No, the creature used that dark fire

as its weapon. It had dissolved my quasi-steel sleeve with a touch.
Creature.

For, yes, while a human shape lurked within, the darkness
surrounding it had never been human. The gaunt figure stood three
meters tall and wore the horns of an elk. Its eyes screamed with
that same darkness, bleeding away everything I'd ever known
which might be good or true.

"Shit!" I scuttled backward, fleeing frantically. I had no doubt
little more than a touch would open my chest or dissolve my skull.

WHUF. WHUF. Wyatt's gear chuffed in the background as he
swore prolifically.

The entity before me whispered. No words, just blasphemous
shadows, things which poisoned the mind.

Bishop! the Adjunct, still holding the aspect of Cap'n Stern,
barked in my mind. ***Watch your shit, son!*** With that, the Adjunct
threw down a crosshair marker on my visual array. Then another.
And a third. Each showed another Irrat moving closer as I
scrambled in the shadows.

"Michael Bishop," chirped a young woman to my left. She
leaned against one of the room's columns. "I can't believe you
don't understand."

"What?" I pushed myself to a standing position, my lone
katana quavering in one hand.

"We can't see you." She turned toward me, her head an umbra
of angry shadows. "The Unity can. You can't hide your thoughts
like you hide your body."

CHHHHhsssSssssshhh... I heard them then, just as before.
Those sharp, sibilant whispers echoed and gamboled behind my
mind. They sounded every bit as clear as the first time I'd heard
them, back when we'd wrecked the *Legacy.*

"Ah, you grasp the truth." A grandfatherly figure spoke with a
rich baritone from behind the elk-horned entity.

But his face. Those eyes spoke of knowledge, discordant and
incomprehensible. His mouth stretched into a rictus grin, the smile

of a man who had gazed into the eyes of eternity and found himself broken on its shadowed shores.

"The Unity isn't something the mind of man can run from. We hear the rambling chaos you call thought. We feel the impressions you feel, your simple emotions. Your mind is like a child playing with clay," he rumbled low in his throat.

Michael? Anya's link came like quicksilver in my mind. *Do you require assistance?*

"You believe we wish you harm," the man continued, "that we are adversaries."

"Aren't we?" I spat at him.

"Naturally not." He clucked. "If we wanted to kill you, we'd already have done so."

I couldn't help but hear Firenzei in my mind as the man spoke.

"They wanted your pathetic asses alive," he crowed. *"All of you. Why do you think I haven't slaughtered you yet?"*

The horned figure whispered again, sharp, undying sounds. They made shapes in my mind, visions that haunted and hunted.

"So what is it you want?" I clung tighter to my katana, knowing the answer in my heart.

"We want to take you home, Michael." This from the young woman, the dark aurora over her burning and beguiling. "It's time. You know it's time."

Kid! Stern growled in my mind but too late.

I'd been so surprised, so overwhelmed by the calm certainty in their demeanor, I hadn't realized the truth.

They'd flanked me.

I yelped as hands took me from behind, hands so strong they lifted me off my feet. I hadn't even known they were there. Three sets of hands—no, four. One grabbed my wrist and twisted. My katana fell to the ground.

They dragged me backward.

"This, then, is the inevitable outcome." The older man walked behind us as they dragged me, kicking and cursing. "Some things are meant to be, Michael Bishop."

The p-pool. The fuc-king lag-goon. Wyatt's link came scattered, broken. I felt his heart pounding.

Asset Guthrie? Anya's link cut into my mind. *What is happening?*

Exquisite, the large man linked back, the thought filled with reverence. *It's beautiful.*

What's going on over there, Guthrie? I flicked off the *Wraith* and squirmed madly, attempting to fight off the pack of Irrats dragging me backward. For a moment, I thought I might pull free…

But no. Fingers like iron cords wrapped around my arms. One squat figure held my right leg and stared at me with eyes that glinted like knives.

I snarled up at the gentleman walking behind us, dignified and calm. His skin glistened from the goop in the incubator. Beside and behind him, the horned beast loped along, shrouded in shadow. To his other side—

"Hello to you, cowboy." The Russian man gave a small, fierce smile. "Hoping you loving coming home."

"Are you serious?" I glared at the older man. "Please don't kill me while making me listen to Petrov here butcher English."

"We aren't killing you. We've explained that." The man's rictus grin formed a tight little line. "Look. Look and see what the future holds, Michael."

They pushed me forward a few more steps, and a veil parted in my mind. Sweetness burned there, a kind of infinite joy and belonging I hadn't understood before.

Kid? A voice I thought I should recognize cracked like a whip in my skull. *You need to focus here.*

They turned me, roughly. The nude young woman, the one with a halo of amber fire, wrested me around while the squat figure

521

pushed down on my shoulder.

I fell to my knees.

"Look," the woman hissed. "See."

I looked. I gasped at the magnificence. Grasped it.

In an instant, I understood.

The Vyriim floated above the cerulean and radiant pool, swimming serenely. In the center, the largest knot of them contained strands as thick as tree trunks that danced and swirled fluidly through the air. Their every motion described beauty, etched an image of glory and wonder in my mind.

Impossible. My eyes grew wide.

The immense age of these creatures rolled over me in a sensation of yawning eternity, like a psychic weight. The infinity of their grace left me in stunned awe.

I felt impossibly small before them, an insignificant ember before a roaring and timeless fire.

Dozens of them gamboled there, perfect and peaceful. The psychic pressure of them drenched me in a syrupy warmth, the way a flower gives off scent.

Across the way, I saw Wyatt gape at the fluid motion of them, the terrible beauty. He'd fallen to his knees in broken amazement. His eye shone like a mirror, and the Tangler hung loose in his fingers.

Others knelt with him. Shambling shapes and graceful figures, men, women, and strangeling mixes. As one, they gazed up at the gyrating beauty; as one, they worshiped.

We couldn't have known, not really. But these were our brothers and sisters, part of the **Unity**.

"It's time to come home, Michael." The haloed woman gazed down on me, smiling with something like affection. "You belong with us. You have always belonged."

A gnarled knot of the angelic forms split off from the main pod, a graceful dance. They took one turn around the pool and then swam toward me, all slick tendril and writhing hook.

This made *sense*. My life fell into place around me, perfect symmetry.

Without any volition of my own, I tilted my head up. I opened my mouth in wonder, in supplication, in desire.

From behind, automatic fire. Cries of pain.

"She's immune!" This cry echoed from kilometers away. "We had no way to—!"

"I told you we needed to handle the witch!" someone snarled, but I didn't bother to see whom.

My entire focus, everything I'd been born for, loomed before me.

It drifted closer, welcoming.

More automatic fire thundered behind me.

The woman to my side shrieked and fell, a splash of sanguine scarlet on the ground.

The little squat man turned and sprinted away from me, growling.

None of those things mattered.

You little shit-stain! Stand up! The angry voice hammered in my mind. *Bishop, you really need to man the fuck up here!*

Michael, a soft voice, a voice like a river's song, whispered in my mind. *Please respond.*

The Vyriim drifted closer, and I smelled the sweetness that wafted off them. True joy bubbled in my heart.

I remembered the **Unity**, that bliss Firenzei held. Soon, I knew, it would belong to me.

Bullets sang over my head, slicing into the undulating mass. Violet and gray ichor splattered from the creatures, and I felt them scream, horror and agony devouring my mind.

"No," I gasped. I stood and took a single step forward, unconsciously reaching out to them.

The Vyriim hissed, malformed little mouths opening and closing where strands met, mutating into a maw. It lurched back from me, fleeing the pain of the bullets.

With it, that syrupy sweetness receded from my mind, pulling back like an ancient and inevitable tide. It left me feeling hollow, incomplete.

Unwhole.

Bishop? a confused drawl whispered in my mind. *What in the hell was that?*

"Michael." A hand fell on my shoulder, pulling me back. I turned and saw a blonde woman th—

Anya. I saw Anya there.

She leaned against one of the columns, obviously not applying all her weight to both legs. She held an automatic pistol in each hand.

I wept and shuddered, yet I couldn't say why.

"Here." She held one out to me. *It is nearly empty, but it is better than nothing.*

An automatic reflex, I took the pistol. I couldn't stop staring at her eyes.

"There!" The cry came from behind us.

Anya turned, raising her weapon.

The crack of gunfire echoed in the room as she slaughtered one of the Irrats.

I wanted... Wyatt linked, still disconnected and lost. *Oh, God.* He pushed himself up, securing his hat on his head.

The figures of several Irrats turned toward him.

Wyatt backed away, realizing our situation. *Initiating spikes. Stand clear.*

Seconds later, I heard the hissing bursts as he set them off. Around him, like icy sculptures, nearly a score of figures stood frozen solid. Wyatt had managed to put his spikes to a terrible function.

I almost felt guilty.

"It is not being over yet," the mad Russian snarled from behind me.

I turned, raising the pistol Anya gave me, and fired.

The man ducked behind whirring machinery and cackled.

Bullets sang and pinged off the metal.

From the corner of my eye, rippling darkness shimmered and sang. I threw myself to one side and whipped the weapon up toward the twilight-clad form.

It whispered again. The horned shape crept toward me, leaning forward on all fours now.

I backed away; it had destroyed my quasi-steel with one swipe, after all.

"We doin' this, Bambi?" I snarled. I brought the weapon forward and—

CRACK! The sound echoed from behind me, from the Broodwell. It sounded like the thundering of the Earth's crust, like tectonic plates grinding into mountains.

Both I and the weird shadow creature stumbled and spun.

Not twelve meters away, a scarlet fire hung in mid-air, softly singing a warbling eldritch song. As I watched, it shimmered and grew, branching into a crackling oval.

"Oh." I grinned at horn-head gleefully. "Things are about to get bad for you."

A second CRACK, followed by a third and fourth scattered around the room. With each, a ruby-colored flame blossomed in midair.

"Hsssssssshhhh." The horned-shadow turned slowly toward those flickering lights. It took a step backward, then two more.

I thought it might bolt.

"That's right." I spun the pistol toward it. "Run away. Run and hide. It's the only way you can survive this."

It snarled at me one last time, then bolted.

In a fit of pique, I pulled the trigger anyway, aiming squarely at the thing's back.

Click.

My eyes went wide as I gaped, first at the weapon and then at the Irrat.

525

It hadn't heard me run dry. It ran into the darkness.

Thank God.

Took 'em long enough. Wyatt punctuated his link with a series of *WHUFs*, spikes meant to cause mischief, I assumed.

The scarlet flames warbled in space and sang a haunted, eldritch melody. As I watched, the flame grew wider, burning on nothingness. It easily stretched taller than I stood.

Assets, the link came as a familiar, slender woman stepped through one of the burning apertures. She wore dark tactical gear that hugged her form.

I toggled on my handshake protocols. This function of my Crown would give me basic information regarding other Assets, more data if I paid them extra attention. The tech allowed a thoroughly intimate knowledge of other Assets, but typically I didn't need much more than name and number.

Brookmyre, Michele, Asset 087, my Crown announced. I couldn't help but chuckle.

"Michele from L.A.," I muttered. "Can you believe—?"

Michele paced fully into the room and peered about.

She didn't see the knot of Vyriim swarming and swimming, a predator darting in the air behind her.

Darting straight for her.

Michele! I moved toward her, toward the mad indigo shine of Wyatt's stasis field. *Behind y—!*

The Vyriim swooped down on her, swifter than a storm.

She met my eye as I linked, started to smile…

And they fell on her, savage and inhuman. Brutal. Hooks shredded, tendrils whipped.

They fell… through her?

Michele spun as she realized what happened, moving her incorporeal form away from the Broodwell and the Vyriim, retreating in momentary confusion. Her body flickered once, a staticy silver light.

The *Spectre.*

I stopped in place, so relieved I almost laughed.

The lady might be hard to work with, but Michele had never been a fool. She'd obviously toggled it before stepping through the aperture and had arrived completely insubstantial, ghostly.

The Vyriim couldn't touch her.

Hey there, Bishop. She reached into one of her pockets, and the static around her fluctuated as she shut the *Spectre* down. *Always starting trouble, aren't you?* She turned and threw a half dozen or so small objects into the room. One landed near me, a small cube.

A *Sibyl*-class drone.

The moment the device landed, the five outward facing sides flashed a searing, blipping emerald. Within the next half second, each drone facet fired several short bursts of viridian plasma, transforming the Broodwell into a laser-light show. In the course of seconds, hundreds and hundreds of sensory scans reached into the room.

Everything those lights touched, they recorded. Details of every surface they came to rest on was transmitted to some Facility database, giving the Designates a picture-perfect model of the room.

Bishop. Petrova. Guthrie, another figure linked as he stepped through the aperture. He wore a suit similar to mine and carried a device shaped vaguely like a crossbow. Behind his head hovered a glowing, sky-blue half-halo—part of the man's equipment.

Hunter, Liam, Asset 306, my Crown announced. Gatekeeper *and extraction Asset.*

We have your conduit queued, the man linked. *Let's begin your extraction.*

I headed for him, Anya, and safety.

At that moment, three other Assets stalked out of the burning gateways. Two men and one woman, each wore dark colors and carried various sharp and horrific bits of reality-altering equipment.

The moment the figures came through the portals, the Vyriim

went absolutely wild. Their serene swimming devolved into a thrashing, gnashing fury.

One of the Irrats screamed, a wail of terrible wrath. Others began to pick up a chant, canting words in a tongue I'd never known.

The room exploded into fire and madness.

2

As Assets, arrogance can be an occasional problem.

We are tools in the hand of the single most powerful organization in history. The Facility, in some form or another, has shaped humanity for nearly a thousand years.

Not all of those were good years.

Assets fight against inhuman Irrationals who would seek to destroy our world from within. We stand against deviant aberrations that would devour it from without. We shape physics like a child molds clay. We work miracles, right before the eyes of baseline humans.

Certainty, hubris would be our weakness.

The instant she activated the *Sibyl*-class drones, Michele toggled on her *Spectre,* a smart play. The Vyriim had been stalking her from the shadows of the room, constantly forming and unforming into different clutches.

The moment she cast the drones outward, a knot of the tendrils swooped toward her. If she hadn't immediately reengaged her packet, the creature would have dragged her away.

Instead, it caught Thomas Cooke, Asset 428.

The man wailed, completely taken off guard by the speed and lethal grace of the aberration.

It wrapped around his legs and pulled him into the air, another tentacle grasping the *Talon* he held, rending it useless.

The Broodwell! Wyatt sent a general link as he dropped a marker on the ichor. *It'll drag him under! It'll take him and—*

The Vyriim ripped off Cooke's arm, the wet sound of tearing muscle drowned by the man's screams. Casually, it removed his second arm. Then came the legs and head. The creature did this methodically, allowing the blood to splatter on the ground.

What? I almost fell to my knees from the sheer horror of it. *What. The. Fuck.*

The Vyriim threw Cooke's pieces down at the Assets below, its motions desultory.

"No!" One of the other Assets, **Watts, Amanda, 651, *Wraith*,** brought her Maverick up toward the snarl of tendrils. Before she pulled the trigger, a savage light shone out from a large male Irrat.

She levitated, struggling as if trapped in viscous amber.

The Irrat stepped closer and raised his other hand. His face locked in a death rictus, he brought his palms closer together. A hateful thrumming sang between them.

That awful light compressed, falling in on itself and the woman it held. It crushed a helpless Watts, reducing her to bloody pulp as she silently screamed.

He released her liquefied corpse to fall to the floor.

As one, the Irrats moved toward Liam and Michele.

Asset 306, the Designate sent in a general link. *Please remain on site until suitable reinforcements can be provided.*

Sure. Liam's frown knitted together. *No problem. Sounds awesome.* With that, he fired the gatekeeper crossbow into the floor at his feet. The quarrel appeared practically identical to one of Wyatt's spikes. At the spot where it jutted from the floor, a scarlet aperture appeared.

The Irrats moved closer.

It only took a moment for the gateway to grow large enough.

Liam fell through and vanished.

What? I turned to Anya. *Did we just lose our extraction?*

I doubt it. She hobbled closer to me, holding onto the mad Russian's dimensional engine. *He would not leave Locale Three without Designate permission.*

"Looks like I'm all alone." Michele gave the dozen Irrats a winsome smile. "And with no weapon."

"You don't understand the power of the Unity." A small figure stepped away from the others, little more than a boy. "You should abandon your shackled masters. They're liars. They don't keep their oaths."

In an instant, Michele became a blur.

The *Adept*, at work. The staticy sparkles around her intensified as she powered down the *Spectre* for an instant.

That instant provided her more than enough time. Michele reached beneath her jacket and pulled two disks, each the size of a dinner plate. With a ferocity and glee that, quite frankly, terrified the shit out of me, she hurled each device like a Frisbee of Doom.

One sailed into the burbling ichor of the Broodwell.

The other twirled directly into a throng of Irrats.

Fucking Tabula Rasa, Stern reported. ***Here's the system settings on those.***

Two large circles appeared over my visual array, scarlet indicators that warned me back.

She fucking did not, Wyatt marveled. *That chick, I swear. She's crazy!*

What is it with the two of you? I asked.

Michele dove to one side, again under the *Spectre*. Three different Irrats lunged for her, but her packets did their duties, and she slipped over them like water over stone.

They're goin', Stern reported. ***Watch yer shit.***

From those circles, two points of brilliant white, phosphorescent magnesium blossomed to burn against my visual array. That light radiated, burning away reality itself.

Murmurs of incredulity gave way to fear, then panic. Irrats swarmed away from those lights, cavemen fleeing the incomprehensible.

With a crashing, crackling eruption, the Tabula Rasa obliterated everything around it.

I had to turn away before it scalded my eyes. Stumbling back from that hellish glow, I almost fell straight into Anya.

An explosion.

A second.

Unforgiving, unnatural cold.

The fields collapsed in on themselves, screaming.

531

Careless bitch! Wyatt linked. *Do you know how close that came?*

I blinked, trying to see what happened. It appeared as if half of the Broodwell had been swallowed by the Rasa, as well as a good percentage of the looming Irrats.

One Irrat lost part of a leg and most of his arm to the swift and decisive slice. He wailed in animal agony, stumbling away from us.

In the chaos and panic, I heard the singing of the gatekeeper crossbow. It fired again and again, but it took me a moment to track where Liam hid.

He crouched in the shadows by the far door, the one Wyatt's Irrational friend had been near.

He fired quarrels into Irrat after Irrat. With each hit, the *Gatekeeper* teleported that target far away.

Offhand, I wondered where Liam sent his offensive porting targets. As far as I knew, it could be the moon.

You have reinforcements, Assets. The chilly voice of Designate Ling rang in our minds. *Incoming now.*

Simultaneously, two figures stalked through the apertures. In that moment, my handshake protocols pinged them.

Jackson, Edward, Asset 572, *Seraph.*

López, Rafael, Asset 811, *Seraph.*

They sent Seraphs? Wyatt raised an eyebrow. *Shit's getting serious.*

Unlike the first wave, these men appeared ready for a desperate, dirty fight. Each wore a tactical vest swathed with bandoliers and heavy packs hung at his belt. In this they appeared like any common soldier or perhaps a member of the SWAT team.

The moment they stepped into the room, they shattered that illusion. They manipulated portions of their visual arrays, affecting system dialogues only they saw.

As the *Seraph* packet drew energetic resources from the Lattice, the packet's coalescence protocols began to take effect.

The energy materialized into silvery-blue exoskeletons, each with two wickedly curved blades extending out beyond the users' right hands.

Asset 306, you are excused, the Designate linked. *Please resume your primary objective.*

Understood, Liam responded. He cocked his head toward Anya and me questioningly.

"I think we're ready," I said. "Although Guthrie's still in the middle of it."

"I'll get him." The *Gatekeeper* headed back toward the fray. "I should be able to extr—"

A rending, tearing sound sliced through our minds, a din like space itself split asunder. That shrill keen sounded louder than the screams of the dying, louder than the bursts of the Tabula Rasa.

It must've been heard across the city. I felt it in my bones. It made my teeth ache.

Wyatt's field.

It twitched and bent. It thrummed, as the drone frenzied within it.

For an instant, it blinked out, vanishing before reappearing.

Buddy, I linked the large man, *give me good news.*

I'm tryin' here, Hoss, he linked distractedly, his mind focused on equations and vectors. *Just hold on a minute.*

As if in response, the field's scream went up an octave, wailing even louder.

I don't think we can hold on, Wyatt. Unconsciously, I took a step back. *I don't think we have a minute.*

3

The wail undulated, bent.

Every set of eyes turned toward Wyatt's stasis field.

The shimmering thing now burned with a violet haze, like a scrum of oil on the surface of a pond. The field no longer formed a dome, but wavered into alien shapes I had no name for.

It pulsed angrily. It whined and raged and buzzed.

Wyatt Guthrie. The Designate spoke across the general channel. *Given energetic readings, we are sending four more* Artisan *Assets into Locale Three. Please compile a patch detailing the design of this construct so we may control the threat.*

Understood. Wyatt heaved a relieved breath at the Designate's certainty. He adjusted the Stetson on his head with a smirk. *I'm pleased it's been helpful.*

Without it, this situation would certainly be terminal. We acknowledge and appreciate the utility of what you've accompl—

In that moment, his field exploded.

Every Vyriim incubator in the room shattered before the onslaught of that screaming, deafening force. Asset and Irrat alike whirled through the air, caught in the furious concussion. Even the Vyriim tumbled sideways, the large creatures unable to stand against the blast. They slammed against the far wall, falling into snarled knots of tendrils.

Anya and I managed to stand far enough away that much of the blast dissipated before it reached us.

Liam, who had been about to step back into the fray to get Wyatt, caught the explosion full on.

He tumbled backward through the air, crashing into the mad Russian's machine.

"Oh no!" I stepped forward, throwing down the pistol I still held. Empty now, I didn't expect it'd help much against what came next.

Burning in the center of the room, the wrathful remnants of the drone flickered menacingly. Indigo light emitted a wide field of energetic radiance for about three meters around it. That violent emanation raged and refracted for a second while galvanic arcs sparked between the edge of the field and the small sphere within.

It hummed and crackled as it built strength.

Um, Wyatt tapped at his keys, staring at the array only he saw. *I show the drone'll get exponentially stronger.*

This is factual, Designate Ling replied.

Designate, anyone fiddling with those field designs needs to pay attention to line 67r through line 89t. Make the noted changes to the axiomatic rate of decay for emanated forces. That should stop the coming explosion.

Thank you, Asset Guthrie, the Designate linked. *We will handle the situation from here.*

"RAIJU DRONE AG-286f HAS SUFFERED TERMINAL DAMAGE!" Screeching echoed around the chamber. "PROTOCOL 17-R ENGAGING. PLEASE CLEAR ALL NON-FACILITY PERSONNEL FROM THE AREA! ESTIMATED EFFECT RADIUS: 745 KILOMETERS."

I couldn't help a small smile. The Designates had taken a play from my own book by letting the Irrats know how bad things had become.

Some of the combatants already knew.

Many Irrats started to scream at the impossible heat radiating from the failing *Raiju* drone. I smelled the sickening scent of cooked flesh and singed hair, along with an undertone of the rotten sea.

The floor buckled beneath that awful light.

Everyone who had managed to resume standing stumbled toward that violent furnace of fury. Even from our position, I saw the building had begun to melt around the drone. The entire thing appeared as if it might collapse inward, melting its way to the sub-basement.

I couldn't help but feel somewhat at fault.

"No." Liam didn't look at me as he spoke, yet I knew I was his intended audience. "This is not our responsibility. Our one job is getting the holy hell out of here." Just then, a silvery gleam caught my eye.

My katana.

It had been knocked around by fighting and eldritch power blasts until it finally came to rest against a wall not two meters away.

Liam moved over to an exhausted Anya, two injectors in hand. As the battle behind us began to rage again, he injected her.

I took the opportunity to jaunt over and grab my sword. I slipped it into its scabbard on my back and returned to find Anya visibly relaxed.

"Okay." Liam brought his right hand up to the odd piece of technology which hovered around the back of his head. A metallic half halo, the thing shone with light the color of the clear blue sky. "Come. On," he whispered, obviously concerned. After a moment he calibrated some unseen variable, pinching at his visual array.

"Can you get him?" I asked with a nod toward Wyatt. He lay close to the drone—too close. I didn't want to see my friend melt into an arrogant pile of sludge.

"Fucking paradox looping," Liam snarled. "But yeah."

A scarlet aperture opened beneath the fallen Wyatt. Surprised, he tumbled through, only to plop out a second fissure which appeared behind Anya.

You okay? Liam stepped over closer to us. *It's getting harder to generate functioning apertures in here. I didn't want to leave your liver behind or anything.*

I need my liver! Wyatt pushed to his feet and patted himself. *Feels like I still have it though.*

Good. Liam nodded. *You're going to want a stiff drink when this is over.*

I'm gonna want several, Wyatt corrected.

In that case, let's move.

With that, Liam ushered us out the door.

Gatekeeper

"Go, go go!" Liam hustled us along briskly.

Or at least as briskly as possible, as we weaved and dodged through the mad melee. Once we passed through the ruined vault door into the hallway beyond, he began to tinker with the half-halo hanging at the back of his head.

"Can we just port out?" Wyatt asked.

"Not yet," Liam muttered, pushing us ahead. "Any more gates and we're risking aberrant vectors in here. I don't mind pushing bad guys into compromised apertures, but they aren't recommended for the rest of us."

"We can push on a bit." Wyatt adjusted his Stetson. "I'm just pleased we're getting an extraction at all."

"We'll find a null-vector zone soon enough," Liam assured us. "Just gotta keep going."

We have incoming Titan-*class Assets,* Designate Ling sent in a general open link. *We are routing* Raptor *and* Gatekeeper-*class Assets to Locale Three, to neutralize the damaged* Raiju *drone.*

"Not our problem." Liam nodded at Anya, giving her a warm smile. "We just need to get that data out of our *Preceptor's* head."

Whatever he'd injected Anya with had already done its magic as she traipsed along quite well for a lady with her kneecap shot.

Not that she'd had any time for the mecha to patch her injuries, instead her pain process halted at her sensory nerves.

She'd limp along just fine.

For a while.

"Watch out." Liam stepped in front of us, the gatekeeper crossbow warbling. He fired a quarrel at a figure I'd completely missed lurking behind a large potted tree.

A perfect shot, straight into the gut.

"Shit!" The man stumbled forward, automatic pistol slipping

from nerveless fingers.

Crimson fire crawled over his form, wailing an odd and eldritch song. He vanished, offensively teleported away in a flash of scarlet fury.

"Good work," Wyatt huffed. I noted the barbarian had a hard time catching his breath.

"It's all about preparation," Liam replied. "We need to take five, man?"

"No, I—"

"Yes," I panted, nodding at Liam.

Wyatt had been shot in the chest less than half an hour ago. The man pushed too hard, even with our reality-altering mecha at work.

"S'all good." Liam smiled. "The Designates need to calibrate our aperture. It'll take 'em a few to configure our back door."

"They weren't exactly expecting us in New York." I kept my eyes trained down the hallway, searching for Irrats or tentacle monsters. In the distance, the pitched battle roared.

"Here's as good a pit stop as any." Liam indicated a sign that read, MEETING ATRIUM THREE.

"Good idea." I nodded and pushed the door open.

A long table ran down the center of a poshly decorated room with a whiteboard at one end. The entire south wall contained windows that overlooked the city.

While Liam and I watched the hall, the room rumbled with the force of small explosions on the levels above.

Absentmindedly, the *Gatekeeper* Asset tapped at the half-halo which hung around the back of his head.

Its blue shine twinkled and shone with every touch.

The extraction conduit is in place. The Designate linked us all at once. *Unfortunately, there is nothing of use in that building. Alterations rendered to the J4 subset of spatial axioms, along with degradation to the thermodynamic axioms from local Irrational technology, mean aberrant vectors are a certainty.*

Certainly altered, Wyatt linked smugly. *This place is weird, even for New York.*

Just tell me when and where, Designate, Liam replied.

We have a conduit a block and a half away that has been used multiple times, and therefore is quite secure. I'm sending the coordinates now. Haste is prescribed.

"Good," Wyatt muttered under his breath. "I'm glad she told us. I wanted to hit the conduit all lackadaisical-like."

"I don't like our options," Liam groused. "Using an elevator while explosions are happening seems like bad mojo."

"But the stairs won't be kind either." I met Anya's eyes. "Even if it's hard to feel pain just now."

"I currently have zero registered pain processes." Anya stared up at me, her eyes glazed.

"Doesn't mean your knee is up to snuff," Wyatt drawled. "You fall down some stairs, you'll break yer head. Then the Designates will never get their data."

"That stairwell is little more than a fire exit," I grumbled. "But it's safer than the elevators. They leave us trapped, sitting targets for automatic weapons. Hell, some Irrat could throw a grenade down the shaft, right on top of us."

"All bad choices. I'll be back." Liam nodded at me. "Hold the fort."

The *Gatekeeper* Asset turned and fired a quarrel into the wall. A rippling circle of crimson light gathered around that quarrel, keening a quiet, haunting song. He stepped through the aperture and vanished.

"Showoff," Wyatt grunted. He leaned back against the wall.

I settled in to keep watch until Liam returned. Surely, I thought, we could go five minutes without dealing with hostile Irrat bullshit.

As it turned out, we couldn't go five minutes without dealing with hostile Irrat bullshit.

"Michael Bishop," a feminine voice purred from down the

passageway. "I'm so pleased to see you again."

Wondering where I'd heard the voice before, I turned back toward the chaos of the Broodwell.

A sleek silhouette of feline femininity lounged along a column.

"Um," I stammered, gaping. "You."

"Yes, Michael. Me." The blonde woman smiled. She held a Glock 32 in her left hand, almost casually. "I trust I won't have to share you this time?"

My mind refused to parse what I saw. While Caprice never gave me a name for the woman, I recognized that smirk. A smile like that could cut a man from across the room.

"How can you be here?" I shook my head, all logic fleeing out of reach. "You were in the bar with Caprice."

"I'm here now." She smiled. "I'm here for you."

"Impossible."

"It's impossible Firenzei found Wyatt Guthrie." She stalked toward me, sleek, elegant. Her eyes devoured me. "Perhaps, for the Unity, nothing is impossible."

The implications baffled me, made space spin.

"Stop!" I barked, holding my katana forward. The woman's pistol far outclassed my single blade, but that didn't occur to me.

I needed to think.

"I don't have to stop." She held her hands out to her sides, the Glock still dangling from her fingers. "That's the joy of it. Michael. I have the Unity. Nothing you could possibly do can stand against it."

The fuck? Wyatt linked. *Bishop, do you know this freak fatale?*

She houses the phage, Michael, Anya warned.

"We have to assume your shackled masters will know all you know," she continued. "That's what this is about."

"Our what?" I felt as if I'd started to drown in this conversation.

"It's not too late." She stared me squarely in the eye, but I got the distinct impression she spoke to someone else. "Send this one with me. If we ally ourselves, the servitors of the Scarlet Star will fail."

"You are one crazy bitch," I muttered.

"This is simple, Michael." She took another step. "You will come with me. You will honor the pacts made by those you serve." She paused, studying my face.

"I don't think so." I met the woman's sensual gaze. "We're leaving. We've learned all about your invasion bullshit."

"No." She tittered, musical. "You will come with me now, or you will come with us later." The smile fell from her face. "The only difference is your suffering."

The woman took another step and opened her mouth to speak again.

She never got the chance.

Automatic fire roared from my left, all iron and fire and thunder. Bullets tore into the woman's stomach and chest, splattering her with crimson.

I turned.

Anya stood there, Firenzei's pistol in hand. She held it trained on the woman, her hand trembling.

The blonde crumpled and fell. Immediately, her midsection began to roil as the Vyriim sought egress.

"Nope." Wyatt stepped forward, the Tangler already singing. With a huffing *WHUF* he fired a spike directly into the corpse.

As Vyriim attempted to squirm free, he pecked at a few of his keys. In an instant, an azure field crackled around the lithe form.

Wyatt dropped the temperature in that space so rapidly it took my breath even from five steps away. The body froze solid in less than an instant, the filthy parasites trapped within.

"You and your dates," the large man muttered.

"I don't know what you're talking about," I declared. "Not a bit."

"She spoke as if she knew you," Anya replied, lowering the weapon. "A friend of yours?"

"Definitely not," I replied, holding up my hand.

As I defended my life choices, Liam walked back to our hallway. The scene through the aperture shifted.

"Okay." The young man combed at his thin beard with his fingers. "I have us a straight shot to the lobby. No stairs." He gestured at the crimson gateway.

"Sounds good to me." I turned to Anya and gestured to the aperture. "Let's go."

Stepping through the aperture felt like gliding through curtains of burning silver. The heat briefly brushed my skin but not long enough to cause any pain. Instead, a light, flickering sensation tingled against my flesh. I heard a soft crackle in my Crown, like the embers of an almost dead fire.

The aperture led straight into the front foyer of the building.

"Oh." A young woman stood in the middle of the foyer, manila folders in hand. She appeared far more like a secretary than a dangerous Irrational criminal.

She gaped at me as we entered the room.

Baseline human. Caution hummed in Anya's link.

Got it, I linked. *Doesn't mean she can't just shoot us.*

The woman stammered, took a step back. Her heavily painted mouth formed a tight little *O.*

"Ma'am." Wyatt bobbed his head at her as we went by.

She only nodded briskly, obviously horrified at his gore-spattered face. I doubted she even knew what happened on the upper floors.

"Lean on me," I told Anya. "You can't feel how badly you're hurt."

Anya nodded her agreement.

As we passed the woman, she grimaced at the blood from my wounds. Her mouth hung open, her eyes wide.

The security guard at the door started as Wyatt came close, limping and bleeding. He lifted his walkie-talkie to his mouth.

"Don't." I swung my katana toward the guard's face. "Put it

down or get fucking stabbed. That simple."

The man dropped the walkie-talkie.

Outside, the first of the sirens wailed. I glanced up sharply as fire trucks swerved in front of the building.

Friends? I glanced at Liam.

Absolutely. He quirked up one side of his mouth. *Open up your primary handshake dialogues as we step outside.*

Already on. I steadied Anya as Liam pushed open the door. She lagged behind, badly. I couldn't help but wonder how much further she could go.

I toggled my dialogues during the Asset-palaooza upstairs.

Good man, Liam responded. *It's a mess out here.*

No sooner did I step outside than those dialogues pinged my first friendly. **Regent, Miriam, Facility Factor 028**, my Crown announced to me as we came close to a young woman. The system outlined her in a gentle white glow, so as to make her impossible to miss. She stood next to a yellow barricade and wore the traditional blues of a New York policewoman.

"This way, sir," she called, waving us forward.

Liam nodded and reached up behind his head. Casually, he pulled the Crown augment from its place, folding it in on itself. That sapphire glow faded as the augment shut down. He held the gatekeeper crossbow down to one side.

Wyatt holstered the business end of the Tangler. Now it only appeared to be a huge technological backpack.

"Miriam?" another cop called out. "You good?"

"It's all good, Thomas," she answered. Miriam touched a small black device on her belt. The scarcest whisper of a hum emitted from it. **"I'm helping these folks get to where they need to be. They're just injured citizens, as you can see."** Her voice carried an arresting ring, somehow augmented by that droning little device.

"Right." Thomas stared squarely at us.

I still carried my katana and remained dressed in a shredded suit. The handkerchief covering Wyatt's missing eye positively screamed with crimson blood. Anya's remaining white tactical gear had been liberally splattered with blood and Vyriim viscera.

Yet Thomas nodded genially.

"You folks get some help. Have a good day." He touched two fingers to the brim of his hat before returning to tend the barrier.

As Miriam led us forward, my Crown pinged more Facility operatives.

Factor Keating stood at the far end of the street, another police officer. Unseen by his comrades, he dispersed gaseous agents designed to calm and soothe the populace around him.

Factor Richter worked with the firemen, linking with Assets inside the building to know where they should focus their attentions.

Dozens of other Factors bustled about, each performing their duties perfectly. Firemen and police made up most of the Factors, but I saw more than one in the ambulances.

I doubted they'd all been sent full dossiers on the direness of our situation. Factors with higher clearance remained rare. Typically, they were simply people. Exceptional people, recruited to serve the largest organization on Earth... but only people.

A matched pair of Facility drones whirred past us overhead. Each remained hidden beneath a *Wraith* packet but had been well armed, just in case things got out of hand. On my visual array, they simply appeared as white shapes—shapes no non-Asset could even see.

"Hoss," Wyatt coughed, pointing. "Looks like shit might be serious."

I turned and my face immediately soured into a frown.

O'Brian, Patrick, my Crown reported. **Facility *Liaison* 760**.

Patrick shook hands with one of the police officers, a potbellied man who likely out-ranked everyone on site. The *Liaison* smiled widely, laughing at something the cop said.

Creepy fuckers, I sent to Wyatt. *There's your Illuminati lizard man, right there..*

Now, Wyatt linked, *you're just jealous. You think the* Liaisons *might be more suave than you are.*

I'm pretty sure they sweat mind-control hormones. I watched as *Liaison* O'Brian clapped the cop on the back and then shook hands with another. *At least when I trick an enemy, I do it the honest, old-fashioned way.*

With invisibility and hyperkinetic reflexes? Wyatt chuckled. *Exactly.*

"This way." Miriam gestured, pushing us past a barrier on the far side of the street. She kept her finger poised at her belt, just in case anyone thought to ask her what, exactly, she thought she was doing.

No one did.

Two more invisible drones sped by.

As I helped Anya step past the barrier, a fashion billboard across the street began to flicker, scintillating and rippling on my visual array. When it stopped, the sign turned black with crimson dataglyphs pulsing at the corners.

THIS IS A STATUS TWO HOT ZONE, the billboard informed us. It flickered again, changing its message.

KNOWN AND WANTED IRRATIONAL TERRORISTS ARE IN PLAY. POSSIBLE ABERRANT INCURSION IN PROGRESS.

"There." Miriam pointed to an out-of-the-way door situated along a crooked alley. "Your extraction conduit."

"Thank you so much, Miriam." Liam smiled at her. "Your help is greatly appreciated."

She beamed at him as my cadre limped our ragged way toward the extraction point. On one hand, we had to be very conspicuous in our tattered state, barring memory alteration. On the other hand—

This *was* New York City.

"Here." I jerked my head toward the alleyway. "Almost home."

Wyatt grinned wearily. "Are you sure you don't want to stop and get a drink?" He chuckled but didn't slow.

Location achieved, Designate. I glanced down the alleyway. *Initiating conduit, Assets.*

Hey, I linked Wyatt. *Take Anya. I'll be right behind.*

Um. Only the slightest pause. *Copy that, Hoss. See you in Neverland.* He gave me a nod before he went through the door.

I glanced at the burning building one last time. A scarlet stylized *S* dominated its front, looming over the now chaotic street.

The building had caught fire quite magnificently, no doubt fueled by a catastrophically failing *Raiju* drone. I hoped the Assets had a handle on that.

If not, we'd lose most of the Atlantic seaboard.

"You're up." Liam smiled at me. "Don't worry about this little scuffle. We've got it handled."

"Right." I gave him a weak smile.

"The data is all you're responsible for, Asset." He clasped my shoulder. "Get debriefed."

"Will comply." I chuckled and gave the man a real smile before I turned to make my way into the conduit.

It parted around me, the sensation like burning silk.

The moment I stepped through, white light flashed, brilliant and stark in my mind. My eyes burned like topazes set aflame.

Michael Bishop, Asset 108. Welcome to Facility 17.

Torpor

I didn't remember being patched up. I didn't remember being taken to Asset Emergency Services, either.

I never remember these things. No Asset does.

"I sometimes think they 'port you straight into some kinda suspended animation," Wyatt once opined while we hid below the deck of an abandoned oil tanker. "I don't rightly remember much about any Facility, do you?"

Those Mexican gangsters have machine guns. I shot him an incredulous stare. *Also, if you haven't noticed, I think most of them might already be corpses.*

"That's the real rub of it." He peeked over the top of a shipping container, both eyes narrowed to slits. "The entire process of passing between 'active Asset' and 'torpor' is pretty confusing. It's like trying to remember someone else's dreams."

You're going to get shot right in your pretty little beard. I put one hand on his shoulder and dragged him down next to me. *At least let me toggle the* Wraith *before I sneak on ahead.*

"Well, now you're acting like you don't think it's weird at all." Wyatt had shrugged.

In all honestly, weird didn't come close to describing what I thought of Facility protocols. Often I found little scraps of silvery consciousness while in AES, moments I remembered well. I also typically recollected the sterile debriefings I underwent with my Designate. Beyond that, my memories of the Facility locations remained tremulant.

This time I woke slowly, drifting my way back through the fog of remembrance. I blinked at the woman standing over me.

She stared at an area of empty space, part of her visual array I assumed. She blew mousy brown hair out of her face.

Gardener, Rachel, my Crown supplied. **Asset 135**.

"Hey." I cleared my throat.

"Good morning, Mr. Bishop." Rachel didn't glance up from her display.

"How—?" I coughed and gave up on speaking. Instead I just gestured at my body.

"We corrected a buildup of cerebrospinal fluid, likely due to alterations rendered to the X9 subset of biological axioms." She glanced to the left of my head, likely reading data outlined there. "Your shoulder and back both sustained significant damage. It also appears as if you've been stung in the abdomen multiple times."

"Yeah." I tried to clear my throat again. "I had a rough day."

"I'll say." She arched one eyebrow. "These injuries seem to indicate an Asset expressing reckless abandon."

"I planned my abandon very well," I groaned.

"I would hate to see you reckless then," she replied, shaking her head.

"Where...?" I sounded as if my throat had been assaulted by tentacle aberrations. "Where are the other members of my cadre?"

"Wyatt Guthrie is in surgery. The damage done to his face and ocular nerve was extensive." She paused. "His stats imply he was intoxicated for much of the dossier." Rachel tapped nothingness in the air in front of her.

And Anya? Linking felt better than talking, by far.

Your Preceptor *will need a knee replacement. The fact that she was able to walk on it is incredible. That procedure is due to take place this afternoon. She is being prepped now.* Rachel fluffed my pillow.

Much better. I managed a small smile. *What about the drone? New York?*

Relax, 108. Your cadre is well. You're set to be released in less than an hour. I'm certain your Designate will debrief you soon.

"Thank you, Rachel."

"You're just going to go and mess up my work again." She shook her head. "I've seen your type, Asset. You think that just

550

because we're miracle workers, you can push your luck."

"You aren't wrong." I smiled at her.

She gave me a thin smile back and left, muttering to herself.

I lay back.

I slept.

2

An indeterminable amount of time later, I began to drift back into myself. The world had gone dreamy, soft. The lights of the hallway glared down mercilessly. I blinked and walked forward through the sterile passage. It felt as if I forgot something, but I couldn't imagine what.

I passed a door to my right and then another. Each appeared identical, constructed of white metal and glass. I didn't feel remotely curious about them however. I knew exactly where I belonged, as if the fact sat squarely in the center of my being.

I opened the third door. The correct door.

Good evening, 108. As always, Designate Ling linked crisply. Neat and professional, she sat behind the table, wearing a dark pencil skirt and a matching vest over her silky top.

I smiled.

She glanced down at her Ordinal slate and traced one lacquered nail across its surface.

"Is it evening?" I checked my system time. Christ, the display showed nearly ten at night.

Ten at night and a day later than I expected.

Stepping inside, I took a seat.

The Designate tapped her slate twice and peered down at a readout I couldn't see.

As always, Michael, you have performed to specification and beyond. This dossier composed a difficult assignment, and yet our reviews of your phaneric records indicate you performed admirably.

Difficult, yes. I nodded. *Definitely an unusual mission.* I met her gaze, noting the faceted darkness of her eyes.

We appreciate the design flaws you discovered in the Raiju *drones.* She raised one artful eyebrow. *Future iterations of all drones will be impossible to damage in the method you used.*

As it happened, that particular tactic saved our lives, I reminded her.

That particular tactic also came close to killing millions of baseline humans, she countered. The tone of her link had gone wintery sharp. *However, the situation did not prove catastrophic. The drone was dealt with summarily.* She tapped her nails against the surface of the desk, clicking like metal on ice.

I'm glad. I smiled at her as I had little more to say on the subject.

I needed a cigarette.

The Designate spent a moment gazing down at her slate and then up into the air above it. Briefly, I saw a scarlet dataglyph pulse upon its surface.

She nodded.

The extensive data from your cadre provides all the required information. We now understand the source of the Irrationality spikes and the technology used. She set the slate down and turned to lean across the table.

I smelled orchids.

I'd like to say I'm glad. However, the things we uncovered have far-reaching ramifications.

The Vyriim. Yes. Her smile appeared quite small. *That ramification is particularly horrific.*

They plan to invade. I doubted she'd respond but I wanted the Designate's take. Even if the Facility decided I needed to know, I would forget as soon as they removed me from duty.

They do. She tapped her fingers on the desk again. In that moment she looked like a predator, lean and feral. *They will not succeed.*

They seem to feel as if we owe them something. Or as if we've made some agreements.

They are incorrect on both counts. That icyness loomed in her link.

Understood. I could rest assured I'd be updated with any

pertinent information the next time my Crown went active.

We know more than they believe. During some of your unfortunate experiences with them, you were connected with me through the soft-sync. We learned much.

Oh. I nodded. *I see.*

There are other ramifications, ones we don't understand yet. She picked up her slate again. *You should be aware that you will be tasked with more missions of this caliber in the future.*

I will? I sat still in my chair, a bit dumbstruck. I had to admit, I'd looked forward to being placed back on the television-psychic taskforce. Hell, even being sent to apprehend Irrat kids beat being castaway in—

We find these events troubling. As you now have experience with Aberration 45717R, you and your cadre will be among the first tasked with dossiers that concern them. Her eyes flickered up at me. *You will also receive a second tier designation.*

A promotion? The idea boggled me.

Your actions were reckless, your choices poorly considered. At almost every turn, you went against protocols. She smiled. *Your stratagems were the last thing the enemy expected.*

Um, thank you? I didn't know how to respond.

For now, you are to be inactivated immediately. Before you leave, a white room will be provided to decommission all your packets and remove your neuralware. Do you have any other questions for us?

In truth, most of my questions would never matter. I knew that. On one topic, I and conspiracy-minded Wyatt agreed: The Facility could be as dodgy with its own Assets as it was with the outside world.

"None I can think of, Designate. I'm ready to be dormant for a while."

Easily arranged. She tapped at her slate and brought up three more dataglyphs. She selected one before indicating the door.

I stood with a nod, then opened the door.

Brilliant white light rained over me. That light bled, it burned. It shone into the heart of me, revealing everything I'd ever been.

As I stepped into it, I heard the Designate's last link.

Thank you, Michael. As always, we wish you well in the days ahead.

3

Sometime around one in the morning, I arrived back on Nob Hill, exhausted. More than anything else, I wanted to get back to my flat, maybe cuddle up with something sweet. I felt foggy and headachy.

I was still bandaged up from the accident. I couldn't believe I hadn't even gotten the son-of-a-bitch's license plate.

Trying to figure out where I'd parked, I meandered around. When I reached into my pocket, my cell began to buzz. It went on for a long time, as if it had somehow just received several messages at once.

Nine missed calls. All from Caprice.

"Michael, I don't know where you went, but I can't believe you stepped out on us like that—"

"Me neither." I almost laughed.

I'd gone outside for a moment to make a call. Caprice set up a legendary evening for us, and I didn't want my buddy Wyatt interrupting me. He and I had a previous engagement, but when Caprice called, I knew my plans would change.

With Caprice, I'd found it important to stay fluid.

When I told him the plan, Wyatt totally understood. He'd wanted in on whatever went down, of course, but then, Wyatt always did.

Dude always had an eye for trouble, and Caprice was definitely trouble.

Then some drunken asshole plowed over me in his Prius.

I was lucky to be alive. An ambulance took me to the hospital and patched me up, but I'd still missed out. Her voicemails told me that much.

"Last call, sexy," she purred. "Let me tell you what we are doing, right now—"

"Fuck. Of all the luck." As I listened to the call, I groaned. The recording had been exquisite. I'd truly missed out on an otherworldly experience.

At last, I found my car.

"Finally. First good luck all evening." I rummaged for my keys. In my jacket pocket, I found a packet of cigarettes.

"Who do you belong to?" I stared at them stupidly for a moment. Were these mine? Something seemed to suggest—

No, I didn't smoke. The EMT must have thought they belonged to me and put them in my pocket. I crumpled them up and threw them in a trashcan by my car.

Smoking's dangerous. Habits like that get a man killed.

Once in the car and on my way, I hit redial on my phone. I hoped Caprice wasn't too mad. Maybe we could meet back up with that blonde tonight—

I frowned. For some reason, that sounded like a bad idea.

"Michael?" Caprice's voice combined desire and concern perfectly.

"Hey, sweetheart."

I grinned as I drove into the night.

Adventure awaited.

###

Next in the Series

Castaway in a hostile reality. Hunted by telepathic zealots. Trapped within an endless, labyrinthine city... Michael Bishop has been captured by forces unknown.

Stricken with amnesia and wandering within dank, unused tunnels, Asset 108 might be in a situation he can't snark or seduce his way out of.

Accompanied by his terminally gorgeous girlfriend, Michael finds himself floundering through firefights at the center of an interdimensional web of schemes.

He doesn't even remember how to use a gun.

A firestorm of bullets and an elegant ruse later, Michael stumbles into an inhuman reality, a terrifying plane of existence far from his own. Now, with a few old friends and none of his fancy technology, Bishop has to navigate a city of intrigue and alien horror.

Inhuman machinations looms in the shadows of this place—schemes that threaten the Facility itself...

The Primary Protocol

Available at Amazon.com

Powered by Patreon

Want more Irrational weirdness? My Patreon page has dozens of free excerpts from my books, and my Patrons get even more! If you'd like a front row seat to all the extra-dimensional adventure, check it out today at Patreon.com/JMGuillen!

About the Author

JM Guillen was just an average Joe working at a Necromancy factory in 2010. One day, while enjoying a grilled cheese sandwich on break, a horrible and completely improbable accident happened!

Oh no!

JM Guillen just so happened to be struck by the emanations of a scarlet star that came into a strange and terrible alignment. He immediately began scrawling forsaken and unpronounceable names into a tome, names granted him by the power within the star.

This book, the Liber Noctiis, drove him irrevocably mad and gifted with uncanny, unearthly power. Today he spends his time creating books of fell power and summoning inhuman beings best left alone. His goal of absolute world domination is almost within his grasp.

Soon, nothing will stop him.

Occasionally, he writes fiction.

You can join his newsletter at his website, www.irrationalworlds.com.

Made in the USA
Middletown, DE
13 December 2019